Fantastic Four®

COUNTDOWN
TO CHAOS

D1711538

®

Fantastic Four®

COUNTDOWN TO CHAOS

PIERCE ASKEGREN

ILLUSTRATIONS BY
PAUL RYAN & JEFF ALBRECHT

BYRON PREISS MULTIMEDIA COMPANY, INC.

NEW YORK

BERKLEY BOULEVARD BOOKS, NEW YORK

FANTASTIC FOUR: COUNTDOWN TO CHAOS

A Berkley Boulevard Book
A Byron Preiss Multimedia Company, Inc. Book

Special thanks to Ginjer Buchanan, Steve Roman,
Michelle LaMarca, Howard Zimmerman, Emily Epstein,
Ursula Ward, Mike Thomas, and Steve Behling.

PRINTING HISTORY
Berkley Boulevard paperback edition/June 1998

The Penguin Putnam World Wide Web site address is
http://www.penguinputnam.com

Check out the Ace science fiction/fantasy newsletter, and much more, at
Club PPI!

Check out the Byron Preiss Multimedia Co., Inc. site on the
World Wide Web:
http://www.byronpreiss.com

ISBN: 0-425-16373-3

BERKLEY BOULEVARD
Berkley Boulevard Books are published by The Berkley Publishing
Group, 200 Madison Avenue, New York, New York 10016.
BERKLEY BOULEVARD and its logo
are trademarks belonging to Berkley Publishing Corporation.

PRINTED IN THE UNITED STATES OF AMERICA

10 9 8 7 6 5 4 3 2 1

In memory of my mother,

Jacqueline Porter Askegren,

who died while this book was in its earliest stages,

but whose lifelong love and encouragement

were what made it possible.

ACKNOWLEDGMENTS

My thanks go to:

Stan Lee and Jack Kirby,
for cocreating every major character in this book
and literally hundreds of others, as well.
Together and apart, they've given me more hours
of reading enjoyment than I can count.

The many writers of the other Marvel novels
and short stories, for creating most
of the minor characters
and institutions that populate these pages.

Keith R.A. DeCandido, editor, for ushering
this work into existence, and for asking me to
write the fershlugginer thing in the first place.

Fantastic Four

COUNTDOWN TO CHAOS

PROLOGUE

I n a room with no doors and no windows, a bank of nine television monitors abruptly clicked to life. They were large-screen monitors, mounted in three rows of three, and held in unified array by a heavy frame. Each television received and presented a different feed—commercial networks, local stations, cable news channels, satellite downlinks, and more. It was 6:00 P.M., local time, and the broadcast media were striving eagerly to distill a world's worth of news into scant minutes of footage and commentary. Nine different images and the sound from nine speakers banished the silent darkness, filling the room instead with a kaleidoscope of pictures and a Babel of sound.

One man watched and listened to it all. His eyes came open even as the first light from the screens reached him, and he stared, unblinking, at the impromptu collage of on-the-scene footage, animated diagrams, and announcers that filled the monitors. He sat unmoving before them and stared at all nine glass surfaces simultaneously, never focusing on a single one, but paying equal attention to each. Nine separate audio tracks reached his ears, all at the same approximate volume, and he listened to them all. He heard the bland tones of analysts and announcers, the measured words of government spokespeople, and the more nervous comments of witnesses and victims. With an ease born of long practice, he correlated the images and sounds, combining them in his mind and then distilling them down to their basic content, the discreet bits of data that suggested so many consequences and possibilities.

The recent accidental death of the Export Commerce Minister in Costa Verde, South America, had been followed by the appointment of his successor, a man whose past was rife with mystery and innuendo. Whispered rumors linked him to the terrorist cabal known as Hydra, an organization known to have a base hidden somewhere within Costa Verde's boundaries. So far, none of the allegations had been proven, but America's State Department did not look on the appointment with pleasure, especially since the office of Export Commerce Minister was a traditional stepping-stone to the Costa Verde presidency.

Merchants in the tiny island nation of Madripoor were selling bootleg software programs at bargain prices to visitors from around the world, many of whom had journeyed to that country specifically to buy them. Too many of the eager patrons later found that their purchases were infested with destructive viruses. The result? Disastrous consequences for private computer users and businesses around the world, and even for certain government organizations that had been foolish enough to avail themselves of the apparent bargain prices. Since Madripoor's prince was of the opinion that the latest International Copyright Convention was "a bag of lies, intended only to protect the haves from the have-nots" and had declined to sign it, other nations were nearly powerless to combat the situation.

A political rally in Virginia turned ugly when a certain well-known radio host made criminal allegations against party officials, prompting a violent demonstration, and the announcement of what promised to be an even more violent counterdemonstration. A counter-counterdemonstration seemed likely, but not certain.

The World Health Organization was frantically raising funds to battle the plague of leukemia sweeping through Eastern Europe, the terrible legacy of a nuclear accident in Hungary five years before. Already, WHO's assets were stretched nearly to the breaking point, forcing the reduction of aid to other nations. Most analysts said that things were sure to get worse before they got better.

Thanks to a major breakthrough in computer-chip technology, Stark Enterprises's stock prices rose sharply and their competitors' plummeted, sending shockwaves through the industry. Already, manufacturing and software companies were desperately seeking new alignments and partnerships. Financial commentators anticipated a ripple effect in mutual funds and pension plans as the value of their investments changed dramatically.

Civil war continued unabated in the small nation of Sylvania, as Gypsy and German factions tore at one another in a paroxysm of "ethnic cleansing" that made the streets run red with blood. Only that nation's close proximity to Latveria and its Gypsy-born ruler kept the conflict from spilling over Sylvania's borders. Thus, the United Nations found itself in the awkward position of relying on the deadliest man in the world, Victor Von Doom, to keep peace in the war-torn region. Reports were that Doom was amused.

The images on the screens changed. Commercials, sports summaries, giggling weather girls—the seated man watched and listened to them all with equal attention. A full ninety-three percent of the information the screens conveyed now was trivia, but even trivia had its uses. A new brand of deodorant, an unexpected soccer triumph, a summer storm—any of them could produce results that few minds could anticipate, and create new opportunities and possibilities.

Actions had consequences, and the consequences had consequences, too—often grotesquely disproportionate to the initiating event. Two weeks before, a horse had stumbled and thrown its rider, killing him and vacating a key political position. Filling that role with a Hydra sympathizer promised to make Costa Verde's relationship with the United States immediately take a turn for the worse. Those worsening relations, along with the fact that Costa Verde's major cash crop was the coca bush, had dire implications for America's inner cities. Many new addictions and deaths there in the years to come could be traced back to a poorly shod horse and the unlucky absence of one cobblestone from the road that it had galloped along. After the fact, even a lesser mind could see the chain of events and make the connection, with enough knowledge and some thought. That lesser mind, however, would never carry the thought process to the next level, or ask the next, logical questions.

Why had that cobblestone been missing from the path of the unfortunate José Gonzalez, horseback riding enthusiast and Export Commerce Minister of Costa Verde?

Chance?

Or something more?

The Thinker smiled.

• • •

Seven years ago:

Reuben Kincaid poured more amber whiskey into his glass, drained it, and then repeated both actions. The booze didn't help. Nothing did. He felt as if there were no room in his mind for the alcohol's sweet numbness, no room for thoughts of anything except for the younger man who sat on the other side of Reuben's desk, paging silently through a sheaf of photographs. His visitor—and the gun that lay on the desk, never more than six inches from Reuben's right hand.

"Nope, not pretty," Michael Brady said. Both men worked for the Roxxon Chemical division of Roxxon Oil, the world's largest petroleum manufacturer. Kincaid was division head; Brady was an up-and-comer, the current corporate golden boy, and obviously gunning for Kincaid's job. Kincaid hated him. Now he hated him some more as the younger man leaned forward and set the photographs on the desk. Brady continued, "I'd hate to see the papers get hold of these."

"I plan to deliver them personally to all the major media," Kincaid replied. His voice was unsteady, but that had less to do with the whiskey he had drunk than with the horror and despair sweeping through him, boiling emotions barely held in check by his simultaneous fury.

"That would be extraordinarily unwise," Brady said. "We can spin the situation as things stand right now. In six weeks, everyone will forget about the incident. If the media sees those—"

"The world's going to see them," Kincaid hissed. "The whole world's going to see what we did to Madripoor."

This time, Brady didn't reply.

"Those poor people," Kincaid continued, close to tears. He picked up the photographs, spread them across the polished oak slab of his desktop. Portraits etched in agony, they were images of men, women, and children, their mouths open in what were obviously screams. Faces were covered with bubbling blisters, eyes were swollen shut, hair was falling out in great, bleeding clumps. Some of the people pictured sought to cover their mouths and noses with scraps of cloth, but the protection was too little and too late, and all the more pathetic in its obvious futility. Nothing in their power could save them from the acidic poisons that were devouring them, from within and without.

Two days before, someone in the tiny island nation of Madripoor had made a terrible mistake and dumped fifty pounds of the right catalytic agent into the wrong processing tank at Roxxon Chemical's newest production plant. Someone else had been derelict in duty, or perhaps a warning system had failed; Kincaid wasn't sure which. He supposed it didn't matter. Either way, the results had been the same. A series of caustic reactions had followed, turning what should have been fertilizer base into something very much like certain chemical warfare agents whose use had been forbidden by international accords. Countless cubic yards of toxic horror had erupted from the site, billowing clouds of corrosive gasses that destroyed all they touched.

"Those poor people," Kincaid repeated. "Fifteen percent of an entire country's population wiped out, another ten percent left blind for life, and you want to sweep it all under the rug?"

Brady shrugged. "Fifteen percent of nothing is still nothing," he said. "Madripoor's a cesspool, a sewer. No one will miss those who died."

"Their families will," Kincaid said softly. "The people who knew them. And we were giving Madripoor a chance to quit being a sewer, remember? Roxxon was going to help them grow a real economy, give them a chance to join the legitimate world. They'll never trust us again, never trust Western business. Can you blame them?"

Brady shrugged again. "So it's back to drug traffic, bootleg software, and counterfeit Rolex watches for Madripoor," he said. "Back to being nothing but a sinkhole. So what? There are plenty of other 'developing countries' eager to do business with Roxxon. We'll find a new patsy."

"No, we won't," Kincaid said. "What we're going to do is tell the world what happened. We'll make whatever amends we can, and we'll hope to God that society can find some way to forgive us for the cut corners, for the rushed training, for the shoddy construction, for the subgrade steel in the containment vessel." He picked up the gun, wrapped his patrician fingers around the cool textured plastic of its grip. "And for the bribes and the kickbacks that made them all possible," he continued.

"How much do you know about the bribes?" Brady asked. He sounded curious.

"Enough. I know that thirty percent of the plant construction funds went directly into the prince's pocket, and another twelve percent went into your Costa Verde bank account. I know about the starvation wages and the botched inspections. God. I know that Roxxon likes to do things this way, but I thought my division was clean." Kincaid paused, composing himself. "Why did you do it, Brady?"

"I didn't," Brady said. He smiled. "You did. You're the boss, remember?"

Kincaid shook his head. "It's not going to be that easy," he said. "You were sloppy. I put the paper trail back together, and followed it to you."

"Oh?" Brady said. "Anyone else who follows it will just find a certain holier-than-thou division head who finally got his delicate hands dirty, and who couldn't stand the shame of discovery. That's the easy answer. Once you've committed suicide, the authorities won't look any further."

He stood.

"Suicide?" Kincaid said. He thumbed back the hammer on his gun. "That's why you think I have this? Not a chance. That's the coward's way out. I'm no coward."

"The media will disagree, and so will the courts," Brady responded. "But neither will ask you for your side of the story." He strode toward his superior. "You won't be available."

Kincaid pulled the trigger, then pulled it again. The gun roared and bullets smashed into the other man's chest. Blood pulsed out of the holes they made, to paint the front of his shirt crimson.

Brady didn't stop, or even pause.

Kincaid shot him some more, but to no avail. Desperately, he threw the gun at Brady's head, but the other man ducked easily. Brady reached for him then, and Kincaid began to scream.

He didn't scream for very long.

Five years ago:

Janos Horvath didn't like the foreign consultant his superiors had hired. The man was old, and bald, and liver-spotted, and weak like American beer. Janos, however, had long ago learned the twin virtues of courtesy and obedience—courtesy to one's guest, and unhesitant obedience to one's masters. The latter, especially, had served him well during the political upheavals that had rocked his native Hungary. If Supervisor Ormsk said to show this Burns person whatever he wanted, Janos was only too willing to comply. Right now, what the American wanted to see was the primary controls for the coolant system that served the decaying nuclear power plant that lay less than twelve kilometers from Janos's native village of Baktakek.

"Excellent," the older man said, gazing at the control panel. It was a greasy assembly of switches and buttons that displayed the effects of more than thirty-five years of continuous use. "Simply excellent," the consultant repeated. He steepled his fingers and grinned.

Burns's reaction puzzled Janos. The Baktakek reactor had been state-of-a-rather-primitive-art back in 1963, when Nikita Khrushchev himself had officiated at its opening; now, the place was little more than a relic, held together with prayers and good intentions. Who could express enthusiasm upon seeing such a thing? He must have let some of his confusion show because Burns answered the unspoken question.

"Here, here, fellow," the older man said. Apparently in an attempt to demonstrate camaraderie, he slapped his guide on the back. Janos barely felt the impact; it was as if a feather had landed there, so light and ineffectual was the blow. "I can tell what you're thinking, my friend," Burns continued. "You're wishing you had one of those newfangled reactors, all sleek and smooth, with accessories and computerized controls, hm?''

Janos nodded. That was exactly what he wished. That was what all of the surrounding province wished—to be freed of this decaying monstrosity, and have something relatively safe in its place. As things stood, however, the best that they could hope for was a modest improvement in security and safety— and Janos was sure than the cost for even that much would be more than poor Hungary could afford. ''Yes,'' he said. ''Of course we wish to modernize. That is why we brought you here.''

Burns shook his head, ruffling the too-long fringe of gray hair that clung to his balding pate. ''No, no, no and no,'' he said. ''Automation and transistors take all the fun out of this business.'' He gestured at the panel of switches. ''These are Korsakov-Lysenko systems, a precise imitation of the Swiss Orten controllers, and I cut my eyeteeth on a set of Ortens. Let me show you a little trick the boys at MIT taught me.''

Before Janos could stop him, Burns leaned closer to the control panel and ran his frail hands over its contours. Faster than Janos would have believed possible, the palsied fingers pressed buttons, flipped switches, and ran vernier controls along their tracks. Then, moving even more swiftly, Burns tapped a series of command codes into the panel's keyboard, stabbed the ENTER key, and stepped back, grinning.

''There we go,'' he said.

The words had barely left his mouth when the sirens began to sound.

Janos suddenly felt very cold. ''What is it?'' he gasped. ''What is this you've done?''

''Shut down the coolant pumps, drained the reactor pool, and withdrawn the control rods,'' Burns said, still grinning. ''Didn't even have to override the safeties. I love this system. It's so user friendly, don't you know?''

''Undo it! Change them back!'' Janos commanded, feeling even colder now. He thought of what would happen when the reactor core reached peak temperatures. He thought of heat measured in the thousands of degrees, of uranium atoms tearing themselves to pieces, releasing a firestorm of free quanta as they frantically sought newer, more stable forms.

He thought of Chernobyl.

He stared at the controls. As if of their own will, his fingers twitched and curled. He tried to remember what Burns had done, which sequences the other man's hands had followed. If he could do the same things, if he could do them in reverse—

"Wouldn't waste my time if I were you," Burns said. "You don't have much of it left. Twenty minutes at most, I would guess, and that's certainly not long enough to deduce the password I installed in your little toys."

Password? Janos moaned. The sirens got louder. Janos could hear frightened shouts in the corridor and the pounding of cheaply shod feet on old concrete as the rest of the power plant staff hastily evacuated. For a moment, he thought of joining them, and then decided that there was no point; he would never be able to reach safety in time.

Again, Burns seemed to anticipate his thoughts. "Seventeen minutes to core meltdown now," the insane American said. "Then we'll see something, I promise you!"

"Undo it!" Janos repeated. "Put it back!" He grabbed the older man's shoulders and began shaking him. "Fix it, before we all die!"

"Die?" Burns said, a quizzical tone in his voice. "Why, I—" A pained expression passed over his wrinkled features. His own hands came up now, and at first, Janos thought he would try to claw his way free—but all that Burns did was clutch his own chest, and emit a pained gasp. "Oh, dear," the American said. "I do believe I'm having a heart attack."

"Heart attack? No, oh no, please no, you can't," Janos begged, releasing his iron grip. "You've got to undo this terrible thing, you must—"

The pained look flared briefly to one that neatly expressed agony, and then faded to something more peaceful. "Yes," Burns said softly. A look of peace flowed across his wrinkled features. "A heart attack. A major cardiac infarction, I do believe."

He collapsed and sprawled on the dirty floor.

Janos made a sound of pain and despair. He dropped to his knees beside the stricken man and looked frantically for some sign of life.

He was still looking fifteen minutes later, when the reactor erupted.

One year ago:

"The representatives of the press are ready, Your Majesty," Schultz said. He stepped closer to the seated king and extended one hand, to help him rise.

King Thisbee sighed and smiled. "The world changes, gentlemen," he said to his guests. "There was a time when the press waited for events. Now, events wait for the press."

The witticism was slight, but surprisingly effective at easing the tension in the lavishly appointed anteroom that led to Sylvania's throneroom. The two other men sharing the room permitted themselves slight smiles, expressions that would have been unthinkable in each other's presence even a month before. A month before that, and they might have been at each other's throats, eagerly trying to kill one another. Now, seated before one of Europe's longest-reigning monarchs, a man who represented a lineage that had ruled, unbroken, for many centuries, they were nearly at ease with one another—but not completely.

"The world changes," Thisbee repeated. He rose, leaning heavily on Schultz's supporting arm. He was an old man, and moved with a cautious precision. "At least, I hope it changes."

"It will, Majesty," one of the others said. "It must." He spoke the Sylvanian dialect without flaw, but with a slight German accent, the legacy of his own lineage. His blond hair and blue eyes were in stark contrast to the darker colors of the other seated man. Otto Batemann's grandparents had been German, residents of the Ghormenghast province, the ownership of which had been bitterly contested by Germany and Sylvania for many centuries. World War II had settled that particular dispute, at least for now, and Germany had ceded

11

the territory to Sylvania as postwar reparations. Still, many Ghormenghast residents thought of themselves as Germans, and that mindset was key to the country's current unrest.

Germans, at least ethnic German Sylvanians, didn't like Gypsies very much—and Gypsies had roamed the green hills of Sylvania for longer even than Thisbee's forefathers had ruled there. Gypsies occupied an exalted place in this part of the world; one of their number had even risen to the throne of neighboring Latveria.

Gregor Samsa, still seated, smiled sardonically, his strong white teeth in stark contrast to his swarthy skin and dark lips. Samsa represented one of the largest and most powerful Gypsy tribes, and looked as comfortable in the tailored suit he now wore as he would have in his more colorful, traditional garb. "If not, we've wasted a great deal of time here these past months, eh, Otto?" he asked. "And I know you hate to waste time."

Otto stood and extended his hand. "Come, Gregor," Batemann said. "Enough of hatred, eh?" He smiled again as the Gypsy's hand clasped his.

Though spoken lightly, the words did not come easily, and nor did the offered handshake. Two headstones in his village cemetery marked the graves of Batemann's brother and cousin, both killed by Gypsy bandits three years before. In revenge, the Batemann family had raided Gypsy camps and burned Gypsy wagons. Such skirmishes were a way of life in the little country, and had become increasingly harsh in recent years. Now, at last, the ethnic German community and the Gypsy fathers had agreed to turn their backs on history, and work together as the next century approached. Respected and admired by both sides as a man of peace and impartiality, King Thisbee had mediated those negotiations and guided them toward success. All that remained now was the royal proclamation that would ratify the agreement, followed by the long, hard job of turning good intentions into reality.

Sylvania was a small nation, but it occupied a position of great strategic importance, bordering as it did both Germany and Latveria. The world paid close attention to what happened there, and the recent outbreaks of ethnic violence had drawn public attention. Now, the castle media room was crowded with correspondents from four continents, and dozens of video cameras stared, unblinking, at the dais where the signing would take place. On the dais, on a polished table, the ornate parchment used for royal proclamations waited, along with a ceremonial pen. A dozen representatives of both the Germans and the Gypsies were scattered through the crowd, eager to witness the ceremony for their own people. All turned attentively as the King entered the room.

Schultz stepped to the microphone. "His Royal Highness, King Thisbee," he announced to the waiting throng.

The room immediately became silent, except for the clicking of camera shutters.

Thisbee looked out at the crowded room and smiled. He rarely spoke at public functions, but today he seemed ready to make an exception. "Please, my friends," he said into a nearby microphone. "Join with me, as Gregor and Sylvania turn a new page in history's book."

More cameras clicked, audible even over the soft murmur of sudden, whispered questions and comments. Correspondents looked quizzically at camera operators, and Germans and Gypsies stared at one another with mingled anticipation and curiosity at the King's words. The fact that Thisbee had spoken at all was unusual enough, but the cryptic nature of his words prompted even more interest.

The fact that he had not mentioned Otto Batemann's name was causing some comment, too.

Thisbee plucked the ceremonial pen from its holder and gripped it in his right hand. He draped one arm across Gregor Samsa's shoulders, an unprecedented public gesture of familiarity for the monarch to make toward a leader of either warring faction.

The soft murmur from the spectators became louder, and even Samsa suddenly looked confused and nervous.

"Gregor, Gregor, Gregor," the king said, smiling broadly. "Did you really believe that I would allow the German interlopers to hold any sway over Sylvania's most beloved denizens?'' He laughed, a short, harsh bark of derision. Then he struck, with far greater speed and force than any man his age should have been able to muster.

Samsa tried to stop him, but he didn't try fast enough, shock and disbelief slowing his response. The Gypsy leader could do little more than cry out in horror as the much-loved and universally respected King of Sylvania stabbed Batemann in the left eye with the ceremonial pen.

Batemann died instantly.

The shouts and screams and anguished pandemonium that filled the room were sudden, hectic and loud, but gave only the faintest hint of the horror that would fill Sylvania's streets in the days to come.

Today:

The cascading tumult of sound and light came to a halt as the nine television monitors went dark and silent. Even as the last images faded, a telephone at the seated man's right buzzed. He plucked the receiver from its rest and brought it to his ear without speaking.

''Thinker?'' a voice said. ''Are you there?'' The words were in English, but spoken with a thick Russian accent.

''Of course I am here,'' the man seated in the darkness replied. With some effort, he kept his voice free of the contempt he felt for all who were his intellectual inferior—a number that included all of the world's populace. ''Report, Kragoff.''

''All proceeds on schedule. Phase One is ninety-seven percent complete. The final counterpart will be in place this week. We are proceeding slightly ahead of schedule. Phase Two—''

''Phase Two need not concern us just now,'' the Thinker said. He paused for a moment, sifting through his flawless memory in order to isolate the details of the current operation. ''Tell me more about the current status of Phase One. I assume the discrepancy is with the New York aspect.''

''Yes,'' Kragoff said. ''In the city. Construction has gone unexpectedly well. The foundation concrete proved to be of a lower grade than the records indicated. We anticipate completion of the access tunnel later today. That should free some assets and have a ripple effect on subsequent tasks.''

The Thinker frowned, an expression that was perfectly at home on his broad features. He had spent an enormous amount of time developing the current schedule, and liked to see milestones met early only slightly less than he liked to see them met late. ''Unacceptable,'' he said. ''Cease excavation or slow it, until the completion hour matches my projections. I want that tunnel completed on time—not early, not late. Punctuality is essential to the success of your assignment.''

Kragoff paused before speaking again. ''Agreed,'' he said slowly. ''I bow to your superior wisdom in such matters.''

The Thinker almost laughed at the frustration in the other man's voice. He understood Kragoff's annoyance. The Russian was unaccustomed to keeping any schedule, let alone one as demanding as this, and no doubt had thought himself doing well by working faster than anticipated. In many cases, that might have been true, but not here and not now. ''And tomorrow?'' he continued.

''On schedule precisely,'' Kragoff responded. ''All goes as you said it would. The explosive charges are in place, and I personally verified the shipping manifests less than an hour ago.''

''Good,'' the Thinker repeated, meaning it. Accurate data was essential to any successful operation, and Kragoff's special abilities made gathering it easy. ''And your servitors?''

This time, there was pleasure and even affection in Kragoff's voice. ''My loyal ones? They are always ready. They never fail me.''

''That pleases me, Kragoff,'' the Thinker said. ''It's good to be surrounded by those who deserve your trust.'' He paused, considering the time, without consulting a clock or watch. He needed neither. ''Call this number again in eighteen hours and forty-two minutes,'' he said. ''We will discuss Phase Two then.''

''Barring unforeseen developments?''

The Thinker smiled again. He thought about a South American street paved in cobblestones, and about one stone in particular, and about the terrible repercussions caused by that stone's absence. He thought about Pedro Gomez, the hapless maintenance worker whose job it had been to inspect that stretch of road for safety before the Export Commerce Minister took his daily ride. Gomez's official superiors had discharged the man, believing he had failed in his rather simple duty.

The Thinker knew the truth—that Gomez had pried the brick loose from its proper place and disposed of it, acting on the commands of his true master.

"Unforeseen developments?" he said into the telephone. His voice held a mocking note. "There will be none."

Driving on Madison Avenue was like being in a parking lot that had, for some reason, decided to move ever-so-slowly north, with many stops and starts as it struggled along though the blustery winter day. Just now, a bit less than a block before the Brooks Brothers store that marked the intersection with Forty-fourth Street, the slow crawl became a standstill again. Luther P. Winwood responded by muttering something impolite as he brought the ChemCo delivery truck he was driving to a halt.

"Is it always this slow?" asked Vic Peck, slumped on the worn upholstery to Luther's right. Peck was a heavyset man in his forties, at least ten years older than Winwood, but his voice had a childish tone to it.

"Always," Winwood said curtly. He didn't like Peck, and figured that the other man had probably been hired as his replacement. That was the problem with ChemCo, and with the rat-faced weasel who ran the shipping desk—no loyalty to the little guys who made the operation work, the rank-and-file who knew which rules to obey and which ones to "forget." Customers had complained about Winwood in the last few months, about tardy deliveries and surly comments. The human rodent in shipping had issued a few written reprimands about paperwork and regulations, and Winwood knew that the higher-ups were looking for a chance to replace him. It stood to reason that they would have an easier time doing that with a fully trained backup driver already on the payroll. Making Winwood train his own replacement was adding insult to injury, but he didn't see any way out of it.

"Man, it's like swimming through mud," Peck said softly. He looked out the van's windows at the cars and trucks surrounding it, at the endless stream of noisy, dirty utility vehicles that carried goods and services through the island metropolis. Slush splashed as tires cut through it. The day was cold enough that both men had kept their windows closed. The glass barriers blocked out some of the city noise, but not all of it.

"Y'get used to it," Winwood said. "It takes a while, but it's not so bad, once you do." He meant it, too; four years of making deliveries for ChemCo ("We're the Chemical Company!") had thoroughly conditioned him to the herky-jerky rhythm of city traffic. If Peck hadn't been doing a ride-along, Winwood would have been as happy as a clam, lightly zoned out and thinking about nothing much. With Peck in the next seat, however, he found he had to think a bit more, and he wasn't enjoying the experience.

Ahead of them, the smiling mascot painted on the back of a donut delivery van moved forward a trifle faster than a snail might move. The mascot was scratched and scarred, and the truck looked like it had seen better days, but Winwood scarcely noticed. He lifted his right foot from the brake and let his own truck's idling engine pull it ahead another ten feet or so before pushing the brake down again.

"Look at that," Peck said. He pointed at another truck, just turning onto Madison from Forty-fourth. "Long Haul. I've seen them every day this week."

Winwood nodded, but didn't say anything. Peck's running commentary simultaneously annoyed, bored, and distracted him, three things he didn't like very much. If he had to think about anything, better it should be a subject of his own choosing. Besides, he already knew plenty about Long Haul Trucking, having worked for them for two years before landing the ChemCo gig. Working for Long Haul was real work, too—hard, physical labor, muscling wooden crates and office furniture in and out of hot, dirty trucks. Typical shifts were ten hours, along regular routes that ran through all five boroughs, with special runs out to Jersey. No vacation, no union, no insurance other than Worker's Compensation. He hoped he wouldn't have to go back to that kind of work when the other shoe finally fell, and Peck inherited the cushy ChemCo billet.

"How long have you been doing this kind of work, Luther?" Peck asked, apparently tired of scrutinizing the steel tide that surrounded them.

"Eight years. Nine, come this spring," Winwood said. "Grew up in the city. My brother wanted me to go into the family business, see the world, but I decided to get a local job, instead."

"Oh? What's your brother doing?"

"Right now, twenty to life at Ryker's," Winwood said, grinning without humor. "Eustace killed an old man, about twelve blocks from here."

Peck didn't seem surprised, which was surprising, itself. "Ryker's, huh?" he said. "I worked there for fourteen years, until about a month ago. I was a correctional officer."

"You mean a guard."

"A correctional officer," Peck repeated. "But there was some trouble. A breakout, some missing evidence. I hadn't done anything wrong, of course—"

"Of course not." Winwood snickered.

"—but I decided to seek career opportunities elsewhere." Peck sounded bitter. "Early retirement gets me a partial pension, and this job—"

There was a sound like muffled thunder, and something hard smashed into the van, moving fast enough to tear through the vehicle's metal skin.

"What the—!" Winwood said, the cracked plastic steering wheel shaking free from his loose grip as the impact shook the truck.

"What was that? What's happening?"

Winwood pushed on the brake, twisted in his seat, and craned his neck to look into the van's cargo area. What he saw didn't make him happy. Something had torn through the vehicle's side panels, making one dinner-plate-sized hole as it came in and another as it exited. Racks lined the freight hold, anchored to the walls, and the missile—whatever it was—had smashed through those too, and the containers they held. Now, liquids of many colors and varying consistencies spewed from shattered carboys and jugs, splashing into pools on the floorboards. Even as Winwood watched, something red and liquid found some other, colorless fluid, and combined with it to release acrid gasses that made his nose sting and his eyes water. A moment later, the roiling cloud was lit from within, as some other combination of chemicals came to incandescent life.

The blood in Winwood's veins suddenly turned to ice. Fire.

They were on fire. Fire was bad. He knew about the unlabelled fifty-gallon drum that lurked back there, just beyond the rippling veil of gasses. The metal cylinder held something quite dangerous, something that ChemCo didn't have a license to carry within city limits, and didn't have the proper container to carry it in, no matter what the circumstances. If the fire found it—when the fire found it—

"We've got to get out of here!" he snapped at Peck.

"But—"

"I said, *get out of here!*" Winwood yelled, bellowing the words over his shoulder even as he popped his door open and tumbled out into traffic. It was cold and clear outside, but he knew that both situations were about to change. The truck lurched as he left it, and started rolling slowly forward again. By some unpleasant coincidence, the surrounding flow had started moving, and he had to dodge cars and trucks and he ran for the sidewalk. Scrambling through the last lane of traffic, he squirmed between two parked cars and looked back to see if Peck had obeyed his frenzied command.

He was just in time to seen the ChemCo truck's front bumper kiss the donut delivery van's rear one, and then to see both vehicles disappear, subsumed by a black-and-orange sphere of flame.

Seven minutes later, Madison Avenue had become an outpost of hell. Thick billows of white gasses rolled between cars and trucks and vans, searing and burning anyone they found. Below them, narrower rivulets of liquid fire traced erratic paths along the wet pavement, found one another, united, then split again, burning channels into the asphalt before dripping into storm drains and sewer gratings. The tendrils of flame lit the artificial fog bank from below, granting the clinging vapors a spectral radiance as they spread, apparent even in the weak afternoon sun.

By now, traffic had halted completely, and the narrow spaces between the stalled vehicles were filled with jostling humanity as frantic drivers and passengers abandoned their vehicles and sought relative safety. It was not an easy quest;

too much smoke, too many gases, too much fire blocked their paths. Feet slipped on the slushy pavement, making the evacuation even more chaotic.

And then there was the noise, a rich, aural tapestry of curses and coughs, of frantic pleas for help from tortured throats that became rawer and rawer with each breath. Fire alarms in neighboring storefronts rang, activated by the clouds of gas and smoke. Somewhere in the clogged municipal artery, a driver, overcome by the airborne toxins, slumped across his car's steering wheel, and the sharp blaring horn joined the cacophony. In the distance, police and fire engine sirens wailed as the city attempted to respond to the disaster, only to find that the streets were too full, too choked to allow direct access.

Beneath the smoke, beneath the gases, in the intersection of Madison and Forty-fourth Street and below the motionless Long Haul truck, a manhole cover moved. It moved by floating upward in a straight line, to hover six inches above the opening it covered. Then it drifted lazily to one side and settled noiselessly to the adjacent asphalt. Two hands that might have been paws groped through the now-open manhole, and then more of a quasi-human figure followed. He had broad shoulders and a head that looked a trifle off-scale, a huge, barrel-like torso, and too-long arms, all of them wrapped in protective garments.

He had the build of a gorilla.

Still only halfway out of the manhole, the newcomer reached upward, and dug gloved fingers into the metal of the truck's undercarriage. It tore with relative ease, so he ripped a sizable section free and set it aside, then reached up again had began clawing at the thick wooden planks of the truck's cargo compartment floor. Those offered more resistance, but not much, and in seconds, the apish newcomer had torn completely through them. He made a grunt of something like satisfaction, then reached further up and pulled himself through the opening into the dimly lit cargo area.

There, someone was waiting. He was a stocky man, wearing a fur-trimmed coat, baggy trousers, and heavy work gloves and boots. At his waist, a leather holster held a weapon. What remained of his hair was snow white and long on the sides, and his blue eyes glinted as they spotted the newcomer.

"Well done, my loyal one," Ivan Kragoff said. "You are precisely on schedule."

The only response was another grunt.

Johnny Storm was fifty stories above Manhattan and heading north when he heard the explosion. He was flying over Madison, following the course of the famous street, but far removed from its choking tide of trucks and cars, buses and motorcycles, pedestrians and bicycle-riding messengers. He was far enough above the dirty asphalt that he heard the blast only as a muffled retort, nearly masked by roaring engines and other traffic noise that echoed up through the concrete walls of the city. He took little note of the blast, his mind still occupied by happier thoughts.

Then he saw the black, roiling clouds of smoke and the bright, flickering fingers of flame clawing their way upward around the jammed traffic below.

He saw the flames as few others could, not just as jagged tendrils of yellow and orange, but as complex, rippling masses of thermal currents, elaborate webs of exothermic chemical reactions that consumed more and more volume as they built upon themselves. Johnny knew that, even as he watched, free oxygen threw itself into the flames, heated and broke from stable molecular pairs into volatile atoms, and then frantically sought new stability by combining with other matter. One result of the two-step process was heat, and lots of it, thermal energy that drew more oxygen to it, repeating the cycle. Unattended, it would keep building, Johnny knew, until it ran out of oxygen or fuel to feed it.

The Human Torch knew a lot about fire.

Johnny drew up short in his flight, stopping above the blaze. He hovered in midair, some three hundred feet above the conflagration. His own fires held him there. Johnny's body was a mass of flame, sheathed in an incandescent plasma that burned but did not consume. The plasma, in turn heated the surrounding air and created a vortex, a constant updraft that fought gravity's pull. Like the fire below, the fires that sheathed his body sought to grow and spread; unlike them, however, his flames were held in check by his own will, controlled and shaped with the ease of long practice. Years before, a chance accident involving cosmic rays had transformed the teenaged Johnny Storm into something that was more than human— grander and more terrible, a creature of the elements, a Human Torch. Now, effortlessly and without conscious thought, the Torch slightly reduced the power of his flame. In instant response, the heated vortex surrounding him cooled a few degrees, and Johnny allowed gravity to pull him downward.

Whatever had happened, it was messy, he realized. At least two vehicles were nothing but blackened twists of metal now, and many more had been damaged by spewing gouts of flame from the central blaze. Newly disenfranchised drivers were trying desperately to make their way to the sidewalks, but they weren't having much luck. Some kind of chemical vapor had erupted from one of the sundered vehicles and spread through the still-crowded streets in puffy billows. They cloaked but did not conceal the rivulets of flame that still burned beneath them. Johnny easily recognized the familiar heat signature, the thermal flux of burning fuel. Gasoline, he decided, and maybe something else. Jet fuel? He wondered for a brief moment how *that* had happened, then shook his head and pushed the thought away. The details could wait for later.

As he dropped, more sounds reached him. The sounds weren't as interesting as the flames, but he noted them nonetheless. Horns and car alarms. The rumbling thunder of the central blaze. Frightened voices. Sirens, distant but getting closer. Shouts of anger and pain and terror. Voices.

"Look! It's the Torch! It's the Human Torch!"

"Help me! Someone help me!"

"The Torch? What good can he do?"

Johnny smiled. He gestured. The roaring pillar of flame that gushed from the intersection of Madison and Forty-fourth rippled and twisted, as if trying to ignore some unheard command. Johnny's smile became slightly tense as he concentrated and gestured again. This time, the column of fire obeyed. In stark defiance of natural law, the raging inferno folded in on itself. It flattened and condensed into a single ribbon of almost blindingly intense radiance, a ribbon that unfurled itself to bridge the gap between the two burning trucks and the Human Torch's right hand. Suddenly, the fire consuming the vehicles burned more cleanly and efficiently, nearing white heat even as it rushed to merge completely with the fiery corona that surrounded Johnny Storm's blazing body. The fire's base burned even more brightly as the sudden increase in heat sped the convection currents that fed it. The sudden flare of life was enough to heat the sundered trucks' frames to incandescence, but the sudden fury was short-lived. In seconds, the entire body of flame was gone, merged with and destroyed by the Human Torch's plasma envelope. A moment after that, and the last dull red glints of heat had faded from the burning truck carcasses as the heated metal cooled, its thermal energy drawn off and absorbed.

In the streets below, cries of fear became cheers, audible even over the wailing sirens that became even louder as emergency service vehicles approached. Here and there on the still-crowded sidewalks, witnesses and bystanders applauded. Johnny liked the sound, and gave himself a second to enjoy it before going back to work. There was more to do, even if the biggest, most pressing problem had been resolved.

Inside the Long Haul truck, the stocky man gestured at a file cabinet, anchored with straps to the truck's inner wall. It was a locking cabinet, the kind used by government contractors to store classified files, with inches-thick walls and a combination lock that qualified it as a safe. "The second drawer," the man said. "Quickly, now."

His companion, the newcomer placed one hand on the second drawer's handle, and braced the other against the first drawer's face. He yanked. Metal shrieked and tore, then there was a sound like a rifle shot as the safe's bolt broke and the drawer came free. Effortlessly, the apish figure pulled out the entire drawer assembly and cradled the heavy mass in his arms. It was filled with files and papers, and a magnetically insulated subcompartment apparently held computer backup tapes.

The sirens outside were getting louder as rescue services found ways to the scene of the disaster. Wisps of off-white gasses were drifting into the truck's interior, and tendrils of flame were visible through the breach in the floorboards, but they weren't as bright or as plentiful as they had been a moment before. The disturbance outside seemed to be lessening a bit more quickly than anticipated. The man wondered why, and then he wondered what impact the new development would have on his timetable.

He looked at his wristwatch, which he wore on a heavy strap on the outside of his left glove. "Three-eleven precisely," the man said. "Satisfactory." His part of the operation was nearly done. Another minute was all he needed.

The truck's other occupant, still carrying his burden, shuffled back to the hole in the floor. He extended his arms and released the file-cabinet drawer. It hung in midair for a moment, suspended by some invisible force; then it drifted downward, angling itself through the torn floorboards and the still-open manhole. The apish figure dropped after it and vanished. The manhole cover rose again, drifted a few feet, then dropped back into place with a satisfying *clang!*

Above, the white-haired man took one final glance about the sundered truck, and then shrugged, as if nothing remained to interest him. A faint expression of concentration flickered across his features, and then he moved downward, too—but not through the opening his underling had created. Instead, he passed through the wood and steel undercarriage as if it were not there, as if it were mere smoke or illusion. Without sound, without comment, without any evident difficulty or pain, the man seeped through the truck's structure, to disappear beneath the scorched asphalt of Madison Avenue.

The entire operation, from start to finish, had taken eight minutes and thirty-four seconds.

The central blaze, though extinguished, had left its mark. A dozen rivulets of liquid fire still marked the streets, and a dozen more splashing puddles of flame burned and boiled holes in the asphalt. They were arrayed in a vaguely circular pattern, the legacy of the original explosion, the last traces of the flaming fuel that the eruption had spat from itself. Whatever had caused it, the blast's work lived on even after it had died. Johnny dropped a bit lower and went to work.

As work went, it wasn't very hard. It took only seconds to draw the flame from the lavalike trails, absorbing the heat energy and incorporating it into his own metabolism. He could do things like this almost without conscious thought. The puddles demanded more attention, however, though not much. Most of them he absorbed as he had the streamers, but one or two, the ones that splashed across other vehicles, he decided to snuff a bit more swiftly. Among the abilities that the cosmic rays had bestowed upon him was the power to control his own flame with pinpoint precision; now, he used tightly focused bolts of plasma to burn off the oxygen near the other flames. Those flames failed instantly, extinguishing as neatly and cleanly as if he had thrown the switch on an electric light. Another second or so, and he had drawn off the residual heat from the pools of combustant, dropping them well below levels that would support burning. As long as no one was foolish enough to play with matches, the stuff was harmless now. Someone else could clean it up, Johnny decided.

That left the disturbance's other bequest, the still-spreading clouds of acrid vapor that clung and stung. The stuff didn't seem to be lethal, but breathing it didn't look like much fun either, and Johnny saw no reason not to deal with it immediately. He descended a bit more and hovered about ten feet above the still-choked streets. His flame was burning more brightly now, stoked by the heat he had absorbed. He had a slight surplus of thermal energy, and this would be a good opportunity to use some of it.

With nearly instinctive control, Johnny relaxed the vortex of heated air that held him aloft. He didn't reduce its temperature or its lifting power, but he let it spread, unspooling from his body in a widening curve. In moments a sprawling system of updrafts and thermal currents surrounded him, extensions of his corona that weren't hot enough to qualify as flame. Another mental command, and the vortex extended downward, cooling another ten or twenty degrees as it did. In moments, the lowest of the thermal currents, scarcely warmer than a summer breeze, had intersected with the clouds of gas that still filled the intersection.

Johnny smiled again.

The chemical fog bank rippled, flowed. It shifted and seemed to boil. Then, slowly, the stuff oozed upward, following the path that Johnny's vortex had created, swept along by the new updraft. Almost immediately, the first wisps of gas threw themselves into Johnny's flame and were consumed. He paid careful attention. This was the critical point. If the gases were flammable, or even explosive—

The chemical fog smoldered, spat, and dissipated as it broke down into something less troublesome. More followed, a spiral column of toxins given form by the convection currents that, in turn, were shaped by Johnny's will. More of the gases burned off, to no apparent bad effect. Johnny wasn't a chemist, but he knew an enormous amount about burning substances and their byproducts, gained through years of applied experience. That experience told him now that burning off the mystery vapor posed no real hazard. He redoubled his efforts and drew more of the roiling vapors toward him.

Four minutes later, the gas cloud gone and his own flame extinguished, he stood in the intersection of Madison and Forty-fourth, shaking hands and kissing babies. "Aw, shucks, ma'am, it was nothing," he said to one particularly attractive dark-haired woman whose car was streaked with scorch marks. "I'll be glad to talk to your insurance agent, but maybe you'd better give me your personal phone number so—"

"Good job, Torch," another voice said, interrupting. A heavy hand clamped down on his shoulder. "Tell you what, we won't even file a grievance with the union."

Startled, Johnny turned. "Excuse me?" he said, annoyed, and then he stopped speaking and grinned.

The firefighter grinned back at him. "Just kidding, Mr. Storm," he said. "That was sweet work. Looks like you didn't even need the cavalry this time." He extended one gloved hand.

Johnny took it. "Thanks, Captain," he said, taking quick note of the other man's rank. "Glad I could help."

"Glad you could, too. I've lived in New York all my life, and this is the first time I've met a super hero."

Johnny thought for a moment about the boiling cloud of flame that had marked the intersection only minutes before, hot enough to boil asphalt and melt steel. For him, it had been no particular challenge, little more than a moment's diversion. But to face it without his powers, with little more than protective clothing and chemical sprays—

Suddenly, he felt a bit embarrassed by all the attention he was getting, by the cheers and applause. "Don't be silly, Captain," he said, shaking the other man's hand with renewed vigor. "You guys are the real heroes."

He was surprised to realize he meant it.

Paraclete, Third Form Instructor of the Genetics Academy, led his students through a narrow corridor and into a broad, empty space. He had been here before, as part of an archeological expedition through the catacombs beneath ancient Attilan. The chamber was a broad circular space, almost like an amphitheater, ringed with gray stone columns and showing no signs of deterioration, despite centuries of disuse. Paraclete found its relative expanse and vaulted ceilings reassuring, especially after an hour or so of leading his charges through rubble-choked passages.

Paraclete didn't like enclosed spaces, a dislike that was part of his legacy as an avianoid Inhuman, marked by the birdlike adaptations common to his kind—a beak, fine feathers instead of body hair, and round eyes that moved quickly and furtively in their shallow sockets. Paraclete could not fly, at least not under his own power, but much of his body had been adapted for flight, so enclosed spaces disturbed him. Perhaps a dozen other of his people, certainly no more than a score of ancient Attilan's populace shared his specific adaptations, in greater or lesser degree. Paraclete could walk the streets of his home city for hours at a time, and never see another face that looked even remotely like his.

He liked that.

"We will pause here," he said, and waited for his thirty listeners to cease murmuring among themselves. They were a mixed lot, ranging from early adolescent to young adult. Half of them were nearly indistinguishable from the humans who had so thoroughly despoiled the Earth—two eyes, two arms, two legs, bilateral symmetry, smooth-skinned, and nearly hairless. And the others—

Ah, the others. Not for the first time, Paraclete gazed out on the attentive and varied features of his charges. To look at them was to look at the true Inhuman race, at all its mystery and majesty. A young male with three fingers on his left hand and six on his right, with reptilian skin and a prehensile tail, stood next to his current paramour, a young female who had pale gray wings and pointed ears. Like Paraclete, she was an avianoid, but without the facial adaptations; she had conventional lips and a conventional nose. Not ten feet away, the girl's brother watched them both carefully, gazing at them with iris-less eyes, his body rustling slightly as the leaves and tendrils that covered him rubbed together. Another male— Tavatar—stood near the class, but separate from it, as was often his wont. Paraclete paused as his eyes met those of the younger man.

Tavatar was, sometimes, something of a troublemaker. He was a brilliant student, but moody and withdrawn, set apart from the others by certain physical limitations. His face was half-hidden by the breathing mask he wore, connected by flexing hoses to a tank on his broad, muscular back. Without the mask and breathing apparatus, he would choke to death, betrayed by the specialized lungs that worked within his chest. But whatever inconvenience Tavatar suffered because of his adaptation, he was well-compensated by the other powers and abilities that were his birthright. Paraclete was sure of that.

There lay the beauty of the Inhuman race, the secret and power and what made it so different from it sister species, the weak and monotonous humans who had inherited the Earth.

Paraclete knew that beauty well. Early in the term, he had accessed the files of each of his students, then read their genetic codes, meditating up and savoring each complex confluence of peptides and proteins. He knew what powers and attributes each had, what hidden potential lay locked with their cells. The diversity was spellbinding, and it was because of his love for such variety that he had pursued a career in the holiest of sciences, genetics. Not as a planner, or even as a researcher—Paraclete's gifts could not justify such exalted ranks—but at least as a teacher, spreading the word and leading others to the light.

"These ruins as a whole date back to the earliest days of the Inhumans, the days when the Kree performed the experiments that resulted in our race," he said, continuing his lecture. The words came from deep within his throat, shaped there by muscles and membranes that compensated for Paraclete's pointed tongue, and lipless mouth. "Those experiments, in part, were attempts to meet the challenge from another star-faring race, the Skrulls."

"The traditional enemies of the Kree," Tavatar said. There was a slight note of challenge in his voice, a note that Paraclete had heard before.

"Not enemies when construction commenced, only competitors," Paraclete corrected. "Though mere cycles later, that rivalry would become hatred, and then ripen into war, for reasons we will discuss at another time."

"Instructor, I have a query," the winged girl said. Her voice was like a song, and Paraclete knew that only his ears could hear all of it, and that only he could appreciate the delicate supersonic *glissando* that gave emphasis to his title.

Paraclete nodded.

"Must competitors be enemies? Must one lead inevitably to the other?" she asked. "On Earth, the humans—"

"You ask a question better posed in your Philosophy session, or Sociology," Paraclete interrupted. "Here, today, we may discuss competition, because that is the handmaiden of genetics, but I cannot teach you of war or morality. I can say, however, that I know of no sentient competitors in the same environmental niche who have not gone to war at least once in their mutual histories. Skrull and Kree, human and Inhuman, Eternal and Deviant. That does not mean that there won't be—can't be—peace between them.''

This time, the girl nodded.

''The Kree built this city,'' Paraclete continued. ''They built it very early in their own history, and it is a pale and primitive place compared to the structures that mark their homeworld or their colony planets, or even our own Attilan. They returned to this place many times over the ensuing eons, however. They had—*have*—many interests on Earth, and have never entirely abandoned it, or this sector of space, even though it is not formally part of the Kree Empire.''

''And we are not subjects of them,'' Tavatar said flatly. ''Not formally.'' The words did not sound sincere as they left his lips.

Paraclete looked at him. There were rumors he had heard about Tavatar, faint whispers of radical politics and twisted allegiances that he found troubling, especially from one as promising as the younger man. Better to nip such heresies in the bud, before they could corrupt the others.

''Correct. We are not their subjects. Our people rule themselves, and we select our leaders and we appoint our kings. You know that, Tavatar.''

''I also know that the creator owns the creation, and that the Kree created us.''

Muttered comments swept through the assembled pupils, gasps and whispers and faint, derisive laughter. Paraclete raised his hands—three-fingered, with claws—for silence; when he had it, he continued.

''Ten thousand standard years ago, the Kree experimented on our ancestors, on 'normal' terrestrial human stock. Their goal was to produce a race of super soldiers for their near-constant wars,'' Paraclete said. ''That much is true. But it is foolish to say that they created us. If you must, say instead they fathered us—and the parent does not own the child.''

''Then we are their heirs, and thus their subjects,'' Tavatar said, with the unfathomable logic of a zealot. His tone was becoming harsher, more strident, and Paraclete began to worry. This was worse than he had suspected. Renewed contact with the Kree in recent years had led to the popularity of certain political dogmas that Paraclete found foolish at best, and dangerous at worst. Too many of the young Inhumans were infatuated with tales of their genesis, with the stories of vast, galaxy-spanning empires and worlds with untold wealth. Against such a glorious backdrop, to such young and uncomprehending eyes, even mighty Attilan began to seem very small, indeed.

"We can talk of this another time, after class," Paraclete said, suddenly determined to change the subject. "I brought you here to discuss heredity—"

"It is heredity of which I speak, and legacies and—"

"I said, *at another time*," Paraclete snapped. He gestured at the walls surrounding his party. "Who can tell me what this resembles?"

"Resembles?" someone asked.

More gently, Paraclete continued, "Yes. Resembles. Many of you have been in a place much like this before, even if you were too young to remember it. Many more will visit such a place, when you reach—" he looked meaningfully at Tavatar "—*maturity*."

Eager, excited answers came, all at one time:

"The Chamber of the Sacred Mists!"

"The Vault of Terrigen!"

"The Place of New Life!"

Eagerly, student after student responded, with a dozen colloquial names for one place, the Inhumans's holiest of holies, the site where their race partook of Terrigen, the secret mutagenic compound that could unlock the power hidden with their genes. Once in each lifetime, an Inhuman might partake of the Terrigen—at birth, with parental consent, or upon achieving adulthood. Some Inhumans were born without special attributes and some were born enhanced, but no one who breathed the sacred mists ever remained the same; each received a different gift from them, a new adaptation or ability or power.

Paraclete's facial structure would not allow him to smile, but he was pleased as he heard the reverential responses. "Yes," he said. "Just so. Our archeologists are still exploring this place, but we believe it may be the very first Theater of Genetics, or at least the first one in this sector of space."

"Then the Kree had the Terrigen from their earliest days?" That was the winged girl speaking again. Paraclete realized that her hand had crept into that of her parareptile suitor. He was surprised that her brother had not noticed.

"We don't know how old this place is. It may date from one of their return visits. And, no, not the Terrigen. The Terrigen is ours alone. The Kree had other ways."

"Better ways," Tavatar said.

Paraclete glared at him. "Student Tavatar," he said, with a carefully measured tone, "you are intelligent and you show great promise, but if you wish to teach class, you will first need to finish your studies and receive your rank and certification. Until then, be silent."

Tavatar continued, as if his teacher had not spoken. "Even in our race's earliest days," he said, "the Kree knew the secrets of genetic transformation. They made us, artfully and well, to serve their purposes and fight their wars. The variety we embody today is the legacy of centuries of ignorance and folly." His tone had become more urgent, and he spoke with an almost military cadence. "This place, built so long ago, is a place much like where we were born, and the secrets of our race lie here, not in Attilan, not at the fumbling hands of fools like you." His face was suddenly covered in a sheen of yellowish perspiration, and he gritted his teeth around the respirator.

Drugs? A seizure? Or something else?

"What—how dare you—" Paraclete forced the words out, suddenly aware that he had lost control of the situation. He didn't like the way the younger Inhuman looked, didn't like the look of concentration rippling across the young, half-hidden features. From his study of Tavatar's genetic code, Paraclete knew that the student possessed certain mental aptitudes, psionic potentials that preliminary evidence said would never awaken, at least not without special cultivation and training.

What if that evidence was wrong?

Paraclete suddenly felt very frightened. Everything was making a certain kind of twisted sense now—Tavatar's moodiness, his sullen arrogance, his recent obsession with his presumed ties to the Kree, to a military culture bent on galactic conquest. How would a young male, already partially isolated by his physical limitations, deal with new perceptions, new abilities, new inputs to a brain that had not been trained to receive them? Could he deal with them at all?

He might well go mad.

It had happened before, Paraclete knew.

"We will return to the matter at hand," he said, trying to regain control. "We have lessons—"

"There is nothing you can teach me, old man," Tavatar snarled. The veins on his neck bulged and throbbed like nervous serpents. The other students were pulling back from him now, frightened. They stepped back even further as Tavatar drew a small valence suppressor from beneath his robes. Paraclete recognized it as a tool from the engineering lab, a tool that could serve double duty as a deadly weapon. Tavatar continued. "I have been here before, and this place has taught me all I need to know."

What did he mean? Psychotic fantasy, or actual experience? Solo exploration of the ruins was strictly forbidden. The Kree had built their city well, and to last, and many dangerous artifacts had been found it its recesses, still working well after years of abandonment. If Tavatar *had* been here before, what had his goals been? What had he learned? Paraclete reached for the portable communicator that hung at his belt, punched the square DISTRESS switch that would send a signal back to Attilan. He didn't bother trying to speak into the device; he knew that he would never have that luxury.

"In olden times," Tavatar continued, "*my* people ruled the stars, and had only to contend with the Skrull vermin, and not with misfit aberrations sullying their gene pool." He raised the weapon, trained it at Paraclete. "When freaks like you would have been executed at birth!"

This was worse than Paraclete could have imagined. "Tavatar," he said, "I beseech you—"

The younger Inhuman squeezed the trigger.

Paraclete felt a sizable portion of his chest and abdomen disappear, dispersed into random ions. He heard the winged girl scream, at a pitch only he could hear, and then he felt himself fall to the dusty stone floor. The impact didn't hurt as much as he might have expected, but he knew that was because his body had already gone into shock. The nerves had shut down; he couldn't feel the wound, couldn't feel the red wetness that he knew had to be gushing from his ruined body, couldn't feel much of anything.

He could still hear, however.

He could hear Tavatar's ravings, and he could feel some faint sense of loss as a once-promising mind collapsed into psychotic ravings. "And now I am here again," Tavatar was saying. "Here to show you the wonder and the way, here to free you from genetic servitude to an outmoded paradigm! Here to show you the way of our makers, the way of the Kree!"

There was a rumbling sound, a grating. It seemed to come from all directions, as stone ground against stone. Paraclete shifted his gaze, saw the walls slide open, ancient slabs of dusty basalt sliding on hidden tracks to reveal banks of complex apparatus, brightly gleaming as if new-made. He had never considered this possibility. No one had. The chamber had been so barren, so empty, that no one had ever dreamed what secrets might lie behind its walls.

No one but Tavatar, evidently. How had he found the equipment? Direct mental perception? He had that aptitude, the teacher remembered, a bit of knowledge gleaned from the younger man's genetic map. Or had the Kree left some kind of hidden psionic marker that only Tavatar could heed? How had he activated the machineries? Direct mental access? His genetic code allowed for that possibility, too. They were all good questions, but Paraclete knew that he would never know their answers.

Someone screamed. Not the girl, but someone else, only to be cut short by the buzz of the valence suppressor, and the thump of another body falling to the floor beyond Paraclete's field of vision. He wondered who else lay dead or dying now, but he found it hard to care.

"No one leaves!" Tavatar shouted. "No one!"

Paraclete tried to look back in his direction, but his eyes didn't want to work anymore. They resisted him as he forced them to move slowly, slowly in their sockets, until he could see Tavatar and some of the others again. He wasn't sure why he bothered; there was nothing he could do, no way he could do anything but try to make each breath last a little longer.

And he wasn't having much success there, either.

A control station of some sort had risen from the floor at Tavatar's feet. As Paraclete watched, the madman yanked his breathing mask free, threw it on the floor, then began pressing switches. "Show you all," he gasped, his breath already coming in ragged bursts as he tried to process normal air. "Undo in a single instant ten thousand years of genetic heresy. All corrected, all fixed, all pure once more—"

"Don't do it!"

"No!"

"Tavatar! Please!"

In a distant kind of way, Paraclete wanted to join in the pleas, but he couldn't—his lungs weren't working at all anymore. Besides, something interesting was happening to his vision. The world was going black at its edges, and rippling waves of darkness were filling his field of view. Things were getting dimmer and dimmer, and the anguished cries were becoming more distant, as if the world itself were going away. He felt some regrets, a vague desire to help, but only faintly, like a half-forgotten dream. Besides, the darkness was so complete now, so all embracing, so inviting.

Something clicked and hummed, and then the humming gave way to screams. As Paraclete's vision continued to fade, he smelled something chemical, like antiseptic mixed with solvents. Light filled the chamber, a radiance that seemed brighter than the sun itself, brilliant enough to give even his dying eyes vision once more, enough to give him one final glimpse at the world he was leaving.

The last thing he saw was the winged girl melting, flowing, the lines of her lean body and her face twisting into new contours. The last thing he heard was a shriek of agony.

He knew whose scream it was.

CHAPTER 2

"I'm gettin' tired'a this," Ben Grimm said. His rumbling voice held a bored, even petulant note. He was standing in the center of a reinforced test chamber on an upper floor of the Fantastic Four's headquarters at Four Freedoms Plaza, squarely in front of a vertical steel slab, padded with black plastic. Behind the slab, mounting it to the wall, was what looked like a simple spring, but he knew that it was something much more complex. The front of the slab was scuffed and split, like a punching bag that had taken a terrific pounding from oversized fists.

The Thing's fists.

"Nonsense, Ben," Reed Richards said calmly. He was seated at the opposite end of the room, behind an equipment console. Right now, he wore a lab jacket over the blue-and-white uniform that was his work clothes as Mr. Fantastic, leader of the Fantastic Four. A tall, lean man with brown hair going white at the sides, he looked thoughtful as he gazed at the readings displayed before him. "Your metabolic levels show no sign of fatigue."

"Listen up, Stretch. I didn't say 'fatigued,' I said 'tired,' " the Thing said. "You've had me hooked up to this gizmo for more than an hour now, and I'm gettin' tired of it." He looked sourly at one of the dozen or so electronic modules glued to his blocky form. They were little turtle-shaped devices, flattened hemispheres with several projections, and their LED indicators seemed to return his stare. Ben snorted softly. His blue eyes moved in their deep sockets and focused on Reed again. "Besides, we've danced this one before, haven't we?" he continued. "Seems to me, I spend half my life doin' tests for you, like a trained circus monkey, and the other half movin' heavy furniture around this dump. I guess that's next, right?"

"I just need a few more readings on the stress tester, Ben," the other man said patiently. "You've got an anomalous spike in your fourth basal—"

"Ya want readings?" the Thing asked. "Read *this*!"

The stonelike orange armor plates that covered Ben Grimm's entire body made a sound like grinding rocks as he brought his hands together. Each had only three fingers and a thumb, but they still laced together well, making a solid, dense mass. The Thing raised both arms until the double fist was above and behind his head.

Richards looked up from his console, an apprehensive expression on his face. He had seen this kind of behavior before. "Ben," he said, "please don't—"

Too late.

The Thing brought his four-fingered hands forward and down again, the big muscles of his back and arms driving them ahead with tremendous force, moving so swiftly that the room's air molecules whistled as his swinging arms displaced them. Ben twisted his body as he struck, so that the double blow met the metal slab from a vector precisely perpendicular to its already battered surface.

There was a sound like thunder, a rumbling crashing noise that could be felt as much as heard. Metal shrieked and tore as the thick steel bowed under the impact. The springlike assembly behind the striking surface compressed, held the force for a moment, and then released it again—or tried to.

Already, the Thing had braced himself for the recoil, and now he braced the slab too, clutching the thick edges of its bent face. His splayed, four-toed feet dug into the test chamber's floor. He grunted softly as the force of his own blow tried to return home, only to find the muscles that had created it blocking its path. Unable to go forward, the spring's energy spent itself instead to the rear, tearing a hole through the test chamber's armored wall and hurling itself into the room beyond. Still moving fast, even as it passed from view, the uncoiling spring tore loose from the slab that Ben still held and kept moving, smashing against and then through another wall. Alarms wailed and sirens rang, masking but not hiding the sound of crashing, tearing metal as the spring struck and rebounded again and again. Finally, somewhere in the distance, it stopped.

The Thing let the battered chunk of padded steel drop. "Did ya get those readings you wanted, Stretch?" he said mildly.

"Ben, that was a perfectly good inertial shunt, and I still

had uses for it," Reed said, clearly annoyed. "You've got to learn that scientific equipment doesn't grow on trees—" His words trailed off into silence as the Thing began to divest himself of the various sensor modules.

Ben did it the easy way. Not bothering to detach the telemetry relays, he simply ran corrugated hands along the mountainous contours of his own body, grinding the electronics modules into dust. Glistening chips of metal and silicate rained to the floor and accumulated in a pile at his feet. Then there was a noise like a small, distant avalanche as he rubbed his hands together to shake loose the last of the dust.

He looked pleased with himself.

"I wish you would learn to control your temper," Reed said.

"This ain't temper, Stretch," the Thing said. "This here's just plain ol' crankiness. I told you I had things to do today, places to go. You promised me this checkup would only take a few minutes. Last time I checked, sixty ain't a few."

"I know, I know," Reed said. He looked at his control panel again. "Still, the new analysis algorithms were yielding some fascinating results."

"Does that mean you're gonna be able to cure me?" The Thing's voice held no note of hope. "I've danced to that one before, too." Suddenly, he looked smaller somehow, as if simply thinking of his lost humanity had taken something more from him. Standing in the midst of the wreckage he had created, his head bowed and his shoulders slumped, he looked in some ways like an unhappy little boy. "Why don't you just give up, Reed?" he asked, in a surprisingly soft voice. "I have."

Years before, the unscheduled test flight of an experimental space ship had had dramatic consequences for its passengers—especially Ben Grimm, the pilot. Cosmic rays, seeping in through the craft's inadequate shielding, had made them all more than human in some ways, and in some ways less—especially for Ben. Reed Richards, the ship's inventor, had gained the power to stretch and mold his body into almost any shape. Susan Storm, now Susan Richards, had been given the power to become invisible, and to create shields and walls of invisible energy. Her brother, Johnny Storm, became the Human Torch. And Ben—

Ben had become a monster.

There was no other word. Freakishly huge, unimaginably strong, covered from head to toe in scaly, rocklike armor, all that had remained recognizably human were his eyes. They peered out at Reed Richards now, blue and intense and vulnerable, from beneath a projecting brow that would have done Frankenstein's monster proud.

"Never gonna be a cure, Stretch. Just false hopes. Give 'em up."

"You can't mean that, Ben," Reed replied. Two steps on elongated legs brought him to the side of his oldest, closest friend, and he placed one white-gloved hand on the Thing's shoulder. "You can't let yourself think that way." Since the fateful day of that journey into outer space, Reed Richards had constantly worked to reverse the change that the cosmic rays had wrought on the other man.

Fingers that could shred steel were oddly gentle as they grasped Mr. Fantastic's wrist and plucked his hand free from the Thing's shoulder. "I mean it, Reed. I'm tired'a foolin' myself."

"Ben—"

The Thing shook his head. "Nah," he said. "You keep playin' with your toys, if you want—but we both know they won't make any difference." He glanced down at himself again. "We both know I'm like this—that I *am* this, forever."

"I don't think that's true, Ben. I don't think the situation is as severe as you think."

"It is," the Thing said. "Severe for me, anyhow. The rest of you got off light—you're still human."

"Are we? Do you really think we're more human than you?"

A puzzled grunt was Ben's only reply.

"Think about it. Do human beings stretch like taffy, or spray fire from their fingertips? Or Sue's force fields and transparency—how many humans have those kind of effects at their command?''

''An' how many look like a walking brickyard, an' juggle pianos when they're bored?'' The sneer was apparent in the Thing's voice, if not on his features.

''Those are changes of degree, Ben—not of kind. Though visually more *evident* than those of the rest of us, your body's mutagenic response to the cosmic rays is actually somewhat less extensive. Your muscles and bones still work much the same way they always did, your blood chemistry is only about forty percent outside of normal parameters, certainly much closer to human norms than my own. Even the tissue that makes up your epithelial armor is closely related to ordinary bone and hair.''

''Oh, yeah, I'm sure. Ever try combing this stuff?''

''I'm serious, Ben. You were a strong man before the launch; you're stronger now. Your endurance and durability have been similarly enhanced, but you had those qualities to begin with, too. I assure you, however, that Johnny couldn't flame on, not even 'just a little bit,' before the launch. I suspect it would be much more difficult to reverse the alterations in his biochemistry, or in Sue's, or in my own, than it will be to change you back.''

'' 'Will'?'' Ben quoted.

''Will,'' Reed repeated. ''We've already had some success,'' he said, referring to several previous attempts, some of which resulted in Ben Grimm temporarily regaining his human form, others that changed the nature of his mutation. ''And we'll have more.''

''False starts,'' the Thing said sadly.

''Not false, Ben. Just starts. I promise you.''

For a long moment, the two men stood silently. Then the Thing glanced glumly at the hole still gaping in the test chamber's armored wall, and through it at the hole in the next wall beyond.

''I did a job on your shunt, didn't I?'' he said ruefully.

''Don't worry about it, Ben. You had to let off some steam, and Tony Stark is coming out with a new model, anyway.''

A wry grin played at the corners of the other man's lips. "I doubt he'll give us much of a trade-in on this one, though."

"Ya want me to hang around and help clean up?"

"No, that can wait. I'm expecting a visitor, and you've got errands, you said."

"Yeah, that's right. Heh. I almost forgot. I have to see a man about a coat."

"As far as I could tell, it was just another fire," Johnny Storm said. There was a slight note of disdain in his voice, as if he had better things to do and was eager to start doing them. "I see a lot of fires. I didn't hang around to check out the causes. I figured that's what the conventional authorities were for." He sounded bored. "You know—details."

The Torch was seated in a reception area on an upper floor of the Fantastic Four's skyscraper headquarters. The man he was speaking to was a husky, muscular African American who wore a conservatively cut dark suit and a subdued tie. His attire, and the studied look of calm on his handsome features marked him as a representative of those conventional authorities to which the Torch had referred. A laminated ID clipped to his jacket pocket identified him more specifically as Doug Deeley, agent of SAFE. A briefcase waited on the floor, near his left foot, and Deeley never took his gaze completely away from it.

"Nothing out of the ordinary, huh?" Deeley continued. His voice held a very faint note of annoyance, but it was almost completely masked by his professional tone. "I don't suppose you saw the holes punched through both sides of the ChemCo truck."

Johnny shrugged, and grinned. "That was a ChemCo truck?" he said. "By the time I got there, it was just a bunch of scorched metal."

"What about the Long Haul trailer? Did you see anything going on there?"

Johnny shrugged again, but this time he didn't grin. "Look, you've got to understand. If there was a Long Haul truck there, it didn't register on me. I saw a problem, and I did what I could to help. I didn't pay much attention to the surroundings; I was worried about the people. Like I said, as long as there wasn't some kind of super-type lurking in the area, I was willing to leave the details for—''

''—the conventional authorities,'' Deeley interrupted. ''I know. I heard.'' His irritation was more obvious now.

Johnny fidgeted a bit, looked at his watch. Then he glanced again at the business card he held. Deeley had given it to him. ''SAFE,'' Johnny said. ''What kind of a name is that?''

''The one they gave us,'' Deeley responded. ''That was before my time, though. I don't know who came up with it; some PR guy, probably. You'll have to ask someone else.''

''Maybe I will,'' the Human Torch said. He was wearing his uniform, the distinctive colors of the Fantastic Four, but on him, the outfit looked like casual clothes, coming as close to being rumpled and shapeless as the tailored, skintight fabric would allow. Now, he raised his left hand, pointed upward. The white cloth of his glove boiled into nothingness, and let a tendril of flame form at the tip of his index finger. The ribbon of fire unfurled itself, twisted in the air, shaped itself into four letters. ''SAFE,'' Johnny repeated, reading his handiwork. ''Alphabet soup, right? What's it stand for?''

''Strategic Action For Emergencies,'' Deeley said patiently. He didn't look as if he liked the Human Torch very much, and he sounded resigned to getting no more information from the younger man. ''We're a federal agency in the Executive Branch, responsible directly to the President himself. You know, Mr. Storm, we've already had this conversation.'' His tone of voice added, *more than once*.

''Oh, that's right,'' Johnny drawled. The letters hung in midair for another moment, then faded away. A flaming tic-tac-toe grid replaced them, and the Torch began filling in the spaces, one at a time. ''You told us about that before.'' A few months previously, SAFE had worked with the Fantastic Four and Spider-Man; the Torch had met Deeley then. Since that time, the SAFE agent had been assigned as the FF's liaison officer, and paid several visits to their headquarters. ''So, do you like working for SAFE?''

"Well enough. Some good folks there."

Trying to hide a lazy smirk, but not trying very hard, Johnny continued, "What's it like, working for Nick Fury?"

"Wouldn't know. You're thinking of another agency. I work for Sean Morgan."

"The big guy with the eye patch and the chin stubble?"

"The big guy with the gray eyes and the crewcut."

Johnny shook his head. "This business," he said. "It's all starting to run together for me. I'm gonna have to get a score-card one of these days."

"I'll messenger one over to you when I get back to the office," Deeley said. "Will wallet-size be okay? We're out of the wall version."

The Torch's mouth opened, but words didn't come out. He closed it, then opened it again, but before he could speak, the elevator doors at the room's far end opened and Susan Richards stepped out. "Johnny Storm," she said, "I have warned you about playing with fire in here!"

"Now, dear," Reed Richards said. "There's really no hazard. Johnny has complete control, and I fireproofed everything on this floor after the unfortunate incident with the—"

"I'm not talking about danger, Reed, I'm talking about manners." Sue turned to face the SAFE agent. "I'm terribly sorry about Johnny, Mr. Deeley. Sometimes he's the perfect little brother—in every sense of the words."

Deeley stood, and extended his hand. "Don't mention it, ma'am. But I certainly wish you folks would start calling me 'Doug.' "

"I'll try," Susan Richards said. "But only if you switch over to 'Sue.' "

"Fair enough, Sue."

"And I guess that makes me 'Reed,' " Reed said dryly, taking Deeley's hand as he released Sue's.

"Good," Deeley said. He extended his hand to the Torch, who took it, shook it once, then dropped it, even as he spun on one heel and began heading towards the room's exit.

"Sorry to greet and run," Johnny said, "But I've got a lunch date with a lovely lady. See you later, Agent Deeley."

A second later, sliding doors whisked shut behind him, and Deeley turned to face his hosts again.

Sue shook her head. "No matter how old he gets, he'll always be sixteen," she said.

Reed looked at their guest. "What can we do for you today, Doug?"

"I was hoping someone would ask," Deeley said, reaching for his briefcase. "Colonel Morgan thinks we have a situation that merits your attention."

"How's the weather outside, there? Winter here yet?" Fritz said. His voice was a raspy whisper, coarsened by many years of cigar smoking, but his tone was both kindly and respectful. "Now raise your arms."

"I dunno about the temperature," Ben said. He meant it. Such things had long since ceased to mean much to him. "It's not snowing." He raised his arms. "Like this?"

"Not so high," Fritz continued. "There." He held one end of the tape measure against the Thing's left wrist, and extended the cloth ribbon to measure the span between Ben's left hand and his spine. "You want a nice tweed this time?"

Ben shook his head. "Doesn't matter. I don't really care what you use, as long as you use enough of it."

"Got some nice British tweed, but it's a little pricy," Fritz continued. He ran the tape from the Thing's shoulders to his ankles, and wrote down another measurement. "I can give you a little break on that, though. I'm not looking to get rich here."

"Do what you gotta, Fritz," Ben said. "I ain't worried about it. Just make me look pretty." He hated buying clothes, but he liked Fritz. He had stumbled onto the older man's small Sixth Avenue haberdashery mere months after becoming the Thing, and he had done much repeat business there in the long years since. The old man was one of the few people on Earth who treated him as if he were still just plain old Ben Grimm— another customer to be served, and measured, and clothed as best as possible, without condescension or fear. Fritz had constructed many garments for Ben's outsized frame, using a great deal of ingenuity to adjust normal tailoring techniques to encompass someone whose proportions had strayed so far from human.

"You're lookin' good already, Mr. Grimm," Fritz said. "I wish half my customers took care of themselves the way you do." He paused, patted Ben gently on the shoulder, affectionately. "How come you need a new overcoat so soon? Something happen to the nice camel's hair I made you last year?"

"Yeah," Ben said glumly. He had liked that coat, at least as much as he liked any of his civilian garb. "About a hundred gallons of sea water, to start with."

"That's not good. Salt water, it's bad for camel's hair. Heck, it's bad for almost anything, except fish." Fritz laughed softly, and wrote down a few more numbers. "I'm just about done here," he said. "No changes, so far."

"Yeah, well, I been watching my diet," the Thing said. "Gotta keep my girlish figure."

"Excuse me," a new voice said. "Aren't you Ben Grimm? You're the Thing, right?"

Ben looked in the seven-foot-tall, three-pane mirror in front of him. He saw three reflections that gazed back at him, each looking like a small chunk of mountain, crushed and shaped by unknown forces into humanlike forms and clad for the moment only in blue wrestler's trunks.

He saw himself.

"Nah, you've mistaken me for someone else," he said. "My name's Jones. I'm one of the Kentucky Joneses."

The newcomer shook his head. He was a young man with thinning hair and a nervous tic, and he looked vaguely familiar, as if Ben had seen him in a newspaper photo. "You can't fool me," he said. "You're the Thing. I've seen you on the news."

Ben didn't say anything.

"This is great," the other man said. "This is just great. I'm Carmine Hamilton!" He extended his hand.

Ben didn't take it. "That supposed to mean something to me?" he asked.

After a too-long moment, Hamilton shrugged, withdrew his hand, and reached into his coat pocket and plucked out a card.

When he offered it, Ben took pity on him and accepted the bit of paper.

"BizNet, huh?" the Thing said. "What's that?"

Hamilton suddenly looked two suit sizes smaller. "Uh—it's my baby, Mr. Grimm. It's my pride and joy. America's newest, and the world's fastest growing online service provider, customized to serve the business and engineering communities. We've got multiple servers in every area code, we've been written up in *Popular Computing* and *Wall Street Journal*, we've got investors ranging from Tony Stark to Bruce W—"

"Computer stuff, huh?" Ben interrupted, grunting the words. He took Hamilton's right hand in his left one, and pressed the card into the other man's suddenly sweating palm.

"Much more than computers, Mr. Grimm, it's a whole new age in technological—"

Gently, or as gently as he could manage, Ben closed Hamilton's fingers, balling the smaller man's hand into a fist around the paper rectangle. Then, for just moment, he held Hamilton's left hand in both of his, enclosing flesh and bone in a cage of rocklike skin and super-strong muscle. He squeezed, but only barely.

"Ouch," Hamilton said.

"I don't *do* computers, Hamilton." Ben opened his hands, released the other man from a grip that could hold tigers. "Now take off. You're bothering me."

Hamilton massaged his fingers, wiggled them. When they were working properly again, he returned the card to his pocket. He laughed softly, wiggled his fingers some more. "Uh—heh, of course, of course," he said. "I know that. Anyone could tell that, just to look at you—"

Ben looked at him.

"Um, I mean—you're a rugged outdoors type, that's what I meant," Hamilton said weakly. He paused.

Ben didn't say anything.

"What I was hoping, Ben—"

Ben's eyes narrowed slightly.

"Ah, Mr. Grimm," Hamilton amended. "What I was hoping, Mr. Grimm, was that you could put me in touch with Reed Richards. Now, there's a man who could appreciate our services. We're doing a new series of TV spots, with celebrity endorsements, and—''

Ben brought his own hands together, tucked one inside the other. Knuckles popped, a sound like bones breaking.

Hamilton, already sweating, began to sweat some more.

Fritz, who had been watching without comment, interrupted. ''Mr. Hamilton,'' he said gently, ''I think Bernie is ready to see you now.'' About twenty feet distant, another man, dressed like Fritz in a black pinstripe suit and similarly bald, beckoned cheerfully with a tailor's chalk. Hamilton saw his opportunity to exit gracefully and took it, striding off with a mock-cheerful, ''Bernie! Buddy!''

Fritz watched him go, and muttered a word Ben didn't recognize.

''What's that, Fritzie?''

''Something I shouldn't say, Mr. Grimm,'' Fritz responded. ''But that Mr. Hamilton, he annoys me. New money and no class, bothering a gent like you—''

Ben smiled. He liked being called a gentleman. ''Aw, don't worry about it,'' he said. ''I'm used to stuff like that. At least he didn't try to sprinkle holy water on me.''

Fritz shrugged, then set his notepad and tape measure aside. ''Wait here a moment, Mr. Grimm. I want to get some fabric swatches. I think you'll like that tweed.'' He walked away. Ben watched him for a moment, then began looking at the shop's other wares.

He was at the sock rack when something that felt like a finger tapped one of his broad shoulders. He spoke without looking behind him, knowing who it had to be. ''Take off, Hamilton,'' he said. ''I ain't in the mood. Find yourself another celebrity playmate.''

The finger tapped again, harder this time, with more force that he would have thought Hamilton capable of mustering. Ben put down a pair of argyle socks that he probably would have been able to wear, once upon a time, and turned. ''Look, I'm tellin' ya—''

A fist smashed into his face.

It was a fist that belonged to a gorilla—literally.

Worse, it was a fist belonging to a specific gorilla, one that he recognized.

"Aw, crud," Ben said. "What are *you* doing here?"

The ape replied by hitting him a second time.

Reed Richards picked up one of the photos that the SAFE agent had offered him and examined it closely. It showed the grim aftermath of a traffic collision, the burned and blackened skeletons of two panel trucks locked together in a final embrace.

"The one in front was a donut truck, though you can't tell it from that picture," Doug Deeley said. "The one behind was from a chemical supply house here in the city—ChemCo."

Reed nodded. They were still in the reception area of Four Freedoms Plaza, only a few minutes after Deeley had emptied his briefcase on a convenient table. "I didn't know ChemCo was authorized to carry aviation fuel within city limits," he said.

"They aren't," Deeley replied grimly. "They didn't have permits for half the other goodies in that shipment, either. But someone knew what they were carrying."

"Knew?" Susan Richards said. "This was deliberate?"

Deeley nodded. He handed her another photograph, similar to one that Reed had plucked from the impromptu display. It showed another truck, bigger than either of the others. It looked like a moving van, half-filled with bulky pieces of furniture, easily recognizable as such even beneath their shrouds of tarpaulin and packing quilts. A series of file cabinets was anchored to one of the trailer's walls, and one of those cabinets had been torn open. Now, it sported a gaping hole where one drawer had been. A similar hole, but larger, scarred the floor of the truck's cargo area. Deeley said, "This truck belongs to an office moving firm, Long Haul. It was about half a block from the ChemCo truck at the time of the incident."

Reed made a thoughtful noise.

"How did SAFE get involved in this, Doug?" Sue asked.

"NYPD and FDNY both called the Bureau of Alcohol, Tobacco, and Firearms. ATF brought in the FBI, the FBI called S.H.I.E.L.D., more out of habit than anything else, I think. S.H.I.E.L.D. kicked it over to us, with a nasty note attached, and we called you." Deeley laughed softly as he used his fingers to tick off one agency name after another, but he didn't seem particularly amused. "There are still a few jurisdictional bugs in the system," he said. "Anyhow, we're all in agreement on one thing. We think that the explosion was engineered so that a person or persons unknown could use it as cover for the raid on the Long Haul truck."

"So much damage? Just to steal some files?" Sue asked.

Deeley nodded. "These files may have been worth it," he said grimly. "This particular load of cargo was the office archives for a high-tech firm in the process of relocating. I know that you've heard of them—Lifestream."

"That's not good," Reed said softly. Lifestream was an advanced biotech firm with shadowy ties to America's intelligence community. A few months before, Lifestream had managed to lose track of one of its own projects, a complex psychoactive substance formulated to repress certain brain functions and stimulate others. It had fallen into the hands of super-criminals who used the names Carnage and the Green Goblin; they, in turn, had nearly unleashed a plague of unending, incurable homicidal mania on the city. Only Spider-Man, with a bit of assistance from Mr. Fantastic, had been able to avert an almost unimaginable catastrophe. In the process, Reed had been able to secure the only surviving sample of the stuff, and verify that the formula had been lost. He was reasonably sure that whatever had been taken from the truck was something else.

But, still. . . .

"What files did they procure?" he asked.

"We don't know," Deeley replied.

"You don't know?" Sue said. "How is that possible? Wasn't there a cargo manifest? Won't they tell you? Don't you have the authority to find out things like that?"

"Well, we think we do," Deeley said slowly. "So does the

President. Lifestream, however, has different ideas, and they're well enough connected that they can drag their feet for a while. We're pushing some buttons and pulling some strings, but we haven't seen any results yet.''

"And you want us to help?" Reed asked. "I don't see how."

Deeley shook his head. "We've got good people working that end of it. Colonel Morgan wants your help on the incident itself. Someone planned this heist very carefully—knew the schedules of the trucks involved, knew what was in the ChemCo truck, and knew what was in the Long Haul truck, even if we still don't. The whole thing started when a shaped explosive charge detonated inside a fire hydrant at that intersection, and effectively turned the valve cover into a small missile that punched through the truck and started the fire." Deeley paused, and pulled another photograph from his briefcase. It was a picture of a surly looking man with blond hair and round, John Lennon glasses. "We're reasonably sure that same someone hired this man to place that charge. His name is Erik Morrison, and he won't tell us who he works for now—but we know that he used to work for the Thinker."

"Oh," Sue said softly. "Oh, my." The Thinker was one of the Fantastic Four's oldest enemies, an enigmatic genius who had challenged them again and again over the years.

Reed nodded. He didn't seem very surprised. "The *modus operandus* fits," he said. "The first time we met the Thinker he had a gang of thugs working for him, and he timed their operations to take advantage of things like exploding water mains—incidents that he engineered himself. Those jobs were usually cover for bigger operations, though, like the time he raided our headquarters."

Deeley said, "That was the Baxter Building, right?" The FF's original headquarters had since been destroyed, and replaced with Four Freedoms Plaza.

"Yes," Reed said. "He had the run of the place long enough to do some real damage, and to steal some data that I would really rather he didn't have. I've upgraded our security measures quite a bit since then, of course. I assume you've checked on the Thinker's current whereabouts? He was in the Vault, last I heard.'' The Vault was a specialized containment facility constructed by federal authorities to hold super-powered criminals. Technically speaking, the Thinker didn't fall into that category, but many of his underlings and agents did, and the Thinker resided in the Vault less to keep him inside than to keep his associates out.

"Still there," Deeley said. "And we can't prove any communication between him and Morrison. But we still think he's behind this."

"I think you're right," Reed said. "And, even if you're not, it won't hurt to assume the worst. The Thinker's a dangerous man, and he bears watching. What do you want us to do?"

"Talk to him, for starters. We sent some agents out to chat, but they came away with nothing. He wouldn't even talk to them, treated them like hamsters or something. You, on the other hand—''

"By 'you,' you mean Reed, right?'' Sue asked. "You want Reed to interrogate him for you?"

"Yes, ma'am. And not really interrogate. *Interview* might be a better term. The way Colonel Morgan figures it, the Thinker believes that he's in your husband's league, mentally, at least."

"He's not," Sue said. She sounded faintly annoyed.

Reed shrugged. "Now, Sue," he said softly.

"At any rate, he might be a little bit more responsive than he was with our people.'' Deeley paused.

"And I'm sure that Colonel Morgan recognizes that the Fantastic Four has a vested interest in keeping tabs on the Thinker,'' Reed said. "He's right. When do you want me to go?"

"I can arrange transport out west at your convenience," Deeley said. "Just give me an hour."

"That won't be necessary, Doug," Reed said. "I can get myself there." He glanced at his watch. "I can take the new Fantasti-Car and be there in two hours. Why don't you call the Vault and get things going at their end?''

"I'll be happy to," Deeley said. "But that's an awful rush. Are you sure you don't—?"

"I'm sure," Reed said firmly. "The sooner this is done with, the better." He glanced at Sue and smiled, his composed features suddenly turning boyish as the expression spread across them. "I promised Sue an evening of dinner and dancing, and not even the Thinker can make me delay that."

The gorilla grunted and threw a third punch, but Ben, finally over his surprise, dodged the blow easily. The hairy fist whistled past him and the ape, suddenly off balance, lurched forward. As it came closer, Ben threw his own fist out in an abrupt, reflexive blow that caught the gorilla on his chin, but only glancingly—still hard enough to break stone, but not enough to do more than daze the anthropoid. This particular gorilla was far stronger than most, strong enough to go toe-to-toe with the Thing. When he recovered and punched the Thing again, the blow was strong enough to make Ben rock back on his feet. "What a revoltin' development this is," the Thing muttered.

The gorilla hit him again and screamed. He bared his teeth in what looked like a grin but was actually a snarl of challenge. The anthropoid had faced the Thing many times in battle, and knew him as a hated enemy.

The feeling was mutual. Now, the Thing hit back, driving the heel of his left hand into the ape's hairy chest with good effect. He didn't worry about holding back the way he might have with a human foe. He hit hard enough to drive the air from the ape's lungs in a great, shuddering gasp, and to send his shaggy form tumbling back and away. Bouncing, rolling, sliding, the gorilla slammed into a display of imported Italian silk ties. Ribbons of cloth and splintered cabinet flew in all directions.

"What is this? What's going on here?" That was Fritz, stepping back into the main sales area, a book of fabric samples in each hand, apparently drawn by the commotion. "What are you doing to my shop?"

"Fritz," Ben yelled. "Run! This is no place for civilians!"

"But—"

"*Run!*"

Fritz ran.

The ape gathered his legs beneath him and sprang at the Thing again. One knee drove deep into Ben's chest, knocking the breath out of him in an explosive gasp, and then, two oversized, super-strong handlike paws clamped down on the scaled expanse of the Thing's neck. The gorilla screamed exultantly, and began to squeeze.

Ben realized that he was in great danger as black spots crept into the edges of his vision. Even he needed to breathe, and the ape was just strong enough to keep him from doing it. With a chance to prepare, the Thing could hold his breath for quite a while, but he hadn't had that chance this time. If the gorilla maintained its grip—

He brought one fist up, hard, into the underside of the ape's jaw, stunning the brute enough to break the stranglehold. The gorilla recovered almost instantly, and punched the Thing in his stomach. Ben ignored the sudden pain that blossomed in his abdomen. The fight at hand didn't worry him; Ben was willing to go one-on-one with any ape on earth, even this one, and was confident that he would come out on top. The superpowered gorilla was reasonably dangerous, but by himself, he wasn't much of a threat for someone like the Thing.

The problem was that the gorilla in question was never a solo act. Some years before, this particular ape had been one of four passengers in a unique space vehicle—a craft launched by the then-Soviet Union's top scientists, in an attempt to duplicate the origin of the Fantastic Four. Unfiltered by Earth's atmosphere, the cosmic rays had worked their magic again, creating superhuman powers where there had been none before. Three of the craft's four occupants had been anthropoids, two apes and a monkey—a gorilla, an orangutan, a baboon. The fourth, the craft's pilot, was the animals' master.

The gorilla punched Ben in the belly again, harder, then clubbed one side of his head with an open-handed blow that was hard enough to make the Thing's ears ring. The ringing got worse when he slammed his brow against the ape's skull in an abrupt head butt—but it didn't get so bad that he couldn't hear a sudden, new voice that came from behind him.

It was one he had expected, given the identity of his simian assailant.

"Grimm? What's the meaning of this? What are you doing here?" Ivan Kragoff demanded, even as Ben turned to face him. He came into the room by stepping through the mirror where the Thing had seen his own reflection only moments before. Kragoff walked through the unbroken pane of glass as if it weren't here, and, in a sense, it wasn't—at least not for him, not now.

"Kragoff, ya bum! *You're* askin' *me* that?" Ben dodged another punch from the gorilla and grabbed for something to throw at the newcomer. His left hand found a small bench, one that he had seen Fritz stand on while searching high shelves. He closed his fingers around it, plucked it from the floor, and threw it, hard, at Kragoff's head.

The impromptu missile didn't do any good, which wasn't particularly surprising. Kragoff's own super power was to make himself insubstantial, to move a step out of phase with the subatomic structure of normal matter. Reed had some fancy words for it, polysyllabic wonders like *pseudo-intangibility* and *psionic quanta base units*, but all that it really meant was the Kragoff couldn't be touched unless he wanted to be. He could make himself a phantom, less material than fog or mist, well beyond almost any threat from the physical world. Now, glass shattered and flew as the stool moved at bullet speed through the man who now called himself the Red Ghost, and smashed into the triple mirror behind him.

Kragoff laughed. In some way that Ben had never understood, the Red Ghost's vocal chords, no matter how immaterial, could interact enough with air to make sounds.

"Turn solid an' fight like a man, Kragoff," the Thing snarled. The gorilla's fist came down again, hard, this time on top of his skull, but Ben barely noticed. The Red Ghost was one of the Fantastic Four's oldest, most treacherous foes, and his mere presence demanded the Thing's near-total attention. Ben could handle the ape's pounding for as long as he had to, but he knew all too well that the Ghost had other threats at his command. "C'mon an' fight," Ben repeated, hoping to goad the villain into making himself vulnerable.

"I think not," the Red Ghost said. A holstered sidearm hung at his left hip, a gun-shaped apparatus with a flaring nozzle. He drew it now. "There is no need for me to sully my hands with the likes of you," Kragoff continued. "Not when I have other means."

Ben eyed him carefully. He had known Kragoff to use a variety of weapons, ranging from smoke bombs to energy beams. Some required that the Red Ghost materialize before using them, making himself at least momentarily vulnerable. Ben's own attributes were physical in nature, not much good against anything he couldn't touch. But if Kragoff phased back in, even for a moment—

The gorilla that he had nearly forgotten snaked one overlong arm around Ben's throat, and then drove a fist into the Thing's back, just above the kidneys. He hit hard enough that the Thing grunted in pain, then threw himself back against the ape. "Calm down, Cheetah," he said angrily, driving one elbow into the animal's soft gut. "You're botherin' me, here. Go find yourself a nice banana."

The Ghost raised his weapon.

The ape clawed at Ben's face, and reached with the other hand for a floor-to-ceiling rack that held men's hats in a variety of styles and sizes. The gorilla grabbed the steel fixture and swung it like a club, cutting through the air in a whistling arc that promised to intersect with the Thing's skull. Ben ducked, and raised one hand to intercept the bludgeon. It broke and bent as it slammed into his rocky hand. Bent—and kept bending, twisting and flowing, wrapping itself around his wrist.

"Aw, crumbs," the Thing said. He knew what this meant, too.

"Excellent," the Red Ghost said, hissing the word in a satisfied tone.

The metal shaft kept bending, winding itself around Ben's forearm and wrist even as the gorilla released it. The shaft's free end formed itself into a jagged spike, then struck at Ben's face like a cobra. The Thing raised his free hand, snatched at the pointed chunk of metal, caught it and held it. It struggled in his grip, twisting and bending and trying to find an exit from his crushing grasp.

The curtains at the rear of the sales area opened. Ben knew that behind them were fitting rooms, a stockroom, and a freight elevator, all rubbing shoulders with the tiny, cramped office where Fritz did his accounts. Right now, however, there almost certainly had to be something more going on back there, because ambling through the parted drapes was an orangutan. Presumably, he was following the same path that the gorilla had taken.

"Here's Huey, an' there's Dewey," Ben snarled at the Red Ghost, as the second ape came on stage. "Now where's Louie, Unca Donald?"

"Your drolleries bore me, Grimm," Kragoff replied. He was still holding his gun, trained in the general direction of the Thing's head. Ben watched him carefully, waiting for some giveaway—anything, no matter how slight—that might tell him that the Ghost had rematerialized. "But, in answer to your question, my baboon is otherwise engaged."

"Yeah, probably to your sister!"

The orangutan gestured with one forepaw. The hat rack twisted and writhed again, moving in response to the magnetic waves that the smaller ape could control. The metal jerked and convulsed, tearing itself out of the Thing's grip, and launching itself again at his head. As it moved, it twisted some more, this time lengthwise. By the time it had wrapped itself around the Thing's neck, it had become something very much like steel cable.

Ben clawed at it, but his fingers were too blunt to do much good against the metal cord that was digging deep into his hard skin. Heavy and thick by normal human standards, it felt like kite string in his oversized hands, too fine for him to grip. The world was turning dark again. Desperately, he tensed his neck muscles, straining against the transformed rack, feeling the metal cut into him, trying to close his windpipe. He made a choking noise.

"Much better," the Red Ghost said. He made an adjustment to his weapon. "This is a nerve gun, Grimm," he continued. "Another product of superior Soviet technology. It suppresses normal dendrite activity. At the proper setting, it can stun, paralyze, render unconscious, or even kill a normal human being." The expression on his face changed slightly, as if he were considering some other factor, and the outlines of his body suddenly became infinitesimally more distinct. "I have no doubt that it will be similarly effective against a monstrosity such as you."

His world nearly black now, the Thing lurched toward the Ghost. The gorilla clawed at him and the band of metal around his neck tightened some more as he stumbled forward. The effort provided futile, and he fell at Kragoff's feet.

The Russian laughed, and tightened his finger around the weapon's trigger.

Ben used the momentum of his fall, added to it, and brought one open hand down, hard, against the worn carpet. The shop's sagging floor rippled and flexed as the shock wave swept through it. The two apes squealed in confusion as they lost their footing on the suddenly flexing floorboards. The shockwave hit Kragoff, too, just as he turned solid, with just enough force to make the gun fly from his hand. The white-haired man stumbled and cursed.

"You'll pay for this, Grimm," Kragoff said.

Ben felt the improvised garrote around his neck relax slightly as the orangutan's concentration—if that was the right word—suddenly weakened. He tore the band of metal free, wadded it into a ball, and threw the lumpy spheroid at the Red Ghost, who still looked reasonably solid. Approximately three inches from its target, the metal ball stopped in midair and hung there, motionless. Ben knew what had stopped it—a wall of magnetic force. The only conclusion to draw was that the orangutan had recovered.

Ben reached for the gun, if only to crush it, but Kragoff reached faster. Even as the Thing's blunt digits touched the device, the Ghost clutched its grip and the renegade scientist took possession of his weapon once more. There was a clicking noise as Ben's finger grazed one switch just hard enough to change its position, and then the gun was beyond his touch once more. "Not fast enough, Grimm," he said exultantly. "Now—"

The watch that he wore on his left wrist chirped.

The Red Ghost cursed. He looked at his weapon, and a disgusted expression spread across is face. Something was apparently wrong with one or more of its settings, due either to impact when it had hit the floor or to Ben's fumbled grab. Kragoff twisted a one knob, flipped a switch.

The watch chirped a second time, more insistently.

"Bah," Kragoff said. "This takes too long."

The gorilla's fists smashed into the Thing again, and the orangutan squealed in challenge as it moved in to join the battle.

"No time for that, my loyal ones," the Red Ghost said. "Leave him for later."

The orangutan shuffled to his side, but the gorilla ignored him, and kept pounding on the still-woozy Thing, who did his best to fight back. "Whatsa matter, Kragoff?" he asked, even as he punched the gorilla again. "Got a bus to catch?"

Kragoff said something more, a string of harsh-sounding syllables that the Thing recognized as Russian. This time, the gorilla obeyed his master's command, and broke off the fight. A second later, the man and his two apes had bounded through the curtained passageway and into the stockroom, back near the fitting rooms and freight elevator.

"That's it, Ghost—pick a fight and then run," the Thing said, doing his best to roar with still-straining lungs. He gave chase to the fleeing trio, stumbling on the sundered flooring as he went after them. They moved faster than he could, however, both because of his bulk and because two attempted strangulations that he had endured in less than three minutes still left him gasping. Half stumbling, half lumbering, he made his way to the stockroom area, just in time to see the freight elevator's doors pop open in response to the orangutan's magnetic command.

The Red Ghost spun on one heel and fired his weapon. Whatever the problem with its setting, he had apparently corrected it. A yellow bolt of energy erupted from the gun muzzle, grazing Ben's left hand even as he threw himself from its path. A tingling feeling swept though the Thing's hand, a pins-and-needles sensation that he remembered from the days when he was just plain Ben Grimm; the feeling of a leg or an arm when it went to sleep. The sensation built and peaked for an instant, and then faded. As it faded, Ben realized that he no longer had any feeling below his left elbow, no control of the muscles that lurked beneath the craggy hide. This went beyond mere numbness; it felt as if his lower arm had died.

He remembered what the Ghost had said about paralysis, and death.

Ahead of him, a third anthropoid had come into view, emerging from one of the fitting rooms. This was the smallest of the Ghost's trio, a baboon with shape-changing powers similar in some ways to Reed's. Just now, the monkey was in its base form, and carrying a submachine gun tucked under one shaggy arm. Behind him came the gorilla, lugging a garment bag that held something about the size and dimensions of a man.

Something that didn't move, didn't struggle.

"Kragoff," the Thing repeated, charging again. He balled his right hand into a fist and raised it.

Kragoff fired once more, and the baboon joined him. Ben dodged the ray blast, but didn't worry about the bullets; his skin was more than proof against such stuff. A hundred or so leaden slugs pounded into him, a staccato stream of bullets that made him stumble slightly, but he continued to drive himself forward. As he staggered, another bolt from the Ghost's gun grazed his right leg. This beam had less effect than the previous one, but it was enough to make him stumble again.

Ahead, the gorilla hopped through the open elevator doors, with the orangutan in close pursuit. Ben reached for something, anything, to throw at the Ghost, and then realized it was a futile effort. Kragoff had gone unsolid again, perhaps to avoid ricochets, and was already oozing through the floor. He was smiling as he slipped from view. That left only the baboon to deal with.

Of course, the baboon had a machine gun.

The trained primate made a snarling noise, then pulled the trigger again. This time, the bullets chewed a path along the walls above Ben's head, just below the ceiling's acoustical tiles. Chips of cinder blocks flew as the bullets bit into them. Ben let himself wonder what the baboon thought he was doing, and then realization dawned as he saw one and then another set of emergency lights explode into glass and metal shrapnel.

"Cut it out, ya danged monkey," Ben demanded, but the baboon ignored him. One last burst of ammunition, and the stockroom's primary lighting was dead, too. Darkness fell, more complete and effective in the enclosed space than the Thing would have believed possible. He took another step forward, but it was a misstep, and stumbled again, then fell. Effectively blind, nearly lame, he struggled to his feet in the darkness. Ahead of him, even over the ringing in his ears, Ben could hear a scratching sound as ape claws found elevator cables, and then a muffled thud as the elevator doors slammed shut again. He knew that they were closing behind the baboon, not in front of him. He lumbered forward, but he knew that he was already too late.

By the time that Fritz returned, with police officers and candles and flashlights, the Ghost's entourage was gone beyond hope of pursuit.

"I pulled the Thinker's file for you," Warden Fingeroth said. "I was just reviewing it a bit. Wanted to be able to talk knowledgeably, you know." He was a slender man with short, brown, slightly curly hair, and a bowtie. He had an annoyingly obsequious manner, at least when playing host; Reed Richards suspected that he was somewhat less pleasant to his line staff. "It's really quite remarkable," Fingeroth continued, sliding the folder across the table for his guest's benefit. "This man has been in and out of various federal penitentiaries for years now, and investigated by everyone from the NYPD to Interpol, and no one has ever determined his real name—or verified any conventional aliases. I mean, it looks ridiculous to list him as 'Thinker, The.'"

"Yes, well, I doubt that such considerations matter much to him," Reed said. He quickly skimmed the thick sheaf of documents, but saw little he hadn't seen before—most recently, during the last hour or so. He had reviewed his own records and some material from SAFE while the Fantasti-Car's computerized guidance system chauffeured him across the country. Most of the Thinker's past crimes had been against members of the Fantastic Four, after all. Clipped to the folder's front flap, however, were some new items—mug shots that were recent, even if the face they presented was quite familiar and little changed since the last time Reed had seen it. He saw unruly brown hair, broad features and a high brow, and deep-set eyes that stared out at him with aloof contempt. This was a face that Richards had come to know well over the years.

In many ways, the Thinker was the Fantastic Four's most mysterious foe. Even after more than a dozen face-to-face encounters, even after studying cases involving the Thinker and other heroes, Reed knew almost nothing about the man. His origins, his history, his motives, and his ultimate goals were all nearly complete unknowns. Physically, he was unprepossessing, of average height and build, with physical strength no greater than might be expected of a man his size who engaged in sporadic, moderate exercise. He had no known special senses or powers.

The Thinker's mind, however, was a different matter altogether. The peculiar genius that lurked behind those brooding eyes was unique, unlike any other Reed had ever encountered—and he had encountered many in his adventurous life. The Thinker was a genius, but of a very special kind.

Victor Von Doom, Latveria's iron-masked ruler, was certainly a genius, even if a twisted one. So were Bruce Banner, and Tony Stark, and Henry Pym, and many others of Reed's acquaintance, undeniably brilliant minds with scores of fundamental breakthroughs to their credit. Richards himself made almost immeasurable advances in scores of interrelated scientific disciplines. That was what defined genius to most people—originality, invention, and discovery, the thinking of thoughts that no one had thought before.

To Reed's knowledge, the Thinker had never had an original idea in his life. Every scheme the man had created, every device he had built, every weapon he had thrown against his enemies had represented a startling elaboration of someone else's work—Reed's included.

Years before, as an experiment, Reed had used DNA synthesis techniques to create an artificial lifeform, a primitive aquatic form resembling a lower-order fish. The Thinker had stolen the notes from that experiment, and a few other items from Reed's lab—and almost immediately created a semi-intelligent, super-powered humanoid enforcer he called his "Awesome Android." Reed, in turn, had examined that creature more than once in the ensuing years, and had always come to the same reluctant conclusion—it embodied precisely the same design principles and data as had his own specimen, but extended and made more complex. It was as if Reed had pointed the way, and the Thinker had followed his lead, but gone much further.

That was the Thinker's genius—to take the work of other, more creative minds, to take isolated facts and bits of data and string them together in constructions that were at once seemingly new and yet utterly without novelty. The Thinker was an inductive genius, and almost certainly the greatest one in the world.

In the folder, between the criminal record and the psychiatric report, Reed found another sheet that interested him. It was a medical report, filled with scribbled notations from the Vault's infirmary staff. He read it carefully. "This says he's been sleeping a lot lately," Reed said.

Fingeroth nodded, head bobbing up and down like a yo-yo. "That's right. Up to twenty hours a day, some days. The guards noticed it first. We have cameras trained on his cell, you know."

Reed knew. The Vault was the nation's highest-security correctional facility. It had to be; many of the most dangerous men and women in America languished within its walls, superpowered individuals whose slightest move could have deadly implications. They merited careful observation.

"How long has this been going on?" Reed asked.

"The sleeping? It's sporadic, but more common in the last six months or so. Some weeks, he sleeps only a few hours a night. Others, it's all we can do to rouse him at meal time. I thought it might be clinical depression, but the medical staff disagrees." Fingeroth sounded annoyed.

"I would tend to agree with them," Reed said softly, reading the rest of the report. "The symptoms aren't quite right. Are there any other anomalies?"

"Maybe not an anomaly, but something. It's not in that file, though. My understanding is that the Thinker is a voracious reader and media junkie. Back when he was in Ryker's Correctional in New York he drove the staff up the wall with library requests for things like science journals and engineering reports. When they wouldn't let him have what he wanted he made do with whatever else he could find."

Reed nodded. That fit. The Thinker's thought processes were characterized by an unrelenting appetite for new data, from whatever source.

"Well, it's the darnedest thing," Fingeroth continued. "Since coming here, he hasn't requested a single newspaper, magazine, book, or videotape. It's like he doesn't care about the rest of the world anymore. Or maybe he's given up."

"I doubt that very much. There must be some other answer," Reed said. "I suppose I'd better see him now."

"Fine. You can use my office."

Reed looked at the warden, somewhat surprised. "Are you sure that's wise?" he asked.

Fingeroth smiled and nodded. "The entire prison is a secure facility, Dr. Richards, and the Thinker doesn't have any physical powers. There's no reason to make yourself uncomfortable while you talk with him."

"If you say so," Reed said. "Does he know I'm coming?"

"SAFE asked us to stick him in an isolation cell after their last interview, and no one has talked to him. Your visit should be a complete surprise."

"Hello, Richards. I rather thought you might pay me a visit." Seated in the well-appointed confines of Fingeroth's office, wearing a prison-issue orange jumpsuit, the Thinker still made a surprisingly imposing figure. His broad features were twisted in a condescending smirk, and he seemed to consider himself the ruler of all he surveyed. Thick metal restraints held his wrist, ankles, and neck, and more chains linked the whole assembly together.

"Are the shackles necessary?" Richards asked.

"Yes sir, they are," the guard replied.

"Warden Fingeroth seemed to think that this man poses no immediate threat."

"Even Warden Fingeroth has to follow some regulations," the guard said. He wore two-tone green armor, a powered metal suit based on Tony Stark's designs for Iron Man. Guardsman armor was standard issue at the Vault, and a wise precaution, given the nature of the prison's population.

"I don't mind the restraints," the Thinker said. "I do mind the audience." Something about the way he gazed at Reed made the room suddenly feel a few degrees cooler.

"This conversation will be recorded, Thinker," Reed said. He gestured at the small audio-video recording device he had set on a convenient table top. "Your privacy's not an issue."

"Be that as it may, there will be no conversation to record until this oaf leaves."

Reed nodded at the Guardsman. "I think I can handle him, son."

After the guard left, the Thinker continued. "You've come a long way, Richards. Running errands for SAFE now, are you?"

"How did you know I was coming?"

The Thinker shrugged. "I've had many boring conversations with sundry government lackeys in the last few days. Apparently, there has been a disturbance in New York, and someone thought I might be able to provide a bit of insight." He smiled. "I chose not to cooperate. It wasn't hard to anticipate that they would try another approach, and even less difficult to predict what that approach would be."

"All right, Thinker," Reed said calmly. "Very clever. How are you at horse races?"

"I've never made an extensive study of the subject, but I do know a bit about horses. I fancy I would do well at gaming, if I chose to."

That much was certainly true. The Thinker was a wizard with odds and astonishingly skilled with statistical projection; with enough data he could probably predict almost anything. Reed had thought more than once that the Thinker could easily have been the world's greatest weatherman.

He decided it was time to change the subject. "How are they treating you here?" He asked the question without really caring what the answer would be.

"Well enough. A roof, four walls, three meals, a place to sleep."

"You've been doing a lot of sleeping."

"And you've been doing some reading, I see. Tell me, does Warden Fingeroth still think I suffer from clinical depression?"

"Probably. I told him he was wrong, but he seemed to like his own diagnosis."

"He would. He has a small mind. Not like mine. Not like yours." The Thinker grinned. "And what do you think of my mental state?"

"I wouldn't care to guess," Reed said slowly. "Besides,

I'm here to ask questions, not to answer them.''

The Thinker nodded again. ''Ask,'' he said agreeably.

''When was the last time you spoke to Erik Morrison?''

''Erik? It has been five years, four months, one week, three days, seven hours and thirteen minutes since last we spoke. That was at Ryker's Correctional Facility, in New York. We were having lunch in the prison cafeteria. He had the corned beef hash with eggs, I chose the vegetable plate and the fruit cup. Ryker's fed us well, at least.''

''You must have liked the food. You waited three months before escaping.''

The Thinker smiled.

''Any idea why Morrison might have engineered an explosion on Madison Avenue this past Monday?''

The Thinker smiled some more.

''It served as the cover for another crime,'' Reed continued. ''That's very much your way of doing things.''

''But I am in prison, locked away where I can hurt no one,'' the Thinker said. He shifted in his seat, enough to make the make the chains that held him rattle and underscore his point. ''And I haven't seen Erik in more than five years.''

This time, Reed made no response.

After a long moment, the Thinker continued. ''I assume the other crime was successful, or you and your new friends would not have paid me these visits,'' he said.

Reed nodded. ''The thieves got what they came for, and what they wanted pointed in your direction, too. Files from a firm engaged in recombinant DNA research.''

''Lifestream?''

''How do you know that?''

The Thinker made no reply, and Reed let himself feel slightly annoyed. This was the worst part of dealing with the Thinker, the almost constant feint-and-parry that characterized even the simplest conversation. The other man seemed to feel a constant need to demonstrate superior knowledge, to prove himself smarter than anyone else, no matter what the topic.

''What does Erik say about the situation?'' the Thinker asked.

"He's not talking."

"Ah. He must be afraid of reprisals. Not a very courageous man, Erik."

"He betrayed you once before, testified in the trial that sent you to Ryker's. They found him two months later at the bottom of a prison airshaft. Both of his legs were broken. You were in solitary confinement at the time, but I imagine you heard about it."

"And now, I gather, Erik has learned from his past mistakes. That is an admirable trait."

Reed shook his head. "If he had learned from his mistakes, he would have gone straight after getting out, instead of going back into the demolition business," he said.

"Not many options are available for an ex-con with a record like Erik's," the Thinker replied smoothly. "Especially not if former associates are eager to exploit one's skills and talents, eager to reward cooperation and to punish refusal." He grinned again.

Irritated now, Reed caught the other man's opaque gaze and held it. "This isn't getting us anywhere," he said. "I'm not sure what you're up to, Thinker, but some aspects are obvious. You've figured out how to run an operation from here, and it must be a big one, or you wouldn't sit here and play these games with me."

"Games?" the Thinker said coolly.

"Games. And I've had enough of them." Reed extended his right arm twenty feet or so to his left and pressed a red button on the underside of the warden's desk. While he waited for the Guardsman to return, he continued. "I'll be back," he said, "and I'll bring some equipment with me and run some tests. I helped design this place, and I made it as proof as possible against people like you. If you've found a loophole in its measures, I want to know."

The door swung open, revealing a Guardsman.

"I'm done here," Reed said.

The guard walked in and attached a leashlike cable to the prisoner's restraint collar. "Come on now, Thinker," he said. "Time to go back to your box."

The Thinker looked at Reed. "A pity our conversation was such a short one," he said. "There are so many things we could discuss. Tell me, Dr. Richards—what kind of research are you performing currently?"

"I can't answer that question, Thinker. But I wish *you* would. What are you working on? What holds your interests these days?"

The Thinker smiled. "Psychohistory still has its charms," he said softly.

"Isn't it *great*?" Jenna Villanueva said, the question ending in a girlish squeal of delight. She made pointers of her index fingers and prodded Johnny with them in an alternating teletype rhythm that he found both pleasant and mildly annoying. "Aren't you *excited* for me?" she continued. "And it's all thanks to *you*." She grinned. "And that, Mr. Storm, is why *I* am buying *you* lunch."

"Aw, c'mon, Jenna," Johnny said, close to embarassment. He took another breath of chill air, and watched a faint cloud of condensation form before his eyes. "It was all in a day's work." The two of them there threading their way though the crowds that filled Madison Avenue's broad sidewalks. Once, twice, three times in fast succession, Johnny saw attractive, unattached women stride by, their charms evident even beneath winter wear. All three noticed him, in turn; two caught his steady gaze, and one smiled at him and winked. Johnny had to wonder if she had recognized him as the Human Torch, or if his own boyish good looks had been the charm. He realized he would never know, but that was okay; not knowing was part of the fun.

Jenna was still at his side, her arm linked through his now, but didn't seem to notice his roving eyes—perhaps because she had been the target of many similar gazes. "Two *years* riding that stupid helicopter, and I finally get an assignment where you can hear my voice!" She proceeded to perform a pretty good impression of a helicopter's *chup-chup-chup* noise. She kept it up just long enough not to be annoying, unmindful of startled looks from other pedestrians.

Until recently, Jenna had been the local traffic reporter for WNN, ''All News Television, All the Time!'' Johnny had met her when a sudden equipment failure in the chopper she rode had sent it plummeting from the sky, and moving fast and hard towards a crowded Central Park. Johnny had pulled both Jenna and her pilot from the falling helicopter before impact, and then worked with his sister, the Invisible Woman, to contain the ensuing explosion and fire. The mildly spectacular rescue had led to newspaper stories, local television coverage, and even a featured interview on the syndicated *Incredible Disasters* news show. That bit of public exposure, in turn, had led to a promotion for Jenna and assignment to a real news beat.

''I get to go to the United Nations World Economics Summit,'' Jenna said, excitedly. ''I get to meet ambassadors and dignitaries from all over the *world*. Pretty good for a little girl from Portland, huh?''

''That's nice,'' Johnny said, barely listening. For a member of the Fantastic Four, accustomed to high adventure and travel to other planets, listening to stuffed shirts drone to one another about economic trends was hardly an appetizing prospect. He could understand Jenna's perspective, though; it was one that he might have shared, years ago, before that test run in an experimental spaceship had transformed him from an average teenager into the Human Torch.

Johnny smiled slightly as he considered how one thing had led to another, and at how his life had changed. For him, the helicopter rescue had been a minor good deed, the kind of work he did almost without thinking. For Jenna, it had not only saved her life, but changed it, perhaps forever.

''Really, Jenna,'' he said. ''I'm glad things are going well, but it's your ability that did it. They wouldn't give you the gig if you couldn't do it.'' They were approaching the intersection of Madison and Forty-fourth, and Johnny had a twinge of sudden surprise. ''Huh,'' he said. ''That's funny.''

He stopped.

Jenna didn't. She kept moving, kept chattering on about her new assignment. She was a strong woman, with a dancer's stride, and she managed to take a few steps before Johnny's arm, looped through hers, drew her up short. "Hey!" she said, more startled than annoyed. "What's the holdup?"

"I just realized where we are," Johnny said. "I was here Monday."

Obviously eager to get moving again, looked slightly annoyed. "And?" she asked.

"There was a fire, a burning truck," Johnny said. "I put it out, like I did your buddy Heather's helicopter." Heather Lee had been the pilot of the WNN chopper.

"And?" Jenna repeated.

Johnny shrugged. "And nothing, I guess. Some government goon came by HQ to ask me about it, though." He smiled. "That didn't happen with your 'copter crash."

Jenna laughed, but as she laughed, she looked at her watch. "We had better hurry," she said. "The reservation is for noon, not noonish."

"Reservation? I thought you said this place was never busy."

"Um, well, it never is. But it's better to be safe."

"Or SAFE," Johnny said, knowing she wouldn't get the joke, and also knowing it wasn't much of one. He looked away from the busy intersection, away from the dirty slush and passing cars that masked the seared asphalt, and started walking again.

A moment later, they were at the restaurant that Jenna had recommended so strongly. Just inside the arched doorway, a young woman with short blonde hair greeted them. "Hello, welcome to Erol's Tea Room," she said cheerfully. "I'm Sandy, your hostess. Table for two?"

"Um, that will be—" Johnny began to say, taking the lead, but Jenna interrupted him.

"No," she said, shaking her head and making her hair ripple and flow like a dark waterfall. "Villanueva, party of two. We reserved a private dining room."

Johnny looked at her in surprise. "We did?" he asked. "That seems a little excessive."

Jenna smiled, flashing strong white teeth in an appealing

smile. "Not really," she said. "This is a special day."

Johnny wondered about her definition of the word as Sandy led the two of them through the nearly empty main dining area, back toward an elaborately embroidered curtain that looked as if it had been purloined from some Turkish mosque, but which probably been manufactured somewhere in Taiwan. Sandy reached out with one slim hand and swept it aside.

"This way to our private party room," she said.

"You first," Jenna said to Johnny. "Wait until you see this place."

Johnny looked at her, then shrugged. Always one to humor a pretty lady, he turned and stepped into room beyond.

Someone was waiting for him there.

"Huh?" Johnny said, suddenly, genuinely startled as he caught sight of the familiar face. "What are *you* doing here?"

Reed took about twenty minutes to work his way through the Vault's security exit interview procedures, and nearly twice that long to escape Warden Fingeroth's oleaginous attentions. The official wanted a debrief on Reed's visit, but didn't get one; Reed had already decided that any report he made would be to SAFE. If Sean Morgan wanted Fingeroth to know what conclusions Mr. Fantastic had drawn, the head of SAFE could tell the annoying little man. After finally prying his hand free from Fingeroth's, Reed climbed back into his Fantasti-Car and launched it into the clear blue sky. A few minutes later, the cockpit control panel display announced that he had left the Vault's airspace.

The Fantasti-Car he rode today was a two-seater, good for quick hops to anywhere on the continent. Reed and Sue regarded it as pretty much their personal vehicle, a status mockingly acknowledged by Ben's nickname for it, "the Honeymoon Special." Like all of the multipurpose craft that shared its name, this particular Fantasti-Car featured a state-of-the-art computerized navigation system, tied in with the federal Geographical Positioning System (GPS) satellite system, to the National Weather Services satellite feeds, and to the mainframe back at Four Freedoms Plaza. Now, Reed was letting the autopilot do the driving for him, while he considered his conversation with the Thinker.

Most of the interview had gone about the way he had expected it to. Reed hadn't said so to Doug Deeley, but his personal view was that nearly any suspicions regarding the Thinker were probably well founded. Reed's various encounters over the years with the enigmatic genius had enabled him to assemble what he thought was a reasonably accurate picture of the other man's capabilities and personality—and that picture was not a pretty one. This particular interview had done nothing to change it. He had come away from the meeting with only two findings that seemed to hold any real promise, the first was that the Thinker had apparently found some way to run or at least monitor an operation from within the Vault. That was alarming enough, but the Thinker's parting comment might just be a cause for greater concern.

Psychohistory still has its charms, the Thinker had said. Five words, spoken casually, or as casually at the Thinker could manage, and yet they carried ominous implications.

Psychohistory was an uncommon term, included in only a few dictionaries. It had been coined by the science fiction writer Isaac Asimov in the late 1940s, as part of the rubric supporting a series of stories. As posited by Asimov, psychohistory was an elaborate form of trends projection, based on the idea that human society followed certain rules and patterns. With enough data, a mind that understood those rules could predict the tide of human events, perhaps even in fine detail. Asimov had proposed the science as a method of prediction, but had also allowed that it could be put to other, more manipulative purposes.

Reed could see how such a discipline would appeal to the Thinker. It was a mechanistic philosophy, one that sought to reduce all human existence to a complex numbers game, and explain away things like random chance and creative insight by making them functions of high-level equations. To the Thinker, a man whose whole approach to life consisted of taking other people's ideas and extrapolating from them, such a belief system would be almost hypnotically attractive. Even

Reed had been intrigued the first time he heard the term in college, and even more intrigued when he read what little he could find about it.

The problem with psychohistory as an applied science was that it demanded immense computational ability, to process enormous amounts of information regarding occurrences and events, and also to extrapolate their effects on one another. Reed wasn't at all sure that such data processing capabilities existed even today, despite the computer revolution of recent years, and despite his own achievements in the related fields of cybernetics and artificial intelligence. Emulating even a single human mind was possible, but almost unimaginably difficult; Reed had a hard time believing that anyone could create a statistical model that would emulate all of human existence. Furthermore, recent advances in chaos theory suggested that the mechanistic philosophy that formed the underpinnings of psychohistory was just flat wrong, and that such complex patterns could never be predicted with any certainty.

On the other hand, if anyone could do such a thing, it would probably be the Thinker. Certainly, his intellectual capabilities and his philosophical bent suited him for the job.

Struck by the thought, and not liking it, Reed pressed a dashboard switch. A computer keyboard slid from a recess in the control panel. Reed entered one password, then another, and opened a direct link to his main computer banks in Four Freedoms Plaza. He began to type, opening data files and running analysis routines, and writing complex equations. In moments, diagrams and elaborate projection curves took form on the control board monitor.

Some time before, he had begun work on a mathematical model that would simulate the random emissions of neutrons in decaying isotopes and their behavior in a meson-rich, high-gravity environment—say, just above the event horizon of a black hole star. It occurred to him now that certain abstract similarities existed between that unfinished study and the Thinker's apparent pet project, in that both involved the superficially random incidence of phenomena that were, in fact, interdependent on a fundamental level. If he could develop the appropriate parameters for data input and quasilinear projection—

The work had a certain hypnotic quality to it. Even at such an early stage in the effort, the first-draft equations had grace and symmetry that invited further study. In mere minutes, Reed found himself entranced by the implications of the Thinker's remarks, and by the possibilities that those implications suggested. They seemed to build on one another in a geometric pattern of reinforcement and contrast that pointed the way towards even more tantalizing possibilities. In moments, he was completely immersed in the task he had set himself, and unmindful of the world around him.

He was so absorbed that he didn't even notice the first, fat snowflakes strike the Fantasti-Car's canopy. He did hear the buzzing sound that followed a few minutes later, however, and there was no way he could miss the wall of whiteness blocking his craft's path through the upper reaches. He felt a sense of genuine disbelief as he recognized the storm for what it was— a blizzard, the kind of storm that could dump feet of snow on the ground in mere hours. Certainly, it wasn't optimal flying weather.

Why hadn't the navigation computer system alerted him earlier?

Reed typed in a final command sequence, and returned the computer keyboard to its recess. He was an accomplished and experienced pilot, and he knew that this kind of flying demanded his total, personal attention. He thumbed a switch, then gripped the steering yoke and waited for the autopilot to release control of the craft to him.

It didn't.

Feeling the faint beginnings of worry, Reed pressed the emergency override and wrenched the steering grip to his right, hard, trying to correct his course before things got worse.

The Fantasti-Car continued on its preset path, straight into the heart of the storm.

Questions raced through Reed's mind, but he pushed them away. Some kind of remote override? Or sabotage? If so, who had done it? When? All those considerations could wait, at least for a while. Right now, his main concern was that he was only a few hundred feet below the stratosphere, racing into bad weather, utterly unable to control the vehicle he rode. Already, ice was building up on fuselage's outer surfaces and weighting the craft down. That meant that other systems were failing, too; ordinarily, the vehicle was more than proof against inclement weather—but not here, and not now apparently. Once more, Reed pushed the thought away.

He was running out of time.

He strapped himself into his seat. Emergency situations called for emergency measures, no matter how little he cared for them. Bailing out in a blizzard was dangerous, but less dangerous than crashing in one. He pushed an armrest button, the big red one labeled EJECT. In seconds, he knew, the canopy would slide back and the seat would leap up and to the left. Automated steering jets would carry him back and away from the storm, and a special parachute would carry him down, hopefully before the worst of the strom hit. He braced himself for the hammer-blow of upward acceleration.

Nothing happened.

Moving quickly, he slithered out of his seat harness without unbuckling it and unlocked the control panel housing. Inside it waited dozens of circuit boards in close array, with narrow access tracks between them. Those tracks were his last chance, Reed knew. He flattened the elastic bone and flesh of this fingers, extended them, and reached into the instrument panel's interior. He knew where the control yokes functional linkages were and how they worked; he had designed them himself. If he could reach them, manipulate them—

It was about then that the futuristic craft's turbine engines, already whining as they labored to breathe the cold, snow-laden air, coughed once and stuttered.

A moment later, they died, and the Fantasti-Car began to fall.

Roxxon Oil Media Center, Texas:

''I don't like the term *hostile takeover*, not even when it's technically accurate,'' the man behind the podium said. He had dark hair that clung to his skull in too-tight curls, and perfect teeth that glinted whitely in the bright lighting. "Roxxon and Acme are partners now. Where we are is what matters, not how we got here." He paused expectantly.

"Mr. Brady! Mr. Brady!"

"Over here, Mr. Brady!"

"One more, Mr. Brady!"

Michael Brady looked out over the reporters crowded in front of the stage. "Last question," he said. He smiled and pointed. "Yes, you in the red," he said.

An attractive blonde wearing *Daily Bugle* press credentials that identified her as Vreni Byrne stood and the chatter surrounding her dropped to a dull murmur. In the sudden relative quiet, she spoke carefully. "Mr. Brady, for the last ten years, you've been spearheading Roxxon's drive into new business areas, both markets and technologies, ever since you were instrumental in Roxxon Chemical's efforts to open the Madripoor market. That effort ended in disaster—"

An expression of mingled regret and annoyance darkened Brady's handsome features. "And tragedy," he said sharply, interrupting. "I'd really rather not talk about those days, if only out of common decency. Kincaid left a family behind, you know."

"Yes, yes, of course," Byrne said, backtracking hastily. "But since that incident, your initiatives have been marked by a series of buyouts, and then layoffs and wage rollbacks, as Roxxon integrates its new acquisitions in the existing conglomerate. You're known for your own personal, aggressive management style. Can Acme Atomics expect to see history repeated as you take charge?"

"Good question," Brady said. "If an obvious one. The answer isn't easy, though. I'm sure there will be some changes in the long run, but for the moment, we plan to let Acme be Acme. The company is a cornerstone of the community, and we'd be crazy to jeopardize that status." He grinned, revealing his flawless teeth again in a remarkably insincere smile. "I don't think the newest members of the Roxxon family have anything to worry about."

Brady then shook his head as more reporters raised their hands and shouted out questions. "Sorry, ladies and gentlemen, but that's the last question." His smile widened. "Give me a chance to play with my new toy, okay?" He turned and left the press conference, nodding politely in response to shouted queries, but saying nothing more.

Byrne looked at her photographer Tom Cox, a short man with tired eyes. "It's like looking at a shark in a business suit," she said, "And a lying shark, at that. If I worked for Acme, I'd start cleaning out my desk now."

"You're not the only one," Cox said. He returned his camera and attachments to their case. "Brady's a real slash-and-burn kind of guy. I covered the press conference when those weasels took over EncycloGraphics. Brady said the same thing then, in almost exactly the same words. 'The Roxxon family.' Two days later, they were handing out walking papers." He shrugged. "I just wish I could buy stock in unemployment. It's the only thing that's going up these days."

CHAPTER 4

Six refrigerator doors lined one kitchen wall. Ben opened the first. A complete ham, still uncut, looked back at him from one of the metal wire shelves. "Oh, baby," the Thing said softly, "come to Poppa." He reached inside, wrapped broad, flat fingers around the ham's shank, and lifted the entire joint of meat to his lips like an ordinary man might heft a turkey drumstick. He took a bite, then chewed thoughtfully, a satisfied and amiable grin splitting his craggy features.

"I'm still waiting," Sue said. The two of them were in the section of Four Freedoms Plaza that was reserved for living quarters, as far as possible from the laboratory facilities and reception area. A half-dozen kitchenettes were available on other floors, but Ben had insisted on coming here to the main kitchen, despite Sue's protests. It was probably just as well; considering the Thing's remarkable capacity for food, only here could he find enough. "I want to know what happened," she continued.

"Sorry," Ben said, swallowing. "Reed grabbed me for his dumb tests before I had breakfast, and talking with the cops at Fritz's used up my lunch time. I'm hungry." He continued his exploration of the refrigerator and found an unopened gallon of milk. He popped off its cap and lifted the bottle to his lips.

"Benjamin J. Grimm, don't you dare," Sue said, an undercurrent of menace in her voice.

Ben looked at her, at the genuine anger flashing in her eyes. He shrugged. He stepped to the main cupboard and found his personal drinking glass, roughly the size of a small punchbowl and with his name stenciled on the front. Moving quickly, he poured the entire bottle of milk into it, then upended the glass over his mouth and drained it with a single gulp. He burped.

"There," he said. "Satisfied? Another glass to clean." He set the drinking glass on the counter and put the empty milk bottle in a recycling bin.

Sue shook her head. "That's beside the point," she said. "Manners count, and if I let you get away with drinking out of the bottle, Johnny and Reed will be next."

Ben looked at her. "Reed? Drinkin' from the bottle?" he asked. "*That* I gotta see."

"That's *still* not the point," Sue snapped, frustrated with Ben's delays. "Now, tell me about what happened."

"I went to Fritz's," Ben said. "Kragoff did, too. I wanted a coat, but I don't think he did." He looked annoyed. "What a crazy world. It's getting so a guy can't even go shoppin' in peace."

"Go on."

"I tussled with Manny, Moe, and Jack," Ben continued. He munched some more ham. "But one of 'em turned out the lights. By the time I could see again, they had taken the elevator to the subbasement."

"So?" Sue prompted.

"So there was some kind of an access tunnel from the elevator shaft to the nearest subway tunnel," Ben said. "New, too. Accordin' to the building engineer, the elevator inspector had been there yesterday, and everything checked out okay. That means the tunnel had been finished sometime last night." He paused. "Of course, Snap, Crackle, and Pop had hopped the first train, along with the Ghost, and were long gone."

"Any idea what they were after?"

Ben shook his head again. "That's the screwy part. The gorilla was carryin' a garment bag that looked pretty full, but Fritz said nothing was missing."

"You could stuff a person into a garment bag," Sue said thoughtfully.

"You could," Ben agreed, "but no one had gone missing. The staff were all there, and so were the customers—just me an' that Hamilton jerk."

"Hamilton?"

"No one important," Ben said. He told his teammate about the BizNet representative. "But the funny thing is, afterwards, he acted as if we hadn't met. He came over to me, did the whole 'I want to meet Reed' song and dance a second time. It was like he didn't remember our earlier chat." By now, Ben had picked the ham bone clean, so he dropped it in the trash and went looking in the refrigerator again. "We got anything sweet here?" he asked. "I'm still hungry."

"There's ice cream in the freezer," Sue said absently. "But

don't take the whole—'' Her words trailed off and she looked at him, annoyed.

Ben had already found the half gallon of walnut-fudge ripple and eaten it, swallowing the frozen block of milk and sugar in a single gulp. Now, he grinned sheepishly at her, or as sheepishly as a human-shaped mountain could. He opened the dishwasher and set his milk glass on the upper rack. ''Sorry,'' he said softly. ''Hungry. Worked up an appetite, rasslin' with them monkeys. Heh.''

Sue glared at him. ''Two of Kragoff's pets are apes, not monkeys,'' she said, but it was obvious that she wanted to say something else, probably something very unpleasant.

Ben shrugged again. ''You sound like Reed,'' he said. ''And where are he and Johnny, anyway? He needs to know about this.''

''Johnny's on a date. Reed's in Colorado,'' Sue said.

''Colorado? What the ding-dong hey is in Colorado?''

''The Vault.'' Quickly, she filled him in on the Lifestream heist and the request from SAFE.

''Huh. Wish I'd had a chance to see Deeley. He's a good guy,'' Ben said. ''I can do without payin' social calls on the Thinker, though. That guy's pure poison.''

''We've handled him before, remember?''

''Yeah, but he's still trouble. An' we've handled Kragoff, too, but he's the one loose now. Shouldn't we call Reed and let him know?''

''I think that can wait,'' Sue said thoughtfully. ''But I'll call Doug and see if SAFE knows anything about Kragoff's whereabouts. It's not like we can do much until he shows his face again. And Reed's probably still busy with the Thinker.''

''Yeah, but the Thinker's behind bars,'' the Thing noted again. ''The Ghost isn't, an' he's pretty tough for a guy who manages a monkey act.'' He laughed sarcastically. ''Geez. The Thinker, the Red Ghost. It's Old Home Week. I wonder if Johnny's run into the Puppet Master.''

Sue considered his point for a moment, while Ben opened and closed cupboards, searching for more to eat and finding it. Potato chips and fruit disappeared into the bulldozer-like maw of his mouth, chewed only once or twice before being swallowed. It was a sight Sue had seem many times before, but she still found it a source of eerie fascination. The changes wrought by cosmic rays on her teammate's metabolism had been many and complex, and had lent an inspiring intensity to his appetite.

"All right," she finally said. "I'll call SAFE first, and then the Vault." She reached for the phone that hung on one kitchen wall. Though conventional in appearance, it was linked to Four Freedoms Plaza's state-of-the-art communication system. The Fantastic Four's hectic lifestyle had long since made automated answering an absolute necessity; only a dozen men and women knew the string of digits that would make this particular telephone ring. People who called the publicly available line would need to work their way though a complex voicemail system, and almost certainly be relayed to the FF's public relations firm.

The phone rang now, a split second before Sue's fingers touched its smooth plastic surface. It emitted the two-tone chirp that announced a call from outside the building.

Ben looked at her, startled. She looked back at him.

The telephone rang again, its tone cut short as Sue answered.

"Hello? Yes, this is she. Who's calling, please?" Sue's fair complexion abruptly went pale as she paused and listened to the caller. "What? That's not—" Her words stopped, and another pause followed. "I see. Yes, yes, we'll be there in an hour or so."

"What's going on?" Ben asked, as she returned the handset to its cradle. "Who was that?"

"Denver Hospital," Sue said, in a distracted tone of voice that was colored by controlled concern. She looked at Ben. "Get another Fantasti-Car ready. We've got to go."

"What?" Ben asked. "Denver Hospital? How the heck did they get our number? An' why?"

"Reed gave it to them," Sue replied. "There's been some sort of accident." She paused, and when she spoke again, there was a catch in her voice, mingled this time with disbelief. "He's been hurt," she said.

"Just banged up a bit," Dr. Behling said some time later and several thousand miles to the west, in Denver Hospital. He was a tall, ungainly scarecrow of a man, slender enough to be called skinny and with an unruly mop of brownish hair. Ben and Sue had taken a very hectic ride across the country in response to his call, putting another, more heavy-duty Fantasti-Car through its paces as they rushed to Reed's side.

Behling's eyes blinked owlishly at Sue from behind thick lenses. "We assigned him the room more for privacy than anything else. Celebrity status, and all that. I'd still like to take a few x-rays, run some tests, but Dr. Richards has declined."

Sue wasn't listening. She was too busy leaning over the pale form that lay in the hospital bed, too busy hugging and kissing the man who was her husband. "Oh, Reed," she said. "What happened?"

"Yeah, Stretch, take a wrong turn at Albuquerque?" the Thing rumbled.

Reed took his lips from Sue's and answered. "Hardly, Ben. I ran into some bad weather, a blizzard. I thought I could ride it out, but I was wrong. The main turbines iced up and failed." He looked pale and drawn, and an adhesive bandage clung to one temple.

"You tried to fly that crate in a blizzard?" Ben asked, disbelieving. "That's crazy. Why didn't you just—"

"It can wait, Ben," Sue said forcefully. Her blonde tresses were still dusted with snowflakes from the walk inside. Now, they were melting, and the droplets glistened like tears on her face.

"But I wanna know why the nav computer—"

"It can wait," she repeated. "All I'm worried about now is making sure Reed's all right."

Ben looked at her for a long moment, then shrugged, moving his shoulders up and then down with studied nonchalance. "Okay," he said mildly. He turned to look at the gawky figure standing at his left. "Maybe I can talk to you. How about it, Doc? Any frostbite on his tootsies?"

Behling blinked at him this time. "As far as I can tell, Dr. Richards is fine. In fact, he's remarkably intact for a man who crashed an aircraft in a snowdrift and waited there for the better part of an hour," he said. "No broken bones."

"He ain't got the kind of bones that break easy," Ben said. "Tie into knots, sure, but not break."

"Yes, well, even so, he has bruises and a sprain, a few minor contusions," Behling continued. "A mild concussion seems likely, but it's hard to tell. I'd really like to take an x-ray to make sure, if just to see what his skeleton looks like." Something of a wistful note had entered his voice.

"I appreciate your scientific curiosity, Doctor, but there will be no x-rays today," Reed said firmly.

Behling looked disappointed.

Reed stood, leaning heavily on Sue, then releasing her as he found his balance again. "Thank you, Doctor, but just let me get home. I have work to do."

Behling frowned. "I wouldn't advise it, Dr. Richards," he said. "I prescribe complete bed rest for the next few days, at least. Even your unique physiognomy—"

"My unique physiognomy is just fine," Reed said, with uncharacteristic testiness. "It's also what saved me. That, and the emergency airbags in the Fantasti-Car."

"Well, at least let me get you a wheelchair. Our insurance carrier requires—"

Reed shook his head, and immediately looked as if he wished he hadn't. A pained expression flickered across his face and he seemed to lose his equilibrium for a moment.

"Men," Sue said softly, but looked at him anxiously.

Ben rolled his eyes back in their sockets and then turned to Behling again. "Pretty hairy driving conditions out there," he said. "Who brought him in? How'd they find him?"

"This may not be New York, but our rescue service personnel are quite competent and accustomed to adverse conditions, Mr. Grimm," Behling said. "Though I must admit that knowing they were on their way to the famous Mr. Fantastic probably sped things up a bit."

"They knew?"

Behling nodded. "The staff at the Vault made a long distance call to 911."

"The Vault?" Sue and Ben said the word together, but only the Thing added a puzzled, "Huh?"

"They were monitoring my progress, apparently," Reed said. "When I dropped off their screens, they called all local rescue services. I'll have to thank Warden Fingeroth for that." He paused before continuing. "But I would like very much to do that from home. Soon. Now."

"Right now's fine with me," Ben said. "I get to drive this time, though." He looked at Sue. "That okay with you?"

She nodded.

"Good. I never want another ride like that last one." Ben looked at Reed and grinned. "You think I'm a daredevil at the wheel, try riding with Susie when she's in a rush."

Sue smiled sheepishly, but Reed didn't respond.

Ben continued. "I can come back in a few days and pick up the wreckage."

"I don't think that will be necessary, Mr. Grimm," Behling said. "Or feasible."

"Huh?"

"After I got off the phone to Mrs. Richards, I spent some time running interference between Dr. Richards and representatives from the National Transportation Safety Board. Just part of our many services here," he said dryly. "They're quite anxious to begin analyzing the debris."

Ben snorted. "Won't happen," he said. "But let 'em try." A sudden thought struck him and he turned his gaze on Reed again. "Some stuff's happened back home that you need to know about," he said. "I ran into—"

"Ben," Sue said, still hovering protectively at her husband's side.

"—but I guess it can wait," the Thing said without missing a beat. "In the meantime, how'd yer little gab session thing with the Thinker go?"

"Fine," Reed replied. "I don't like to say it, but I think he's in the clear this time."

Ben snorted. "I agree with the doc," he said. "You musta hit your head on something."

Conrad Mandible (Yale, Class of '58) stepped from the shower and toweled himself dry. He shrugged into the hotel's trade-marked burgundy bathrobe and stepped into the fuzzy yellow slippers his wife had given him for his birthday, the ones with rabbits on the toes. He shook his head. Blanche amazed him. Even after thirty-five years of marriage, three and a half de-cades of moving in increasingly elevated circles of govern-ment and society, she was still in so many ways the giggling teenager he had courted.

Mandible was a tall man with silver hair and a lean build only just now going to seed. His new role as Special Econom-ics Advisor to the President was gradually undoing the work of many years of regular workouts in the gym. The job meant too many sixteen-hour days, too many seemingly endless meetings, too much travel and too many conferences in too many cities. But when the President had made the request, Mandible had known what his answer had to be. Still, when his term was over, when the request came again—if it came—

There was a knock.

"Yes?" Mandible asked, speaking loudly enough to be heard through the door as he ran a comb through his still-damp hair.

"Room service," came the reply, which was only a slight surprise. Mandible had ordered a late lunch before stepping into the shower, and the hotel was known for excellent service.

"Come on in," he answered, barely finishing the words before the door swung inward. "I was just freshening up. You guys made good . . ."

His words trailed off into shocked silence.

"Roast beef sandwich on pumpernickel, mustard," a voice said. "House salad, creamy Italian dressing, lobster bisque. Coffee, black, decaffeinated. Cheesecake with cherries."

Mandible heard the words, but paid no attention to them. Instead, he stared in stunned shock at the man wheeling the chromed service cart into the VIP suite.

The newcomer was a tall man with silver hair and a lean build only just now going to seed. He wore a burgundy bathrobe and his feet filled fuzzy yellow slippers with rabbits on the toes. His face was a familiar one, a face that looked back at Mandible only moments before from the shower-fogged mirror.

"What—you—I—" Mandible said to his doppelgänger, some corner of his mind dimly aware of how foolish he must sound.

"Precisely," the newcomer said, still speaking with Mandible's voice.

"Enough chatter," someone else said, speaking with a slight accent. "We have a timetable, after all."

Another man had entered the room, a not-very-tall man in some kind of a costume. Mandible recognized him in a vague sort of way from half-remembered newspaper stories. The Crimson Ghost? The Red Phantom?

Whoever he was, he was holding some kind of gun.

"Quickly now, my loyal one," the man said to someone still waiting in the corridor. "I have need of you."

Yet another figure came through the door, moving in an awkward gait somewhere between a shuffle and a waddle. It had long arms and a pendulous belly, both covered with fur, and dark eyes that glinted ominously from beneath a receding brow. It was an orangutan, and it bared its teeth slightly as it ambled toward Mandible.

As the ape came closer, Mandible looked back at the man with the gun. The name finally drifted up from somewhere in his brain. "You're the Red Ghost," he said.

The balding man smiled, pulling his lips back to reveal uneven teeth set in a disturbing grin. "Correct," he said, somehow managing to hiss the word. "And you are an obstructionist appendage of the outmoded capitalist state." He raised the weapon. "Were circumstances only slightly different, I would now be leading you and others like you to your execution."

"No! Wait!"

The Red Ghost shook his head. "No rhetoric, no futile

pleas," he said. "Instead, sleep." He squeezed the trigger.

A moment later, the man who looked like Conrad Mandible munched quietly on the roast beef sandwich as the orangutan tended to his counterpart. With surprising dexterity, the ape wrapped the unconscious man in what looked like yards of plastic tape, and then hoisted his limp, unprotesting burden to one shoulder.

"Excellent," the Red Ghost said, looking at his Rolex. "Precisely on schedule. If the other team has done its part, all pieces are in play now."

The replacement Conrad Mandible said nothing, but nodded and continued eating. The ape shuffled towards the door. As he got closer, he gestured with one paw, and the knob twisted, clicked without benefit of physical contact. The door swung open and the ape walked through it. The door swung shut behind him, moving as if by itself.

"Review his papers," the Ghost said to the room's only other occupant. He gestured at a leather valise that waited on the room's desk. "Alert us if they diverge from expectations."

"Mandible" nodded again.

For a moment, the Red Ghost looked as if he were about to say something more. Then, even as his wristwatch chirped softly, he shrugged, turned, and walked through the door.

He didn't bother opening it first.

Four Freedoms Plaza was one of the most secure buildings on Earth, bristling with alarm systems and defensive measures that were sufficient to fend off almost any of the Fantastic Four's many enemies. Before leaving for Denver, and not knowing how long they would be there, Ben had placed all of those systems on a high alert status, in view of the Red Ghost's recent appearance in the city. Now, even as he brought the Fantasti-Car in for a landing, he could see on his dash monitor that those systems had been reset to idle standby. As a section of the tower's rooftop slid back to receive him, and as he brought the Fantasti-Car in for a perfect vertical landing, Ben saw the reason for the new alarm status: Johnny was standing in the hangar area, a concerned expression on his youthful features.

The Fantasti-Car's turbine lift engines slowed and stopped. Smaller electrical motors whined softly, and the futuristic craft taxied into its assigned stall in the hangar area. Most of Four Freedoms Plaza's top floor was devoted to vehicle storage and launch areas, and the Fantasti-Car that Sue and Ben had flown to Denver was only one of many. Once it had parked, the vehicle's canopy slid back and the passengers deplaned.

"What happened?" Johnny asked his partners anxiously. "I got Sue's note, but it didn't say much. Is Reed okay?"

"I'm fine, Johnny," Reed said, but he seemed to be speaking to his wife as much as to his brother-in-law. "A few bruises, that's all."

"And a concussion," Sue said tartly.

"Concussion?" Johnny asked.

"I don't have a concussion," Reed said.

"You don't know that, Reed," Sue said.

"I think I know enough to—"

"Hush!"

Reed hushed, but shot a sour look at Johnny and Ben as his wife led him towards a waiting elevator. She was emphatically extolling the merits of bed rest and Reed was equally emphatically denying he needed any when the metal doors slid shut behind them.

"Banged up, huh?" Johnny asked Ben.

"Must be," the Thing said. "He was a grouch the whole way back, an' he's not actin' too friendly now."

"What happened?"

"He ran into a blizzard on the way back from Colorado—"

"Colorado?" Johnny interrupted. "What was he doing in Colorado!?"

Ben told him, and then continued. "He tried to ride the storm. Unfortunately, he tried to ride it out in the Honeymoon Special."

"A blizzard? In that thing? Ouch."

"Yeah, ouch," Ben agreed. He stepped to the workstation nearest his landing area and pressed a few switches. "It musta taken him by surprise. I checked with the National Weather

Service and they said it was some kind of freak meteorological event.''

Behind Ben, a panel in the service bay slid back, and a wheeled device the approximate size of a large dog emerged. It brought a flexible armored hose with it. Rolling up to the Fantasti-Car's fuselage, the machine attached the hose to a recessed fitting in the craft's hull. As the refueling process began, the robot turned its attentions to another access panel near the cockpit.

The wheeled robot, and others like it, was as close as the FF came to maintaining a ground crew for its impressive aerial fleet. For the next twenty minutes or so, it would refuel the craft, examine the vehicle for damage or excessive wear, and run various diagnostic programs. Later, Ben would review its reports and almost certainly verify them himself, but for now, he didn't mind letting machines do the donkey work.

"What did Reed say?" Johnny asked.

"Not much; Sue wouldn't let him. Mama Richards is in Mother Hen mode now, big time."

"She gets like that sometimes."

"Yeah, but I wish she'd let me get a word in edgewise. There's stuff Reed needs to know about." Briefly, Ben told Johnny about his morning encounter with the Red Ghost and his super apes at the haberdashery.

"Kragoff, huh?" the Torch said. "That's a name we haven't heard in a while."

"Yeah, and one I coulda gone without hearin' for a while longer. Still, I think Reed should know what happened, and I wanna tell him, but Sue says I gotta leave Stretch be fer a while."

"Did you call the cops?"

Ben looked sourly at his younger teammate. "Didn't have to. A baboon with a machine gun has a way of drawin' attention." He glanced at the workstation display panel and nodded at the reading he saw there. "Gonna call Deeley later and find out if SAFE has anything on the Ghost, though. Guy like that's hard to keep in jail."

There was a whirring noise and a click as the automated

service unit disengaged from the Fantasti-Car. As it rolled back to its cubby, the machine paused in front of Ben for a moment. Another whir, another click, and a diskette popped out of a slot on its gleaming metal surface.

"Thanks, Jeeves," Ben said, taking the bit of plastic. The diskette held the results of various diagnostic checks, and a complete download of the Fantasti-Car's trip log. The machine made no response, but parked itself in its storage space. A moment later, the wall panel had slid shut again.

"What about you, hotshot?" Ben asked.

"What about me?"

"Kinda surprised you're here. I thought you were spending the day with your lady love."

Johnny snorted derisively. "Lady love?" he said. "Jenna? We're just friends, and I'm beginning to think not very good ones, at that."

"How so?"

"Aw, she pulled a fast one on me today. We were supposed to go to lunch, and she sprung a little surprise on me. Seems her boss asked her to try and arrange an 'exclusive' interview with me for WNN."

"And you ain't interested?"

"It's not like that, Ben," Johnny said, obviously still annoyed at whatever had happened earlier. "I don't like being used, and I don't like walking into a fancy restaurant and finding a local news anchor waiting for me."

"Heh. Them's the breaks, kiddo. Carmine Hamilton wasn't looking to chat with me, either."

Johnny didn't say anything. Ben looked at him. The kid looked genuinely sad.

"Did you at least get a decent lunch out of the deal?" the Thing asked.

"It was okay. Why?"

"Because I didn't. And there's a dozen frozen pizzas in the icebox. I guess I could spare you one, if you asked real nice."

Johnny laughed. "We live in New York, pizzeria capital of the world, and you want to do frozen. If you don't want to go out, why don't we just order delivery?"

"Because the last time we did that, the delivery boy turned out to be the point man for another Skrull invasion."

"Good point," Johnny said, nodding.

They began walking toward the elevator.

Consciousness returned slowly. It did not return all at once, but came to him in fits and starts—brief glimpses and phantom sounds that faded in and out as he tried to waken. By the time he realized that he was able to keep his eyes open, he wanted to close them again.

He was aware enough now to realize how badly his head hurt, a dull, deep-seated throb that suggested a concussion. He had a sour taste in his mouth that he recognized as a symptom of dehydration and shock, and a soreness in his chest that pulsed in time with his breathing. For a brief moment, he considered relinquishing consciousness again, in hopes that he would feel better when he woke, but he was awake enough to analyze that option and assess it as a bad one.

Acting more on need than desire, he took a deep breath and sat up. The world spun crazily around him as he moved. After a sickening moment of vertigo, it righted itself, and he took stock of his surroundings.

He was seated on the edge of a cot, on the same thin mattress that had held him while he slept. Gray stone block walls surrounded him, and yellowish light shone down from a ceiling fixture. To his left was a small washstand; to his right, a door made of steel bars. Beyond it, he could see a corridor and more doors, but the other spaces in this particular cell block looked dark and empty.

What had happened?

He remembered gleaming controls and roaring engines, then the sickening sensation of freefall, then the sudden shock of impact as the fall ended. He remembered metal breaking and tearing, and he remembered a great deal of pain as he bounced about the cockpit's confines.

There was another memory, too—a tantalizing image that hung at the periphery of his memory, indistinct but undeniable. He tried to focus on it, but the details would not come. In those last moments of consciousness, in the seconds before the white world outside his craft had given way to darkness, he had seen something picking its way towards him through the snowdrifts. Humanlike but not human, it had been indistinct and shadowy, a gray blot against the whiteness raging outside. Even so, there had been something familiar about its build and stride. Now, he struggled with his uncooperative memory, certain that the figure had been key to his current situation. He massaged his temples, thinking. If he could only remember—

"Awake, huh?" The voice had a hollow, mechanical ring to it.

He looked up from his thoughts. An armored figure stood outside the cell door, green metal gleaming even in the dull lighting.

"Yes, yes, I—"

"Shut up," the Guardsman said. "No questions." He knelt to open a slot in the cell door, and slid a tray though it, bearing covered dishes. "Chow time. I'll come back in an hour for the tray. When I do, stand at attention well away from the door, and don't make any funny moves. If you do, I'll come down on you, hard."

The armored figure turned and walked away, metal boots ringing as they struck the concrete slab floor.

Reed Richards watched him go.

CHAPTER 5

Seated on his bunk, the Thinker watched intently but silently as two Guardsmen strode past the force field that served as the door to his Vault cell. One of the two-tone, green metal-covered figures glanced in the Thinker's direction, but said nothing. There would have been no point. Other prisoners tried to make small talk with patrolling guards, or issued threats to them. The Thinker did neither. He viewed such things as beneath him.

Now, as the two armored men left his field of view, the Thinker laid back on his bunk and composed himself, with his arms at his side and his legs straight. His breathing slowed and became more shallow, and his heartbeat dropped to a fraction of its normal rate. Beginning with his extremities, he willed the muscle groups to relax and go limp. A wave of serenity passed through him, a flowing sensation of tranquility and relaxation, and he closed his eyes.

When he opened them again, he was somewhere else—or, rather, his consciousness was.

Hidden in folds of the Thinker's brain were molecule-sized microchips, linked by undetectably fine superconductor filaments, each component much too small to be detected with even the most sensitive surveillance equipment available. That apparatus, combined with his own considerable force of will, enabled the Thinker to transfer his mind from one body to another. Though crafted entirely of synthetic materials, the shell that housed him now was a duplicate of his original frame, perfect in every detail. The Thinker's real body had a six-inch scar on his left ankle, a pale reminder of a childhood injury. This body had the same scar, and so did more than a hundred other duplicate Thinkers, cached in secret places around the world. With but a moment's thought, the Thinker could shift his mind from this body to another, more easily than most people could change clothes. All the while, his birthform would wait for him in Colorado, safe and secure from his enemies, and guarded by the full might of the United States government. The Thinker found that aspect of the situation more than a trifle amusing.

At the moment, however, he had no time for such considerations. The body he wore now sat in a room without windows, in a comfortable chair positioned before nine darkened television screens set in a wooden framework, above a bank of complex controls. This room, too, had duplicates across the world, one in each of the Thinker's various laboratory complexes. He used them to access mass media, to gather the day-to-day information that he found useful for certain of his endeavors, and to issue commands to the underlings who shaped those endeavors. This particular room, however, served another purpose equally well. It made a good meeting place.

In front of the seated Thinker, the nine television screens remained dark, and yet an image seemed to form in them. Flashes of color and form appeared, as something passed though the glass barrier as if it were not there. Arms, legs, head, torso—all emerged and became visible, their passage having no noticeable effect on the equipment that was now, suddenly, behind the newcomer instead of before him.

"Hello, Thinker," the Red Ghost said.

"Hello, Kragoff," the Thinker said. He slid his chair back along its floor tracks as the newcomer emerged from the television screens. "Precisely on time, too. Excellent."

The Red Ghost smiled, and made a mocking half-bow. "Punctuality is a virtue," the Russian said. "Or so I am told."

The Thinker nodded in acknowledgment. Having wasted enough time on pleasantries, he turned his attentions to business. "Report," he said.

"Everything is in place. I personally installed the genuine Mandible in his cell at the New Jersey facility."

The Thinker nodded. "Reed Richards is in custody now, as well. He and Mandible were the last two of the current batch."

"That's good. We've accomplished much, these past months."

"Years," the Thinker corrected. "I have been pursuing this exercise for many years, long before you became part of the operation. I laid down the original statistical matrices more than a decade ago. After Richards's initial advances in DNA synthesis and lifeform manufacture made such things feasible, I created my first android and the initial duplicates, and began putting them in place." He paused. "Reed Richards is a man of considerable genius, but remarkably limited vision. For so very long, he has believed that I undertook my original raid on his facilities with nothing more than simple larceny in mind. In all our encounters in all the years since, he has never divined the slightest hint of the master plan underlying all of my schemes. He has not had the faintest glimpse of the operation that his discoveries have made possible."

"Richards is still dangerous," the Red Ghost said edgily. "I would greatly prefer that we liquidate him."

"As you liquidated Ben Grimm at the haberdashery?"

"That was a fluke, and I was not prepared for it," the Red Ghost snapped. "You did not tell me he would be there."

"True enough," the Thinker said, not sounding as if he liked the admission. "His presence was unforseen. I monitor the Fantastic Four's activities with considerable attention, and I saw nothing that would prompt the Thing's proximity during the Hamilton abduction."

The Red Ghost snickered. "Perhaps Grimm needed a new overcoat," he said.

The Thinker shot him a baleful glance. "Be amused if you wish," he said, "but understand that the Fantastic Four now know that you are active in New York once more. That complicates matters."

"Simplify them again, then. Dispose of Richards, rather than risk his escape."

"No," the Thinker said, irritated now, and letting his irritation show. He made a steeple of his fingers and fixed Kragoff with a steady gaze. "We have had this discussion before. We need the information that the ersatz Richards can gather. His is a remarkably difficult mind to emulate, and having the original in our custody greatly improves the odds more than it does with the other abuctees. The cybernetic relays in Richards's cell provide useful input for the duplicate's thought processes, and decrease the likelihood of discovery to less than seven percent."

"And if he escapes our custody?"

"He will not escape," the Thinker said in clipped tones. "I

have nullified his powers. Without them, his physical prowess is no greater than those of an ordinary man. For Reed Richards, in his present state, iron bars and stone walls do a prison make. He is no longer a threat.''

Kragoff shook his head. ''I disagree,'' the Russian said. ''As long as he lives, Reed Richards is a threat. That lesson, at least, I have learned. As the Americans say, I have learned it the hard way.''

''He will live just long enough to play his part. He will see our efforts succeed, and witness the dawn of a new day,'' the Thinker said. ''I do not believe he will care for it.''

Behind the Red Ghost, the nine television screens clicked to life, prompted by an unspoken command from the Thinker. On them, forming one complete image, a computer-animated globe seemed to spin. It was perfect in every detail, resembling a satellite photograph, but too detailed to be one. Spinning slowly, it revealed the world's seas and continents with razor-keen precision, unobscured by cloud cover. On the globe's land masses, a network of glowing green lines defined national boundaries and provincial borders. One continent after another came into view from the west, and then disappeared again beyond the eastern horizon, only to return again in a matter of seconds.

On those land masses other symbols glowed. They were starred highlights in a dozen other colors, distinct from the boundaries and borders. Most markers were clustered around major population centers. New York, Tokyo, Moscow, Beijing, Tel Aviv, and Hong Kong bore so many glowing indicators that the tiny spots of light had merged into irregular blobs of light. From other nations, such as Sylvania, Hungary, Greece, and Korea, only isolated telltales shone, glinting starkly from sporadic locales.

The Thinker gestured at the northern portion of America's eastern seaboard, specifically at New York. The city's outlines were barely discernible under a cloud of the shining sparks. ''With the last of the counterparts in place,'' the Thinker said, ''we are at an even one thousand. One thousand men and women, all of them my agents. They move undetected among the world's five billion. Together, they are the fulcrum on which I shall move the world.''

"We," the Red Ghost corrected.

The Thinker nodded. *"We* shall move the world," he said. "Forgive me. I have worked on this plan for many years. Your role in this, though certainly vital, is still a recent development.''

Kragoff did not respond.

"One thousand men and women," the Thinker repeated. "Five hundred individuals would have sufficed, if they were the right five hundred, and if no unknown factors intervened. Doubling that number effectively eliminates any chance of failure, no matter what forces might unknowingly move against us. Six hundred eleven men and three hundred eighty-nine women. One thousand agents in all walks of life, chosen and placed and poised to make the choices and take the actions that I direct, and to prompt the consequences I desire. They will guide human history into a path more conducive to my goals.''

"And mine," the Ghost interjected.

The Thinker nodded again. As he did, the image on the monitor array changed, as the globe stopped spinning and reversed its course for a few degrees of arc before stopping again. On the screen, green lines defined a sprawling territory that stretched across two continents. This country, too, hosted the bright indicators, perhaps a hundred of them, scattered across the land's contours like toys in a child's playroom.

The Red Ghost smiled at the sight. "Mother Russia," he said softly, and then murmured more words in his own language.

"Remember, Kragoff," the Thinker said. "I reward accomplishment, not impertinence.''

The Ghost looked at him.

"Russia will be yours, as promised," the Thinker continued. "I leave to you how you will administer your rule.''

Kragoff shrugged. "I have been in nearly constant contact with URSA for the past year," he said, naming a clandestine organization dedicated to returning the former USSR's Communist government to power. "Since joining you in your endeavor."

"And I gather that you finally convinced them of your veracity?"

"With some difficulty," Kragoff said. "URSA's new Director of Internal Activities, Dina Rosengaus, is a rather wary woman. My refusal to provide her with the specifics of this operation does not endear me to her, but she has balanced it against my proven service to our homeland's previous, proper regime." Before becoming the Ghost, Kragoff had been among the Soviet Union's leading researchers, awarded many decorations by the Communist government for his scientific orthodoxy. "Ultimately, trust and hope triumphed over doubt, as they always must. URSA stands ready to shape order from chaos."

"Replacing her will be unnecessary, then. I will recycle the duplicate."

The Ghost nodded in acknowledgment, then continued. "URSA's ranks include many skilled administrators and charismatic leaders who have found themselves sadly disenfranchised by the changing political climate." His thin, bloodless lips curled in disgust as he spoke the last words, but then he smiled again. "They stand ready to restore the dictatorship of the proletariat, and prepare the world once more for the inevitable advent of the classless society. I will give Russia to URSA, and then URSA will give Russia Communism once more—and also bestow upon me certain authorities and privileges of rank."

"A fair exchange, I think."

"Easy words, for a man who will control the remainder of the world." Despite the words, there was no hint of challenge now in Kragoff's voice, but only respectful acknowledgment.

"*Control* might not be the proper word," the Thinker said. He paused. "*Study* is more appropriate, I think." He gazed at the nine screens, at the tiled image of a world that had suddenly started spinning again. "Yes. Study," he repeated. "And to study anything properly, one must perform certain experiments." He paused. "Many, many experiments."

• • •

The prison cell seemed ordinary enough—a cot and wash-stand, four stone block walls, concrete slab floor, a plaster ceiling, and a standard prison-issue barred door. That last barrier should have posed no great obstacle to anyone with a body as flexible and malleable as Reed Richards's was. Under ordinary circumstances, he would have extended himself through the spaces between the bars and escaped easily, but these were not ordinary circumstances. Just now, Reed was trapped as effectively as any of the Vault's denizens.

If this was the Vault, a force field would have augmented the door's steel bars, and provided an impenetrable barrier. That wasn't the case here, however. Something about the place kept Reed's powers from working. He suspected that the something in question was a neutralizer array, perhaps installed behind one of the cell's stone walls. Dr. Doom had used something similar on him recently, to good effect. Doom's device, installed in a collar locked around Reed's neck, had worked by suppressing the specific neural impulses that controlled his superhuman stretching ability. Now, his unknown captor had accomplished much the same effect. Presumably, Reed's capability was still there, locked inside his irradiated cellular structure, but beyond his ability to control. He was powerless now.

Other options remained available, however.

Reed spent the first day of his imprisonment researching the specifics of his confinement while he regained his strength. He paced the length and width of his cell to measure it, and examined its sparse furnishings carefully. There wasn't much to examine, but he went over the cot and washstand thoroughly, noting each aspect and filing the information away in his mind.

The prison itself was nearly barren, and it followed a routine as mundane and unbroken as any Reed could imagine. The Guardsman—or *a* Guardsman—brought food at regular intervals, and returned at equally regular intervals to retrieve the tray. Reed timed them carefully, using the electronic wristwatch that was an integral feature of his costume's left white glove.

By the time the Guardsman had delivered his third meal, Reed was reasonably sure that the armored attendant was not a true Guardsman at all. It seemed to be a semiautonomous robot, with a limited number of response routines programmed into its circuits. Certainly, it showed no ability or inclination to respond to questions or comments, and something was subtly wrong about the way it moved, and about the angles where its limbs joined its torso. Whatever was inside that metal suit didn't have a human skeleton, but more likely possessed a mechanical armature of some sort. If it was a robot, that suggested some possibilities.

The third meal served was supper, apparently put together by someone of a vegetarian bent—an assortment of steamed vegetables, tasteless bread, and soy milk. The Guardsman provided it on a tray with two plates and a handled mug, along with a spoon, and a fork, and a blunt knife. An hour later, when the robot retrieved the tray and dishes, the knife and the fork were missing, but the Guardsman did not seem to notice. That suggested some promising possibilities to Reed, bits of knowledge that were at least as valuable as the two utensils he had tucked into the waistband of his uniform.

By themselves, of course, they were of only limited use. Certainly, neither piece of cheap metal would do any good against the Guardsman's armor, so using them as weapons was out of the question. Reed knew of other uses for them, however.

For several hours, Reed ran the knife's rounded tip against the rough concrete that mortared the wall's stone blocks together. Whoever had built the place had elected to spend somewhat more on construction than on outfitting the dining facilities; the concrete was tough, and hard enough to stand up against the steady stroking. That was good. In fairly short order, Reed had reshaped the blade into something like a screwdriver.

Footsteps rang out as metal boots slammed against the corridor's concrete floor.

Reed looked up, only slightly surprised. Whoever had built this place had obviously patterned it loosely after the Vault, as if familiar with that place's regimented procedures. Assuming he was still in the Mountain time zone, it was nearly 2100 hours now, which was when Vault regulations called for lights out.

"Lights out in ten minutes," the Guardsman said.

"Would you like a fresh turnip?" Reed asked. "I have plenty." He didn't bother to hide the tool he had so painstakingly made. He wanted to determine if the Guardsman would notice it, or react.

"Shut up, mister," came the reply. "None of your lip. Lights out in ten." The Guardsman strode down the corridor, continuing its rounds.

Reed nodded. That much, at least, was good, and consistent with his initial hypothesis. Obviously, the Guardsman was a robot, one with only limited cognitive capabilities, programmed with a set of canned responses to various cues. It had no ability to recognize a non sequitur, let alone respond to it. Even better, the fact that neither the robot nor anyone else had interrupted his work meant that Reed was almost certainly not under any kind of round-the-clock surveillance. Had this been the real Vault, two staffed cameras would have monitored his every move, and his purloined prize would long since have been confiscated. During his examination of the cell, Reed had seen three likely routes of escape; these two new bits of knowledge optimized one and made the other two less attractive, though still possible. Now, he examined his makeshift screwdriver carefully and considered his next step.

Ten minutes later, darkness fell. He waited another five minutes for his eyes to adjust, and then he went back to work.

"Reed, you aren't supposed to be in here," Sue Richards said, annoyance and concern equally evident in her voice. She stood in the doorway to one of the several prototyping facilities in Four Freedoms Plaza. It combined the best features of a workshop and a proving ground, and enabled Reed Richards to turn his ideas into reality, then test their utility.

"Hmmm?" the lean man behind the workbench replied. A vaguely distracted look flowed across his thoughtful features.

He turned off a small welding torch and set it aside, then slid thick-lensed protective goggles up and away, revealing his brown eyes. "Did you say something, dear?"

Sue looked at him for a long moment, but didn't reply.

Shoulders shrugged eloquently, the goggles slid back into place, and the torch clicked back to life, as gloved hands played its flame along the interior of a medium-sized piece of apparatus. A similar piece of equipment, apparently completed, waited on a nearby table.

"Reed," Sue repeated, a genuinely angry tone in her voice this time.

Again, goggles slid back and again the torch died, set down this time with an air of finality. "Yes, Sue?"

"You're supposed to be in bed," she said. "Dr. Behling prescribed at least three days of total bed rest, and I promised to supervise you closely. I haven't been able to get you to lie down for ten minutes since we got back from Denver. First, you spend an entire day at the main computer workstation—"

He smiled. "Just something that occurred to me in the hospital," he said. "I wanted to check some fourth-order physics equations against some data we gathered the last time we went into the Negative Zone."

Sue continued as if he hadn't spoken. "And then, you spent most of the night locked in the genetics lab—"

"I had started some test sequences running before I left for the Vault and I had to check them. They might be germane to Ben's situation."

Sue shook her head. Hands on hips, a stern expression on her face, she cut an imposing figure "Uh-uh," she said. "That's not good enough. You won't do Ben any good if you work yourself to death. You won't do any of us any good." Her voice softened. "You certainly won't do *me* any good."

The lean man smiled. "I'm sorry, my darling," he said. "Just let me finish up this assembly, and then I'll make it up to you."

Sue looked at him pensively. "How long before you're finished?" she asked.

"One hour, maybe two." He thumbed the torch's ignition switch. The flame sputtered to life, and he slid his protective goggles back into place again. "The first one is finished, and this one's almost done. I want to—"

Sue shook her head again. "Still not good enough," she said. Her voice raised. "Ben, Johnny!" she called. "He won't listen to reason!"

She stepped out of the doorway and further into the lab space. Almost immediately, two figures joined her, as the Thing and the Human Torch flanked their teammate.

"C'mon, Stretch," the Thing said. He sounded patient, if slightly bored. "Doc Behling says its beddy-bye time, and Benjamin J. Grimm, RN, is here to fill the prescription, even if I have to drag you back to your quarters kicking and screaming."

The welding torch clicked off again, and white-gloved hands removed the goggles and set them aside.

"C'mon, Reed," the Torch said. "We've played this game before, every time you get a bug up your rear about some new gadget. You know the rules by now."

"You're being unreasonable," came the mild reply. The access panel on the piece of equipment clicked shut, and the clamps holding it in place opened as one finger pressed a button. "I think I know my own limitations better than any conventional—"

Ben shook his head as he interrupted. "No way," he said. "No arguments. I ain't gonna give you a chance to convince me of anything. I just got off the horn to Denver, and Behling was plenty ticked when I told him you hadn't hit the sack yet."

"I hate to say it, but Ben's right, Reed," Johnny said. "Concussions are serious business."

"I keep telling all of you, I don't have a concussion. I'm fine."

"Yeah, well, keep actin' the way you are, an' I can change that situation."

"Ben," Sue said. "Threats won't help matters."

"Aw, c'mon, Susie, I'm just kiddin', you know I'm just—"

Ben went abruptly silent as a blinding radiance filled the room. There was a crackling noise, like an electrical discharge, and the air was suddenly sharp with the scent of ozone. Space itself seemed to twist and fold, and then, in the center of the glare, something seemed to emerge from nowhere.

Six somethings.

Five of the half-dozen materializing forms were human, or at least humanoid. One was a tall man, clad in a black and gray costume with a lightning bolt motif and pleated glider wings. A metal antenna, looking like a tuning fork, was attached to the masking hood of his costume. Next to him, her arm linked through his, stood an attractive woman, statuesque and with classically beautiful features that were framed by a mask and by a rippling, flowing curtain of red hair.

Three other forms shimmered, became more distinct. They were a man with green skin and fishlike scales, and another, bigger man whose legs ended in hooves instead of feet. Beside them was the fifth newcomer, a slender man wearing green and white, and whose head seemed slightly too large for his body.

The Fantastic Four stared at the new arrivals with a look of mingled recognition and surprise.

The sixth, last figure to become visible was in no way human, and grotesque enough to make even the scaled man look mundane. It looked like an enormous bulldog, nearly the size of a small car, with an antenna-like tendril growing from his brow. Now, even as the dog became visible, the glare surrounding the entire party ebbed and faded. In mere instants, it collapsed into a pale nimbus of energy that coalesced around the dog and then disappeared. From start to finish, the whole process had taken only seconds, and then silence abruptly filled the room, only to be broken by the Thing's disbelieving voice.

"I don't believe it," he said. "The Inhumans? What the ding-dong hey are you guys doing here?"

"We seek your aid, Ben Grimm," Medusa said. "Aid for us, and for the future of our entire race."

· · ·

From Fred Raven's America, *WNN News-Talk Radio, Washington, D.C.:*

"—and if you don't like it, go live somewhere else! Like that would make a difference these days! The whole world's going to hell in a handbasket! At least this land I love is going there a bit slower!"

"You don't love anything, Fred! All you know how to do is hate! You're just—"

"Enough of that noise, folks! Half past the hour on the Fred Raven show, and that sounds like a good time to move on to the next caller. Wayne from Virginia, you're rantin' with Raven!"

"Fred, what's happened to you?"

"Watcha mean, Wayne-man? Speak to me."

"I've listened to you for years, ever since you were a local drive-time show, and I've really enjoyed—"

"Glad to have you, Wayne, but make your point, and make it fast. I'm trying to do a radio show here. Lotta people want to complain. Lotta people think the ol' Raven's stepped on their toes."

"Me included, Fred. What's happened to you? You used to be a pretty thoughtful guy—conservative, sure, but rational. I liked a lot of what you had to say. But now—it's like you've gone off the deep end in the last year or so. I mean, c'mon Fred, sealing the borders? Revoking visas and passports? Listen to what you're proposing! You go on the national airwaves and you talk about deporting anyone who's not at least a second generation citizen, for God's sake! That's beyond reactionary, beyond xenophobic—it's just plain fascist."

"Yeah? So what's your point? Times are tough, buddy, and tough times call for tough measures. We do things my way, and at least the trains will run on time. Wouldn't that be nice, hmmm?"

"It's like you've become someone else."

"Not me that's changing, Wayne. The world's becoming a different place. That's how I feel, and most of my listeners agree."

"People like you are making it different, Fred. You used to

talk about America as a place that combined the best of all nations. You used to talk about people of all colors, all creeds, all nationalities working together to solve our problems. How can we do that when you keep driving us apart? Your show's national now—think what a difference you could make! Instead, you're just being a divisive, disruptive, dangerous—"

"Y'know, Wayne, you're right on one point. I have changed a tad over the years. Maybe I've grown up a bit, maybe I've just gotten smarter, but mostly, I've gotten more realistic. Most of the problems that face society today *can* be solved—just not by the way you think. Get rid of trouble-makers, and you get rid of troubles, I say."

"Fred, you can't believe that! You—"

"What a sourpuss! Next call! Billy from North Carolina! You're rantin' with Raven!"

CHAPTER 6

Reed Richards had always been good with tools, even improvised ones. As a child of eight, he had once completely disassembled his father's antique pocket watch and then put it back together, using only two sewing needles and a pair of tweezers he had made by reshaping a hairpin. His father had learned about Reed's work only after noticing that the watch had begun to keep better time. Now, working quickly with the tools he had created from the dinner utensils, Reed set about dismantling his cell's only piece of furniture, the cot.

It didn't take him long to do the job. Bending the fork's tines and twisting them together had given him a primitive but useable wrench, and the knife's now-squared tip did double duty as a screwdriver and as a prying tool. The flatware's metal was soft and bent easily, but Reed was perfectly willing to bend it back into shape again and again, and to apply his makeshift tools where they would do the most good. In less than an hour, he had reduced the bed's frame to its component parts, making it a pile of long and short pieces of metal, and an assortment of nuts and slotted bolts. He examined each piece of steel closely, flexing the long pieces and comparing the short ones to the gap between his cell door's bars. When he was satisfied that they could serve him the way he wanted, he set them aside and moved on to the next step.

As originally constructed, the bunk had been little more than a square frame with stubby legs made of tubular steel. It had no slats; instead, a heavy-gauge wire mesh supported the thin mattress. Working quickly, Reed unwound the wires, straightened them as best he could, and then began twisting their ends together to form a continuous length of about fifty feet. The wire resisted his efforts, but he persisted, and forced the springy stuff to do what he wanted. This phase took longer than dismantling the cot had, and was less interesting, but it was just as essential. After a while, his fingers found the rhythm of their task and needed little guidance as he worked, so he could turn his mind to other things.

The others had to be worried about him, he knew. It was difficult to be certain, but his best guess was that he had been held prisoner for two days now—ample time for his absence to be noted and for a search to begin. Knowing Sue, she was already moving heaven and Earth to find him, and Johnny and Ben were no doubt hard-pressed to keep up with her.

Unless his unknown captor had taken them, too.

What had been done once could be done again. Even now, a powerless Sue or Johnny or Ben could be sitting in a similar cell, working on some type of escape plan.

Or they could all be dead.

He didn't like to think about that possibility. The others were a tough and resilient lot, but whoever had captured him had shown cunning and considerable assets, and was no doubt dangerous. Worse, though his unknown captor had gone to some trouble to keep him alive, he might not place such a high value on other members of the Fantastic Four. Reed's main suspect at the moment was still the Thinker, and he knew several possible reasons why the Thinker would want a live Reed Richards as a captive—and not all of those reasons applied to his teammates. The Thinker had uses for Reed's mind, for his intellect and knowledge, uses that pertained less well to the Invisible Woman, the Human Torch, and the Thing. If he—if anyone—had decided that the other members of the Fantastic Four were expendable—

It wouldn't do any good to worry, he knew. If they were captives, he would need to free them. If they were casualties, he would need to avenge them. He could do neither from where he was now.

Reed reached for another length of wire and found none. He had spliced the last two pieces together, and the resulting length was ready for the next step. That was good, if only because his fingers were beginning to ache from the monotonous work. He reached for the piece of pipe that he had chosen from among the cot's four legs, the one that seemed slightly shorter than the others, and began to wind the wire he had so painstakingly assembled around it. He placed each loop close to the next, wrapping them all as tightly as he could. He started at one end of the pipe and worked his way along its length. When he reached its end, he started winding again, in the opposite direction, wrapping a second layer of coils over the first, and then a third.

The work was tiresome, but necessary. He did it with considerable precision and remarkably little attention, just moving his hands in a steady, almost robotic pattern that laid a thick layer of wire over the pipe's cylindrical surface. As he worked, he thought, but not about his work, and not about his teammates.

Instead, he considered yet again the Thinker's parting comments, and what the other man might have meant.

"The Academy elders summoned us, in desperate search of aid, and now we come to you," Medusa concluded simply. She and her fellow Inhumans still stood in the ample space of the prototyping workshop where they had first arrived, despite invitations from Sue to adjourn the meeting to a more comfortable area of the skyscraper headquarters. This was anything but a social call, Medusa had explained, and time was of the essence.

She had then spent twenty hasty moments speaking for her silent husband, the Inhumans' king, Black Bolt. In hurried tones, she had told a terrible tale of betrayal and horror near their home city of Attilan, and of a maddened student named Tavatar who had turned ancient machinery on his fellow students. Tavatar, perhaps without meaning to, had slain a third of his classmates and subjected the rest to agonizing transformation.

"We Inhumans are not a fecund race," Medusa said. "Each of our young is prized, beyond price. To lose so many of them, to lose them all at once—"

"They are in suspended animation now, awaiting our return," Karnak said softly. He was Medusa's cousin, a lean man of average height, slender and with thoughtful features. His every motion, however, no matter how slight, suggested an unusual combination of physical might and effortless grace. "But the horror that Tavatar unleashed eats at them still," he continued, "slowed but not stopped by the desperate measures we have taken."

"They will die," another voice said. It came from the lips of the tallest of the Royal Family, the one whose curved legs ended in hooves. He was Gorgon. "And if, perchance, they survive, they will wish they had not," he continued. "Tavatar's mischief has somehow hyperactivated the Terrigen residue in their flesh. The process continues, despite our best efforts to stop it. The mutations they endure now are not pleasant ones. The third of the students who died are dead because they became things that could not survive in any natural environment."

"What about this Tavatar nutjob?" the Thing asked. "What happened with him?"

"Dead," came the response from the green-scaled Inhuman, Triton. He spoke with grim satisfaction—and with a rancor uncommon for the aquatic Inhuman who typically thought kindly of others. "He stood closest to the genetic accelerator when he activated it, and his own DNA structure was overwhelmed almost immediately, developing him into primordial matter—undifferentiated slime. A fitting end for one who tampered with the forbidden."

"Yeah, well, lemme tell you about a chick named Pandora someday," Ben said. He ran the blunt fingers of one hand along the thick fur that clung to the neck of Lockjaw, the Inhumans's gigantic bulldog. The oversized pet wagged his stub tail frantically and tried to lick Ben's face. "C'mon, c'mon, cut it out," the Thing responded, but he didn't pull back from the animal's sloppy affection.

Visits from the Inhumans were rare, and almost never casual. Since the star-faring Kree had created them ten millennia before, they had dwelled apart from mainstream humanity in their hidden city, a part of the human race, but apart from it.

Most Inhumans, and each member of the Royal Family, had his or her own super powers, the legacy of those experiments. Black Bolt, king of the Inhumans, could fly and manipulate a wide range of energy forms, though his power carried with it the curse of silence, for even the slightest whisper from Black Bolt's powerful voice could cause devastation. Medusa, his consort, had total physical control over her own steel-hard, super-strong hair, and could use each strand of the flowing mane like a prehensile appendage. She had known the Fantastic Four the longest of any of her people, and had even served briefly as a team member, when circumstances had forced Sue to take a leave of absence.

Karnak, called by some the Shatterer, possessed heightened sensibilities and enhanced strength, and the ability to determine any physical object's single weakest point. Gorgon's hooflike feet could administer thunderous shockwaves of almost unbelievable force. Triton's entire body was adapted for aquatic living, to such an extent that Reed Richards had been forced to develop miniaturized life-support equipment so that he could survive in an air environment. Even the Royal Family's pet, Lockjaw possessed a special power, and his was among the most amazing—instantaneous teleportation, even across interplanetary distances. It was Lockjaw who had brought the Inhumans to Four Freedoms Plaza from their far-off, hidden land.

"We'll help, of course," Sue said. "Won't we, Reed?" She looked to her left at Reed, who still stood at his workbench and who nodded in easy agreement. He seemed about to speak when Johnny interrupted.

"What do you want us to do?" he asked. "I know that Reed's done some work with Terrigen samples, but your people must know even more about it. How can we do anything they can't?"

Both Triton and Karnak opened their mouths to answer, but Black Bolt gestured for silence, and then gestured again at Medusa, signing his wishes to her. As his wife, and in view of her special association with the Fantastic Four, it was her role to speak.

A lock of the attractive woman's flowing red hair reached into a pouch at her belt and drew out a small crystal. Another tendril touched a stud at the crystal's base, and her hosts blinked in surprise as a three-dimensional image formed in midair before them. The image was of a creature that looked more apelike than human. His eyes were set deeply beneath protective brow ridges and his entire face was covered with a thick fur. He looked like a primitive hominid, but something about the way his eyes shone suggested great intelligence.

"This is Pilose, our last hope," Medusa said. "Ten standard years ago, he was an instructor at the Genetics Academy, and Attilan's most renowned healer."

"An' what's he doin' these days?" Ben drawled. "Test subject at a barber college?"

"He lives in self-imposed exile, in the Himalayas, suffering in solitude and in silence. Ten years ago, his wife perished in a laboratory accident. Pilose, blaming himself, took a vow of silence and exiled himself from our city, to dwell alone in the wilderness forever."

Johnny asked, "How come you're so eager to find him now? What's he know that the rest of your braintrust doesn't?"

"Yeah," Ben interjected. "He sounds like a real antisocial type."

"The Royal Family has always honored his vow of solitude," Medusa said, "but we cannot do so now. Like nearly all of our people, Pilose has a special power—but his is one that offers both menace and salvation." She paused, as if trying to find the appropriate words. "The Terrigen is strong in Pilose," she said, "and at least partially under his control. He can use it to reverse the changes it has wrought in others, to regress them to their earlier, pre-enhancement state. We hope he can do the same for Tavatar's victims."

A long moment of silence followed as the Fantastic Four considered the import of what Medusa had said. The Inhumans had based much of their culture on their artificially evolved prowess, and many of the rankings in their society derived from the Terrigen-induced super powers that most members wielded. Any Inhuman, or anyone else, who could reverse that evolution and remove those powers could do unimaginable damage to the Inhumans's way of life, if he so chose.

"I ain't surprised you guys were happy to see him go," Ben said dryly. "Not the kind of guys you folks want under-foot."

"Ben," Sue interrupted. "That was uncalled for."

Medusa smiled slightly. "Uncalled for, but true," she said. "Pilose was—is—a peaceful, studious sort, but many of the Genetics Academy found his presence unnerving, and even frightening. Under the direction of a less kindly will than his, such powers could be devastating to our way of life. The elders were not eager to petition for his return, not even in this, our time of trouble."

"You say he can cure the kids?"

"We don't know that he can, Ben," Medusa said simply. "We only know that we cannot."

"How can we help?" Sue asked.

"Yeah, we're not exactly Himalayan tour guides."

"We've already tried the mountains, Grimm," Gorgon muttered. "He is not there."

Medusa shot a glance at her cousin. "I speak for Black Bolt," she said crisply. "But Gorgon is correct. There is no sign of Pilose in the land of his exile. Not even Karnak's heightened senses could find his trace. We spoke with many of the local villagers, but they could not help us. It seems that Pilose closely resembles a creature of their local legends—"

"The Abdominal Snowman," Ben said.

"That's *abominable*, you dodo," Johnny said. "The Yeti."

Medusa nodded. "—and as so often happens," she continued, "rumor serves as a mask for truth. None of the sightings or report bore the fruit we need so desperately."

"How can we help?" Sue repeated.

Medusa pressed the crystal's stud again, and the image of Pilose faded. She tucked the tiny projector back in her belt-pouch and pulled out a folded sheet of paper. "One of the Sherpa guides we contacted in our search said that we were the second expedition to that area in only a few months, and that the other had been led by a Russian."

"Russian?" Ben said.

"He also said that the other expedition had been successful, and captured a specimen of the Yeti."

"Strange. Something like that should have made world headlines," Sue said. She glanced at Mr. Fantastic, still standing quietly at his workstation. "Have you heard anything about that, dear?"

Reed Richards made no reply.

Medusa unfolded the piece of paper. "We would like very much to speak to the man who led the expedition," she continued. "The guide did not have a name, or a photograph, but he was able to make a drawing for us." She held the picture up for display. "This is who we seek."

The sketch was surprisingly good, drawn by someone with both talent and skill. The face it presented to them was of a balding man, with broad, flat features twisted in an angry scowl. Long hair clung to the sides of his skull, and even in the drawing, his eyes seemed to smolder with inner fury.

"Kragoff," Ben snarled.

"Kragoff?" Medusa responded eagerly. "You know him? Can you take us to him? Where is he?"

The Thing nodded. "Oh, I know the bum all right. I ran into him just the other day, too," he said. He turned to look at his teammates. "Like I been trying to tell you, Reed, I—"

"Ben Grimm," Karnak interrupted suddenly, speaking in a low, urgent tone.

"Just a second here, I'm tryin' to—"

Black Bolt raised one arm again, gesturing for Karnak to be silent, and Medusa laid her hand on her cousin's wrist, underscoring their king's command. Karnak ignored them both, but continued to speak, even as he stared intently at the man who stood behind the workbench.

"Ben Grimm," Karnak repeated. "Surely you do not think that this is the real Reed Richards?"

With blinding speed, "Reed" drove one white-gloved fist into the Inhuman's face.

Somewhere else, the real Reed Richards took the longest of his salvaged bolts, threaded a nut onto it, and inserted the two items into the cot leg's open end. The bolt caught and held, its progress blocked by the small shims Reed had already placed inside the metal tube. He tapped the protruding head a few times to make sure that the nut was wedged in place, and then he twisted the bolt. It spun easily, alternately extending and retracting from its new home. Reed nodded, then stepped over to his cell's door and continued his work.

The cell door's vertical bars intersected a bit more than halfway down with a pair of horizontal ones. That meant the lower section was shorter than the upper, which would make things a little bit harder, but not much. Squatting in front of the door, Reed inserted the gadget he had made between two of the bars. With the bolt retracted, it fit into place easily. He had improvised a swivel for the tube's other end from pieces of the washstand's faucet; now, he took the rubber washers he had scavenged from the same plumbing and placed them between the swivel's base and the bar's surface, and did the same with the bolt head. The bits of rubber provided some traction, enough so that the swivel base and the bolt head remained stationary as he spun the device's wire-reinforced shaft. The bolt extended itself a bit more and pressed harder against the metal bar, holding Reed's creation in place as he took his hands from it. He was almost done now.

There was still some wire left. He used it now to lash the bed's two long rails together so that they would reinforce one another. More wire held the paired rails to the modified cot leg, at an angle perpendicular to the tube's axis, positioned so that most of its length extended into the cell and upward. When he was done, the end of the assembly was a good foot above Reed's head, and slightly more than that distance from the ceiling. That gave him about six feet of leverage, enough to do the job.

Reed reached up, wrapped gloved fingers around the paired rails and pulled, applying slow, steady pressure. The improvised lever swung, and as it moved, the modified cot leg spun on its swivel, forcing the bolt in its other end outward. Metal grated, strained, and for a moment, Reed thought the end holding the bolt would split—but the wire reinforcing the tube held, and something else gave, instead.

The cell door's bars moved apart slowly.

Reed was a lean man, but stronger than his build suggested.

The work the Fantastic Four did, the work that he had made his life, demanded that he be in top physical condition. Now, even without his powers, even after two days' imprisonment, he was quite strong enough to operate the reverse turnbuckle he had so painstakingly built. Twice, he had to remove and reposition the lever; once, the spreader slipped and had to be put back in place. Even with those delays, it took him less time to use the device than it had taken him to make it. After an hour of careful effort, the gap between the bars was wide enough for him to struggle through it. Two minutes after that, and he was in the corridor outside his cell, at the cost of some scrapes and sore muscles.

The soreness went away as he moved away from his cell's confines. He took three steps and felt the familiar sensation almost immediately, a rippling wave of sudden vitality that swept though him as his cosmic-ray charged cells came to full life once more. It felt good. Still walking, he flexed his fingers, extended them six inches and then six more, then let them retract back to normal proportions. He yawned, letting the muscles and bones of his face flow like wax and he distended his jaw and closed it again. He arched his back and stretched, bending almost double as he did so, and he smiled. All stiffness and soreness fled, and he felt suddenly energized as his full attributes returned to him.

The accident that gave the Fantastic Four their powers had occurred years before, and Reed had long since become accustomed to the easy freedom his elastic body gave him. Losing that freedom, even temporarily, was never much fun, and served only to remind him how confining and unforgiving a place the physical world could be. Now however, his body was as unfettered as his mind, and he felt ready for anything.

He heard something, then, the grading sound that metal boots make on a stone floor, followed by five words spoken in a commanding tone. "Hold it right there, Mister!"

The words came from behind him, spoken in a voice so familiar that Reed didn't bother to turn around and see who had spoken. Instead, he stretched and flowed and twisted, moving just in time from the path of a plasma bolt that raced past him and dug deep into the corridor's stone floor. Bits of rock, half-molten and half-seared, were still falling back to the floor as Reed turned to face his attacker.

It was a Guardsman robot. The same one that had served him his meals? Or another? Reed didn't know, and he didn't care. The object of the exercise right now was to keep out of its reach, and avoid being targeted by the plasma projectors in the thing's hands. Moreover, he had to stop its assault before it could summon reinforcements; the little that Reed had seen of this place suggested a sizable installation, and he didn't want to find out the hard way how many armored troops were available to keep order.

"Keep your hands above your head and don't move a muscle," the Guardsman said. Without giving Reed a chance to comply, it fired again, this time in a slashing trajectory that cut through the air at about the level of Reed's head.

Or where Reed's head had been.

Moving quickly, Reed compressed most of his body's mass along his vertical axis, condensing himself into a squat, roundish shape. Even as the robot tried to blast him again, Reed kicked hard against the floor. The resilient nature of his muscles allowed him to add the momentum of his downward compression the force of his leap, launching him from the floor at an angle. When he hit the ceiling, he pushed off from it again, adding a hard thrust from the muscles of his arms. Again and again he repeated the maneuver, bouncing from wall to wall.

"Hey, lights out," the robot yelled, apparently having nothing in its vocal response selection that was appropriate to the situation. Its armed response moves were in somewhat better shape, even if not quite good enough. The armored figure did the best it could to follow Reed's erratic trajectory, and spewed white fire from its hands in a futile attempt to destroy him. The plasma bolts found walls and gouged them, found steel bars and melted them; the corridor was soon filled with heat and the stink of burning.

"I don't want any lip from you!" the robot roared, as one blast found a ceiling light fixture, releasing a cascade of blue-white sparks.

Reed bounced again, landing this time behind the robot, and reverting to a more humanoid configuration as he did. He extended his arms, stretching one into a long, looping coil that wrapped around the robot's thorax section. With a sudden, convulsive jerk, he yanked his arm back, hard. The motion was just enough to make the robot twist and spin, until it faced Reed again.

"Stand at attention," the robot said. Something about its voice suggested desperation, but Reed was reasonably certain that this unit was not advanced enough for such emotions. "Don't make any funny moves," the robot continued, raising one hand to fire another plasma burst. "If you do, I'll come down on you, hard."

Reed's other arm, meanwhile, had stretched into one of the sundered cells and his elongated fingers had grasped a sizable length of cell bar, sheared off neatly at each end by stray plasma blasts. He had noticed it a few bounces earlier, and thought it might prove useful.

Now, he swung it like a baseball bat and hit the Guardsman robot in the head with it. It connected with a satisfactory ringing sound and a resonant impact that made the piece of steel vibrate in Reed's grasp.

The pseudo-Guardsman kept talking. "Do like I say and—"

Reed swung a second time, then a third, putting every erg of strength into the blows. They made loud, clanging noises that reverberated in the corridor.

"—et rien va te faire du mal!"

The last blow had scrambled the robot's vocabulary chips, Reed realized, and done enough damage to reset its language defaults. It had done something else, too. The third smashing impact been enough to rock the Guardsman's masked head back on its moorings, bending the mechanical man's neck far enough back to expose the overlapping plates of its jaw and throat assemblies. Reed wondered how closely the robot matched its human counterparts at the Vault. He knew that the Guardsman armor plans featured a design flaw, one that he had been working with federal authorities to correct. The robot's unknown maker had closely duplicated the armor and weaponry; had he duplicated the weaknesses, too?

There was only one way to find out.

With practiced speed, Reed shifted his grip on the metal bludgeon. He elongated his arms again and then retracted them, using the elastic snap of his muscles to bring the metal shaft up, fast and hard. He had already noticed that one end of the severed pole came to something like a point, and this was what he drove toward the exposed underside of the Guardsman's metal jaw.

White fire erupted from the Guardsman's right hand, a searing burst that Reed was hard pressed to dodge. More metal boiled and more stone burned, but none of the energies found Reed's elastic flesh.

The spear he had improvised found its target, though.

The not-very-sharp point caught the robot's jaw just behind the chin, where the third and fourth segments of the jaw assembly met and overlapped. It was a standard design approach for armored suits, Reed knew. The problem with it, at least in the case of the Guardsman armor, was that the overlapping plates didn't overlap quite enough.

The broken bar punched through the faulty joint, drove upward into the helmet's interior, stabbing into the space that would have held a person's head. This Guardsman obviously kept something else there, however: apparently its central processing unit.

Sparks flew. A dozen French syllables erupted from the robot's voice box, and its body convulsed. The Guardsman's steel hands closed into fists and then opened again to claw the empty air. The damage had apparently blinded the robot, and it lashed out without any obvious target or goals. Reed dodged its blows easily and stepped back to see what happened next.

That was when the robot's joints locked. It fell forward, the weight of its fall driving the makeshift spear completely through its head and releasing another geyser of sparks. A howl of static roared from the machine's vocoder, and then faded.

When it faded completely, Reed could hear something else.

Footsteps.

Heavy footsteps, the kind feet shod in metal made, as armored boots slammed against stone floors.

Reinforcements were on the way.

CHAPTER 7

Ben Grimm's first thought was that Reed did have a concussion, and a fairly severe one; his second thought was the sick realization that Karnak was right, and that his oldest, closest friend had been replaced by an impostor. No doubt the Inhuman's heightened levels of awareness had enabled him to perceive some discrepancy in the duplicate's behavior that was invisible to other eyes.

For a split second, he wondered who had done the job. Heaven knew that there were plenty of parties with the ability to field a duplicate, and with the kind of agenda that such an effort would support—but that consideration could wait. The time for that kind of thought was gone, swept away by circumstance. Now, Ben saw ''Reed's'' hands grip the items on the workbench and lift them. There was something about the way the familiar-looking man moved, something about the resolute expression his face wore as he lifted the two devices.

"Susie, heads up!" Ben yelled the words, even though he knew they were probably unnecessary. Already, Karnak and the rest of the Inhumans had dropped back, giving the Fantastic Four the chance to strike. The Royal Family's members were all skilled fighters who had worked with the FF before, but they obviously recognized that their numbers could cause problems in the workshop's confined space. Right now, the Invisible Woman had a clear field to attack, but Ben fleetingly wondered if the impostor's uncanny resemblance to the man she loved might make Sue hesitate to use her powers against him. Then that particular concern passed, as he saw the shock and surprise on his teammate's face fade, to be replaced by something more like fury.

"Reed" was stretching now, flattening his torso and pulling back to avoid a lighting-fast strike from Karnak. The Inhuman's flashing hands cut towards the impostor's midsection, but missed their target. As the ersatz Mr. Fantastic dodged, he pressed buttons on the devices he held. Instantly, they changed, housing sections sliding back to reveal gaping muzzles.

"Those are guns," Ben yelled, angry at himself for stating the obvious even as the first wave of plasma sprayed in Sue's general direction. Sprayed—and then splashed in midair, mere inches from the Invisible Woman, as it struck one of her transparent force fields. The incandescent blob of energy flowed along an unseen curved surface, spreading itself thin and then dissipating completely. Even as it faded, "Reed" turned his attentions elsewhere. The two portable energy cannons he held were suddenly trained on the Inhumans, specifically on Triton.

The impostor smiled, his features flowing into an expression of cruel anticipation that seemed remarkably inappropriate to the man whose face he wore.

Ben threw himself at "Reed." His own mass and bulky proportions made moving quickly difficult, but not impossible. He did the best he could. As he jumped, he reached out, trying to grab and wreck the weapons before his quarry could fire them.

He was only half successful.

Ben's left hand found one gun barrel, crushed it. Even as he squeezed the metal housing into a broken lump, "Reed" fired the weapon again. Its path blocked, with nowhere to go, the surge of high-energy plasma turned itself on the gun's interior. A muffled concussion ensued as the weapon tore itself to pieces, the force of the blast smothered by the Thing's rocklike flesh. Ben gave a reflexive grunt of pain, scarcely less loud than the explosion itself.

Rocked by the Thing's attack, the impostor tottered and almost fell. The shot from his other gun went wild and stabbed a hole through one workshop wall. Triton, well clear of the blast, nonetheless watched warily and hung back as the impostor raised the remaining weapon again. Ben didn't blame the aquatic Inhuman; he knew from experience that the scaled man was good in a fight, but in this kind of battle, Triton was quite literally out of his element.

Besides, given the option, Ben had a hunch this fracas was one he might pass up, too.

Now, even as the fake Reed trained his weapon on the cluster of human and Inhuman figures suddenly swarming toward him, he also raised the broken remnants of the first handcannon. He brought the twisted mass of metal down hard on the roof of Ben's skull. The force of the blow was surprisingly great enough to make the Thing wince and blink his eyes in a futile attempt to banish the black spots that suddenly swam before his eyes. Whoever the impostor was, whatever he was made of, he was much stronger than the real Reed Richards, almost strong enough to knock out the Thing.

"Watch out, guys an' gals," the Thing said. He had to force the words out, even as he struggled to regain his equilibrium. "He's tougher than he looks."

"Reed" fired again. Once more, the incandescent bolts splashed against something transparent. This time, however, the unseen barrier was only inches away from the gun's muzzle, and the spurts of plasma conformed to a curved concave surface. The bubble of protective energy had formed around the gun instead of around its target.

"I read you, Ben," Sue said. A look of concentration flowed across her features, as she contracted the force field surrounding the fake Reed's plasma cannon. The fire it had trapped burned more brightly as the space in which it burned became smaller. "I don't like doing this," Sue said to the impostor. "Surrender, whoever you are, or I'll be forced to—"

"Reed's" lips pulled back in a ruthless grin, and he pulled the trigger again.

Sue shrugged, looking resigned and but not terribly unhappy about the situation. The transparent force bubble contracted some more, turning the weapon's energy back on itself. Now, the field's volume was small enough that the metal of the gun's housing twisted and bent.

"—do this," Sue finished, squeezing some more.

The gun exploded and seared the hand that held it.

As it did, Sue said softly, "You had your chance."

The impostor screamed in pain, and its screams sounded in Reed's voice.

Reflexively, Sue dropped the force barrier. Ragged chunks of red-hot metal fell to the floor and smoldered. Empty now, the impostor's right hand was a broken, twisted thing. Mr. Fantastic's glove had protected the intruder, but not enough.

"Looks like that's taken the fight out of him," the Thing rumbled. He didn't sound as if he meant it. "Whoever he is."

"I don't think so, Ben," Medusa said. She was watching the fallen impostor carefully.

The maimed hand was reshaping itself, flowing and growing as it became something new. The broken fingers blended together and fused, and then became indistinguishable from one another as the skin thickened and turned gray. The final ragged fragments of white fabric split and fell away, as the remnants of what had been the impostor's hand became something else entirely. In moments, what had been a hand holding a weapon had become a weapon itself.

Now, it was a hammer, studded with cruel spikes.

"Definitely not Reed," the Thing said, as the bludgeon lashed out at him. Reed could do many interesting things with his body, but this kind of transformation was beyond even his abilities. Ben dodged the blow and let it strike the flooring instead. "Okay, that does it, the kid gloves are off," he continued, as if they had ever been on, and came out swinging.

His first blow caught "Reed" on the side of his head. The impostor's elastic neck stretched to impossible length and then snapped his head back into place, like a gigantic rubber band. When the head rebounded, however, the face it bore had changed, too, with flesh and bone alike shifted into new configurations.

The impostor's mouth opened to impossible extremes, then opened some more, as if the grinning head were trying to turn itself inside out. Needle-sharp teeth, each of them several inches long, grew abruptly from the upper and lower jaw. Ben raised his fist to strike again, but before he could, the gaping mouth came down on him. Instantly, it engulfed his entire left wrist in a razored bite. Teeth splintered and broke, but enough remained intact to dig deeply into the stony plates that covered the Thing's body and make a sound like snow tires grinding on clean pavement.

"Yeesh," Ben said. It hurt. He flailed the captured hand, trying to break the grisly grip. It did no good. "I said it before, an' I'll say it again—what a revoltin' development this is!"

Waves of change continued to ripple and flow through the impostor's convulsing body. Almost unrecognizable now from its previous state as Mr. Fantastic's twin, the intruder was fast becoming a mass of deadly weaponry. Spiked hammers sprouted from both wrists, and razor-edged plates suddenly erupted from its body. They shredded and tore the already tattered remnants of the famous costume the impostor wore. Still with his jaws locked on Ben's wrist, the creature nonetheless lashed out at anyone within his considerable reach.

Ben took his free hand, grasped the top of the fake Reed's head. He gripped solidly and began to pull, but was unable to dislodge the creature's grip. He pulled some more, and then the flesh and bone of the impostor's skull abruptly softened. It flowed around the Thing's blunt digits and then hardened like concrete.

The fake Reed made a hissing, gurgling noise that it might have meant as laughter.

"Aw, man," the Thing said. Both his hands were trapped now. "This just gets worse an' worse!"

The impostor continued the attack, lashing out at the Fantastic Four and at the Inhumans. A long, ropy tendril wrapped itself around Gorgon's neck, seeking to strangle him. In these close quarters, the hooved Inhuman's shockwave power was of only limited use. Worse, it was a very real hazard to his fellows, so he had to rely on his superhuman strength to struggle against the monster's embrace—a struggle that seemed futile. Another tendril wound completely around Karnak, binding his arms so tightly that he could not strike. The spiked hammers that had been the impostor's hands pounded at Lockjaw, and at Medusa, who used her flowing locks to restrain the club that swung in her direction. One of the fake Reed's legs became more like a tentacle and grasped Triton, dragging him toward the cutting surfaces that sprouted now from the monster's body. Cries of mingled pain and surprise filled the small room as struggling combatants sought to defend themselves. No matter how hard they struggled, the creature seemed to grow stronger and stronger.

The hissing, gurgling noise that came from the creature's

mouth became louder, and then something else joined it—a chemical smell that stung the nose and made the eyes water. Ben felt a sudden burning sensation on his arm, and gaped in surprise.

The fake Reed's clutching mouth had begun to drool a corrosive foam, some kind of acidic solvent that was eating its way even into the durable body armor of the Thing's rocky orange skin. At first, Ben scarcely felt it, then he felt a twinge of pain, the kind of pain that he knew would get worse, fast.

It did.

"Hey," the Thing yelled, as the acid ate into him. "Hey! I could use a hand here!"

Susan Richards spun in his direction. She had been helping Triton free himself, and now the aquatic Inhuman stumbled back as Sue turned her attention in the Thing's direction.

"I see it, Ben," she called. "I've got it." A split second's thought, and another bubble of force field energy formed, this one conforming closely to the contours of the creature's head and face. Trapped by the invisible, impenetrable barrier, the corrosive acid foam ceased working on Ben's flesh. Instead, the bubbling stuff backed up and splashed against the impostor's features. The creature seemed scarcely to notice.

"Good goin', Suze," the Thing said. "An' now, for my next magical trick . . ." His words faded into silence as he gritted his teeth and flexed the big muscles of his shoulders and arms. This time, he wasn't seeking to free his embedded fingers, but to use the grip they gave him. He twisted, hard. There was a wrenching, breaking noise, like the sound pottery makes when struck by a hammer. "Reed's" eyes rolled back in their sockets and more teeth broke, then the creature's grip came free. As it did, the shock and pain were enough to relax the bone and muscle that held Ben's fingers, and then that grip, too, released.

"Ben, drop it and get away," Medusa yelled. For the first time since her arrival, her voice held the note of command. "Move! Now!"

Ben obeyed, as much because he was tired of fighting the creature as his affection and respect for Medusa. He shoved the head away from him. Apparently recovered from the pain he had caused it, the fake Reed snarled and spat at him as he stepped back from it. Ordinarily, the Thing didn't like walking away from a fight, but this time, a moment later, he was glad he had.

That was when another bolt of energy split the air. It was a coherent pulse of modulated electrons, shaped and fired from the antenna on Black Bolt's brow. The withering blast of energy stabbed deeply into the head of the being that had pretended to be Reed Richards. A moment earlier, a half-inch to the left, and the blast might have struck the Thing instead— but Black Bolt was a master of precision in all matters, and his aim was true.

The impostor convulsed in what was probably agony. Like a film playing backwards, it undid its transformation of moments before. Its extended limbs receded, and it regained some approximation of human form even as it writhed and spasmed on the workshop floor. After a long moment, it wore Mr. Fantastic's face once more. Then the familiar eyes closed and the being lay still.

"That should shut down its central nervous system," Medusa said. "Now, unless there's some kind of a failsafe—"

The creature exploded.

As explosions went, it wasn't much—little more than a moment of flash and thunder, enough to destroy the impostor's body, reducing it to ashen fragments. Certainly, the blast wasn't enough to tear through the invisible wall of energy that Susan Richards had reflexively thrown between the defeated creature and her allies. As the thunder faded away, she spoke.

"Two days," the Invisible Woman said softly, scarcely audible above the last echoes.

"Two days?" Johnny asked, standing by her side.

She nodded. "Whatever this, this *thing* was—"

Ben grunted softly in protest at her choice of words.

Sue ignored him. "—it's had the run of the place for two days. Heaven only knows what it was doing here, what damage it managed to do."

"That ain't the problem right now, Susie."

"Of course its not, Ben. Or, at least, not the only problem."
Sue turned to face the Inhumans and spoke in businesslike
tones. "Medusa, I'm sorry. The situation in Attilan will have
to wait until we find Reed."

"But—" Gorgon said.

Black Bolt signed for silence, and shot his wife a look
freighted with meaning.

"Of course it must wait, at least for now; the students can
survive at least another standard day in their current state,"
Medusa said. "Reed is a friend and an ally, and whoever has
taken him has earned our enmity."

"Perhaps even more to the point," Karnak said, "Reed
Richards, alone of all your race, possesses the secret of the
Terrigen, and has studied its mysteries." He paused, and gestured at the impostor's remains. "This entity," he continued,
"may have stolen that secret, and we must know what its
masters have learned before we can rest easy again."

Medusa said, "We will do all within out power to help,
Sue."

The Invisible Woman nodded. "I was hoping you would
feel that way." Her blue eyes were burning with an inner fire,
and anger had made her face pale. "I think Johnny and Ben
will agree when I say that nothing's going to stop me from
finding whoever took my husband from me." She paused.
"Nothing, and no one."

A man who can take twenty-foot strides is a man who can
cover a lot of territory quickly. Reed Richards could keep to
that pace and better it by literally bouncing from the walls as
he made his way though the mystery prison's corridors. He
stretched and rebounded, and extended his legs in great, loping
strides that served well to keep him ahead of the Guardsman
robots that followed him in hot pursuit.

"All right, Mister! This is your last warning!"

"Lights out in ten, and I mean it!"

"Don't give me any of your lip!"

The robots threw inappropriate imprecations at him as they
gave chase, doing their programmed best to deal with what

was obviously an unanticipated situation. In the moment before taking evasive action, Reed had hastily taken a rough
count of the green security units that followed him. He had
counted twenty, too many to fight, but also too many to work
effectively in the relatively cramped confines of the prison
corridors. Apparently never intended to serve as a unified
fighting force, the robots got in the way of each other, and
only two or three could target him at any given moment.

They were still deadly, though. Bouncing, stretching, twisting, it was all Reed could do to evade them and to dodge their
plasma bolts while taking careful note of his surroundings.

Now that he was outside his cell, the place looked even
more familiar. It looked like the reduced-security wing of the
Vault, where the government stored a certain class of career
criminals after stripping them of the weaponry that made them
deadly. In the real Vault, these cells might have held people
like the Trapster and the Shocker, inmates who were ingenious
but not geniuses, felons who needed the tools of their trade to
present a serious threat. If those cells were equipped with
psionic power suppressors like the one in his quarters—devices that Reed did not believe the federal government possessed—they would make effective cages even for individuals
whose powers were innate and not optional add-ons. Here and
now however, the cells were empty, shadowed recesses behind
barred doors.

Reed had to wonder who they were intended to hold.

"Move a muscle, and I'll come down on you, hard!"

"Don't give me any of your lip!"

"Freeze! Put your hands on your head!"

The robots were getting closer, close enough that the floor
shook from their footsteps. A plasma bolt seared the air to the
immediate left of Reed's head, close enough to singe one lock
of his brown hair, and the air filled with ozone's electric stink.
He extended his neck three feet or so, well out of the beam's
path, then extended his arms, reaching for the hallway ceiling.
Elongated fingers found a support member anchoring a light
fixture, and wrapped around it. Reed contracted the elastic
flesh and bones of his body and let himself be pulled upward.

The robot commandos stormed past and below him, and he dropped to the floor again and bounced down a side corridor.

The entire place had a look of being unfinished. Some of the cells were still in varying stages of construction, their barred doors were hung but not yet equipped with locks. A kitchen area was half-filled with still-uncrated appliances, and had only one stove and one refrigerator unpacked and installed. One hallway lay dark and shadowed, leading nowhere, with unstrung cables dangling from ceiling conduits. Reed's tentative conclusion was that his unknown captors had stashed him in the most convenient location, supposedly secure, while they pursued other goals. With a bit of luck, he hoped to prove their strategy a flawed one, and do so in fairly short order.

Abruptly, steel fingers closed on his shoulders, digging deep in an unbreakable grasp, reminding Reed that his surroundings had drawn too much of his attention. He had slowed in his flight, not much, but enough to make a dangerous difference. Giving a cry of pain, Reed reflexively relaxed muscle and bone, oozing out of the sudden grip even as he spun his head to assess the situation.

Two of the robots had apparently separated from the main posse and doubled back until they found him. Now, one of them raised its hands and threw more white fire. Reed dodged again, stretching and twisting, then arched himself backward and extended himself behind his pursuers.

"None of your tricks, Mister!"

"I said, lights out!"

Reed did not respond to the computer-synthesized diatribes that erupted from the pair's mechanical larynxes. Instead, he gripped the ankles of one of the two robots. The Guardsman he had chosen was in midstride when he made his play. It had most of its weight on its left leg, so he chose to work with the right one first. He twisted it and pulled, making the Guardsman stumble a bit, and then stumble some more as he yanked again. The robot spun and fell against its fellow, so it staggered and paused in its headlong rush.

Immediately, Reed turned his attentions to the second robot. It was already firing another plasma burst from its left hand, so Reed grabbed its left wrist and pulled, hard. Still recovering from the unexpected collision, the pseudo-Guardsman offered little resistance as Reed trained its weapon at a new target.

The head of the fallen robot promptly exploded.

As if reacting to what it had been tricked into doing, the surviving robot tore itself free from Reed's grasp and fired again. It was fast, but Reed was faster; with the ease born of long experience, he twisted out of the blast's path. As he dodged a second burst and a third, he decided that he had learned about as much as he was likely to from his impromptu tour of the place. Besides, he could hear thundering footfalls again, sure indicators that the rest of the robots were getting close again.

He brought one foot up, hard, and kicked the Guardsman robot in its expressionless face. As the robot staggered backward, Reed ripped a ventilator grille from its frame, and threw himself into the darkness beyond. In seconds, he was where the robot could not follow.

"It would help things if you told us what we're looking for, Mrs. Richards," Sean Morgan said. He was a lean man with strong features and fair, close-cropped hair. Just now, his voice held a note of patience that didn't quite track with the probing expression in the wintry gray eyes that gazed out at Sue from the communicator viewscreen. Behind him in the image, she could see the cramped confines of his office, a cluttered space that was surprisingly small and utilitarian for the head of a national intelligence agency.

"I can't, Colonel," Sue said. "I don't know, myself." She had already decided to keep her husband's substitution a secret for as long as possible, at least from conventional authorities. She had nothing but respect for SAFE and the new federal agency's accomplishments in recent months, but the Fantastic Four had a long history of looking after its own. When and if she thought that SAFE had to know what had happened, the organization was only a phone call away. For now, however, she preferred to call on Morgan only for information, and let the Fantastic Four and the Inhumans work together in using that data. "This is more of a general inquiry, background questions on some things that have come to our attention. Kind of like when you sent Reed to the Vault, remember?"

Morgan looked at her a moment before speaking. "I wanted to talk some more to Dr. Richards about that visit," he said. "I'm still waiting for a formal report."

The former Green Beret's wait was far from done, Sue realized, with graveyard humor, and he didn't seem to be a patient man. "I'm sure you'll get one," she said. "Reed's very busy—"

"I'm well aware that he is, ma'am, and I know that he agreed to conduct the interview as a courtesy to us, and I appreciate it. Still, I need more than a single phone call."

"So he did call you?" Sue asked the question almost reflexively, and almost immediately wished she had not.

If the query surprised Morgan, he didn't say so. "From the hospital. Said that the Thinker seemed to check out okay, and that he couldn't make any connection between him and the Lifestream case." He paused. "That surprised me."

"It surprised a lot of people," Sue said dryly. The Thinker was the logical suspect for most aspects of the current situation. He was known to be especially adept at creating artificial lifeforms, and the duplicate Mr. Fantastic could easily have been his handiwork. There was more to investigate on that front, too, and she had already taken steps in that direction. "I'll let Reed know your concerns."

"Where is he now, Mrs. Richards? Can you patch me through to him?"

Sue shook her head. "No," she said. "He can't be disturbed." She had met Morgan before, but under more hectic circumstances, ones in which he had not displayed such an aggressive curiosity. Calling him now was beginning to look less and less like a good idea, but what was done was done.

"I see," Morgan said. He still didn't seem surprised. "What's your interest in Denver Hospital?"

"Just curious. They seemed awfully aggressive in running tests on Reed, almost too interested." Her real thought was that a fully-equipped hospital would have made an ideal site to switch the real Reed Richards with his duplicate, but she didn't say that.

Morgan looked at her. "You obviously don't spend much time in conventional medical facilities," he said.

Sue didn't respond; she was only too aware that her pretext for requesting data was a bit weak, but she also knew that repeated justifications would only serve to make it sound even weaker.

"I have an agent in the area already," Morgan continued. "Performing liaison service with the NTSB team investigating your wrecked Fantasti-Car." Despite the FF's best efforts to the contrary, the National Transportation Safety Board had claimed jurisdiction on the crashed vehicle, and was busily analyzing the wreckage. Ben had been forced to accept the promise that SAFE would work to ensure that the futuristic vehicle's secrets remained secret. "I can have him pay a call on the hospital and shake some trees. I'll let you know what falls out."

"Thank you."

"My pleasure, Mrs. Richards," Morgan said, but the sentiment sounded less than wholeheartedly sincere. "One of the joys of working with a limited budget is cultivating a good working relationship with the super hero community."

Despite herself, Sue smiled. There was something about the man's turn of phrase that she liked. He had a remarkably polite way of pointing out that one hand washed the other. "Speaking of the NTSB," she continued, "Have they found anything yet? Any idea what caused the wreck?"

Morgan turned from the communicator, and the word MUTE flashed silently in the corner of Sue's screen as the SAFE head spoke to someone she couldn't see. A moment later, he resumed the conversation. "Stress fracture in the third turbine assembly," he said. "Probably induced by the subzero winds. The NTSB thinks its nothing exceptional, but Agent Deeley doesn't agree. He says temperature variances were well within your craft's tolerances, or should have been. I'll fax you a copy of the report."

"Thank you," Sue said.

"I've got something else for you, too. Agent Deeley says that Mr. Grimm was asking after Ivan Kragoff." Morgan said the name with an almost casual detachment, but Sue could see him watching closely for her response.

"The Red Ghost," she said. She had almost forgotten about that incident, in all the excitement that had followed. "Ben ran into him at a clothing store Monday."

"Right. Seems the State Department worked out some kind of prisoner swap about six months ago, and remanded Kragoff into Russian custody. He dropped out of sight about six weeks later. That may just be a lack of good data on our part; the Russians are very cooperative these days, but their internal security's a mess. They can't tell us what they don't know."

"And now, he's in New York." Sue thought about the sketch that Medusa had shown her, but didn't mention it.

"My guess is, he's been in the area for a while, at least intermittently. I finally got a DNA analysis report back from FBI Forensics regarding the Lifestream heist. I'll send you a copy of that, too. We found a tuft of hair on the crime scene, and it matches with Kragoff's pet gorilla."

"That's a surprise," Sue said, meaning it. Still, it made a degree of sense. Even if the Thinker had somehow mastermined the crime, someone had to actually commit it.

Morgan gazed at her steadily for a long moment, an unfathomable expression in his gray eyes. "Mrs. Richards," he finally said, "just what is going on here?"

"Nothing I can talk about at the moment," she said. "There are security concerns."

Morgan's upper lip twitched. "I know a little bit about security," he said. "Anything I can help you with?"

Sue shook her head. "No, I—"

Morgan interrupted her. "I'm going to have to cut this short, then," he said. "You folks apparently have your hands full; so do I, these days."

Sue understood the comment. SAFE was still a relatively new agency. After maintaining a very low profile for the better part of a year, it had abruptly become very public during a recent confrontation between the Hulk and URSA, an orga-

nization of crazed Russian reactionaries. No doubt, Morgan
was being called upon to answer a lot of questions these days.
"I appreciate your time, Colonel."

"Appreciate this, too, then," Morgan said. "I answer directly to the President, and he has asked that SAFE extend
every possible courtesy to the Fantastic Four. I'm happy to go
along with that, in view of your long service to our country,
and to the world. Without your services, the entire planet
would be speaking Latverian by now."

Sue bristled slightly at the oblique reference to Dr. Doom,
whom the FF had been fighting long before SAFE was more
than a dream in some bureaucrat's heart, but she decided to
let Morgan speak his piece.

"That said," the SAFE honcho continued, "cooperation is
a two-way street, and there are limits to how far it can go in
either direction. For my part, I expect to be notified in a timely
manner of any matters that fall under SAFE's jurisdiction."
His upper lip twitched again. "I should point out that I have
a very generous notion of what that jurisdiction comprises."

Sue nodded, irritated but wary. "Of course you do," she
said.

"Would you like to hear my notion of what constitutes a
timely manner?"

The words came in Morgan's typical, professional tone, but
their implications made Sue's eyes narrow in anger. The Fantastic Four had been in business for a long time, enjoying
considerable freedom from government oversight, and she saw
no reason to change the situation. "I hardly think that will be
necessary, Colonel," she said stiffly. "We're all on the same
team."

"Yes," Morgan said. "Yes, we are. Morgan out." The
screen went blank as he broke the connection. Even as the last
of the image faded, the fax machine to Sue's left began to spit
sheets of paper into a waiting basket.

The air circulation system proved to be a moderately complex
network of ductwork connecting at least three levels of the
facility with a central vertical shaft, punctuated frequently by
ventilator grids. Reed slithered through the convoluted spaces,

pausing periodically to peer out between the louvers and see what else the facility had to offer.

For the most part, there wasn't much, just more shadowed cages and brightly lit corridors. Several times he saw the robots continuing their patrols; twice, the robots saw him, too, and fired at their elusive target, blasting holes in the walls and in the ducts behind them. Both times, Reed tensed his rubbery body into a helical configuration, then released it, literally springing from the path of the deadly beams before they could strike him. Smoldering chips of scorched metal and stone caught him and stung him as he continued exploring the mystery prison, but he ignored them; he was looking for something.

After long minutes of rapid searching, he found it.

Rounding one bend in the conduits, he peered again through a grilled opening. He was pleased to see several blank computer screens looking back at him. Pressing himself against the grate, Reed relaxed the cohesion of his body's molecules to the absolute minimum possible and then drooled himself into the room.

It proved to be some kind of data processing center, half-filled with computer consoles. The setup looked familiar, even too familiar; Reed realized with some annoyance that much of it was a close match with the equipment in the FF's original headquarters, the Baxter Building. He added the fact to the increasing body of evidence against the Thinker, then went to work.

A pair of reinforced blast doors separated the room from the rest of the facility. Reed closed them and reprogrammed their access codes. He knew that they wouldn't stand long against a concerted attack by the Guardsmen, if and when the robots found him, but was reasonably confident that they would last long enough. He began pressing ON switches and went to work.

A file from the computer's housekeeping program provided an isometric diagram of the place. Reed studied the layout carefully as it filled the monitor screen. The complex had five levels, filled mostly with prison cells and utility spaces. He pressed some more keys, and added another level of detail to the computer drawing, a diagrammatic representation of electronic circuitry lurking behind the walls. As he had suspected, most of the cells were armed with psionic suppressors like the one that had been used on him. They held something else, too, some kind of data pickup network that extended throughout the complex. Reed realized with some surprise that he stood now at the center of that network, where all the trunk lines came together and merged. Whatever the system was, its heart was the room he occupied now, and, presumably, processing the information it gathered was the primary duty of the computers that surrounded him. Reed wondered just what that information was, and where it was going. He opened more system files and diagnostic routines, and began reviewing them.

Neither question had an easy answer. Whoever had designed this place was a communication systems genius, or had access to one. Multiple banks of processors took the data from the input network, combined it into discreet frames, compressed them, and then spat them out as a scrambled feed. The system also served as a relay station for external signals along conventional datalinks, incorporating them into the total feed. Reed recognized several standard system protocols that his own communications network used, but the system here accessed them only on a passive, receiving basis; it didn't use anything he recognized as a transmit medium. Instead, the signal's track carried it to what looked like a bank of gravimetric transducers. The message packets went in one end, and came out—

Where?

Reed pondered the question. He knew that it was theoretically possible to use gravity waves to carry data, but doing so on a planetary surface raised significant technical problems. Even stipulating the development of an effective gravity wave generator, any modulation of those waves would be overwhelmed by Earth's greater gravity field. Distinguishing the message from the surrounding, unmodulated field would be fantastically difficult. The technique was best suited for communication over interplanetary or interstellar distance, against a more diffuse and less intrusive backdrop of system noise.

There were other possibilities, of course. Gravity's properties were intimately bound up with the curvature of space itself. Warping space, as he had done more than once, produced associated gravitational anomalies, often so minuscule as to be nearly undetectable, but undeniably present. Feeding those anomalies back through the wrinkles in space that had created them would effectively circumvent the intervening distance and sidestep the issue of interference. Gravimetric transducers would do the job nicely, and, tied to a sufficiently advanced communication system, could probably encode the anomalies to carry information. In theory, at least, such an approach would be well suited for relaying extensive bodies of complex data with almost no transmission lag.

But what kind of data?

Reed found an entry point in the datastream, isolated a file, and copied it. He opened the copy and gazed thoughtfully at what the monitor's screen revealed. He saw ten jagged wave patterns, traced against a grid background; field after field of tabulated numbers; and twenty or more strings of alphanumeric characters. None of them were labeled, but all marched in a precision lockstep across his screen, held together in a single frame format. Together, they encompassed one tenth of one second in scanning time, according to the time-date stamp at the top of the screen. Something about the data frames looked naggingly familiar, as if he had seen similar displays in the past in a different format, but he couldn't be certain. Whatever the information was, it was complex and fast changing, and the time that he had taken to examine one frame, a hundred more had made their way to their intended recipient.

Reed saw no reason to let the process continue.

He made his way through the computer's user interface to its operating system's control screen. One by one, he shut down the routines that fed processing commands to the data network and the transducers. With gratifying promptness, the datastream stopped.

He heard a sound then, audible even over the background

hum of computers and processors. It resonated through the doorway behind him: a tapping sound, gentle at first and then more emphatic, the sound that metal fingers made as they entered numbers into a keypad.

The robots had found him, or were about to.

Reed entered more commands, opened more files. What he saw was interesting, but fragmentary. There was an encoded timeline, running seven years into the past and three into the future, with dated milestones. The icons used on the timeline adhered to no system he had ever seen before, and the labels appended to them were in some kind of code he could not read. There was something special about the marker for today's date. It was larger than any of the others and followed by a long string of odd-looking symbols. It could be a simple calendar marker, one that moved forward with the march of time, but that seemed doubtful. It looked to him more like a special flag, indicating a key event or events. Something was happening today, something important, at least to whomever had crafted this timeline. Reed was good with puzzles and he was reasonably certain that he could decode today's label and determine just what the big event was, given time.

He didn't have that time, however. He knew that the robots would run out of patience quickly.

Another file offered a world map, a high-resolution schematic of the Earth's land masses, divided by bright lines into their component states. On those land masses, other symbols glowed. They were starred highlights in a dozen other colors, distinct from the boundaries and borders. Most markers were clustered around major population centers. New York, Tokyo, Moscow, Beijing, Tel Aviv, and Hong Kong bore so many glowing indicators that the tiny spots of light had merged into irregular blobs of light. From other nations, such as Sylvania, Hungary, Greece, and Korea, only isolated telltales shone, glinting starkly from sporadic locales.

Reed looked at the map, wondering what the symbols meant, what message they held. He tapped a few more keys on the control panel and the image abruptly became more complex as another layer of detail imposed itself on the spinning globe. The tiny spots of light were now accompanied by blocks containing symbols, in the same alphabet as on the timeline. One block in particular caught his attention, a red square in the Atlantic northeast. An arrow ran from it to New York City, and the block itself was filled with symbols that were a precise match to the ones that marked today's date on the timeline. Whatever was happening today, it was happening in New York.

Of course, things were happening here, too.

The air filled with a dull thunder and the armored blast doors shook in their frame as something struck them, hard. Reed was reasonably sure that the impact came from steel fists. The robots were trying to beat the barrier down, rather than cut through it. Reed's best guess was that they were reluctant to blast through it for fear of damaging the equipment banks. He didn't imagine that the reluctance would last long.

Reed had already tried to find the security force's central control matrix and failed. Apparently it resided on another system. Instead of looking for it again, he began downloading data files on onto a recordable CD, selecting items that looked the most promising. The filenames for the timeline, the world map, and several dozen of the timestamped dataframes appeared in a "to copy" list and a status bar blinked into existence. The computer's disk drive clicked and hummed as it copied his selections.

More pounding, more thunder. One of the paired doors twisted and bent in its frame, and bowed inward an inch or so. At first, Reed thought the metal slab would tear free from its tracks, but the deep grooves held. Then something struck its other side again, and the door bent some more.

The disk drive at his left chimed, signifying the completion of its task. Reed opened the drive, lifted out the disk, then tucked it into his costume's waistband. He entered more commands into the keyboard and pulled up the diagrams of the mystery prison's layout again. This time, he didn't bother with the wiring diagrams or the network designs; instead, he concentrated on ventilator ducts and access tunnels, looking eagerly for a path to the outside, preferably one that would accept him and not his pursuers. After a moment, he found a promising candidate.

Metal shrieked and tore, and wrinkled back like burning paper as white fire seared though it. The robots, or their master, had apparently decided to accept the risk of damaging the computer center. Reed dodged the first burst and extended himself upward again. His fingers found an access panel in the ceiling, one that he now knew led to a specific utility tunnel. He opened it and pulled himself inside.

"All right, Mister! End of the line!"

"You had your warning!"

"Here, you're just another con doing hard time!"

Reed raced through the access spaces. His quick review of the diagrams had identified an air inlet for the circulation system, a duct some thirty inches in diameter, a veritable thoroughfare for someone with his malleable physique. It connected to several access passages, evidently intended for repair work. He slithered along the utility tunnel's dusty length, increasing his speed as plasma bursts chewed through the ceiling below his boulevard and sought to find him.

Apparently, the robots were no longer concerned with their facility's well-being, but only with Reed's lack of same.

Left, then right and up. The tunnel was dark and he guided his progress through it mostly by sense of touch. His excellent memory took care of the rest; even a brief glimpse at the map a moment before had fixed the image in his brain. The vertical shaft he followed now became an angled one, then took a short turn and broadened slightly. As Reed flowed along it, he felt the dusty air begin to move, too. He was getting closer to an exit point and farther from the prison's main spaces. Already, the snarl of plasma blasts were distant and muffled.

Left again, then down, until a fine-mesh screen blocked his path. He could see it, palely illuminated by faint light that came from somewhere in the distance. Any of the grille's spaces were sufficient for his fluid body, but not for the CD he still held, so he ripped the thing from its frame and kept going. A moment later, the tunnel twisted downward and its metal walls gave way to finished stone. The air was fresh and clean now, and his path was well-lit. Ahead of him, the outside world showed through an irregular, roughly circular opening. Reed anchored himself with his feet and stretched down, extruding the upper part of his body into the outdoors.

Bright sunlight found his eyes and made them sting. Fresh air, sweeter and cleaner by far than what he was accustomed to, filled his lungs. He twisted again, turned, looked behind himself.

Abraham Lincoln gazed back at him, benign and calm.

Reed gazed at the giant stone face, at the blue ribbon of his own body extending from the sixteenth President's left nostril. Despite himself, despite the grim prison he had escaped, and despite the ominous implications of the discoveries he had made there, he smiled as he realized what he had done.

He had escaped from Mount Rushmore.

After slithering the rest of the way out of Honest Abe's nose, Reed took a half-dozen twenty-foot strides, moving away from the gigantic monument so that he could see it in its entirety. The sculpted mountain was the genuine article, all right. Incredibly, the Thinker, or whoever had built the hidden prison, had built it inside one of the world's most famous landmarks. Reed shook his head in astonishment. In many ways, this was more amazing than any of his other discoveries. Constructing such a stronghold in a public place was an impressive, if baffling accomplishment, almost as incredible as what housed it. He looked at the four faces that had been carved so painstakingly from the living rock.

Lincoln. Washington. Roosevelt. Jefferson. Four men who had shaped a nation, and who, in so doing, had shaped their world, as well. Lincoln, especially, had always intrigued Reed. A humble boy of poor beginnings, he had risen to power and guided a young nation through its Civil War, an agonizing upheaval in social mores with repercussions that were still being felt to this day. Who could have realized what road Lincoln was embarking upon, when he lay close to the fire and read his first books? Such humble beginnings for such an influential man . . .

Startled, Reed let his mind seize on that thought and consider its implications, and then factored them in with the other information he had already gathered. Sometimes, it worked like this, in science and in life: sometimes, an apparently unrelated bit of data or observation cast new light and pointed the way to hidden answers. It happened that way now, as a dozen disparate puzzle pieces finally clicked together in his mind and formed a disturbing whole. An icy feeling swept through Reed as he suddenly realized why that format of the datafiles had seemed so familiar, and how they related to the timeline and the map. Abruptly, he knew what was going on, and who had to be behind it.

The datafiles had been consolidated engram reports, integrated data detailing emotional and cognitive responses. Reed had worked with such files before, when developing artificial intelligence systems.

The Thinker had built more than a few AI systems of his own in years gone by. He had placed those systems in a wide variety of platforms, ranging from murderous robots to synthetic lifeforms. He had even constructed artificial duplicates of specific individuals, the Fantastic Four included, and used them as impostors, to good effect. Reed had no doubt that such creations would find their performances greatly enhanced by a direct link to the personality patterns of their templates. That would require the constant monitoring and near-instantaneous communication of complex data, of course, but the system he had accessed a few minutes before had appeared equal to the job.

Just whose thought patterns had the system inside Rushmore been beaming to an unknown destination?

His own?

There was another point to consider. Psychohistory was the study of society, and an exercise in trends projection carried to a logical extreme. What if someone could not merely project those trends, but shape them? What if someone could dictate the decisions that made the world, and nudge all of society into a new path of his choosing? The logistical problems associated with execution were breathtaking, but the conception was simple enough. Socioeconomic trends followed a logarithmic trend, and a little push at the right point could yield wildly disproportionate results. If you were patient, and if you could control the right people, you could remake civilization.

Or end it.

What shape might the world take if the Thinker were its architect?

Reed pushed that thought from his mind, at least for now, and went looking for help. He didn't know, couldn't know, how much time he had, but he was sure it wasn't very much.

The Thing said, "I say we head out to the Vault and shake the Thinker up and down until he gives with the skinny on this caper." He was lumbering through the halls of Four Freedoms Plaza, making good time as he approached the monitor room. "We know he's behind it, right?"

Beside him, Sue shook her head. "We don't *know* anything of the sort," she said. "It looks like a Thinker plot, and it sounds like a Thinker plot—"

"So it is a Thinker plot," the Thing interrupted. "An' I say, we go to the Vault, an' we—"

"No." There was a new tone in the way Sue spoke as she uttered the single syllable as the last shreds of patience and accommodation wore away, leaving behind only the voice of command. "We aren't going to the Vault, at least not yet, and that's final."

"But—"

"But, nothing. I reviewed the Vault's security records earlier, and then I called Warden Fingeroth. He says that the Thinker is in some kind of a coma."

"Huh?"

"I talked to the prison infirmary, too. He's been having a problem with catalepsy for months, but they thought they had it under control. About sixteen hours ago, though, he went to sleep and they can't wake him up."

"Huh," the Thing repeated. "Must be a trick. Bet I could wake him up."

"That's not what they say at the Vault."

"So he started something before they caught him last time. He's a real weasel, and good at stuff like that."

A few yards before their destination, Sue stopped walking. Ben continued for two or three giant-sized paces before he realized he was now alone. He turned around and rejoined Sue, who glared at him.

"Okay," he finally said. "I'll listen."

Speaking in a low, clear voice that would brook no interruption, Sue listed their priorities. "First," she said, "we find Reed. That's what matters most right now."

Ben nodded.

"After we find Reed, or if we can't find him, we'll track down the Red Ghost, unless we've found him already. Whatever's going on, Kragoff is part of it."

Ben nodded again.

"If we can't find Reed or the Ghost, or if we can't find them fast, we'll try something else, maybe the Thinker."

"An' I shake him some, right?"

"Right," Sue said, finally letting half a smile form on her face. "Ben, I know you're worried, but this is the only way. We have to look for Reed first, and for whoever has him. One place we know he isn't is the Vault."

Ben took a deep breath, and then released it. He and Reed Richards had been friends since their days as college roommates, and close friends, too, despite their occasional squabbles; it often seemed to Ben that he had always known the scientific genius. He sometimes had to remind himself how important Richards was to others.

"Okay, Susie," he said. "Your call."

"Good," she responded. "I've had enough of people second-guessing me today."

Ben grunted quizzically.

"Sean Morgan," Sue said, making the name an explanation. "He gave me a message for you, by the way."

"Oh yeah?"

She continued talking as they started walking again. She told him about the NTSB's report on the fallen Fantasti-Car and about Doug Deeley's disagreement with that report, and she filled him in on Ivan Kragoff's recent history. By the time she finished, they passed through the doorway of the monitor room, where the Fantastic Four kept a wide variety of surveillance and analysis equipment.

Karnak greeted them. "Welcome," he said, looking up from his work. He was seated behind a console, the long, graceful fingers of his gloved hands resting on a keyboard. Medusa stood beside him "We were preparing to summon you."

"I hope that's good news," Sue said.

"Not completely," another voice said. It came from Johnny, seated at another console. "I tapped into the Pentagon's surveillance satellite network and walked up and down the spectrum, but I can't find anything out of the ordinary. Of course, I'm not sure just what we're looking for, but—"

"Incongruities," Karnak said. "Discrepancies in the information that these devices can detect."

"Too bad Reed ain't here," Ben said. "He can really make these gadgets sing."

"If Reed were here, we wouldn't need to look for him," the Torch said sourly.

Ben shot him an angry glance.

"The situation is complicated by the fact that many of the most potentially useful scanners appear to have been sabotaged," Karnak continued.

Medusa agreed. "I can think of a dozen ways to track Reed with instruments as sensitive as these," she said. "I'm sure you can, too, Sue. His brainwave patterns, his metabolic signature, even the pattern of his DNA encoding—they're all on file, and all distinctive" She gestured at another bank of equipment. "This device, for example, ties in with your government's scientific research satellites and can apparently track organic sources of radiation."

"That's a GammaTrac," Sue said. "Intended to monitor folks like the Hulk. SAFE's idea, but Reed provided some technical input and then built his own."

"Well, with minor adjustments, it could be attuned to detect the cosmic radiation trapped in Reed Richards's cellular structure."

"Sounds good to me," Ben said. "Go for it."

Karnak shook his head. "That is not possible. I sensed a—a *wrongness* in the device. Medusa helped me assess it."

"The calibration tables have been altered, along with their backups," the red-haired Inhuman said. "My guess is that the duplicate did it."

"Probably," Sue replied. "He spent some time in here yesterday."

"Without correct ones," Medusa continued, "we cannot reset the tracking device to find Reed, and none of us know enough about the underlying machine code to re-create what we need."

"None of us are Reed, you mean," Johnny said. He didn't look happy.

"So we need Reed to find Reed," Sue said. "We're back to that."

"Perhaps," Karnak said. "Perhaps not." He stood and stepped to another console. "Your equipment is not familiar to me, but with help from Johnny and Medusa, I was able to develop some findings of interest." His fingers danced on the keyboard and a wall display lit. It presented a Mercator projection of the world with all major land masses clearly defined.

"You're gonna have to narrow things down a bit, Karnak," Ben said.

As if in response, Karnak pressed another button. Four orange circles appeared on the screen, superimposed over the land masses. To one side of the display, a pop-up window appeared, listing four names that matched the geographic loci—Bayonne, New Jersey; Mount Rushmore National Monument, South Dakota; a site in the Alaskan tundra, just inside the Arctic Circle; and an island in the South Seas.

"Ben Grimm and I talked about this earlier," Karnak said.

"That was while you were on the phone," the Thing said, in response to Sue's questioning glance.

"Your main communications matrix has been sabotaged, too," Karnak continued, "but not as severely. We were able to verify numerous coded telemetry transmissions during the last two standard days, to these locations. Apparently, the counterpart was sending some manner of data downloads. I can't find any common factor uniting all four, or strategic significance to any of them; they may simply be relay stations. Johnny says the Pentagon's surveillance satellites don't show anything pertinent at these sites. But—''

He entered another series of command sequences. Three more symbols appeared on the screen, green stars that overlapped the orange circles at the New Jersey, South Seas and South Dakota sites.

Johnny looked surprised.

''Black Bolt found these, using the gravimetric sensors in the subspace lab,'' Karnak said. ''To be honest, I am not certain what prompted him to look. He is a skilled researcher, and his powers give him an affinity for—''

''Wait a minute!'' Johnny said. ''Gravimetrics? Subspace? You didn't tell me anything about this.''

''Medusa explained it to me only moments ago,'' Karnak said. He pointed at the stars. ''These represent distortions in the space-time continuum, ripples in the fabric of space itself. I thought at first they were singularities, but they seem to be some other kind of anomaly, probably artificial.''

''Warps? Like Lockjaw creates?'' Sue asked.

''No,'' Karnak said. ''These are much smaller, too small for the passage of physical matter. They are at the absolute bottom threshold of long-range detectability, though quantum theory says that even smaller ones are possible. My best guess is that these might be adequate to transfer data, but nothing more than that.''

''But they correlate with the telemetry sites.''

''Precisely,'' Karnak said. ''It occurs to me that such a capability would be a useful adjunct to a communications system, especially if we assume that there are other such anomalies we cannot detect from here. They might be entry points for another data network.''

''Well, they've got to mean something,'' Ben said. ''Seems to me—hey!''

On the screen, one of the three green stars had vanished.

''Is this a live display?'' Sue asked, a new urgency in her tone.

Karnak nodded. "It's tied directly to the equipment in the subspace lab," he said.

"Then, if what you say is correct, Mount Rushmore just hung up the phone."

Karnak nodded again. "If what I say is correct," he agreed pointedly.

"Ben," Sue said, "get a Fantasti-Car ready. You and Johnny are going to New Jersey."

"We are?" both men said simultaneously.

"Karnak will give you the coordinates," Sue continued, speaking in the tones of a woman accustomed to command. "Take him and Gorgon with you. The rest of us will head for the South Seas."

"But what about the other two sites?" Ben asked.

Sue shook her head. "We've got to go with the odds," she said. "More activity at the first two sites means more likelihood we'll find someone who can lead us to Reed." She paused, and when she spoke again, she did not sound as if she liked saying what she did. "Besides, we have to face facts. Whatever this is, it's big. Four sites scattered across the world, high-level genetic engineering, and artificial lifeforms good enough to create a duplicate Reed. Think about that. Reed's replacement must have had a radically different physical structure to do the things it did, and yet it passed through our internal security systems undetected."

"Fooled you, too," Johnny said.

Sue nodded in reluctant agreement. "But it also spent most of the last two days evading me, remember?" she said. "Burying itself in lab work. I don't imagine 'Reed' talked much to you two, either."

Johnny's and Ben's silence was mute acknowledgment of her point.

Sue continued, "Then there's the possibility that someone has stolen the secret of the Terrigen. It's frightening to think how things could add up. Reed's still our first priority, but his disappearance may just be the tip of the iceberg."

"I still say this has the Thinker's fingerprints all over it," Ben said.

Sue ignored him. She looked at Karnak and Black Bolt, who had just entered the room. "It also seems likely that we'll find Kragoff at one of these sites, or at least, clues that will lead us to him. Do you agree?"

"It seems logical," Karnak said.

Black Bolt made a gesture.

"Agreed, then," Sue said. "We leave at once."

"Ruined," Oscar Paltrow said. He said the words softly. He spoke softly because speaking softly made it easier for him to keep from crying, and he did not want his wife to see him cry, at least not yet. Actually, he didn't want his wife to see him at all, but he supposed he owed her the opportunity, if only in return for long years of reasonably faithful marriage. "I'm ruined. We're ruined."

"What is it?" Aspidistra asked. "What's wrong?"

"We're ruined," Oscar repeated. This time, the tears came, and he realized with some surprise that he didn't mind. They coursed down his face in salty, forking rivulets, following the line of his jaw, then splashing against the expensive fabric of the suit he had worn to work today. He scarcely noticed.

"You're going to ruin that suit," Aspidistra observed. "And it's an Armani." She seemed to be speaking only to say something, anything, rather than directly confront the weeping man in front of her.

"Doesn't matter," Oscar said. "Nothing matters. We're broke, Aspidistra. Ruined."

"Broke?"

Oscar nodded. "Something happened at the Tokyo Stock Exchange yesterday. The computers burped, a power surge, I don't know. When they got the computers back online, something was wrong. They didn't catch it until today, but the damage was already done."

Comprehension dawned on Aspidistra's face, and then anger. "Tokyo? You've been playing the market again? Not after that debacle with Acme Atomics! Oscar, you promised me, you *promised*!"

"I know, I know. But it was a golden deal, golden. Now

that they've fought back the rebels, the Sylvanians want to contract to rebuild their capital city. I knew who had the winning bid for that contract, Aspidistra. I knew which company's stock would triple in value.''

Aspidistra didn't say anything.

"And I knew how to buy on margin, or I thought I did." He set a CD jewel case on the table. It bore the colorful label of a popular financial management software package. "I was online with Tokyo when the glitch hit," he said. "Remember this? Picked it up cheap, that last trip to Madripoor." He paused, ran one hand through his thinning hair. "Or maybe not cheap. It's bogus, counterfeit, bootleg. I found that out today. Something's wrong with it. A flaw in the code that overrides the safeties, raises order levels. The burp at the TSE did something to it, switched it on, I don't know. By the time I realized what had happened, I was on the hook for seven million." He repeated the words, almost as if savoring them. "Seven. Million. Dollars."

Aspidistra still didn't say anything. She just stared at him.

"We're bankrupt, Aspidistra. Ruined."

Aspidistra then spoke five words that she uttered calmly, even primly.

"Oscar," she said, "I want a divorce."

CHAPTER 8

Founded in the 1870s, the Chesney Products Company had once been among the leading heavy equipment manufacturing concerns in the American northeast. Ezekial Chesney, the company's founder, had left the joy of invention to others and satisfied himself with the work of construction and distribution. Edison, Whitney, Ford, and other titans of industry had subcontracted work to Chesney's factories and entrusted it to his network of railroad lines and canal barges. Foundries had competed eagerly for Chesney's business and countless immigrant hands had knocked on his door as America's newest denizens sought work. If the Chesney name had never become quite so well known as Carnegie or Gould or Hearst, it was nonetheless quite famous in its own prosaic way. Chesney died of gout in 1899, but the children he left behind took charge of the company and continued to enjoy the good life.

The Great Depression had changed that.

It had brought an end to the Chesney fortune, as it ended so many others. One by one, the businesses that Chesney served closed their doors; one by one, Chesney's factories followed suit, as the flow of work slowed to a trickle, and the trickle became a drought. The railroads reclaimed their leases and the canal companies severed their contracts, but that was all right; the Chesney company no longer had products to ship. In one terrible year, the business that old Ezekial Chesney had so painstakingly built was gone, its key assets folded into other, hardier companies. By the time World War II's manufacturing boom had jump-started the American economy, all that remained of the once-mighty Chesney empire were two lonely outposts, twin decaying warehouses that provided Ezekial's great-grandchildren with a modest annuity.

One of them was in Bayonne, New Jersey.

"Looks like a prime candidate for urban renewal," Johnny Storm said. He was perched on the rear deck of his Fantasti-Car module. He looked especially boyish now, dangling his feet over the deck's edge. That specialized craft, in turn, hovered some three hundred feet above and to one side of the storage building's pigeon-stained tarpaper roof. "That is, if this place were a bit more urban,'' the Torch continued, gazing down at the surrounding blocks of depots and industrial buildings.

"Yeah, well, maybe I took a wrong turn," Ben said. He was seated in the lead module of the same T-shaped vehicle, and communicated with his three passengers via a control panel intercom. As he spoke, he pushed buttons on the elaborate dashboard. "An' I wish you'd park your butt in the seat where it belongs. Yer givin' me the willies sittin' there."

"Save the willies for someone who can't fly," Johnny responded. "If I fall, I'll catch myself. Just tell me what comes next." Neither Gorgon nor Karnak, seated in the sidecars, attempted to join in on the conversation. Instead, Gorgon scowled angrily at the building that was their goal, and Karnak studied it thoughtfully. They had hung here in midair for nearly a minute now, while their pilot took the lay of the land.

"Surface scan checks out," Ben said thoughtfully. He read the display before him silently, then spoke again. "Hundred-year-old bricks an' mortar, timbers, planking—they built this place in the old days, before steel frames came in, an' before fire codes made 'em mandatory. I'm surprised this joint wasn't shut down a long time ago."

"Hey, it's New Jersey," Johnny said. "Some people say that about the whole state."

The Thing grunted and pressed some more buttons.

"Ben," Karnak said softly. "You said, *surface scan.*"

The Thing nodded, even though he knew that the Inhuman would not see it. "Yup," he said. "What's underneath is more interesting, though. I'm getting some electromagnetic emissions. It doesn't seem to be any kind of a transmission system, just static, but whoever's in there, they're using a lot of power." He pressed another key, waited a second, and the whistled softly at what his screen revealed. "Sonar imaging's complete now, but fuzzy. Too much background noise, I guess." He paused again. "Huh."

"What?" Johnny asked.

"I'm gettin' a modulated signal now, some kinda probe. We're being scanned," Ben said. He brought the Fantasti-Car closer to the moldering pile and worked his controls some more. They were directly over the building now. "They know we're here," the Thing continued. "I'm goin' in, get a better look."

"What's it show, Ben?" Johnny asked, as the Fantasti-Car drifted downward.

"I dunno for sure. The building itself is hard to read, but underneath is another story. Some kinda hollow spaces under the building. Center area's pretty big, but the extremities branch off—" He paused as the realization struck him. "Hey! It looks like a dad-blasted subway station!"

"Let someone else take a look," the Torch said. He scrambled back into his seat. "Patch the feed back here, big guy."

"You've all got it now," Ben said, complying. "Karnak, Gorgon, take a look."

"Tunnels, all right," Johnny said. An image had filled his dashboard screen. "And that one on the left of the display looks like it heads back to the city."

"Hmph. That prolly explains what happened with the Red Ghost the other day," Ben said. "If they've connected a private access route to the city system, he can come an' go as he pleases. Sometimes he rides a city train, sometimes he rides one of his own."

Karnak said, "I concur, Ben. I propose we—"

His words stopped abruptly, and when he spoke again, the lean Inhuman sounded far more agitated than was his usual wont. "Gorgon," he said, "don't!"

"Bah," the hooved Inhuman said, his words carried not by the Fantasti-Car's intercom system, but by the whipping winds that surrounded the hovering vehicle. He had climbed out onto the deck of his passenger module and stood now at its edge. The huge muscles of his distinctive legs tensed and flexed. "We're wasting time," he continued. "The sooner we solve this puzzle, the sooner we help the students."

"Don't do it, Gorgon," Johnny yelled, fire flickering into existence around his body. He reached in the Inhuman's general direction and stood, moving quickly.

He didn't move quickly enough.

Gorgon's legs bent, their animal-like joints bending into sharp angles, and the hooves that served him as feet skittered and slid along the craft's gleaming fuselage as his center of gravity shifted. Then Gorgon's bent legs straightened again in a sudden, convulsive release of power. Gorgon went up, and then down, falling like a meteor toward the Chesney warehouse.

The force of his leap was enough to make the Fanasti-Car buck and rock in midair after he launched himself, and Ben had to yank on its steering yoke hard as he guided the vehicle back into stability. "Great," he muttered. "Just great. He's actin' like me, for cryin' out loud!"

Gorgon fell in a trajectory that almost immediately became precisely perpendicular to the Earth's surface, he fell with a speed that seemed, impossibly, greater than gravity alone could justify. As he fell, he brought his arms close to his sides and made his body as straight a line as his anatomy would allow, reducing wind drag to a bare minimum. Only the ripple of his hair and garments bore testimony to the terrific speed with which his body cut through the air. In what seemed like a split second, his hooved feet found the warehouse roof.

As they did, there was a sound like thunder.

Most Inhumans had as their birthright specialized adaptations that set them apart from mainstream humanity. Many of them—and all of the Royal Family—had what the outside world termed super powers, unique abilities and aptitudes that they honed through constant practice.

Gorgon's power was more spectacular than most, and far more brutal. He could stamp his feet and release devastating shockwaves. The massive muscles that corded his twisted legs and the super-dense bones that gave them their shape were only symptoms of that ability, and not the prime source of his power. That came not only from muscle and bone, but an innate ability to release shattering forces, raw waves of kinetic force that he could shape and control. Now, striking his target like a thunderbolt from on high, guided by the twin forces of gravity and muscle, he let the power that was his legacy surge forth.

The warehouse's roof rippled like a stormy sea as the tidal wave of force fanned out from the point of impact. Weathered mortar crumbled into dust, and bricks exploded into dust as Gorgon's power found them. The warehouse's front wall, grimy but whole until now, writhed and tore away from the structure. It fell mostly in one piece, a rippling curtain of debris that shattered completely as it struck the streets below. Gorgon, ordinarily the most dour of Inhumans, stood near the edge of the rumpled roof, and looked positively pleased at the destruction he had wrought. He beckoned at the others to join him.

"Gorgon," Ben yelled, genuinely angry, as he bought the Fanasti-Car closer to the ruined warehouse, "what the heck was that supposed to prove?"

"Prove?" Karnak asked. "Perhaps nothing. But my cousin has certainly revealed something." He pointed.

Ben and Johnny looked. The face that the Chesney warehouse presented now to the world looked very much the aftermath of a car-bomb explosion. The roof was a wrinkled carpet of wreckage and the building's entire front façade had torn away, unmasking the building's structural members. Unlike a conventional bomb blast, however, Gorgon's advent on the scene had kicked up comparatively little dust and airborne debris to obscure things. What little there was, was already settling, and the Chesney's interior was becoming visible.

Ben had seen more than a few warehouses before. He knew what he would have expected to see inside this one, a cavernous area divided into only a few levels and housing tiers of storage areas. Certainly, the hasty scan he had taken with the Fanasti-Car's inboard sensors hadn't indicated anything to the contrary.

They hadn't said anything about the cages.

Ben stared at what Gorgon had revealed. The building's exposed interior didn't track at all with what his equipment had indicated. The difference was so great that he had to suspect that the electronic feed he had detected earlier was some kind of cloaking system. Contrary to the sensors' reports, the warehouse was level upon level of jail cells, barred cubicles that looked liked they belonged in a municipal prison. From where Ben sat, they looked empty, but he recognized the there was no way he could see them all; the disguised Bastille was simply too large. Besides, there was the matter of its foundations, and the network of tunnels detected below.

"I recommend we explore this place," Karnak said. He was still in his seat, but the Human Torch had already disembarked from the Fantasti-Car and hung in midair, wreathed in flames and staring in astonishment at what Gorgon had unveiled.

Still stunned, Ben tried to reply to Karnak, but it wasn't easy. Something was wrong with his mouth. After a moment's thought, he realized that his jaw was gaping open. With a deliberate effort, he shut it, and shaped the words.

"I second the motion," he said softly.

"I appreciate this, Dr. Scheer," Reed said to the nondescript man seated in the wood-paneled stationwagon. The car was parked on the highway shoulder, not far from where Reed had flagged it down. Reed himself was perched on the car's hood, a cell phone in one hand, the other punching digits into its keypad. Reed had flagged down the car after his own wrist communicator had failed to function properly. Apparently it had been damaged, either in the Fantasti-Car crash or by his captors.

"Hey, no problem," Scheer replied. He was a low-key man of average build. A moment before, he had identified himself as a psychologist with a government background. That explanation went a long way toward explaining the steady composure he had exhibited when Mr. Fantastic came loping towards him on twenty-foot legs. "That's why I got it, for emergencies. And I suspect that any call someone like you has to place in a hurry is an emergency."

"That's a reasonable conclusion," Reed said. He took the phone from his ear and looked at it, puzzled.

"Something wrong? That's one of the new digital jobs, good anywhere. I got it because they're supposed to be more secure."

"They are. It's very difficult to intercept a digital signal."

Reed made the comment in a distracted tone of voice as he tried a second toll-free phone number, and then a third. The only response was a busy signal, which was impossible. The communications matrix at Four Freedoms Plaza had a voice-mail system with effectively unlimited capacity. Even if no one was home at the moment, he should have been able to leave a message. He had hoped to find Sue or one of the others, to arrange reinforcements and a ride home, but something seemed to be wrong in New York, too. Reed thought for a moment, considering his options.

"Can I offer you a ride?" Scheer asked.

Reed looked at him. Ordinarily, he would have insisted on privacy and a reasonably secure line for the call he was about to make, but something about Scheer's quiet demeanor suggested that he could be trusted. Besides, the psychiatrist was unlikely to believe the story he was about to overhear. "No, thank you," he said, "but I'll have to ask your forbearance for a few minutes longer. My home numbers don't answer, so I'll have to call someone else, and it's a long-distance call. I'll reimburse you for the charges, of course."

Scheer made a soft chuckle. "Don't be silly," he said. "And take your time. I'm not going anywhere."

"I am, and soon, I hope," Reed said, dialing the number that would connect him to Sean Morgan's direct line.

Sue watched Medusa lean down and whisper something in Lockjaw's ear. The oversized dog wagged his tail in a convulsion of delight. Medusa whispered something more and scratched the underside of his neck. Lockjaw licked her face.

"Are we ready?" Sue asked.

"I think so," Medusa said. Already a cloud of energy was forming around the antenna-like tendril that sprouted from Lockjaw's brow. "He knows what he has to do."

"Okay. But before we go, I want to take another precaution," Sue said. "This will seem odd at first, but I think its wise." Her strong features twisted slightly as she concentrated, and waves of energy swept out from her body and broke against Black Bolt, Triton and the others. The cosmic rays that had made the Fantastic Four what they were had given Sue the ability to make herself invisible, through an application of an exotic energy wave form. Later developments had given her more control over the strange effect, allowing her to shape the energy into solid, transparent barriers—or to make others invisible, too. Now, even before Lockjaw gathered the energy to depart, he and the Inhumans seemed to vanish, fading from view as Sue's power found them.

"We don't know what we're getting into," the Invisible Woman said. "No sense in losing the advantage of surprise."

Then Four Freedoms Plaza disappeared, as well.

Rather, it seemed to.

Sue knew what had really happened, of course. Like his masters, Lockjaw had an Inhuman gift of his own. That gift was the power to punch holes through space and time, effectively annihilating distance as he folded reality back on itself and then passed through the openings he created. Lockjaw could teleport himself and his passengers across almost unimaginable distances. She had no idea what the upper limits of his range were, but she knew that he had made trips to and from the moon's dusty surface, which meant he could move at least a quarter of a million miles. For Lockjaw, the trip to the South Seas was scarcely more trouble than a walk around the block, and considerably swifter.

A split second before, Sue had stood in the air-conditioned, white-paneled spaces of Four Freedoms Plaza. Now she and the Inhumans became real again half a world away, in what looked more than a little like a high-security prison.

Everywhere Sue looked she saw cages. She and her companions stood in a broad central area, flanked at each end by heavy steel doors, and easily a hundred feet below a featureless black ceiling. Ten levels of broad catwalks connected by stairways ran along the walls that surrounded her, and beyond the walkways were cell doors.

Beyond the cell doors were people.

Sue could see them, at least the ones in the cells closest to her. Men and women, young and old, people of all races, each languished alone in tiny, Spartan cubicles, each furnished only with a washstand and a bunk. That in itself was strange. Sue's career track had shown her the insides of many prisons, and all of them had been segregated by sex.

Whoever the inmates here were, they had been inside for a while. The air was heavy with the rank odor of too many people kept too close together, even though Sue could hear the whir of an industrial-strength air circulation system. The captives didn't wear the uniform of any prison she recognized, but they did wear drab, utilitarian coveralls that made them all look somewhat alike, despite their disparate builds and complexions. Sue craned her head, looking eagerly for the familiar face of her husband, but realized after a moment that no cell as conventional as these was likely to hold her Mr. Fantastic.

"What—what is this place?" Medusa's voice asked softly, easily as stunned as Sue. She had taken stock of the situation even as Sue had done the same, and was similarly mystified. "It looks like a prison."

"I don't know. The coordinates I gave you for Lockjaw were for a small island in the South Seas."

"And that is where we are," Triton said. He spoke with calm assurance. "The sea is near us. I can feel it, even here, even behind barriers of rock and steel." The aquatic Inhuman paused, considering cues that no one else in the party could perceive. "We are on an island, above sea level, since the surrounding water is below us. Lockjaw has served us well."

"I didn't mean to imply—" Sue started to say, and then she stopped, her words interrupted by someone else.

"Hello! Hello! Is someone out there!?" The words, called out in a voice both eager and desperate. "Please! Whoever you are, you've got to help us!"

One of the prisoners had overheard their whispered conversation, Sue realized. That was the only explanation; she had masked even the incandescent discharge that accompanied Lockjaw's trans-spatial jumps. She looked around, saw a middle-aged man with amber glasses staring anxiously in her general direction. He sounded vaguely familiar, and Sue studied his features carefully. Without the shapeless coverall, with a more carefully styled hair and a trimmed beard, he would be a dead ringer for Fred Raven, a syndicated radio talk-show host whom Sue had always found annoying in the extreme.

That was impossible, of course. This man had obviously been here for quite some time, and Sue had seen Raven in person only a week before, at a reception for a charity collecting for the survivors of the Baktakek Incident. She remembered being surprised that a man with beliefs as xenophobic as Raven's had participated in a charity for Hungarians, even for Hungarian children. Naturally, he had spent most of his time there making sarcastic, inappropriate responses to reasonable questions.

"I know someone is out there," the familiar voice called again, "I can hear you! You've got to help us! You've got to help me! I'm an important man! I got connections! I got my own radio show, for cryin' out loud!"

It *was* Fred Raven.

But if this was Raven, who was the man she had chatted with tensely the week before? Someone had crafted a near-duplicate of Reed, and apparently one of Raven; how many other counterparts had been made and put in place? Why? Who were these people? How many of them had someone or something else living their lives, in the world outside?

The questions were still racing through her mind when Raven's voice was drowned out by countless other exhortations.

"Who is it? Who's out there?"

"Please! I've got a husband, I've got children!"

"Thank God! Someone's here to save us!"

"Get me out of here! I beg you, get me out of here!"

Spurred by Raven's shouted pleas, the other prison's other denizens had joined in the din. They stood at their cell doors now, shouting, pleading, demanding, beckoning, stamping their feet so hard that the catwalk support braces flexed and creaked. The anguish cries soon became indistinguishable from one another, merging into a drone that throbbed strongly enough to make Sue's ears hurt. She still knew what they were saying, though, no matter that she could not make out the words, no matter that those words were in dozens of languages. All around her, men and women of all ages and from all the various flavors of humanity were asking her for one thing.

Help. They wanted her help, needed it.

She could not ignore them.

Sue let the cloaking screen of invisibility energy drop. Black Bolt, Medusa, Triton, Lockjaw, and Sue appeared as if from nowhere, and their abrupt advent on the scene was enough to shock the prison's occupants into silence. Somehow, impossibly, the sudden silence held an undercurrent of hope and expectation, and Sue knew why. The Inhumans were not well known to the world at large, but the Fantastic Four were. The uniform that she wore marked her a member of the world's premier super hero team, known and respected in every nation. The prisoners might not recognize her companions, but they knew who she was, knew that she would help them, or die trying.

Another moment's concentration, and more invisibility energy formed around Sue. This time, it took solid form and created a column of energy beneath her feet, a platform that grew and pushed her upward. In seconds, she was many yards above the concrete slab floor, apparently hovering in midair. From the ringed cells, hundred of pairs of eyes stared at her anxiously as she spoke.

"Listen to me, please," she said, her clear, confident voice carrying well and echoing from brick and steel. She spoke calmly and soothingly, so that everyone, even prisoners who could not understand English, could get some sense of reassurance. "We're here to help you. I don't know what this place is, or who has done this to you, but all of you will be free soon. I promise you that."

More cries split the air, exultantly this time. Sue let the people cheer and clap for long seconds, not for her own gratification but to allow them some release of tension. Then she raised her hand for silence, and got it. "My friends and I will help you, but we need some answers to some questions, first. Please, trust me, and be patient for a few moments."

"But—I want out now," an elderly Latin-looking woman

on the third level said, her soft voice audible in the near-silence. "I've been here for months!"

Months? Sue wondered in shock how long this situation had been going on. When had had this prison had been built?

"Months, hah!" a rail-slender Asiatic man on the top floor said derisively. "Try years, lady! Three of 'em! Ever since I got married! They took me on my wedding day!"

Years?

More voices called out, as prisoners suddenly embarked on a bizarre game of one-upsmanship. Weeks, days, months, years—the spans of time the captives called out were mind-boggling, both in their duration and in their variety. One waiflike woman had arrived only three days before; a beefy-looking man with bristling white eyebrows claimed to have been in his cell for six and a half years. Whoever was doing this, whatever their goal, the program of abduction and presumable replacement had been going on for a very long time, indeed. Baffled by the sudden avalanche of unasked-for information, Sue raised her hands again for silence.

"You'll all be free soon, I promise," she repeated. "Free to go home, to return to your lives. You have my word on that."

From the ground level below, Fred Raven's sardonic voice drifted up to find her ears. "Nice talk, lady! But I hope you've got something better than talk to use on the robots!"

"Robots?" Sue asked, genuinely puzzled.

As if on cue, the steel doors at one end of the common area slide open and gleaming forms marched into view.

"Those robots," Raven said, managing to get the words in before the thundering footsteps drowned out his voice.

"All right then, I'll defer to your judgment, but that deferral is only good for twelve hours," Sean Morgan said into the telephone he held. He spoke in measured tones that carried well, even in the controlled chaos that surrounded him. As he spoke, he kept a watchful eye on the men and women scurrying about the SAFE staging area, readying special-use vehicles and running weaponry though test cycles. "After that,

I call out the Marines." He paused. "No, I wasn't speaking figuratively." He paused again. "I hope not, too. Morgan out."

"Bad news, I take it," Nefertiti Jones said, her laconic tone an odd contrast with her military bearing.

Morgan broke the connection and looked at the African-American woman wearing battle armor who stood before him. She had attractive features and close cropped hair, and right now her intelligent eyes were lit with curiosity. She had stood at attention for the entire telephone call, Morgan realized with some surprise. That had been nearly thirty minutes, longer than he usually allowed himself to stay on the phone.

On reflection, he realized that it hadn't been a very long call at all, considering its import.

"It's always bad news," he said sourly. "That was Reed Richards."

It was Jones's turn to look surprised now. A moment before, the SAFE officer had been preparing to lead an expedition to the Vault, ostensibly as part of a training exercise, but actually to investigate the site's security measures. Something about Susan Richards's earlier conversation hadn't sat quite right with Sean Morgan, especially in light of her husband's mysterious reticence regarding his trip and interview session. Morgan was by nature a suspicious man, and a few phone conversations with Warden Fingeroth hadn't done much to set those suspicions to rest, especially after the official had explained that the Thinker was once more in one of his mysterious trances. He had prepared a list of questions and passed it to Jones, confident that she could shake some answers loose.

Literally, if necessary.

"So the so-called training exercise is off?" she asked. "Too bad; my kid brother works out there."

Morgan shook his head. He was still thinking about what Mr. Fantastic had told him, about an outlandish plot involving human duplicates placed in positions of power and influence. He thought about an obscure discipline called psychohistory, and the one man on earth who might be able to make it work. That man happened to be one who viewed most of his fellow human beings as little more than lab rats, and the world itself as a particularly complex maze.

He thought about the Thinker.

"Not off," he told Jones. "Changed. We're moving into a support mode." The words he spoke didn't please him, but he saw no way around them. A big part of his management technique had always been to set personal interests aside and find the best person to do the job, any job. Now, he saw no other option than to put that belief in practice yet again, even if it meant stepping back from his own duties. He wanted desperately to dispatch every force at his command, but Mr. Fantastic had convinced him that other, more subtle measures were what the situation demanded. "Richards is taking the lead on this," he said. "At least, he is for a while."

Jones blinked in surprise, something she didn't do very often. Morgan took a moment he really couldn't spare and balanced priorities against resources. He considered the orders he had issued in the last few frenzied hours. "I need a name," he said. "Someone who's checked out on the *Whippet* and won't embarrass us in front of the Fantastic Four."

"There's Clyde. He's attached to my team for this mission, though."

Morgan nodded. "He'll do. When we're done here, send him to me. Tell him to lose the battle suit, though; he won't have room." The *Whippet* was a high-speed, two-seat special utility vehicle, unique to SAFE but loosely based on designs by Reed Richards. Capable of supersonic flight, it represented the end result of a series of tradeoffs involving fuel consumption and payload capacity. The tiny craft's cabin had barely enough space for two people, let alone two people and a suit of armor, no matter how compact.

"What about the rest of the unit?" Jones asked. Her voice held a note of self-interest. SAFE's Special Tactical Squad was her pet project, a team of heavy-weapons specialists trained for all contingencies. A few months before, she had led a dozen SAFE agents in a raid on a Hydra-held space station; one month ago, the same twelve plus another three had dealt with the Super-Skrull. Those men and women now formed the core of her dedicated unit. They were twenty in number now, and waited on the Helicarrier's flight deck. "What about the Vault?"

Morgan shook his head. Richards's report had changed everything. "I'll take the Colorado run," he said.

"You told Richards you'd wait twelve hours."

"I told Richards I'd wait twelve hours before bringing in the Marines," Morgan said. He wasn't smiling. "I didn't promise anything else. I don't know how yet, but the Thinker is up to something big. I want a presence in Warden Finger-oth's backyard, with enough muscle to make that presence meaningful."

"I could take care of that," Jones said.

"Not this time," Morgan responded. "I've got something else for you, though, another mess to clean up." He paused. "Tell me, Nef, have you ever been to Mount Rushmore?"

Jones blinked again.

It looked to Ben Grimm as if some crazed penologist had commandeered the Chesney Products Warehouse, gutted it, and built a prison inside it according to his own exacting specifications. All that Gorgon's shockwave had done was to peel the aging façade from its clandestinely reinforced interior and reveal the other structure hidden within. The building's once-cavernous interior had been divided into six levels of concrete slab floors, supported by massive steel beams, and linked by stairwells and elevators. Each of the six levels was further divided into multiple cell blocks, and row after row of barred doors faced out on dusty corridors. Each of the tiny cubicles was stark and empty, bereft even of a washstand or bunk.

"Looks to me like someone's trying to corner the jail cell market," Ben muttered. He, Johnny, Gorgon, and Karnak had entered the building at its top and were working their way to the lower levels, trudging through hallways and down staircases, neither of which had been damaged by the shattering impact of Gorgon's landing. The outer walls were mostly gone now, however, and the afternoon sun could penetrate the building and compensate for the nonfunctional lighting. Those rays came into the building at a sharp angle, alternately split and blocked by elements of the interior structure, so that the path they followed was sometimes brightly lit and sometimes deeply shadowed.

Whoever had built this place had built it to last. At first, they examined each cell they passed, looking for some clue to the identity of that secret builder, but after a dozen fruitless examinations of a dozen identical enclosures, all had tired of the game and agreed to spot-check instead. One thing was certain, however—whoever had done the job liked steel and concrete, and had plenty of both.

"Why would anyone construct such a place?" Gorgon asked. Even he seemed stunned by what he had revealed. "Who would build it and then abandon it?"

"Looks unfinished to me, not abandoned," Johnny said. "It's just empty. Maybe the owner stepped out."

"I agree with the Torch," Karnak said. The party of four had reached the ground floor now. Beyond a set of steel security doors, still more empty cells waited. Ahead of them, another turn in the stairs led toward the building's foundations. "There is life in this place. I can sense it."

Ben looked at him thoughtfully. Unlike most members of his race, Karnak's special abilities were largely the result of many years of training. Through intense study and exercise, he had refined his conventional senses and awakened others within himself. If Karnak thought there was more to this place than what they had seen so far, Ben was willing to believe him. It was the contemplative Inhuman who had first spotted the fake Reed, after all.

Reed.

It had been many long minutes since Ben had thought the name, mainly because it made him worry, and worrying wouldn't do anyone any good right now. Reed Richards had been Ben's closest friend for his entire adult life, closer to him in many ways than the few remaining members of his own family. In college, they had made an odd pair of buddies, the patrician scholar and the rough-and-tumble football player. Nonetheless, they had been fast friends ever since, and it actually frightened Ben to think that someone had been able to capture Reed so easily. The dignified, thoughtful man was the heart and soul of the Fantastic Four, Sue's husband, and the only authority figure that Johnny paid much attention to. If he was gone . . .

"Keep going?" he asked the others. All of them nodded, so he took the lead, setting one four-toed foot on the first step of the next flight. A minute or so later, another pair of doors blocked their path. Ben shrugged, pressed one hand flat against the painted metal surface, and pushed. Steel split and tore with a gratifying shriek, and the door fell forward, to reveal—

More jail cells.

"Aw, crumbs," Ben said. "How big *is* this place, anyhow?"

This level was different, though. The halls were brightly lit with ceiling fixtures and the hallway floor showed scuff marks and wear. Some of the cells seemed to be in various stages of construction or modification; and a few open ones held building supplies—mortar, cinder blocks, tools, pipes, and huge spools of cable.

"Okay," Ben said. "Home improvement." He thought about the other cells above, the featureless cubicles they had trudged past only moments before. "Someone's building himself a prison. They built the infrastructure first, starting at the bottom and working their way up. Guess that means we keep working our way down." He was annoyed, and let the emotion sound in his voice. Something about this place was getting on his nerves.

They were standing in the intersection of two corridors now, sort of an indoor crossroads. Gorgon swung his head and looked down each hallway, at the dozens of identical cells he could see receding into the distance. The underground section of the citadel seemed to cover more area than the upper levels, and the ends of the corridors he could see were impressively distant. "But who has undertaken such a project?" he asked. "And what connection does he have with the impostor who claimed to be your leader?"

"Dunno. The answer is probably downstairs—huh?" Ben's

words halted as Karnak raised his hand for silence.

"We are not alone," the shorter man said softly.

Ben looked at him quizzically.

Karnak gestured again, pointing silently at one ear.

Ben listened. Now, he could hear the sound, too. Soft and whispery, it echoed oddly against the hard concrete and steel surfaces of the prison's corridors, so that it seemed to come from all directions at once. It sounded vaguely like footsteps on flooring, but the cadence was wrong—more like a shuffle than a step, and it wasn't the clean, hard sound that shod feet make.

"Paws," Karnak said softly.

He was right, Ben realized, as the sound grew in volume. It was the sound that an animal's paws make as they strike a harder surface—not one set of paws, but many. Now that he knew what he heard, he could distinguish the individual footfalls, pick them out from the background noise and the echoes. The effect was oddly unnerving, even for a man who had led a life of adventure like the Thing.

"Ready, Johnny?" he asked his teammate. That was when he briefly glimpsed a shaggy shape at the end of one hall, a humanoid form that bounded across from one cross-corridor to another. It moved too quickly to be seen clearly, but Ben saw it well enough, and knew what it was.

A gorilla.

And, even in the brief glimpse he had been granted, it looked like a mighty familiar gorilla.

Karnak and Gorgon had both dropped into defensive crouches and stood back to back, facing opposing corridors. Karnak's features were a mask of concentration, but Gorgon's face held a quizzical expression that became even more intense as he saw what Ben had seen.

"Pilose?" the hooved Inhuman said softly.

"Nah," Ben said. Another form had shuffled into view, not trying to hide itself from his gaze. Smaller and squatter than the first ape, it was so heavy that it nearly waddled as it approached the four men. Ben watched warily as the familiar-looking orangutan came closer. He was sure now that he recognized both of the simians, members of the set he had warred with earlier in the week. This time, though, the advantage of numbers was on his side, so the battle promised to be a shorter one. Alone, he had made fairly short work of the Red Ghost's super-powered pets; with Karnak, Gorgon, and Johnny on his side, the empowered animals should pose no real challenge at all. "Not hardly," he continued. "But close. Kragoff's got some other irons in the fire, a trio of—"

That was when he saw the second gorilla, and then the third, both entering from another side corridor. They looked exactly alike, and exactly like the first. A moment later, a second orangutan that looked identical to the first joined them, and then a baboon.

"Uh oh," Ben said softly. This didn't look good, not good at all. He glanced down another corridor, where more anthropoids were gathering. Gorillas, orangutans, baboons—a dozen or more of each, all precise matches for various members of the Red Ghost's goon squad. Possible explanations for the bizarre tableau raced through his mind, none of them very attractive, but one of them especially ominous.

If the Thinker had duplicated Reed, what was to keep him from copying Kragoff's super-powered pets, too? Moreover, what was to keep him from doing it again and again?

Yet another gorilla came into view, and then a pair of orangutans, all of them getting closer. They were coming from all directions now, blocking off any path that might lead to an exit.

"What is this, Grimm?" Gorgon asked. "What are all these apes doing here?" The simian crowd was growing rapidly, and getting closer. The nearest of the gorillas was less than six meters from the hooved Inhuman and stood there silently, unblinking, as if awaiting a cue. Behind it, more anthropoids lurked, their hunched forms huddled close together. They looked annoyingly complacent, undisturbed either by their fellows or by the four strangers in their midst. At least fifty of them were in view now, and still more were joining the throng. Already their numbers were sufficient to block the corridors and completely surround the invading quartet.

The odds had shifted somewhat now, the Thing realized, and not for the better.

"Well, technically, the littler guys aren't apes, they're monkeys," Ben found himself saying, and immediately wished he hadn't. Intended as a wisecrack, the comment was yet another reminder of the reason they had come to this strange place, the missing member of the Fantastic Four. That was the kind of comment Reed would make, and Reed wasn't here. "But they're all dangerous. They got super-powers. The big boys are strong, the orangutans are living magnets, an' the baboons can change shape like Silly Putty."

"Silly Putty?" Gorgon asked.

Ben didn't answer. A thought had struck him. Most animals had an instinctive fear of fire, and Kragoff's pets, despite their powers, had never been an exception to that rule. Presumably, these apparent duplicates would feel the same. He turned to face his partner, and was startled to realize that the Human Torch was not already ablaze. "Johnny," he said urgently. "We need to hold these things off! Flame on an' lay down a firebreak, an' quick!"

Johnny looked back at him, suddenly ashen-faced. Sweat beaded on his brow. "Ben," he said. "I'm trying, and I can't! My powers don't work! Can't you feel it, too? Something about this place keeps my powers from working!"

The words had barely left his lips when the hirsute horde charged.

"This is an unfortunate development," the Thinker said. He was gazing at a monitor screen, at phosphor images of costumed figures locked in combat with an anthropoid horde. The much-hated Thing was busily tying an elastic baboon into knots, and his hooved companion, the big man with the metal visor, was making short work of a gorilla. Behind them, a man wearing green and white had felled another gorilla with a single karate blow to its receding brow. Whoever Grimm's new friends were, they were good at what they did. "The remaining members of the Fantastic Four should have been unable to discover this site," the Thinker continued. "Now, I calculate an eighty percent likelihood that they will reach the lower levels and storm this chamber.''

"Not so, my friend," the Red Ghost responded, standing at the Thinker's side. He sounded almost jovial, and was showing his bad teeth in a broad grin. "You underestimate the defenses we have mustered. Many times, my loyal ones have defeated Richards's accursed quartet. Now, surely, these duplicates we created will overwhelm Grimm and his strange companions, if only through sheer force of numbers.''

"No," came the reply. "They are but apes, and unequal to the task we have set them.''

The Ghost bridled, and muttered a few harsh syllables in his native language. "Do not belittle them," he continued, still enthusiastic. "They are the products of Soviet super science, the end result of many long years of conditioning and training. Why, the gorillas alone—''

His words broke off into silence as he watched the Thing lash out at his assailants. Two mutated fists struck twin fur-covered jaws, and the pair of gorillas slumped the floor, unconscious or dead.

"Your own charges may be doughty warriors, but we optimized these to serve other duties," the Thinker said. "They have all the powers of the originals, but little of their experience. Most of the training these units received was of another sort.''

"But the template process should have—''

The Thinker shook his head, a gesture he disliked in others, but one that he essayed out of consideration for the Ghost. He was well aware that his mental superiority intimidated the Russian, but for this partnership to work, it was essential that Kragoff at least feel a degree of fellowship with him. If that fellowship required that he lessen his demeanor temporarily, he was willing to make the sacrifice. "No," he said. "The replication parameters were set differently for these. The overlay process has less to do with basic skills than with cognitive patterns. Human beings are complex, annoying things, less simple to predict than apes and monkeys. It is far easier to emulate people if we have the originals available to serve as patterns. That is why we retained Richards and Mandible and the others, and that is why our deployed counterparts have gone undetected.''

''Most of them. The Reed Richards duplicate failed.''

''Incorrect and irrelevant. It did its job. The data it relayed from Four Freedoms Plaza is proving invaluable.''

''Not irrelevant. Its discovery set our enemies on our trail.''

''True enough,'' the Thinker conceded. ''But the positive factors far outweigh the negative. The mutagenic formula that our agent provided is a close match to the biochemical residue I found in that hairy specimen you retrieved from Tibet. It is a catalytic agent of remarkable power. Judicious application of it will enable me to upgrade the elements of the Enforcement Unit by no less than seven hundred percent.''

''What about the material from Lifestream?''

''Adequate and useful, but far outclassed by what we have found elsewhere. The primary goal of that theft was to draw Richards's attention, however, so that we could capture him. In that, it was an unqualified success.''

''And, at least, we can still liquidate Richards, now that there is no longer a reason not to.''

For a long moment, the Thinker did not respond to the comment. Instead, he continued gazing at the monitor, watching as four human—or quasihuman—intruders battled the defending forces. Grimm and the two strangers were doing most of the fighting, and were hampered by the de-powered Johnny Storm in the midst. That much was fortunate, at least. Consideration for their powerless companion was slowing the invaders' progress considerably.

But not stopping it.

The Thinker decided that the time had come to tell Kragoff the rest of the bad news.

''Richards escaped our custody sixty-seven minutes and thirteen seconds ago,'' he said. ''He breached his cell, evaded the security forces, and exited the facility.''

The Ghost said some more things in Russian. He spoke rapidly and with great vehemence, pacing back and forth and gesturing angrily. The Thinker let the other man rant for forty-three seconds and then interrupted.

"I should inform you," he said, "that I speak Russian flawlessly, as I do all languages. Your comments do not please me."

The Ghost abruptly fell silent.

The Thinker forced back the fury he suddenly felt building inside him. He hated anger, as he hated all irrational things. "Another unforeseen development, and another unfortunate one, I concede," he said. He nodded again. "However, we had him long enough that his duplicate could perform its duties. We learned much in the time we had him."

"How much did he learn from us?" the Ghost asked angrily. "What does he know now?"

"Not enough. That base had not been brought fully online yet, and served primarily as a relay site for the data network. That, and the subspace transceiver were the only core systems up and running."

"If Richards knows anything, he knows too much," said the Ghost. He sounded fretful now. "Have we taken steps to apprehend him anew?"

"We don't need him. Additionally, appropriate assets are not available at the moment. I used a Enforcement Unit prototype to capture him originally. That prototype is back at the Arctic base now, undergoing modification with the rest of its fellows."

"What about the Guardsmen robots? Why not send them after him?"

The Red Ghost had an inappropriately demanding tone in his voice, but the Thinker decided to indulge him by responding. "The simulacra Guardsmen draw on localized broadcast power, like the authentic units. They can't leave the Rushmore base. That's one reason I elected not to use similar units at our other sites, and why I held that facility in reserve. Its primary purpose has always been to hold the various so-called super heroes after our designs have reached fruition." The Thinker smiled slightly. "The world will have little else to do with them then."

Kragoff grunted.

The Thinker continued, "Federal authorities will doubtless be on the site to investigate shortly. There is nothing there that should lead them to our other redoubts, but I am accelerating the schedule nonetheless. The mutagen our agent found in Richards's data files will save me months of work, but we have no more room in the schedule for unforeseen developments."

"What do you want me to do?" the Red Ghost asked. He tapped the nerve gun that hung at his side. "I could go after Richards, or join the battle against Grimm."

"No. Neither is necessary. They cannot stop us now. The crisis point is in only a few hours; after that, the trends we've set in motion will be unstoppable. Even if Grimm and his fellows prevail here, it will take more time than that to deal with what they find. By the time they discover the real Mandible and return him to his life, the false one will have done its work." The Thinker stepped to a control panel and began entering command sequences into the keyboard there. Typing was one of the few physical activities that gave him pleasure, and he had deliberately configured his computers to use a manual interface rather than a vocal or mental one. "I have some files on the network here that I would prefer remain mine alone. I will rendezvous with you at the Arctic base in four hours and three minutes, after I have dealt with them."

"Do you need a ride?"

"No," the Thinker said. He had kept much from Kragoff, chief among them the secret of his multiple bodies; his partner did not, could not know how easily the Thinker could leave this place. "I have my own methods. Gather up your pets and be on your way; time is short."

Not looking very happy about the situation, the Red Ghost shrugged his broad shoulders. His outline wavered slightly, and his colors paled almost imperceptibly as he went insubstantial. Gravity tugged him gently downward, through the command center's tiled floor and the support members that held it. In seconds, the Thinker knew, Kragoff would be on the New Jersey citadel's bottom level, near the holding pens for his bestial underlings and only seconds away from escape. That was good. The Russian had been very useful in the campaign thus far, and promised to have other uses in the future.

The Thinker paused in his typing long enough to access another video feed, one that he had not shown to the Ghost, lest he panic the Russian. The image displayed came from cameras in the South Seas island base, and it showed Susan Richards and her companions conversing with the prisoners his forces held there. That was bad news, bad enough to make a lesser mind feel fear. The South Seas installation was defended, true, and even now, security forces were on their way to deal with the intruders. However, the Fantastic Four's new allies had already demonstrated physical reourcefulness greater than he had anticipated, and it was safe to assume that the Invisible Woman's contingent was as good as that of Ben Grimm's odd little grouping.

The identities of those other costumed adventurers troubled the Thinker. He recognized Medusa from her stay with the Fantastic Four some years before, but why had she returned? And the others with her—who were they? How had they reached the South Seas site so quickly? Over the years, the Thinker had gathered tantalizing tidbits of data about another human race, a super-powered offshoot of *homo sapiens*. Supposedly, Medusa was a representative of that race; were these others more of their number? At any rate, their presence was yet another unanticipated development.

Unforeseen developments had a tendency to make the Thinker feel something remarkably like nervousness.

It was entirely too possible that Susan Richards would reach that distant site's command center, the equivalent of the room where the Thinker stood now. It would be the work of only a moment to beam his consciousness there and eliminate any secrets that were inappropiate for their eyes, but the impending setback still irritated him. If the invaders freed his prisoners on that island, they would almost immediately move them beyond range of the relays built into the prison walls. After that, three hundred and seven of his duplicates stationed in the Southern Hemisphere would immediately experience a ten percent degradation in their ability to play their parts. That deterioration would continue for several hours; some of the units would shut down completely. Even the ones that survived would soon be supplanted by the original individuals. Three hundred and seven of the Thinker's agents would be gone, replaced by those they had replaced. All he could hope for now was that his operatives had done their work sufficiently well already; obviously, they would serve him no more in the future.

His typing done, the Thinker settled into a comfortable chair and composed himself. This particular artificial body, like the one in the South Seas, included a self-destruct capability sufficient to reduce it to ash. He closed his eyes, and began the practiced sequence of mental exercises that would send his consciousness on its way. By the time the intruders found this room, he would be long gone, both in body and in mind. There was still much work to do, and he was running out of time.

Of course, according to his calculations, so was human civilization.

Reed Richards looked up as the odd-looking craft dropped out of the cloud-flecked afternoon sky and came to a perfect landing a hundred feet or so from Wendell Scheer's stationwagon. He was quite familiar with the *Whippet*, having contributed a bit of design work to its development. The ungainly vehicle looked something like a praying mantis with jet engines attached, with two oversized, supercharged turbines. They rotated on frictionless gimbals and could move though seventy degrees of arc. The ship's fuselage was studded with jointed landing gear that had a leglike appearance, and that could shift into a number of different configurations for vertical landings on irregular terrain.

As the *Whippet*'s turbines dropped into idle mode, its cockpit canopy slid back to reveal a freckled man with red hair who wore a distinctive, quasimilitary uniform.

"Someone call a cab?" the SAFE agent said, loud enough to be heard above the engines' now-muted roar.

"That would be me," Reed answered. He turned to face

Scheer. "Thanks again," he said. "You really didn't have to wait." He extended one hand.

Scheer shook it. "Don't be silly," he said. "The world owes you folks plenty, certainly much more than the use of a cell phone."

Reed smiled and nodded. "Well, all the same, thanks. I also appreciate your promise not to tell anyone what's going on."

Sheer made a twisted grin at the reference to the conversation he had overheard. "C'mon, who would believe me?"

Reed turned away. He stretched his legs to a length that would allow him to enter the *Whippet*'s cramped cockpit easily, and then slithered into the seat behind the pilot. As he strapped himself in, the SAFE agent passed him a leather folder containing credentials.

Reed looked at the ornate metal badge and the accompanying identification card. What he read startled him. He said, "I don't suppose you're any relation to—?"

The red-haired man shook his head. "Nope. Everyone asks that."

"It must cause some confusion for a man in your line of work, Agent Fury."

"That's an understatment," the pilot said. The canopy dome had clicked into place again, and power built in the *Whippet*'s engines. "And, please, call me Clyde. Even Colonel Morgan does."

"He's a practical man," Reed responded. "What has he told you?"

"I take you where you want to go, and I go there with you, no matter what."

"That last part may change," Mr. Fantastic said dryly. "But we can start with a trip to New York."

"Okay," Clyde said. He twisted a throttle and pulled the steering yoke back. In instant response, the *Whippet* threw itself upward. Accleration pushed both men back into their padded seats. The cockpit filled with a clattering noise as the jointed landing gear retreated to present a more aerodynamically efficient profile to the world. "Any particular address?"

The *Whippet* was moving faster now, upward and east,

moving so swiftly that the landscape below merged into a blur, all boundaries and definition lost as it faded into a single, greater whole. Reed watched the world race by as he responded. "Four Freedoms Plaza, to start with. I have some data that needs processing."

"Okay. I'll radio ahead for clearance now and get it out of the way," Clyde said. "The Big Apple's a madhouse today. The UN's got that Economics Council going." He picked up a microphone and began talking into it.

Reed barely heard him, still struck by his last words. His interests in current affairs related more to scientific developments than to politics or economics, but even he had heard of the planned international summit. Delegates from every UN member were expected to attend, along with guests from some nonmember lands, as the world's governments met to address the economic trends that would shape the next century. Today was the day that America's special representative was to address the Grand Assembly, and Reed found his mind suddenly filled with the possibilities that such an occasion presented.

Clyde had just returned his microphone to its rest. Reed reached forward, tapped him on the shoulder. "Better call back," he said. "Slight change of plans. We need to stop by the UN first."

CHAPTER 9

The horde of gorillas, orangutans, and baboons advanced toward the Thing and his companions, moving in a rough approximation of unison that seemed almost like an animal parody of military formation. One of the lead apes gestured, and a steel bar tore itself from a cell door and came whistling toward Karnak. It moved fast, but he moved faster; the diminutive Inhuman raised one hand in a sharp, hard-angled blow that struck the metal shaft precisely two inches past its midpoint. The force of the blow passed from his hand and into the steel, and resonated along the bar's length with exactly enough force to make the whirling chunk of metal shatter. Startled, the ape relaxed the magnetic waves it controlled and let the fragments of metal fall. By then, Karnak had turned his attention to other matters.

"They have the advantage of numbers," he observed to his companions. As he spoke, his left foot swung up in a high kick that intersected neatly with the chin of a baboon swinging from above by its prehensile tail.

"Tell me about it," Ben snapped. A gorilla had shouldered two of its fellows aside in a rush to get at him. Now the Thing accommodated the ape by driving his fist into its midsection, striking the super-strong simian with enough force to drive the air from the ape's lungs. "Must be two hundred here."

"I count one hundred and ninety-eight of them, sixty-six sets of three," Karnak continued. Gorgon had fallen, knocked down by two gorillas. Karnak went to his aid, delivering precisely placed karate chops to the back of the apes' skulls, rendering them unconscious.

"Whatever," Ben muttered. Another baboon bounced toward him, its plastic body twisting and flowing into a serpentine noose that moved toward his neck at great speed. Ben caught the animal before it could reach him, tied it into a knot, and threw it aside. The baboon chattered and shrieked as it went whirling away into the distance.

The four men had their hands full, especially the Thing, Gorgon, and Karnak. Stripped of his powers, Johnny was at a terrible disadvantage, and could do little more than keep out of his partners' way.

Ben had to wonder about that, even as he punched and smashed and pounded at the apes and monkeys surrounding him. Why had the Torch's powers failed? Why hadn't his own, or the Inhumans'? Words spoken to him by Reed—by the *real* Reed—only a few days before came back to him now. Reed had said that the changes the cosmic rays wrought on his body were actually less extensive than the ones that had turned Johnny into the Human Torch. Was that the explanation? Apparently something about this place was damping Johnny's power and not his own. He could understand why it didn't work on Karnak or Gorgon; their powers derived from another source, and had been honed by genetic manipulation and intensive training. Johnny's flame and his own strength had the same origin point, however, and it seemed to Ben that whatever canceled one should cancel the other. Or had Reed been right? Was he actually closer to base-normal human, and somehow below the threshold of the mysterious override?

"Look out, Ben," Johnny yelled from behind him, but words had less impact as a warning than as a distraction. Ben blinked and flinched, and let his guard down for a split second.

It was enough time to for another baboon to attack. The creature had turned itself into something like a carpenter's vise and it threw itself at the Thing's head now. It closed itself on his brow and clamped down. The pressure increased rapidly, and Ben could feel the orange scales of his body's outer skin split and crumble.

It hurt. It hurt a great deal, as a matter of fact, fast reaching levels of pain that he would have thought beyond a baboon's ability to inflict. Ben brought both hands up to get the monkey off his head. As he did, he dropped his guard and opened himself up for other attacks, but there was nothing to be done. If the baboon continued, there was a very real danger that his bones would start breaking next.

He clawed and he tore at the beast's pseudometal body and managed to dislodge its grip even as a pair of hairy fists slammed into his belly. A gorilla? Almost certainly, judging from the force of the blow, but Ben didn't look to check just yet. More pain, more shock, but he focused past them both and concentrated on ripping the baboon from his temples. The monkey squealed and began to revert to its base form, but before it finished, while it was still something very much like tool steel, Ben brought it down on the attacking gorilla's head. The anthropoid gave a muffled grunt and fell to the floor unconscious. Ben tossed the smaller, struggling baboon over his shoulder and returned to the fray.

"We cannot continue this for long," Gorgon said. As he spoke, the Inhuman brought one of this hooved feet down on the toes of an orangutan and then drove a big-knuckled fist into the ape's jaw. In his own way, he was nearly as strong as the Thing, but he was beginning to sound winded. "They will wear us down eventually."

"Yeah, I hear you talkin'," Ben said. He punched two gorillas on their chins as he reluctantly acknowledged the truth of his companion's words. There were just too many assailants. All that worked in his party's favor at the moment was these animals were not as good at armed assault as the Red Ghost's own Winken, Blinken, and Nod. Maybe Kragoff hadn't had time to train the carbon copies yet. On the other hand, with the odds at five-to-one, the attackers went a long way toward making up in numbers what they lacked in skill.

He looked around, desperately. The clawing, biting, fighting pack of primates had herded the quartet ten yards or so down one corridor, far enough to bring another pair of armored doors into view. He slapped down another orangutan and knocked two gorillas' heads together, then pointed at the portal. Whatever lay beyond it had to be better than what they faced now. "Gorgon! We need to make a break for it! Can you clear a path?"

Gorgon nodded. "Be prepared to move quickly," he told his companions. "Any respite this gains us will be brief."

"We'll move, we'll move," Ben said. "Just do it!"

Gorgon's left hoof came down hard, much harder than when he had broken the orangutan's toes. The corridor's floor shook and rippled, flexing like a snapped tablecloth as the shock waves flowed through it. The rippling wavefront swept out primarily in the direction that Gorgon had intended, down the corridor that led to the doors. Disoriented, the apes and monkeys in its path fell like tenpins in a bowling alley. They toppled into walls and against each other, and immediately began struggling to regain their feet. "Go now!" Gorgon yelled.

A too-long moment later, Gorgon and the Thing had torn the door open, then slammed it back shut behind them. Then came the struggle to hold the hinged slabs of metal in place and block out the sea of pursuers surging on the other side—not an easy task, since a third of those pursuers were super-strong gorillas. There had been no time to fumble with keypads or access codes; the act of forcing the door had snapped the thick bolts that held it shut. Gorgon and the Thing held it in place while Johnny and Karnak looked fruitlessly for some way to brace it.

"We—we could almost handle 'em in here," Ben said. They were in the anteroom for another wing of the prison, a relatively confined space. Beyond it, Ben could see still more corridors and jail cells, facing out to much higher ceilings.

However, these cells weren't empty.

"Help us! Please help us!"

"Save us!"

"Who are you? Please! Help!"

A cacophony of voices rang out as the prisoners in the cells shrieked and shouted, speaking in a dozen or more languages. A veritable forest of hands and arms reached from barred cell doors, waving like tree limbs in the wind as scores of prisoners pleaded for release. Footsteps pounded on hard floors and drinking vessels rapped against the doors' bars, making a cascading, clattering noise that almost drowned out the calls for aid.

Almost, but not quite.

Even as the din built to deafening levels, one voice seemed to separate itself from the wall of sound, cutting through the background noise, to reach Ben's ear with remarkable clarity. The words he heard were spoken in a familiar voice, and he glanced in their direction, only to realize with astonishment that they were spoken by someone he knew.

"Ben," a bedraggled Johnny Storm called, his boyish features framed by cruel iron bars. "Ben, thank God you're here! You've got to help me get out of here!"

Johnny? He had been at Ben's side only moments before. How had he gotten himself into this fix so quickly? Ben blinked in amazement, then blinked again as two costumed figures reentered the vestibule where he stood.

"We will have to make our stand here," Karnak said. "I had no luck finding a brace for the door."

"That's right," the flameless Human Torch said. "Nothing to be had."

Ben looked from the prisoner to him and then back again, twice. "What the—" he said softly. "How—"

The blue-clad figure standing beside Karnak followed Ben's line of sight, and saw what the Thing saw. He looked at the prisoner who wore his face, at the white-gloved hands that clawed the air futilely. Perhaps he heard the call for help in what should have been his own voice. The apparent Human Torch smiled slightly, and shrugged.

Several things happened then, so swiftly that they could not be separated into a clear-cut sequence:

One or more gorillas, perhaps several, pounded on the door behind Ben's and Gorgon's back, their combined impact enough to make even the braced metal tremble.

Ben now knew why "Johnny's" powers didn't work—because "Johnny" hadn't wanted them to. He realized how the facsimile Reed, with its hidden capabilities and booby traps, had gotten past Four Freedoms Plaza's complex security devices. Obviously, the Human Torch had let him in, by resetting the alarms and failsafes. Equally obviously, it hadn't been the real Human Torch who had done the job. It had been another duplicate, more precise than the Richards version, exact enough to fool even Karnak's enhanced senses.

Apish fists slammed into the metal barricade again. This time, when the metal trembled, as under assault by some other, less physical force. Magnetism?

"Johnny's" body burst into flames, the unstable molecule fabric of his costume boiling away and becoming part of his corona. The smile on the ersatz Human Torch's face became a smirk as Karnak stepped back in surprise.

"Johnny? What—?" the slender man in the green-and-white costume said. He had not seen the prisoner yet.

"Not Johnny," Ben said, through gritted teeth as the metal behind him twisted and bent, and as more thundering impacts resonated through it to reach him. "Not Johnny, just another crummy duplicate."

Gorgon's hooves, braced against the stone slab floor, dug deep groves in the rock and unrelenting force pushed them forward.

The metal doors, punished beyond endurance, ripped free of their frames, swept aside by animal muscle and magnetic force. The apish horde stormed the tiny space, driving Gorgon and Ben forward.

An ugly smile flowed across what looked like the Human Torch as the creature that had replaced Johnny Storm reached with flaming arms for the Thing.

"I just wish you would tell me why we're here," Clyde said to Reed. The two men were moving at something close to a run through a carpeted hallway on the seventh floor of the Grand Assembly building, fresh from a hectic hovercraft ride. "Colonel Morgan said to follow your lead—"

"Then follow it," Reed said, with uncharacteristic curtness. He was moving fast, but not as fast as he was able; partly out of consideration for the other man and partly because his elastic muscles still throbbed with fatigue, a memento of his escape from the Mount Rushmore prison. He was taking normal strides, not the seven-league steps that were his typical wont. His expression, though composed, seemed slightly distracted, as if he were considering issues beyond the SAFE agent's ken. "I don't have time to explain, and we have to get there at precisely the right—ah. *Now*." He came to an abrupt stop in front of a polished teak door, featureless except for a discreet number plate. This was the office that had been assigned to Conrad Mandible for use during the summit.

"Keep an eye on him, Clyde," Reed said. "He doesn't

leave unless I say he can leave.'' After Clyde nodded, Reed brought the knuckles of his left fist down on the door's glistening surface. Almost immediately, a trim young woman with neatly coifed hair opened the door.

Reed didn't bother to introduce himself, but let his famous uniform do the job. He had made a few calls while en route to resolve the logistics of his visit, and he didn't expect much trouble from the support staff. The woman smiled politely, but the expression didn't quite mask the tone of condescension in her voice. ''Oh, Dr. Richards,'' she said. ''Colonel Morgan told us you were on your way. Mr. Mandible has been waiting.'' She emphasized the last word and waved both men through the open door and into a medium-sized office that apparently did double duty as a waiting room for visiting dignitaries.

A rolltop desk stood in one corner, and framed paintings shared wall space with half a dozen television monitors. Each glass screen displayed the same image with a different network logo superimposed, a single shot of the UN Grand Assembly from a shared camera. A tall man stood near the desk, gazing at the screens.

''You'll have to be brief,'' the woman said, ''Mr. Mandible has a very busy schedule.'' As Reed and Clyde entered the office, she left them alone with the Special Economics Advisor to the President.

Mandible had silver hair and craggy features. He positively reeked of Old Money—tailored suit, a Yale class ring, and a gold signet with matching Rolex—with easy grace and effortless manners mingled with a faint air of constant, unwavering condescension. ''Richards,'' he said, extending his hand. Reed shook the hand once, released it. Mandible didn't seem to notice the SAFE agent who stood nearby, and focused instead on his more famous visitor. ''We just have a moment, I'm afraid. I'm only seeing you now at the President's personal request. I address the General Assembly in five minutes.''

''That's what we want to speak to you about,'' Reed said. ''The content of that address.''

Mandible looked at him and smiled slightly. ''I view economic policy as something close to a science, Dr. Richards, but I wasn't aware that it was one that you studied.''

This time, Reed smiled. ''I study almost everything,'' he said. ''Now, as to the content of that speech—''

''I really don't have time to discuss it in detail. If you'd like to meet afterward, we can talk then, but not now. You can watch the presentation from here if you'd like, or I can have Miss Jamison give you a copy of my notes.''

Richards shook his head. ''I don't have time, either, Mr. Mandible. You'll have to spare me a moment to answer a single question.''

Mandible nodded, then sighed. ''But it will have to be on the fly,'' he said, leaning down to pick up his briefcase. ''Can you walk with me?''

''No,'' the SAFE agent said. His hand hovered near his still-holstered sidearm. ''No, sir, we can't.''

Mandible looked at him, then at Richards. He set the briefcase down again. ''Ask,'' he said flatly.

''The world is at an interesting juncture just now, Mandible. Civil wars, new technologies, shifting political alliances. We're turning the corner on so many issues—but that could change. It's hard to imagine how much harm a single incautious remark could cause, especially here, with the whole world watching.'' Reed paused. ''Tell me, Mandible, what would happen if you were to announce that the U.S. government will seek to resolve its own financial difficulties by declaring a fifteen-year moratorium on all debt payments, to all creditors, regardless of whether public or private?''

Mandible tensed, and the red flush of anger colored his features. ''What you're suggesting is monstrous, absolutely monstrous. It wouldn't resolve anything, just create a shockwave that could effectively destroy the world economy. The President—Mister, the *United States of America* would never dream of doing such a thing!''

''I didn't ask what would happen if the United States did it,'' Reed replied, levelly. His expression was carefully attentive now, like a scientist watching an experiment run its course. "I asked what would happen if you were to make the announcement."

"Mandible" leapt at him.

There had been a time, not so very long ago, when Ben Grimm and Johnny Storm's friendly rivalry had expressed itself, not in verbal repartee, wisecracks, and japes, but in physical conflict. A rough equivalent of adolescent roughhousing, their good-natured tussling had done more than a little property damage, in the FF's headquarters and elsewhere, but had inflicted no real injury. Of course, that had been years ago, when both men had been younger, and before their powers had matured completely.

That was then; this was now.

A blast of white-hot plasma surged from the false Johnny Storm's fingertips and splashed against Ben's face. He ducked his head and closed his eyes just in time, but he could still feel the fire bathing him. He knew that even his super-tough skin could not last long against such an onslaught.

"Gorgon," he called. "You an' Karnak are gonna have to hold your own. I'll take care of this Johnny-come-lately." As he spoke, he tore a slab of stone from the flooring beneath his feet, raised it above his head, and threw it in the general direction of his ersatz teammate.

"You and what army, you ugly lump?" the Torch called back. The voice could have been Johnny's, and so could the words, the kind of invective that had been exchanged freely by the two over the years of their association. In the past, however, there had been some humor and even affection to undercut the venom.

There was none now.

The Torch dodged the chunk of rock and redirected his flame at it, which was what Ben had really wanted—something to draw the duplicate's fire. The stone exploded in midair and rained ash on the combatants, but Ben scarcely noticed. All around him, however, apes and monkeys shrieked in panic at the rampant flames. That was good, at least, Ben realized. If the anthropoid army continued to panic, Karnak and Gorgon might be able to last until he could finish with the fake Torch.

That looked like it might take a few minutes, however.

"C'mon down here an' fight like a man, ya crummy matchstick," Ben yelled at "Johnny," who was hovering just out of his reach. Instead of obeying, the Torch threw more gouts of plasma down at him. Ben dodged the first and the second, but the third caught him squarely in the chest, burning into and scarring the heavy orange scales there.

The pain of the flame blast lent fury to Ben's movements. Again he reached for the floor, and again he tore pieces free. This time they were broad, flat chunks, like flagstones. He brought the two rocks together in front of himself, fast and hard. They broke and crumbled under the impact, but not before finishing the job Ben had assigned them. Even as the stone fragments rained to the floor, the air that the two stones had displaced rushed out and up. The stones' legacy wasn't enough to snuff the Torch's flame, but the wall of wind did destabilize and make the fiery figure falter in its trajectory.

That was what Ben had wanted.

"Mebbe I ain't no Hulk," the Thing said, gathering his legs beneath him and tensing their muscles. "But I can jump with the best of 'em." He straightened his legs in a sudden, convulsive motion and reached up with his hands. A split second later, protected only by their own dense armor, his hands closed on the fake Torch's wrists.

At first, if felt as if he had tried to grab handfuls of the sun itself, so searing and penetrating was the heat. Then the pain faded slightly, as the seal his iron grip made around the flaming figure's form kept oxygen from reaching the Torch's skin, and snuffed the flames beneath his fingers. Those flames died, but only those; the fires that raged along the artificial creature's hand and forearm blazed unabated.

"Play with fire, you'll get burned, Thing," the false Torch said, even as the Thing and gravity dragged him back down.

"Don't care," the Thing mumbled. There was more pain, more flame as man and pseudoman struck the floor, and as the false Torch's fire stabilized again. All around him, the air was filled with the squeal of apes and monkeys, and the sound of flesh striking flesh. Karnak? Or were the apes fighting among themselves? Ben didn't know, and at the moment, he didn't care, either. Beneath his feet, shockwaves swept through what remained of the floor, doubtless the product of Gorgon's hooves, but Ben didn't care much about that, either. All that mattered was defeating whatever it was that had stolen his friend's face—and probably stolen his friend, too.

Ben threw his weight against the Torch, shouldering him into a nearby stone wall. The ersatz Johnny Storm struggled in his iron grip, but couldn't break free; apparently, he had none of the fake Reed's extra capabilities.

"Now who's not fighting fair?" the creature said with Johnny Storm's voice.

"Don't have to fight fair with somethin' like you," the Thing said, the words barely more than grunts. It was getting harder to maintain his grip. The scales on his hands were thick and tough, but they were beginning to break down as heat poured into him. "You don't deserve bein' fought fair," he continued.

One of the Thing's hands released its grip. With a liquid cry of delight, the Torch clawed for his face with blazing fingers. Again, Ben closed his eyes and again he ducked his head, so that the projecting ridge of his brow might give the rest of his face a moment's protection. With his now-free hand, he groped to his left, until his blunt fingers found what they sought.

Metal. An iron bar, part of a cell door, its coolness a welcome surprise as it conducted heat away from his smoldering palm and fingers. Grunting again, he tore the steel shaft free and raised it above his head like a caveman's club.

Instantly, the Torch quit clawing at his face.

"Let's see how tough you really are," Ben said.

"Don't do it, Ben, please," the familiar voice said, so desperate that Ben opened his eyes in response. The figure he held was no longer flaming, and Johnny Storm's eyes stared at him from Johnny Storm's face, and Johnny Storm's voice burst from Johnny Storm's lips. "You'll kill me!"

He was right, Ben realized grimly. The fury driving him

now was enough to make him kill, almost enough to make him enjoy it. He almost didn't care. Fury and disgust roiled in him, and contempt at the false Torch for this final desperate ploy. Two close friends had been taken from him and imprisoned or worse, and someone had to pay for those crimes.

He drew the club back even further.

"You'll kill me," he captive repeated, genuine terror in its stolen voice.

"No, he won't," someone else said from behind the Thing, in the same voice as the being before him.

Johnny's voice.

Startled, Ben turned. To his astonishment, he saw that the real Torch was free now, the lock on his cell shattered, presumably by Karnak. His incandescent figure stood less than twenty feet away.

"Put him in there, Ben," Johnny said. He gestured at what had been his cell. "Something about the cell snuffs my power. It should do the same to him."

What felt like his first smile in days spread across the Thing's craggy features. Like a child might treat a rag doll, he threw the fake Torch from him. The creature's blue-suited body burst into flame again as he was released, but the effect was too little, too late. Momentum carried the fake Johnny Storm into the cell, and the new flames died instantly.

"Some kinda power dampin' whatsis in there," Ben observed. "Like the one Doom used on Reed a coupla months ago."

Johnny nodded, but didn't say anything as he welded the cell door shut. His duplicate was equally silent, and glowered wordlessly at the two men.

"Wondered about that guy for a while," Ben said gruffly. He watched the real Torch finish his work. "Seemed too smart to be you."

"Har har," replied the authentic Johnny Storm. "I missed you, too."

"Yeah, well," the Thing said awkwardly. He looked around himself. The hallway was littered with unconscious apes, and dozens of prisoners stood at their cell doors, apparently dazed by the battle they had just witnessed. One section of hall was penned off by a lattice of flame, apparently more of Johnny's work, and frightened anthropoids looked out from behind it. In a corner, Karnak and Gorgon spoke softly to one another.

"It's good to see ya, matchstick," Ben said. "How'd you get here, anyway? We were looking for Reed."

"It's a long story," Johnny said. "About a lunch date that I kept with the wrong person, and about another guest that crashed the party. I've been here ever since."

"Huh. There's got to be more to it than that."

Johnny smiled. He shrugged. He pointed at another prison cell. "You don't believe me," he said, "ask her."

"Hello, Mr. Grimm," the real Jenna Villanueva said. "Nice to see you again, I guess."

The Thing looked at the Torch, genuinely impressed. "Even in jail, you find a girl," he said sourly.

"I try, Ben, I try," Johnny said, then his grin faded and he suddenly looked much older. "Now, what's this about Reed?"

Lockjaw growled softly as the robots marched in perfect formation through the open doors and toward his Inhuman masters and the lone member of the Fantastic Four who was with them. There were approximately fifty of them, all with gleaming metal surfaces, all with blunt-fingered hands and faceplates cast in a grim parody of human features.

Sue had seen robots like these before, even if the others had not. The shining death machines were similar to ones that the Thinker had deployed against the Fantastic Four long years before. The similarity was so precise, in fact, that she took it as the final piece of evidence she needed to change her mental label of the Thinker from *suspect* to *culprit*. Whatever was going on here, it had to be the enigmatic mastermind's handiwork. The truck hijacking in New York, the elaborate program of abduction and replacement, the vast facility here, and the army of death marching toward her now—they were all clues that pointed at a very specific individual, one who supposedly was languishing in a Colorado jail cell even now. Suddenly, she wished she had taken Ben's approach first.

But if they had, she realized, they might never have found these poor people.

"These units are dangerous," she warned her companions as the first line of attack came closer. "We have to take them down, and fast."

"Agreed," Medusa said. One of the robots turned at the sound of her voice and sprayed fire from its eyes. Medusa dodged the twin beams of incandescent energy and leaned closer to the humanoid machine. The robot fired again, and she drove one booted heel into the joint of its left ankle, making it stumble slightly so that the death-beam went wild and missed Medusa. As the automaton kept moving, a tendril of her scarlet locks extended itself and found a joint in the mechanical man's exoskeleton, slipped inside, then flexed. A second later, something inside the robot clicked and its joints locked, and then it pitched forward and fell on the floor, motionless.

"Their internal workings seem relatively simple, however, at least by the standards of their kind," Medusa observed. "If anyone else is interested, their central relay switches are in the upper thorax."

"Hey, watch where you point that thing," Fred Raven's angry voice rang out.

Sue turned to see what he was talking about, and understood instantly. The blast that hadn't struck Medusa had struck Raven's cell, searing through the upper bars of the door and scarring the space's gray stone walls. The talk show host had thrown himself from the path of the beam, but she knew full well he could not count on dodging subsequent volleys.

Nor could the other prisoners, Sue realized.

"Sue, watch out!" Medusa called.

She turned back just in time to see one robot's oversized hands lash out in her direction. Instinctively, Sue threw a bubble of invisibility energy around the thing's head and then contracted it. The metal cranium collapsed with gratifying immediacy. "We've got to be careful of collateral damage."

"Agreed," called Triton, to her left. Though not in his preferred environment, the aquatically adapted Inhuman was still a force to contend with. Inhumans in general were stronger than humans, and a literal lifetime of swimming the world's seas, even in crushing pressures, had built up Triton's strength still more. Also, he was a skilled fighter himself, a veteran of many battles, and knew how to use his magnificently conditioned body to best effect. Now, he drove the heel of one hand into a robot's jaw, hard enough to stagger it, and stepped from its path as it stumbled past him. As it lurched by, Triton smashed one elbow into the back of its metal skull and knocked the thing the rest of the way to the floor. "Perhaps you can deal with that, Sue?" As Triton spoke, he jumped up and came down with both feet on the robot's back. The mechanical man convulsed once, then fell still.

"Yes, I think so," the Invisible Woman said. She sent waves of energy out once more, extending them farther than before, encompassing a greater volume. Another mental command, and the energy solidified, condensing into a wall of force that hung, invisible, scant inches from the barred doors of the inmates' cells. "I can protect them for as long as it takes," she continued, "but I can't be much help otherwise while I'm doing it. The field will drop if I lose concentration."

"Keep it up for another moment," Medusa said. "But be ready to reconfigure the field quickly." She had toppled another robot, this time by tripping it, and watched with grim satisfaction as Triton smashed its skull. Medusa dodged another ray blast and looked in the direction of her husband and liege. "Black Bolt is almost ready."

Sue looked in the same direction. Black Bolt, the unspeaking leader of the Inhumans, stood apart from his fellows. A look of intense concentration was on his face and the air around him seemed to waver and dance, like the haze that forms above heated roadbeds on a summer day.

Sue knew what was going to happen then, and prepared herself.

Triton and Medusa continued fighting the robots, but less to destroy them than to keep them from reaching Sue and Black Bolt. They dodged energy beams, pounded on the robots, and tricked the automatons into lashing out at each other more than once. Lockjaw helped, too, herding the humanoid machines toward the two fighters, unmindful of the blows they rained upon him. It wasn't as difficult as it should have been; as Medusa had noted, these were simple things, relatively speaking, and many generations older than any the Thinker was likely to create now. They relied on brute force, not cunning. Metal fists lashed out and energy beams seared the prison air, but to remarkably little sum effect. Nearly a fifth of the robots had already fallen when Medusa yelled another command.

By then, too, the haze surrounding Black Bolt had coalesced into a crackling nimbus of energy around the antenna on his forehead.

"Sue," she called. "Now!"

The Invisible Woman flexed a few mental muscles. The force field that hung before the hapless prisoners' cells collapsed as she recalled its energy. Instead, she swiftly constructed a smaller, denser field that surrounded the remaining robots, and opened an aperture in it that faced Black Bolt. Even as she created the gap, a stabbing lance of energy seared through it, bathing the host of robots in a blinding radiance.

Black Bolt had many apparent powers, Sue knew, but most of them involved the manipulation of electron flow. He could harness the power of that fundamental particle to a wide variety of effects, ranging from elaborate matter manipulation to wholesale destruction. Now, he contented himself with a pulsing burst of phased electrons that fanned out as it penetrated Sue's force field. It became a coursing, rippling curtain of energy that lit the robots' brutish forms and made sparks dance along their contours. It built in intensity, becoming bright enough that the robots were hard to see, and then faded.

When it was gone, the robots remained, but were unmoving.

Sue dropped the force field. "Erased their operating system software, I assume?"

Black Bolt gestured and Medusa nodded. "Similar to what he did to the facsimile Reed in New York," she said. "They will trouble us no more."

Sue stared down at the unmoving forms. "Okay," she said.

"But there might be more. We need to get these people out of here. Medusa, can you see to them?"

"I'll look for exits," Triton said.

Sue nodded. "Good. Then Black Bolt and I can look for Reed."

As Mandible leapt at Reed, he changed. The skin of his face and hands flushed and grew more taut; and his bodily contours changed subtly, noticeable even beneath the drape of his tailored suit, as if muscles were finding new configurations. Even the bones of his body seemed to reshape themselves, his arms and legs became longer, growing an inch or two beyond the cuffs of his shirt and trousers.

Whatever was happening, Reed didn't like the looks of it. As he extended his own legs and writhed out of Mandible's path, he shouted a warning. "Clyde, be careful, he's shifting into some kind of overdrive!"

The fingers of Mandible's left hand, longer and needle-pointed now, grazed the skin of Reed's neck, just below the line of his jaw. Reflexively, Mr. Fantastic stretched a bit more, moving away from the pointed digits. As he dodged, he re-shaped his own right hand into a blunt mass, expanding his palm and wrist, contracting his fingers until they were scarcely visible. The bone and muscle of his right arm suddenly went flexible, then stretched and flowed, swinging up and around like a tentacle. A split second later, the club that Reed Richards had made of his right hand smashed down against the back of Mandible's skull.

The ersatz economics advisor scarcely seemed to notice the impact. The force of his leap still carrying him forward, he drew his arms and legs close to his body. He hit the floor and somersaulted, moving forward in a rolling tumble in the general direction of the door.

Clyde, raising his energy pistol, yelled, "He's trying to escape!"

He was wrong.

Mandible came out of his somersault as he reached the closed door. His feet lashed out and smashed into the polished wooden slab. Kicking hard, he leaped backwards in an impossible backflip that threw him in the SAFE agent's direction. Whatever it was that served him as bone and muscle flexed and bent until his head spun backward and he faced his target.

Clyde's finger tightened on his weapon's trigger.

Mandible's arms twisted around now, spinning into sockets that were suddenly many times more flexible than those of an ordinary human being. The fingers of one hand clamped tightly down on Clyde's right wrist.

Clyde gave an involuntary cry of pain and shock as Mandible's sudden grip wrenched his gun hand around to a new target. Even as Clyde squeezed the trigger, even as he realized Mandible's intentions, the gun fired, spitting white-hot energy plasma, at Reed Richards.

Mr. Fantastic stretched out of the ray's path before it could sear him. He stretched some more, extending the fingers of his hands into long, looping tentacles that dug deep into the muscular contours of Mandible's body and grabbed him. "I've got him, Clyde," Richards said.

In instant response to the words and the attack, Mandible's head spun on its mooring once more, this time to face Richards. The dignified features smiled, revealing flawless teeth that suddenly looked much sharper than they had before.

The exposed teeth began to grow.

Mandible's fingers flexed again, further bending the wrist they held. There was a popping noise. Clyde gave another cry of pain as his own fingers went limp and his pistol fell to the floor.

Reed yanked back, pulling Mandible toward him and away from Clyde. Far from resisting, Mandible cooperated, adding the power of his own muscles to Reed's efforts. He threw himself at Mr. Fantastic, his mouth opening wider and wider. Reed tumbled back, stretching and flowing to evade him, but now Mandible was clawing at him. Mandible had some leverage, and the advantage of surprise that his sudden reconfiguration had given him. Sharp fingers dug into the flesh of Reed's shoulders, and sharper teeth sought his throat.

Reed released his grip, flattened his hands against Mandible's chest, and shoved. It didn't do any good. Whatever Mandible's other attributes, he had some measure of enhanced strength, and was absolutely willing to use it. Already, he held Reed's shoulder's so tightly that Mr. Fantastic was effectively unable to ooze from his grasp. Now, Mandible's jaw distended even more, and glistening droplets formed on his exposed teeth. Some of them flowed and merged, then dropped from the tip of one pointed canine. The bead of liquid fell. It found the carpet, ate a hole through it, then kept eating a path into the flooring below.

Reed tensed the muscles of his forearms, shoved again. This time, it did some good, but not enough; the best he could do was slow Mandible's advance. He reshaped the muscle and bone of his legs, brought them up and under his attacker. It was hard to get any purchase, though, and Mandible was bearing down on him with greater and greater strength. Reed felt the other man's muscles tense, as if for an even greater effort.

A flash of light and a buzzing noise filled the room, followed by the smell of something burning. The hands digging deep into Richards's shoulders clutched more tightly, and then released. Mandible reared back, convulsed, and fell. As he fell, the ferocious expression on his patrician features faded, and the lines of his body shifted once more. By the time his now-limp form struck the floor, he once again looked precisely like the President's Special Economics Advisor.

Rather, he looked like the Special Economics Advisor would look, if he had a hole burned through his chest.

Reed looked at Clyde. "Nice shooting," he said.

White-lipped with pain, the SAFE agent nodded. His right hand still hung limply from a broken wrist, but the fingers of his left gripped his government-issue energy pistol. "Good thing I'm ambidextrous," he said grimly.

Reed nodded. He reached for Mandible's briefcase. "Will you be okay by yourself for a few minutes?" he asked.

"By myself?" Clyde repeated. He shook his head. "If you go, I go with you. Morgan's orders."

Reed had opened the briefcase and found Mandible's text. He read it hastily, and realized without any great surprise that his guess about the speech's content had been correct. He looked up from the papers and shook his head. "We're running out of time," he told the SAFE agent. "UN Security will need some questions answered. You need medical attention for that wrist, and I need someone to keep any eye on this—" he paused, "this *thing* until I can send someone for it. I'll square things with your boss."

Clyde looked at the still form sprawled on the office floor. He nodded, then sat in one of the guest chairs. "Can do," he said, and trained his energy pistol on the facsimile Mandible. "Don't want any more surprises."

"Good," Reed said. "I'll take the *Whippet*. You can pick it up at Four Freedoms Plaza later." He looked at what was left of the false Conrad Mandible. "I just hope they aren't all this tough," he said.

Clyde nodded, but didn't take his eyes from his gun's target. There was no sense in taking chances.

"I was on *Incredible Disasters*?" Jenna said. She sounded surprised, but pleasantly so. "I got assigned to cover an economics council at the *UN*?"

"Well, sort of," Johnny responded. He had helped the others free the prisoners from their cages. Now, Ben was at the Fantasti-Car arranging for the conventional authorities to take charge of the erstwhile captives, and the two Inhumans were exploring the remainder of the complex. So far, the news was bad: no sign of Reed, and a dozen or more computers with wiped hard drives. Whoever had created this place had left very few clues behind.

As for himself, he was still trying to digest Ben's update of a very complex situation, and he was also taking a moment to talk with the one of those prisoners whom he knew personally.

Jenna looked at him, a baffled expression on her tired features. Her time behind bars had done little to abrade her natural beauty. White teeth flashed as she looked at Johnny skeptically and repeated his words. "Sort of?" she asked.

"Well, it wasn't you," Johnny answered, feeling both awkward and confused. "What's the last time you remember seeing me?"

"We had lunch at that dreadful Coffee Bean place."

"We had lunch twice after that, and dinner, too. Or I guess we didn't. That must have been your substitute." Johnny paused a moment, thinking. "What was the last thing you remember before coming here?"

"Someone mugged me outside the studio. He was a weird looking guy, bald with white sidewalls, and the gun he had looked like some kind of kid's toy. He pointed it at me, I woke up here. Those horrible gorillas kept bringing me meals, but no one—not even the other prisoners—had any idea why we were here or who had taken us."

"That was the Red Ghost who mugged you," Johnny said. "He was waiting for me in Erol's Tea Room, too."

"Huh?"

"Never mind. I'll tell you about it later." Johnny smiled. "Maybe over lunch?"

"Well, I don't know what my calendar is like for next week," Jenna started to say, but someone interrupted her.

"Hey! Hotshot! You an' the cutie cut out the mushy stuff," the Thing said. "We gotta get goin'." He nodded at Jenna and pantomimed tipping a hat that he wasn't wearing at the moment. They had met before, during the same midair rescue that had brought her and Johnny together. "Ms. V., if you don't mind, I'll ask you to wait upstairs with the others. There's a flock'a SAFE agents on their way to debrief you folks, an' start straightenin' things out." He paused. "I think that's gonna take a while."

"SAFE?" Jenna asked.

"They'll explain that, too," the Thing assured her. He glanced at the Torch again. "Feel up to a trip, squirt?"

Johnny nodded. "You couldn't make me stay behind," the Torch said. "Where are we going?"

"This place is like Disneyland," Ben responded. "Another ride behind every corner. There's a tunnel connecting it to Manhattan, an' another connecting it to a rocket launch pad about a mile east. Karnak and Gorgon are waiting for us there."

"A rocket launch pad? In New Jersey?"

"Yup. A little one, disguised as a tank farm. Some kind of suborbital personnel missile. Spaces for two of 'em, but one's gone. I figger the site manager here took it. Prolly Kragoff. He likes rockets almost as much as he likes apes."

"And boobytraps, don't forget."

Ben nodded. "I didn't. He gimmicked the control surfaces so that the buggy would go off course in a hurry an' crash. I ungimmicked 'em." The amiable tone left his voice. "It's preprogrammed with launch coordinates that match the third site that the fake Reed was yakkin' at. Whoever was here is there now, an' we'll be there, too."

"Yeah, but where are we going?"

"North."

"Move carefully, now, please," Sue said. "No crowding, there's plenty of room."

The tide of humanity moved past her, obedient but eager to reach the outside. Ten minutes of searching had found an exit from the South Seas citadel, a broad passageway and staircase that led outdoors. The prison proved to be a multilevel complex that sprawled incongruously in a semitropic paradise of palm trees and coconuts. At first, she had been reluctant to escort her charges from their cages, knowing that she would have to leave them outside unattended, but she and the Inhumans had decided that the erstwhile prisoners were safer at liberty than they were indoors. All around her now, men and women blinked as they saw the sun again, and breathed deeply of the fresh air. A single look at their smiling faces proved to her satisfaction that she had made the right decision.

She just wished Reed's face were among the ones she saw now.

"What's next, lady?" Fred Raven said testily. "You aren't gonna just leave us here, are you?"

"That's exactly what I'm going to do, Mr. Raven," Sue said, almost pleased to realize that she disliked the real radio host as much as she had disliked his substitute. "The weather is nice, there's potable water in the pond," she continued, pointing at the tranquil body of water. "I wouldn't advise you going back inside unless a storm comes up, though.'' She was reasonably certain that last of the jailhouse robots had been destroyed, but there was no need to tempt fate. ''We'll send someone for you soon, I promise.''

''That—that's not what I meant,'' Raven said, suddenly unsure of himself. ''I guess I meant, what happens next?'' He paused, and when he spoke again, there was a tremor in his voice. ''How do we get our lives back?''

Sue looked at him, then at the others. She looked at men and women who had been held prisoner for periods that ranged from days to years, at over three hundred interrupted lives. She saw the questioning look in their eyes, and realized that she had no answer. ''I don't know,'' she said. ''We'll do everything we can to help, I promise you, but I don't have an easy answer to that question.''

There was another question that begged answering too. Even if no one had voiced it specifically, she knew that it was on everyone's mind.

How many other sites like this were scattered across the world?

Raven didn't say anything more, but her honesty had apparently satisfied him. He just looked at her sadly, and trudged off to join the other freed prisoners. They muttered and whispered among themselves, and Sue suddenly felt a need to give them their privacy again.

Medusa gave her the opportunity. ''Sue?'' she said, framed in the citadel's exit. ''I think we're ready.''

The two women went back inside, heading back toward its center. After defeating the robots but before freeing their captives, the search party had quickly explored the installation. They had found other cells, empty and occupied, and kitchens and food storage spaces. Apparently, the security robots had done double duty as chefs and servers.

The place's lowest floor had proved to hold the prize, however, a compact command center filled with computers and data processors. The others were there now, and looked up from their work as Medusa and Sue returned.

''Nothing,'' Triton said. ''Someone or something has wiped

the files, and recently. There are no clues here that I can find."
Black Bolt nodded in agreement, and Sue's heart sank.

What now?

Lockjaw whined. His nose twitched as he sniffed at something Sue had noticed earlier. It was a pile of ashes, the only untidiness that she had seen in the prison's almost antiseptic environment.

"What is it?" she asked.

Lockjaw whined again. A nimbus of energy began to form around the antenna on his brow, a sure sign that he wanted to depart.

"He has caught a scent," Medusa said.

The Inhumans' giant dog had almost preternatural tracking powers, Sue knew, powers that stretched across even interdimensional distances. But what trace had he found now? Reed's? Or one belonging to whoever had taken him?

There was only one way to find out.

"Quickly," she said, stepping close to the dog. The others joined her almost immediately. "Let's see where he takes us."

Then the world disappeared again.

Doug Deeley was waiting for Reed, standing beside a hovercraft he had parked on Four Freedoms Plaza's rooftop landing pad. The vehicle was a small one, and left plenty of space for the *Whippet* to land. Even as that craft's canopy slid back and Reed exited, a sliding trapdoor near Deeley's feet opened. It revealed a short flight of stairs that led to the Fantastic Four's top-floor hangar. Deeley was on the first of those steps even before Reed was on the second.

"Hello, Doug," Mr. Fantastic said. "I assume Morgan briefed you."

Deeley nodded. "Sure did. Seems hard to believe, though. That wasn't you they brought home from Denver a few days ago?"

"No," Reed said. "Any word on the others? I couldn't raise them on the communicators, and it doesn't look like anyone's home."

"No idea where they are, sir. Mrs. Richards called the colonel earlier, asked some questions he didn't like much. That's the last I've heard.''

Reed nodded. By now, he had reached a computer terminal, one of literally hundreds scattered throughout the Fantastic Four's headquarters. He tapped keys and opened files. "Gone, and it looks like they didn't go alone," he said, answering his own question. "Left a note, though. They went to New Jersey—"

"New Jersey?" Deeley interrupted.

"—and the South Seas." Reed spoke in clipped tones as he reviewed the data displayed on his screen. "Reasonable choices, even logical ones, since they were looking for me and had to go where there was the most activity." He tapped some more keys. "Not the right choice, though," he said. He looked up at the SAFE agent. "Most times, you want to go with anomaly. It's the discrepant member of a given set that offers the most promise."

"I don't know what you mean, but it sounds to me like they were more worried about finding you than about finding whoever is behind this."

"Good point," Reed said. A CD-ROM drive on the computer opened itself and he put the disk he had recorded in Mount Rushmore into it. Reed pushed an ENTER key and pointed at the computer's screen, even as a scrolling list of names began to fill it. "When this is done running, you need to take the results to Colonel Morgan. It should take about twenty minutes to run the search. The computer can give you a file version and hard copy. Guard them both with your life."

"What am I guarding? That is, if I'm cleared to know." Deeley said the words with no trace of humor or sarcasm, only honest curiousity.

"I started work a couple of days ago on an application that would apply statistical projection principles to pseudochaotic events, like human society."

" 'Pseudochaotic'?"

"I'll explain later, and it doesn't matter right now. Basically, I'm doing what the Thinker did, but I'm doing it in reverse, tracing events to their causes. It's always easier that way. The computer is running that program against the list of sites that I appropriated at the Thinker's South Dakota hide-away, and against an international telephone number database and news media files. You should end up with a list of individuals who have," he paused, "perhaps a seventy percent likelihood of being among his agents. Not certain, but it will have to do."

"World leaders? Scientists? Political thinkers?"

"Mostly not, no. Leaders have less power than most people realize, Doug, and the so-called little people have more. Look at the impact a garbage strike can have on society, or on the local economy. Think about how many lives were impacted by that traffic jam, when the ChemCo truck burned. That happened partly because some clerk didn't get the proper permits or the appropriate containers to ship hazardous chemicals. Think how many appointments were missed, how many deliveries weren't made, how many chance enounters just didn't happen—and how many did. Little things add up. Raindrops wash away mountains, given enough time."

"Oh-kay," Deeley said, plainly skeptical. "And these raindrops you're listing—we alert the appropriate authorities and arrest them, right?"

"Absolutely not," Reed responded. He had moved away from the terminal now and was opening an equipment cabinet that ran along the far wall. Deeley had to move quickly to keep pace with him. "A government agency, arresting individuals in all walks of life, without any apparent reason? That could cause a social shockwave, and do the Thinker's work for him. Keep an eye on those people, but keep it secret, and don't move unless you absolutely have to."

"Like you did with Mandible?"

"You heard about that?" Reed said, and he pulled item after item from the open cabinet and stowed them in a padded case. "Good. Exactly like I did with Mandible. Wait until you can't wait any longer, but act before they do." He snapped the case shut and opened a drawer. Half a dozen pairs of white gloves lay inside. Reed peeled off the gloves he wore and replaced them. He closed the drawer again.

"What are you going to do?" Deeley said. Already, Reed was taking long strides away from him, toward another hangar bay, deep in shadows. "Try to round up the others?"

"No," Reed said again. "No time for that. Besides, the way these things work, they'll probably be waiting for me when I reach the Arctic."

"Arctic?" Deeley repeated the word, puzzled. He didn't sound as if he liked being puzzled.

"The Thinker's main base, I think. Kragoff's, too, I suppose, but he's obviously a junior partner in this exercise." Reed pushed some buttons and a different section of roof slid open. Daylight spilled in, illuminating a silvery, disk-shaped craft resting on stubby legs. It was thirty or more feet in diameter, and its smooth contours were almost featureless, marred only by a few, almost invisible seams and joints.

"That's a flying saucer," Deeley said, genuine delight pushing puzzlement aside as he got his first look at the exotic vehicle. "I mean, it's really a flying saucer. Where did you get a flying saucer?"

The dome-shaped canopy split into sections and retracted. The craft hummed, but only faintly, as hidden engines came to life. "Spoils of war," Reed said, "from one of the Fantastic Four's first cases. A group of Skrulls wanted to take over Earth. We convinced them not to." He stretched up and into the vehicle. "It's the best tool for this job, though."

"A flying saucer, from outer space," the SAFE agent repeated softly. He was a former test pilot and obviously held a soft spot for flying machines. "I've never ridden in a flying saucer."

"Maybe next time," Reed said. "Just make sure you get that list to Morgan."

The canopy sections slid back into place and the craft's stubby legs retracted into its fuselage. Even without them to hold it, the disk-shaped vehicle remained where it was, several feet above the hangar floor. Then several feet became many, and the faint hum became a louder one. The Skrull flying saucer moved upward, through the open roof, and into the sky.

Moving north and moving fast, it was lost to view in seconds.

Morrie Kalman moved his computer's mouse to the left, and its cursor mirrored the motion until it rested on the icon he had selected, a hard-to-read little ''B,'' surrounded by a checkerboard pattern that was supposed to suggest a net, but that looked more to Morrie like the decorative border on certain comic book covers of his youth. Obediently, the computer pulled up a sign-on screen, already filled in with his name. Morrie took his hand from the mouse and used the computer's keyboard to enter his password. A half-dozen asterisks appeared, an internal modem made its *boop-boop-boop* noise, and then the sign-in screen gave way to precisely what Morrie had not wanted to see.

NAME OR PASSWORD INCORRECT, the computer told him, PLEASE TRY AGAIN.

Morrie said a bad word in Yiddish. His facility for his parents' language was limited, and three-quarters of it was curses, but he had been making much use of that limited vocabulary of late. ''Still can't get in,'' he continued. ''Three days, and I can't get into BizNet!'' The company he named was one of the new specialty Internet service providers, specializing in high-tech companies. Morrie himself was an entrepreneur, a niche marketer who sold a variety of specialized products, and whose business had been one of BizNet's first customers.

''I called Tech Support a dozen times,'' his personal assistant said. Her name was Kim Ryan, and she was a trim little woman whose blonde hair came from a bottle but whose green eyes seemed to come from heaven. ''They confirm your password and account, and they say nothing's wrong at their end. They say you should try again.''

''What are they saying to umpty-thousand other customers who call to make the same complaint?'' Morrie asked, his voice rising.

Kim shrugged her perfect shoulders. ''Dunno,'' she said. ''But that's their story, and they're sticking to it. I talked with Carmine Hamilton himself.''

Morrie shook his head in amazement—only Kimmie would take a complaint about a *faklempt* password to the head of the company—as he stared blackly at the screen confronting him.

"Hey, don't burst a blood vessel, chief," Kim said. "I have calls out to all the other Internet providers, and they say they can have us up and running in hours. All we have to do is choose."

"I did choose," Morrie snapped, genuine anger in his voice, an emotion that was unusual for the gregarious little man. "I chose BizNet. I got a dozen technology exchange accounts that they service, and their e-mail address is on all my business cards. Kimmie, the business we're in relies on trends, and we can't afford to lose three days just because some dope screwed up a line of code!" He pointed at a brightly colored carton sitting on his cluttered desk. "I got a hundred thousand supersonic, olive oil emulsifiers sitting in a warehouse, and another hundred thousand on their way to customers. I can't access the orders for the ones I have, and I can't bill for the ones I've shipped. What the heck am I supposed to do? What the heck is America supposed to do, for cryin' out loud?"

"Calm down, for starters," Kim said. "Your competitors are in the same boat. And a lot of them ship stuff that's more important," she paused and Morrie shot her a glance freighted with meaning, then continued, "*even* more important than the Emulsitron 3000."

Morrie Kalman went back to scowling at the uncooperative computer. "I could learn to hate technology," he said softly.

"You're not the only one," Kim replied.

hardly regard this as an unforeseen development," the Red Ghost was saying. Anger, confusion and his own thick Russian accent lent an odd cadence to his words. He was in the command center of the Thinker's Arctic facility, surrounded by banks of equipment and display. He had arrived there via shuttle rocket two hours before, only to find the Thinker already waiting for him. That had been a surprise, and not entirely a welcome one. The ease and speed with which his partner moved from site to site baffled and annoyed the Russian, and he had commented on it more than once. "The New Jersey facility is a complete loss. The real Torch and the real Reed Richards are both at large, and even Grimm must have some idea now of what we are doing. And now, this!"

The Thinker ignored him, something he had been doing more and more of late. Instead, he gazed thoughtfully at an array of nine television monitors displaying the feed from surveillance cameras stationed at various points within the facility. Seven showed winding, empty corridors, hewn from living rock and lit by recessed lamps. They connected various storage areas and laboratory facilities that the Thinker had constructed beneath the frozen tundra, with great difficulty and at even greater expense. One screen showed a secured cage immediately adjacent to the Thinker's genetics research laboratory. The cage's sole occupant looked something like a man and something like one of Kragoff's pets, and the creature stared somberly back at the Thinker from the viewscreen. The Thinker had the distinct and unsettling feeling that the specimen Kragoff had retrieved from Tibet knew that it was being watched, and was doing its best to watch back. This wasn't the first time the pseudo-Yeti had surprised him, over and above the mysterious substance he had found hidden in its cellular structure. More than once, the captive had exhibited distinct signs of human-level intelligence, but a complete unwillingness to communicate, no matter what the impetus the Thinker applied—and he had applied many.

That didn't matter just now, however. What showed in the ninth screen monitor did.

Two of the Fantastic Four, the Thing and what was apparently the real Human Torch, were making their way along the perimeter corridors, accompanied by their outré companions. They were less than three sections from the main passageway that led directly to this command center. The facility was divided into seven sectors, arbitrarily tagged for reference purposes with the various colors of the spectrum. Grimm and company were in Sector Blue, the transport station, where their commandeered rocket shuttle had landed seventeen minutes and thirty-four seconds before, and they were making good time as they explored his facility. The Thinker had been monitoring their progress quite carefully since becoming aware of their presence.

That presence did not please him, but that was not what irked him most. His utmost concern was now that two of his greatest enemies had found this hidden redoubt, which had taken him so long to design and provision.

"You were to disable the second shuttle," he finally said, if only to shut up the still-babbling Red Ghost. "They used it to get here, however. How?"

Kragoff fell silent for a moment. When he spoke again, it was with less vehemence. "I decalibrated the propulsion's steering vanes, so that the navigation computer's commands would yield invalid responses."

That was the problem with Kragoff, the Thinker realized yet again. He had enountered this failing many times in the last few years. The Russian never seemed able to see the most effective means of dealing with a problem. Better he had erased the vehicle's computers, or rigged it to explode. Instead, he had tried to be clever, despite the fact that he had so little aptitude for such quick-wittedness.

"I do not know how they were able to follow me here," the Ghost concluded, much of the bluster gone from his voice.

"Perhaps one of Grimm's companions discovered your modifications to the craft and made corrections," the Thinker said. "I do not believe that the Thing's intelligence is sufficient to the task." He paused. "It does not matter greatly. He has to perish ultimately, anyway, and his companions have done nothing to merit our mercy. If we eliminate them now, all will be well. The essential part of our work is done already.''

''The flashpoint is that close?''

The Thinker looked at him, genuine and unaccustomed astonishment in his voice. ''Flashpoint? You still do not understand fully, do you, Kragoff? You think the plan will come to fruition that swiftly? You think that the revolution starts today?''

''Eh?''

''There is no 'flashpoint,' nothing as simple as that.''

''But—your plan—all we've done—'' the Ghost sputtered. ''You said today was the crisis—''

The Thinker took something like pity on his partner. ''Crisis, yes. We are dealing with long-term trends here, slow forces take years to shape and years longer to redirect. Today is the day that they become set and permanent. We have spent years, and I have spent even more time, unweaving the warp and woof of human society. Faith in the economy, in one's nation, in technology, in leaders, in the commonality of humankind, in the future itself—these form the infrastructure on which society rests. My agents—our agents—have worked unceasingly for more than seven years to erode and damage that infrastructure. Soon, it will collapse completely. Only inertia maintains it now, the brute momentum that drives most of the human experience.''

''And once Mandible's speech—''

''Mandible did not deliver his speech. I do not know why. In and of itself, that does not matter.''

''But—''

''Our Mandible did not deliver his speech, but nor did the real one. The attendee nations will note that, speculate on the reason, worry about it, wonder what America's plans are. That will sow doubt and discontent, and work for us, even if not to the extent we wanted.''

''Until they find the real Mandible, and he undoes it.''

''Nonsense.'' The Thinker spat the word, indulging himself with a display of genuine emotion. ''You still do not understand. It cannot be undone, any more than a Presidential retraction could have undone the speech I wrote for our substitute. The wrong message has been sent and cannot be recalled. Another brick has been plucked from the foundation walls of civilization—a smaller brick than we intended, true, but small actions can have large consequences. Remember a single bullet fired in Sarajevo, a bullet that killed only one man. Remember World War I.''

"But—all along, you've told me today is the crisis point."

"Of course. 'Crisis' as in 'cross,' as in 'crossroads.' The trends I have shaped and orchestrated so carefully overlap and reinforce one another with special intensity today. Civilization stands at a corner, Kragoff. We need stay the course for only a few more hours to put the world on its new path and send it on its way. The vast, unthinking horde of humanity will wake up tomorrow not in a world that has collapsed—but they will see the sun rise on a world where total social collapse is inevitable, and certain to occur within less than thirty-four months.''

"Feh. Like Lenin, like Marx, you speak in high rhetoric that has little to do with the common man. Give me me Khrushchev, give me the dictatorship of the proletariat and a world that I can understand."

"You shall have it," the Thinker assured him. "Not much remains to occur, for the world to turn its corner. Famine— or at least the rumor of famine—is imminent in the former Soviet Union, stemming from some unfortunate mistakes made by the Junior Under-Minister of Agriculture. The World Health Organization and others of its ilk will be unable to offer aid, preoccupied as they are by the survivors of the Baktakek Incident. One Internet provider has shut down completely, and two more will fail as they try to take up the slack. Thanks to the injudicious actions of one Carmine Hamilton, nearly seven percent of America's commercial e-mail accounts will fail. Madripoor stands at the brink of revolution, as the disabled underclass seeks to find a voice in running society. The refugees from that revolution will strain the resources of a dozen nations before the year is done. These are the events that will bring the world to its knees, Kragoff, and give you the simpler place you so desire. The so-called authorities cannot reverse the trends I have directed, and I calculate less than a twenty percent likelihood that they can affect those trends in any meaningful way.''

"Someone has to have some idea what is happening," Kragoff said. "Grimm and the others have breached our bases. We are exposed."

"So? The crisis is here. Any steps the authorities are likely to take to offset it—arresting our agents, revealing them—will only precipitate the climax. Suspicion, distrust, lack of faith—these are my tools. Revealing to the human herd a thousand synthetic vipers in its midst will spread terror, not alleviate it." The Thinker smiled. "The fall of civilization will be long and hard," he said, "but it is imminent, I assure you."

Kragoff nodded. "What of the Fantastic Four?" he asked.

"They and their compatriots have caused us much inconvenience today," came the response. The Thinker glanced at the sixth monitor screen, his attention drawn by a sudden flash, the same teleportation effect he had noted earlier. Susan Richards and her new associates had arrived in Sector Orange, while Grimm's party was in Sector Green now. "I think it only appropriate that we kill them now, while we have the opportunity. I will have the Enforcement Unit up and online within twenty-seven minutes. The intruders will serve as an appropriate test of their capabilities."

"Bah. You and your androids," Kragoff said. "They are but toys. A real man does his own killing."

The Thinker looked at him coolly. "I have my androids, you have your apes," he said. "But if you wish to take a direct hand, feel free." He smiled, a sour grin that looked more sincere than his typical grimace of pleasure. "But be quick with it. I have work to do, and your opportunity will not last long."

"I dunno what this place is," Ben said, "but I know I don't like it."

Neither Johnny nor the others had much to say to that. They

looked silently at him with mingled expressions of annoyance and fatigue. They had arrived at a small rocket port perhaps a mile distant from where they stood now. Many yards of twisting corridor had led from that place to this. Ben showed less fatigue than the other three, presumably because of his superhuman strength and stamina. Even Karnak and Gorgon, though far tougher than any ordinary human, had been worn down a bit by the battle with the apes.

Ben just wished he knew where they were going now. Whoever had built this place had built it big; it promised to be even more extensive than the fortress hidden inside the Chesney Products Warehouse. What looked like countless miles of corridors had been hewn from the living rock, and studded with small recessed lamps that cast a watery glow. The chambers they had passed held a variety of facilities and supplies, and huge banks of elaborate equipment whose purpose he could only guess, though some of it looked vaguely similar to items he had seen at Four Freedoms Plaza. That could wait, though; he was less concerned with the place's furnishing than with its owner.

"Notice somethin' funny, kid?" he asked Johnny.

"Funny isn't a word I feel like using," the Torch responded. He still looked tired and worn, and he sounded edgy. His enforced vacation had done nothing for Johnny Storm's spirits.

"Okay, put it another way. We're lookin' for Reed, right?" Johnny nodded.

"No cages here," Ben said softly. "Notice that?"

"Oh," came the response. Then, after a pause, "No."

"Here," Karnak said, gesturing. "This is where we should go." He pointed at a side corridor that branched off from the main avenue.

Ben looked at him. He had come to trust the slender Inhuman's enhanced perceptions, but this was a bit much. To come to a strange place, to start issuing directions . . . "You're sure about this?" he asked.

"If Karnak says go, we go," Gorgon announced. His voice held a stubborn note.

"I ain't arguin', I'm just askin'," Ben said.

Karnak repeated the words. "This is where we should go," he said. "There is a—a *rightness* about this passage. It matches our needs." He paused. "It is difficult to explain, but I know that this is where we should go."

"If Karnak says—" Gorgon started again.

"Yeah, yeah, yeah," Ben interrupted. He made a mock bow. "After you."

Together, the motley quartet turned the corner and strode along a new direction into the dimly lit gloom.

"It's some kind of genetics lab," Sue said, as reality came into focus again around her. She and her companions had materialized in a vaulted space, half-filled with equipment consoles and displays. Along one wall ran a series of tanklike devices that reminded her of oversized incubators. "It looks a little bit like the one in Four Freedoms Plaza. Why has Lockjaw brought us here?"

The oversized dog whined in response.

"The residue he scented in the other facility was organic," Triton reminded her. "Perhaps this is its point of origin."

"Could be. I wonder if this is where the Thinker constructs his duplicates."

"That seems likely," Medusa said.

Sue continued. "I'm still worried about my husband. We've got to find—"

"Pilose!" Medusa said the name in a gasp. "We've found Pilose!"

Sue looked where the red-tressed Inhuman pointed, at a cell on the opposite wall. Inside, an apelike creature watched them silently. He wore no clothing or ornament, and he was big and muscular. Pilose, if it was Pilose, looked like he could cause trouble if he wanted to. Sue felt a brief misgiving as Black Bolt stepped to the cubicle and placed gloved hands on its barred door.

"Um," she said. "Are you sure—"

Metal groaned and tore, and then Black Bolt set the sundered door aside. The cell's sole occupant scrambled out instantly.

And bowed.

He dropped to his knees before Black Bolt, averting his face from the view of the Inhumans' ruler. As Sue watched, Black Bolt did something she had never seen him do before. He dropped to his knees, too, and placed his hands on the hairy one's shoulders. He stared at the freed captive, an intent expression on his face.

After a long moment, Pilose raised his head and gazed back at his king.

"Rise, Pilose," Medusa said softly. "We have come to beseech your aid, not to command your obedience." For more than a minute, she spoke to the apish Inhuman, explaining the horror that had put them on his trail, detailing the terrible need for him back in Attilan. "For ten long years, we have honored your vow," she said. "Renounce it now, and aid us."

Pilose looked at her, and then at the others. For the first time, Sue noticed the intelligent gleam that lit his eyes. The ape-man's gaze locked with hers for a moment, and then returned to Medusa.

"Renounce your vow, if not of silence, at least of solitude," Medusa said. "Your liege beseeches you."

Pilose nodded, and the tension seemed to flow from Medusa's body. "Good," she said, "We can—"

Lockjaw growled.

"You can die, whoever you are," a new voice snarled. "You, and your atavistic friend!" The Red Ghost phased through the rear wall of Pilose's cell, a look of something very much like delight on his face. "And, at long last, at least one member of the Fantastic Four can perish, as well!" He raised a futuristic pistol and squeezed its trigger. A lance of yellow fire raced from it in the Invisible Woman's direction, only to splash against an unseen barrier before it reached her.

"You might as well give up now, Kragoff," Sue said. She could see that he was alone. "You're playing out of your league here. Without your apes, you can't last against the five—the *six* of us."

Kragoff fired his ray gun again, this time at Medusa. She twisted and dodged, then leaped at him, only to give a cry of surprise as she passed completely through his immaterial body. "Hah!" the Red Ghost said. "It seems we have an impasse. And, as for my loyal ones—"

Where Kragoff had strode but moments ago, aloof and unmindful of the physical world's barriers, something more material followed. Heavy blocks split and broke, and huge, hair-covered fists came into view as the barrier they strove against crumbled. An instant later, the Red Ghost's superstrong gorilla came into the lab space, followed by the communist's other simian servitors.

"An impasse no longer, I think," the Red Ghost said, smiling. "I'll finish you, and then I will leave this place and find your partners. My loyal ones can see to your outlandish associates, but I reserve for myself the pleasure of killing the Fantastic Four."

Sue frowned. The expression in her intense blue eyes shifted from anger to concentration as she tried something she had not done in years. Again, waves of invisibility energy rippled out from her brain, this time to form a barrier around Kragoff's body. "You're not going anywhere," she said grimly. "Not until you tell me what this place is and where you have my husband—and probably not even then."

Kragoff laughed again. "I know what you are trying, but it is futile." He stepped forward. "You cannot stop me—" His words became an exclamation of pain as he encountered Sue's force field.

"I said, you're not going anywhere," she repeated. Beads of perspiration formed on her brow. This was the hard part. The Ghost derived his power from the same source as she did, the mysterious cosmic rays that swept through the trackless reaches of outer space. Both had gained their abilities under similar circumstances, and Reed had commented once that both relied on similar forms of energy to implement those abilities.

"Feh," Kragoff said. He holstered his pistol and drew back one fist. "You will not stop me."

He punched the invisible barrier that blocked his path.

Sue winced. At this range, she could adjust her force field to contain even the Red Ghost's intangible form, but at a cost. The field's energies were an extension of her own being. The pain she felt now came not from physical impact—brute force was not the Ghost's forté—but the nerve-jangling interference their two kinds of energy imposed on one another. The only consolation was that, whatever she felt, the Russian felt something similar. She was a seasoned fighter; he was a lab scientist whose main super power enabled him to avoid physical contact. Her stamina was likely to be greater than his. If she could outlast him—

She could.

"Bah," Kragoff said, plainly hurting and frustrated to find himself effectively physical again. "Enough of this. It is beneath me to sully my hands so." He gazed through the transparent barrier, at the attentive anthropoids who awaited his command. "Deal with them, my loyal ones! Do not let them—"

His words trailed off into silence as he saw the results of his command.

The gorilla, taking the lead, leapt at Black Bolt. In instant response, the fingers of Black Bolt's right hand closed into a fist, a fist that raced toward the ape's hairy jaw. Low and flat, the sound of flesh meeting flesh sounded loudly in the quiet lab, and the ape flew backwards, lifted entirely off its feet by the force of Black Bolt's blow. End over end the ape tumbled, then smashed into a bank of equipment with a thunderous crash. Dust rose, then settled.

The ape didn't get up.

Kragoff stared at his largest pet's silent form, a horrified expression on his face.

The orangutan and baboon whimpered in fear, plainly terrified by the power they had witnessed. They cowered in the shadows and offered no challenge.

"Only one blow," the Red Ghost said softly, a wondering, even stunned sound in his voice. "With a single blow—"

A familiar voice sounded from behind Sue. "That'd be his

famous Master Blow. Hurts, too. I felt it once, back before me and ol' forkhead here became pals.''

Sue turned to face the speaker, startled, but not so startled that she let the field holding Kragoff drop. "Ben," she said, as the Thing, the Torch, Karnak, and Gorgon entered the lab.

Or four men who looked like them did.

"Heya, Susie," the Thing rumbled. "Looks like you got your hands full."

Sue looked at him, a thousand questions racing through her mind, doubting queries that needed answers. Anyone who could field a replacement Reed could probably make more duplicates.

"Pilose," Gorgon said, catching sight of the figure who stood beside Black Bolt.

Sue gestured for him to stay back. "No closer," she said.

The Thing looked at her quizzically.

"Sis, you won't believe what happened," the Torch said eagerly. "In New Jersey—"

"Not now, squirt," the Thing said. "Make sure we know who's who, first."

Sue looked at him, thinking. When was the last time she had seen the inarguable real Thing? After a tense moment, she spoke. "What had you just eaten when the phone rang?" she asked.

"A ham an' some ice cream," Ben said. He sounded wary. "An' what did you yell at me about?"

"Yell? I didn't—Oh. You wanted to drink milk out of the bottle instead of a glass," Sue said, with a smile. "Ben, it's so good to see you. How did you get here?"

The next few minutes were filled with hurried explanations and discussion as the two bands compared notes. Finally, Karnak gestured for silence.

"We are agreed, then," he said. "We see this through to its end."

"Bah," Gorgon said. "I still think that Lockjaw should take Pilose back to Attilan, so that he can save the students."

The apish Inhuman shook his head adamantly.

"Pilose has earned the right to face the one who has inflicted this indignity upon him," Medusa said. "More, he has earned a place at our side."

"But—" Gorgon said. He fell silent as Black Bolt glanced at him.

"What about Kragoff?" Johnny asked. The Russian had remained silent despite their best efforts to interrogate him, refusing to answer any question, no matter how trivial. Now, he glared exultantly at his enemies from behind the Invisible Woman's force field. "What are we gonna do about him?"

"Nothing," the Red Ghost said, exultantly. "You can restrain me with this field, but you cannot hurt me, cannot harm me. I am beyond your petty powers."

"Izzat so?" the Thing asked. He ambled in the Russian's direction, until he was close to the field's perimeter. "Guess you got a point, there," he continued, staring thoughtfully at the prisoner.

"Of course, I am correct, you outmoded appendage of the old world order! You cannot—"

"Susie, now!" the Thing said.

Sue dropped the force field. Moving faster than the eye could follow, the Thing's right fist lashed out in a short, sharp arc that ended at the point of Kragoff's jaw. The blow struck home when it would do the most good, in the brief moment between Sue dropping her field and Kragoff turning unsolid once more.

"Done," the Thing agreed, as the Red Ghost fell to the floor in an unconscious heap. He turned to look at Sue. "Let's go," he said. "He'll keep for a while."

"Yeah," Johnny said, looking at the unconsious form sprawled on the floor. "Like a year, I think."

Years ago, it had taken Reed Richards more than six months to figure out the various control and surveillance systems in the Skrull flying saucer, and another month to modify them to suit his own purposes. The effort paid off now, as it had so many times before. Hovering some one hundred feet above the sprawling complex he had found just inside the Arctic Circle, he considered the information his monitors presented.

The place was huge, easily the size of a city block. A low, broad structure was its heart, camouflaged to avoid satellite surveillance. More than a mile of corridors wound beneath the surrounding tundra. Heaven only knew how much damage its creator had done to the permafrost and the local environment, but that issue would have to wait.

His ability to scan the site's interior was limited. Some kind of cloaking field was in effect, but some interesting energy signatures were getting through. Perhaps predictably, they were focused in the central structure. It seemed likely that he would find what he sought there.

The saucer dropped eighty feet and its cockpit opened. Bitter cold shrieked with delight as it gained admittance, but Reed barely noticed. The unique fabric of his costume offered considerable protection against the elements, and his own inherent resilience helped quite a bit, too. Low over the installation's roof, he activated the craft's autopilot and stretched his neck to survey the structure below him. He was looking for a promising access shaft or inlet. After a moment, he found one.

With one twenty-foot stride, Mr. Fantastic set out to do some exploring.

The Thinker pushed some buttons, and his nine-screen display once more changed the images it presented. Grimm, Storm, and the others faded from view. Taking their place were nine different shots of the same tableau. In a broad, vaulted chamber at the installation's center one hundred figures stood unmoving. They stood in ten rows of ten each, arrayed in a formation that seemed more geometric than military. Their identical forms looked blocky and unfinished, all blunt and square-edged, like ingots of metal that had not yet taken their final shape. They were the elements of his Enforcement Unit, the core of the army with which he intended to impose his will on a chaotic world.

Years before, the Thinker had deliberately emerged from equally deliberate obscurity to take charge of the New York mobs. He had done this less for profit than for power, and to create a context in which he could slake his relentless thirst for knowledge. He had led his forces in a series of raids that had stretched the cities resources to the limit. Erik Morrison had worked for him then, even as he had only a few days before, when he engineered the blast that made the Lifestream heist feasible. More to the point, however, his gangland army had enabled him to raid the Baxter Building, the Fantastic Four's original headquarters, and appropriate the genetics data that had made a foundation for so many efforts in the years that followed. His first creation to benefit from the purloined data had been his Awesome Android, a ten-foot-tall, genetically adaptable, utterly subservient artificial lifeform. More than once, this creature had battled the entire Fantastic Four to a standstill.

One hundred Awesome Androids presently stood before the Thinker's surveillance cameras.

The Thinker touched the keyboard before him. The center monitor screen went blank, then filled with a diagnostic report. It read as he had expected. Life signs, genetic configuration, conditioned responses, all were precisely on track with his projections. For more than a week, this installation's mainframe had fine-tuned and optimized the artificial lifeforms that stood before him, readying them for what was to come.

They were ready now.

The Thinker entered another command sequence. Yellowish mists oozed up from the amphitheater's floor. This was his synthesized version of the mysterious mutagenic substance he had found hidden in the Tibet specimen's cellular structure. The files stolen from Richards's computers had offered a close match to it, and some details about how it worked, and the Thinker had spent long hours reconciling the two bodies of data. Now, that work was about to be rewarded.

The yellow mist billowed up from the floor, cloaking the elements of the Enforcement Unit in thick, clinging clouds. The Thinker waited forty-two seconds and then activated the chamber's exhaust fan. As the clouds dissipated, he could see that they had done their work. The androids were changing, their harsh lines of their brutish forms twisting and flowing, and becoming something new.

The Thinker looked at his work, and he saw that it was good. As he watched, it became better.

The hole that Kragoff's super-strong gorilla had punched in Pilose's cell wall connected the genetics lab to yet another passageway. This was a wider corridor than any that the two search parties had experienced. This corridor was higher and more brightly lit, and showed signs of having carried more traffic in recent times.

"Looks like we found the Interstate," Ben said. He and Black Bolt, as the powerhouses of the current grouping, had taken the lead and were moving along the tiled expanse at a good pace.

"I think you're right, Ben," Sue responded. "But look at this place—it must be as big as the Pentagon!"

"Probably serves a similar purpose," Johnny noted. "I guess even world-conquering madmen need a place to hang their hat."

"Or hats," Ben said sourly. "Lot's of 'em. Sue's right. I been in towns smaller than this place." So far, they had passed literally dozens of side corridors, all opening onto other store-rooms and work spaces. "We're gonna have to come back here later an' do some plain an' fancy dismantling."

"That can wait until we've found Reed," Sue said tightly, "or whoever took him."

For a long moment Ben said nothing, perhaps taken aback by the emotion in his teammate's voice. He didn't give voice to concern that had been growing in him for a while.

What if they didn't find Reed? Not now, not ever? So far, there had been no sign of the missing scientist. None of the captives in New Jersey or at the South Seas facility had seen him.

What if that meant he would never be seen again?

Ben pushed the thought from his mind. "Still say we gotta plan ahead," he muttered. "Can't let a place like this stand."

Black Bolt glanced at Medusa, and she nodded in acknowledgment of his silent message before continuing. "It won't, Ben," she said softly.

"Huh?" Ben looked at the suddenly resolute expressions on the faces of the Inhuman Royal Family members.

"Whoever built this place has committed crimes against our people. He will be punished for that."

"Oh," Ben said, considering the implications of her words, but he didn't find those implications unattractive. After a moment, he continued. "Okay. Just don't do nothin' rash. We got a lotta ground to cover before we swing the wreckin' ball."

"Fair enough."

The passageway continued in what was essentially a straight line, at a slight upward incline. The rocket he and the others had ridden to the place had landed in an underground docking facility, so Ben knew that he had entered the place at a point well below ground level. Now, however, he suspected that they were back on the surface, or even above it. As they followed the passage, the side corridors became less frequent, as did the branches they could see from those corridors. Presumably, they were nearing the heart of the complex, with less room for the spiderweblike branchings that all had noticed earlier. Still, they had seen no sign of life since abandoning Kragoff and his pets. Despite the scuff marks on the floors and walls, there seemed to be no occupants in the strange place.

"I don't get it," Ben said. "We've walked more than a mile now, all of it indoors, an' no one's shown his or her face. Who the heck would build a joint like this and then leave it empty?"

"Not Kragoff, that's for sure," Johnny said. "This is out of his league—way out."

Abruptly, Karnak gestured for silence. "We are not alone," he said softly.

"Huh?" Ben grunted.

Karnak pressed the sensitive fingers of one hand to a nearby section of wall. "Beyond this wall, something calls to me," he said. "I cannot be certain, but I seem to sense—"

He paused, a look of concentration on his features. "Yes," he said. "The Terrigen." He tapped the wall with a fingertip as he named the greatest of the Inhumans' secrets. "Behind this wall, there is the Terrigen, or something very much like it."

The others looked at him expectantly. Finally, Ben said, "Well? What are ya waitin' for?"

Karnak's right hand came back and then forward in a short, sharp arc. It stuck the wall in a chopping motion, like a karate chop, but it struck with more power and precision than any normal human could muster. It struck the wall precisely at its weakest point, moving with exactly the right force to make full use of that point. The heavy stone broke and fell away, revealing a dimly lit space behind it.

Ben looked into the gap. Something looked back at him with red eyes that were lit with fury. An animal cry of challenge echoed in the confined spaces, and something with green-scaled skin launched itself though the gap, reaching for Ben's throat with razored claws. A blob of fire spat from the creature's mouth without finding a target, and then the monster made another roaring call to battle. Almost immediately, similar cries sounded from behind it.

"Crumbs," the Thing said softly. "I knew we'd covered a lot of territory, but I didn't think we'd reached Japan!" Even as he spoke, something that looked very much like Godzilla came charging towards him.

A moment later, more of the quasireptilian creatures followed, all identical to the first.

The monsters were about ten feet tall each, strong, quick, and deadly. They spat fire and moved with an eerie grace.

None of these factors mattered much to Ben at the moment. The claws that were closing around his neck did. He made a strangled noise and lashed out with both fists. One of the two blows connected solidly, smashing into the creature's jaw and making its head snap backwards. Ben hit it again, hard enough this time to make it release its grip, and then stumbled out of its reach. He pressed one hand to his own throat, then lifted it free and examined his fingers. No blood. That much was good, at least. The monster had done some damage, but not enough to matter.

"These guys are tough," he warned the others. "Watch out!"

"Thanks, Ben," Johnny snapped. Two of the pocket Godzillas had cornered him. "I needed that bit of advice and insight!" The Human Torch's body was in flames now, and those flames abruptly flared nova-bright. The two monsters gave howls of pain and moved away from him, looking for other prey.

More creatures were boiling out of the broken wall, slithering and hopping and climbing over one another in their mad rush to get to the invaders. So far, that was all that worked in the favor of the FF and Inhumans—the monsters kept getting in their own way. It was like a grim replay of the battle against the apes in New Jersey.

"Nice goin', Karnak," the Thing said, punching another of the brutes. "Remind me never to ask you for directions again."

To his left, the slim Inhuman delivered another karate-like blow to a monster's forehead. His hand found a nerve ganglion or other weak spot. The creature fell, unconscious. Karnak did not bother to respond to the Thing's comment, but kept fighting.

"Give it a rest, Ben," Sue said. She was staying close to one wall, to protect her own back, but now three of the creatures had her surrounded. Fire spewed from their mouths and splashed against one of her invisible force fields inches from her face. Then, as Ben watched, she vanished completely. Baffled, the monsters gave roars of confusion and rage, and then stumbled off.

Sue's voice sounded in Ben's ear, from very close by. "We're holding our own," the Invisible Woman said, "but not much more than that, and we can't do it for long." Susan Richards's trim body abruptly condensed out of nothingness as she leaned closer to her teammate. "I can shield all of us, if need be, but that won't solve the problem. I have an idea, though." She continued talking, outlining her improvised plan.

Ben listened, but he paid attention to the conflict warring around him. Johnny had his flame under complete control now, a tightly focused vortex of localized heat that burned only his adversaries, and not his allies. Black Bolt and Gorgon were acquitting themselves well against the beasts, using a coordinated combination of Master Blows and shockwaves to devastate the creatures. Karnak had felled two of them, and was going for a third. Lockjaw, true to his name, had clamped down on one reptilian leg and refused to let go. Medusa and Triton, not quite as strong as their kinsmen, nonetheless each stood over felled brutes. And Pilose—

As Ben watched in astonishment, the apelike Inhuman leaned into the embrace of one of the monsters, reached up with hairy hand, and touched it once, gently, in the middle of its scaled forehead.

The monster changed. The lines of its body softened and flowed, becoming at once something even less natural looking and yet more familiar. Where a refugee from a Japanese monster movie had stood a moment before, there now stood a blocky gray form, a clumsy, unfinished looking thing.

It was the Thinker's so-called Awesome Android, or its twin.

Medusa's words came back to Ben, drifting up from his memory.

"The Terrigen is strong in Pilose," she had said, a world away and a lifetime ago. *"And at least partially under his*

control. He can use it to reverse the changes it has wrought in others."

The substitute Reed Richards had done his work well, Ben realized. It had provided the Inhumans' greatest secret to one of the Fantastic Four's oldest foes.

Sue had finished her instructions and had vanished again from his side. Ben counted silently to twenty-five, to give her time to make her way to Black Bolt's side, where he knew she would whisper similar directions. He knocked down another monster and made his way to the passageway wall, near the breach that Karnak's blow had created. A moment after he had reached his assigned space, he saw Sue turn visible once more. She gestured at him from across the crowded corridor, and he nodded in response.

"Ya ready, Silent Sam?" he called to Black Bolt, and the Inhumans' ruler also nodded. A second later, two different fists lashed out, striking support members in perfect unison.

"Duck for cover, guys," the Thing yelled, hoping the androids could not understand him.

Reinforced concrete shattered easily enough beneath superhuman strength as his and Black Bolt's combined strength brought the walls tumbling down. More precisely, what was left of the wall collapsed, and brought the ceiling with it. An avalanche of concrete and steel cascaded onto the melée. It fell on the monsters, and not on the humans or Inhumans who had struggled out of its way at the last instant. Enough structural material fell to plug the breach, and to pin most of the creatures who had already passed though it.

"Johnny," Sue's voice rang out again. "Now!'

Fire boiled from Johnny's fingertips, and searing waves of plasma played over the tumbled debris, melting and fusing it. A moment later, the majority of the creatures were encased in a solid, shapeless mass.

"That's the worst of it," Medusa said, panting.

"Is it?" Triton responded. "I think not." He pointed.

One of the creatures, only half trapped by wall's remains, shuddered and shook. It made no move to free itself, but its outlines twisted and flowed, then twisted some more. The artificial rock that pinned it began to smolder again, and the rock's outlines shifted, too.

Another moment passed, and where there had been one monster, now there were two, both clawing their way free.

"Well, that's a new twist," the Thing said.

"They can reproduce," Sue said tightly.

Karnak nodded. "They absorb mass to do so," he said.

The others said nothing, but only watched in horror as the fused heap of building blocks, girders, and monsters began to smolder and twitch.

The end was near, the Thinker realized, with more than a few regrets. His television monitors, tuned once more to news feeds from around the world, told the story.

Or rather, they told him that there was no story.

According to his best estimates, a dozen trends should have met and reinforced one another today, and given evidence that the turning point had come. Oh, there would be no gross, large-scale collapse like that fool Kragoff had looked for, but certain minor events should nonetheless have transpired, sure indicators that his time had come. Outrage at the UN, proclamations from Sylvania's or Costa Verde's governments, food riots in Madripoor—the world's media should have announced the occurrence of at least two of them. One would have been promising; three would have served as clear-cut indicators of his success.

Instead, nothing. The world gave no sign of collapse, imminent or incremental. Impossibly, his most elaborate plan had failed.

A voice drew his attention. "They defeated me," said the Red Ghost, entering through one wall, "through force of numbers and treachery."

The Thinker recognized his words as a lie, but chose to ignore it. "All is lost," he said dispassionately. "The master plan has failed. We may be able to secure this facility, but to no true avail. Even if we destroy the intruders, others will follow."

"All is *lost*?" Kragoff repeated, all braggadocio gone,

swept away by the three small words. "But, all our efforts, all our time—"

"Not wasted. We work well together, Kragoff," the Thinker said, shaping his own lie carefully. Much depended on the Red Ghost believing him. "We will work together again."

Kragoff stared at him, still in something very much like shock.

"Go now," the Thinker said gently. "Use one of the escape rockets. Save yourself, while there is time. I will follow."

As the Red Ghost fled, the Thinker began typing commands into a keyboard. The computers at this location held much data, including the secrets he had wrested from Richards's processors. If he could relay those files to another stronghold . . .

Again, something drew his attention; this time, it was a sound, the noise a ventilator grille made when being removed from its frame. It came from above him. The Thinker looked upward, just in time to see an impossibly elongated, white-gloved hand reached into the room.

"Richards," he said softly.

He had run out of time.

He stopped his typing, and satisfied himself with the simpler task of pushing a red key on a nearby console. Then the Thinker closed his eyes and felt a familiar sensation sweep through him as his body's artificial metabolism shifted into self-destruct mode.

When he opened his eyes again, he was somewhere else.

The androids were reproducing like bacteria now, devouring the surrounding mass and converting it into new androids. At first, Sue and the rest had contended against the new monsters, but the odds became too great almost immediately. Even Pi-lose had found his special abilities quickly outstripped. Clawing, kicking, biting, spitting fire, the creatures massed against the intruders in their midst. Only Sue's invisible force field offered any protection at all, and she knew that she couldn't keep it up forever. Already, her domed field was buried beneath a mass of crawling pseudoreptile flesh.

"This is disastrous," Karnak said, "a perversion of the Terrigen. At the rate these creatures are reproducing, they will overwhelm the entire planet soon."

"I know that, Karnak," Sue said testily.

"Go easy on him, Susie, he's right," Ben said. "We gotta do something."

Sue thought for a moment. "If I drop the field for a moment, we can—"

Her right glove buzzed.

Her heart suddenly in her mouth, Sue pushed a hidden switch at the glove's wrist, activating its built-in short range communicator. "Hello?" she said.

"Sue, this is Reed," the much-loved voice said, almost bringing tears to her eyes.

"Holy cats! It's Stretch!" Ben said, a grin splitting his craggy features. "Hey, Reed—"

Sue motioned for him to be silent. It was hard enough to hear over the background roars of the monsters. "Yes, Reed," she said. For a moment, a fleeting doubt crossed her mind, but she pushed it away. She might as well trust the caller; there was no way that things could get worse. "Where are you?"

"I'm in the facility's command center. We've got to get out of here, and quickly. Someone's activated a destruct sequence."

"Um, Reed, there's a problem with that."

"The enhanced androids? I know. I can see them on the surveillance system, and I can take care of them for you. Brace yourselves and close your eyes, all of you."

Sue looked at the others. "It's Reed," she said. "Close your eyes, all of you. He's going to—"

A strobing brilliance filled the world. It seemed to come from nowhere and everywhere, and even through her eyelids she could see its hypnotic pulsation. There was something strangely soothing about the sudden rhythmic glare. Five seconds passed, then ten. Around her, the sounds of struggling monsters faded into silence. Sue found herself wanting to open her eyes and see what had happened, but she fought the impulse. Fifteen seconds passed, then twenty—

The light faded, and a familiar voice replaced it.

"You can all open your eyes now," Reed said.

Sue did. The lean, handsome man who was her life stood in a nearby doorway, returning a piece of equipment to a small case he carried. "That was a phased strobe effect, keyed to their artificial nervous systems. It should hold them for about six minu—"

His words ended abruptly as Sue threw herself at him, and pressed her mouth to his. Unmindful of the others, uncaring of the unconscious monsters that still littered the passageway, she held tight to him, unwilling ever to let him go again.

The next two minutes were filled with hurried explanations. Reed told the others briefly about his own escape and how he had followed them to the Arctic site. "But we have to get out of here quickly," he said. "The monsters will awake in," he looked at his watch, "in four minutes. We have to get out of here, and then find some way to deal with them before they spread to—"

"Black Bolt will deal with them," Medusa said. "And with this place. It holds too many of our peoples' secrets, facts, and formulae that cannot be allowed to become common knowledge. We trust you, of course, but if the Terrigen fell again into the wrong hands—"

"Of course, Medusa," Reed said. He thought a moment. "I have transportation waiting outside. It will be a little cramped, but it should suffice."

"Lockjaw can take us from this place."

Reed shook his head. "I'll beg your indulgence on that one," he said. "One more loose end needs tying up. Lockjaw can help me with that, if you'll allow it."

"Of course," Medusa said, ignoring a pointed glance from Gorgon. "Anything for the leader of the Fantastic Four."

"Thank you," Reed said. He turned to face the Thing. "Ben, you'll find the Skrull saucer waiting outside. Give these good people a ride to New York. I'll meet you in Four Freedoms Plaza."

"How soon?" the Thing rumbled. "We got a lot to talk about, and Medusa's folks have problems of their own."

"I'll be there in an hour," Reed said. "I'm not going far, just to Colorado."

There are sounds that are too loud to be heard.

There are sounds louder than thunder, louder than the death throes of Krakatoa, louder than the roar that echoed above Alamagordo and Hiroshima combined. There are sounds so loud that they sunder the very air that carries them, ripping molecules apart into their component atoms, and then heating those atoms to incandescence with the fury of their passage. There are sounds that are too loud not just for the human ear or any instrument of human measure, but too loud for physical matter itself to bear.

Such was the sound of Black Bolt's voice.

Years before, the Terrigen had shown the young Black Bolt a cruel generosity. It had given him a variety of powers. He could fly by creating resonant currents in the gravitic field. He could destroy solid matter and, to a lesser degree, restructure it, by redirecting the valence bonds that held it together. He could channel raw energy into the flesh and bone of his body, increasing their strength and his own to levels that matched the power of the Thing himself.

What he could not do was speak, at least not safely. The base harmonic of his voice carried with it another energy waveform, a quasisonic effect with almost limitless destructive potential. For Black Bolt, to speak was to destroy.

He spoke now, standing in the midst of the hidden citadel, after waiting some fifteen minutes for his friends and family to leave this place.

One word? Two? Only Black Bolt knew. There was no one else to hear, and no one who might have heard could have survived. Any who had remained close enough would have perished in the shockwave long before they could have distinguished the sounds that Black Bolt's lips shaped. Like ripples from a pebble cast into a pond, the waves of destruction swept outward from where he stood.

Mortar and stone exploded as the shockwaves touched them, disintegrating into dust and less than dust. Metal support members and armor plate alike split and tore and broke, smashed into shrapnel almost instantly. Tunnels collapsed as the walls that defined them crumbled and fell. Heavy banks of equipment that had taken long years to configure tore themselves free from their moorings, smashed into one another, then shattered completely. The data processors that held the secret of the Terrigen splintered and broke, and the chemical synthesizers that had given that secret physical form followed suit, their contents boiling away into nothingness as Black Bolt's voice found them.

In the amphitheater, the quasireptilian androids—seven hundred and sixteen of them now—ceased their reproductive frenzy as the blast's first effect caught them. Incredibly, the artificial tissues of their bodies were strong enough that at least some survived the initial onslaught. More incredibly, some small percentage of that number had retained consciousness and even awareness. Howling with rage and pain, the few survivors dragged themselves in the general direction of their doom's architect, eager to avenge their fellows, eager to avenge themselves.

Black Bolt spoke again.

This time, he spoke more loudly, more forcefully, and so the ensuing destruction was complete. This time, the withering waves of annihilation spawned by his Terrigen-adapted larynx transcended the cohesive limits of matter itself. This time, those waves turned their fury on the valence bonds that locked atom to atom, and shattered those ties. Molecules split and broke, reduced to free atoms that frantically sought new stability in their energy-charged environment. They sought it by combining with their fellows into new configurations, only to find chaos again as the destruction continued. The process replayed itself again and again until there was nothing left to destroy.

This time, when the last echoes of his terrible voice had faded, none remained to savor the silence except Black Bolt. Attilan's king stood where the Thinker's fortress had stood, where a vast sea of monomolecular dust now stretched, too finely divided to quality as solid matter. Whipped into roiling currents by energies of his voice and by the chill Arctic wind, the stuff eddied and splashed at Black Bolt's feet.

He stood in its midst a long moment, considering the destruction he had wrought. Then, silent once more, he flew to join the others.

Warden Fingeroth looked up as the Guardsman escorted the Thinker into his office. "Thank you, Jones," he said to the armored corrections officer. "That will be all. You can leave now."

"Sir, regulations say—"

"I know what they say, Jones," the warden repeated. "And I said, you can leave now."

"Yes, sir," the Guardsman said. He disconnected the leash-like tether from the Thinker's shackles and left the room. The door whisked shut behind him.

The Thinker looked at Fingeroth.

"Would you like a cigar?" the bow-tied bureaucrat said, gesturing at a humidor on his desk.

The Thinker shook his head.

"Anything else? You must be uncomfortable," Fingeroth said, genuine concern apparent in his voice. He reached into his desk drawer and pulled out a device that looked like a television remote control. He pressed a button, and the electronic locks in the Thinker's chains clicked open. Immediately, the restraints fell to the floor. The Thinker smiled and settled into an easy chair. "Report," he commanded the warden.

"Everything goes as scheduled," Fingeroth responded. "The transport will be ready in thirty minutes. I've already completed the paperwork."

"Which cover story did you use?"

"You're being transferred to another prison, since you don't pose a physical threat and we need the space. Your lawyers have been notified. So has the Department of Justice, but I've seen to it that they've already lost the paperwork."

"Satisfactory."

"The pilot is a replacement, of course. He'll deal with your guards and take you wherever you want to go."

As the Thinker listened, something between a smile and a smirk flowed across his broad features. The failure of the current operation was a disaster, of course, and the end of untold hours of effort on his part, but all was not lost. The Thing, the Invisible Woman, the Torch, the Inhumans—none of them had the wits to guess his most closely kept secret. None of them knew about his own duplicate bodies, or about the electronic chip implanted in his brain. As long as his greatest secrets were safe, he could begin anew. That was the point of the current exercise.

The Thinker knew that Richards suspected that he had some method of communicating from his Vault cell to the outside world. He also knew that not even Richards could have deduced the extent of those communications. That situation could change, of course. By now, no doubt, Richards and his compatriots were on their way here, to investigate the Thinker's situation. Before that happened, before Richards could think things through, certain exercises demanded completion—

Space rippled, tore, folded back. Light filled the office, along with a crackling noise and the scent of ozone. The Thinker blinked in the glare, and when his eyes cleared, he could see two newcomers standing in the office's luxuriously appointed spaces.

They were Richards and that giant monster dog he had seen earlier. The Thinker abruptly realized what was the source of the teleportation effect Susan Richards and her friends had used to travel. He filed the fact away for future reference.

Fingeroth gave a squawk of dismay and reached again into the still-open desk drawer. He had found a pistol and half-raised it when Richards's white-gloved fist smashed into his face. The impact was hard enough to send the slender man tumbling back and down. When he hit the floor, his eyes blinked twice, then closed.

"That was hardly necessary," the Thinker said. He watched, unmoving, as the gigantic dog approached him to sniff inquisitively and then growl. Despite himself, he felt beads of sweat form on his brow.

"Perhaps, but I wanted to be sure," Richards responded. "I've had enough trouble with your little toys. I couldn't run the risk that this one was augmented, too."

The Thinker smiled. "I have no idea what you're talking about," he lied calmly.

"I doubt that very much, Thinker. SAFE tells me they found the real Warden Fingeroth in a prison cell in New Jersey."

"Precisely where he belongs. The corruption of public officials is a terrible thing," the Thinker said. More sweat formed on his brow now, and his face became a mask of concentration.

Richards ignored him. Instead, he turned his attention to a small apparatus he held in his other hand, about twice the size of a cellular phone. He pressed recessed buttons in rapid succession and peered closely at a small liquid crystal diode display.

The Thinker watched him, but did not pay him his full attention. Most of his will was concentrated now on the task of composing himself. The familiar exercises were less easy in this surrounding tumult, but still possible. His breathing had already slowed, and his heartbeat was dropping in response to his mental commands. Now, beginning with his extremities, he willed skeletal muscle groups to relax and go limp. The familiar feeling of serenity swept though him, the welcome sensation of tranquillity and relaxation. He closed his eyes.

When he opened them again, he was still in Warden Fingeroth's office, still less than twenty feet from the man he suddenly realized he hated most in all the world.

Richards tapped the device he held. "I ran a quick check of local energy spectra," he said. "Most of what I found was about what I expected, but I also found some kind of carrier wave in the psionic band. I'm not sure of its purpose, but I'm reasonably certain of its source." He paused. "You."

The Thinker made careful study of the expression on Richards's face, of the tone in his voice. This was the crucial moment. How much did Richards know? What conclusions had he drawn? The answers to those questions were frought with implications.

"My best guess is some kind of communications matrix," Richards said. "Some way for you to get messages into and out of your cell."

His words pleased the Thinker. A moment before, he had calculated nearly a forty-eight percent chance that he had been found out completely; Richards's conclusions, though close to the truth, were not entirely accurate. The carrier wave was much more than what his adversary said, of course. It was the enabling signal for the Thinker's network of duplicate bodies. Without it, the microchips in his brain were little more than silicate bits.

"But I can make further studies later," Mr. Fantastic continued. He set the device he held onto Fingeroth's desk. "I've blocked that band for the surrounding six miles," he said. "Whatever you were doing with it, you won't be doing it anymore."

The Thinker shrugged. "I repeat, I have no idea what you're talking about," he said, but there was no pleasure in his voice now.

The office door slid open. Two men walked through it. One wore the two-tone green armor that was the uniform of the Vault's security staff. The other was tall and well-built, with humorless gray eyes and close-cropped fair hair. He wore a black skintight uniform, and a heavy sidearm hung at his belt.

The Thinker abruptly looked even more annoyed than usual.

"Hello, Colonel," Reed Richards said. "You made good time."

"Hello, Dr. Richards," Sean Morgan responded. "I was already in the neighborhood when I got your call."

Reed nodded in acknowledgment. "Good," he said. "I assume that was no coincidence. I'll leave the Thinker with you, then. I hope you didn't come alone."

Morgan almost smiled. "Oh, I brought backup," he said. He gestured at the office window, and both the Thinker and Richards looked where he pointed. Hanging against the cloudless blue sky was something that looked like a cross between an aircraft carrier and a dirigible, a huge, blunt shape that was gun-metal gray and held aloft by oversized helicopter blades. The exotic craft was the SAFE Helicarrier, the airborn fortress that served as the agency's mobile command center and tactical headquarters. "You can't see them from here," Morgan continued, "but I've got seven armored personnel carriers at the main entrance, too, on loan from the National Guard." He looked thoughtfully at Richards. "The Marines are on standby, but we can't use them inside the national borders, except in time of war, anyhow."

"You guys really mean business," the Guardsman commented. He had stepped over to the Thinker's side and was reattaching the prisoner's shackles. The prisoner moved neither to cooperate nor to resist.

Morgan glanced in the Guardsman's direction. "I always mean business," he said mildly. "And for the duration, I'm your boss, so you mean business, too." He looked back at Richards. "I'll be running the show here at the Vault for a while, Doctor," he continued. "The President wants me to oversee figuring out who's who and what's what. This place is chock full of the worst people on Earth. I'm not leaving it be until I'm sure that everyone who is supposed to be here is, and every one of its security measures is back online. I also have enough agents available to replace every staff member, if necessary."

"I doubt that will be necessary, but you have some careful screening ahead of you," Reed said. "Fingeroth probably isn't the only duplicate on site. Someone in the motor pool tampered with the Fantasti-Car I used to get here before, I think. Keep an eye on the Thinker, though, and he won't be able to issue commands to any others, here or anywhere else. I'm reasonably sure he's the real McCoy." Reed passed the device he held to Morgan, who took it without comment. Quickly, Mr. Fantastic explained the apparatus was and what it did, and his suspicions concerning the Thinker. As he spoke, Lockjaw loped back across the room to stand at his side. The antenna on the dog's forehead began to glow faintly as he gathered the energy to depart.

When Richards finished speaking, Morgan nodded. "That fits. We did some research on this guy. I found at least a dozen crimes in the last three years that fit his M.O. perfectly, and at least four reliable sightings of him, at times when he was supposed to be behind bars."

"Is that so?" Richards asked. He looked again at the Thinker, who wore his restraint harness once more. "That's very interesting."

The Thinker studiously ignored him.

"Well. I think I have a bit more research to do myself, then," Reed continued. He ran gloved fingers along Lockjaw's furred neck. The dog waved its stub tail in response. "I'll be in touch, Colonel," Mr. Fantastic said. "I'll let you know if I learn anything."

"Same here," Morgan replied.

Then the man he spoke to was gone, swept away in in the blinding glare of energy that marked Lockjaw's interdimensional jumps.

Four Freedoms Plaza, New York:

"**A**nd, again, we are in the debt of the Fantastic Four, Reed Richards," Medusa's image said from the viewscreen. She was speaking from the Inhumans' far-off city of Attilan. Behind her stood Black Bolt, listening silently as she spoke his words. "Paraclete's students and Inhuman society owe you more than can ever be repaid."

"Not at all, Medusa," Reed responded. He was in the communications room at Four Freedoms Plaza, flanked by his own teammates. The preceding few days had been hectic ones, as they tied up the loose ends of the very extensive adventure. "I'm very pleased that you found Pilose, and even more pleased that he could help those who had been stricken, but the presence of you and the others is what turned the tide against the Thinker." He paused and smiled. "If there were a debt to pay, it would be ours."

Medusa smiled, too. Of all the Inhumans, she had known the Fantastic Four longest, initially as an enemy, then as an ally, and then as a member. She was well accustomed to Reed's sometimes pontifical manner. "Enough compliments, then," she said. "Simply accept the thanks of a friend."

"Of course. And I hope you will do the same," Reed said, breaking the connection.

" 'The presence of you and the others is what turned the tide against the Thinker,' " the Thing rumbled in the closest he could come to a singsong voice. "You make it sound like the rest of us were along for the ride."

"Don't be silly, Ben," Sue said. "Reed's right. If Black Bolt hadn't destroyed that Arctic base, we'd still be fighting androids." She paused. "The rest of the world probably would be, too."

"Reed's always right," Ben said, mock petulance still in his voice. "If big brain is so smart, how come no one's been able to figger out how the Thinker ran this deal?"

"Ben!"

"It's a reasonable question, Sue, but not one I can answer," Mr. Fantastic interjected. "Remember, even though circumstantial evidence and the M.O. make the Thinker's involvement seem obvious, none of us ever actually saw him anywhere, except in the Vault.'' He paused again. ''The connection is there, but not the proof of it.''

''So he was runnin' it from inside the joint,'' Ben said. ''You found some kinda radio connection, right? He set things up before he went up the river, an' then all he had to do was pull strings.''

Reed shook his head. ''I found a nonmodulated carrier wave in the quasipsionic band,'' he said. ''It could be the basis for a communications system, but I think there's more to the story. I can't help but think that his periods of comalike sleep are part of the solution to this mystery.''

''The mystery can wait,'' Sue said. She smiled. ''We're days late for dinner and dancing, Mr. Fantastic. You promised me a night on the town when you got back.''

''Please, Sue,'' Reed said. ''Not tonight. I've got so much work to catch up on—''

Johnny interrupted. ''What I want to know, is how did they capture you? They got me at lunch, when I was distracted—''

''An' we've all met the distraction,'' Ben added sourly.

Johnny continued, as if he had not spoken. ''But how did they get you?''

''Sabotage to the turbine blades, by a member of the Vault motor pool, a member who was actually one of the Thinker's creations. He and Warden Fingeroth were the only two at that site, according to Morgan's people, but they were enough.''

''An' that was enough to make you crash?''

''No, Ben, not at all—but it was enough to make the Fantasti-Car vulnerable to the blizzard,'' Reed said. The half-remembered image from the confused moments after impact drifted up from his subconscious again, and this time he recognized the hulking gray form. ''He had one of his androids, the base version, waiting for me at at the crash site. After that, it was just a matter of replacing me with the prepared duplicate. He knew that the substitute Johnny had already managed its end of the arrangement.''

''How'd the critter know where to wait?'' Ben asked.

"The Thinker knew where I would crash, because he knew about the storm in advance. He could easily have been the world's greatest weatherman. In fact, I wouldn't be surprised to learn that he engineered the Lifestream theft specifically to prompt my visit, just in time for the storm to hit."

"An' what tripped him up? Other than us?"

"Himself. Ego. Vanity." Reed said the three words quickly, with almost a staccato rhythm. "His comment about psycho-history is what brought him down. He likes to think of himself as beyond human emotions, but, in the end, it was his very human vanity that destroyed his greatest plan."

"Hey, I just thought of something," Johnny said. His voice sounded like the voice of a man who had made a great discovery. "The world's been going to hell in a handbasket these past couple years. Unemployment, crime, conflict, poverty—how much of that can be laid at the Thinker's door?"

"Not all of it," Reed said.

"But some."

"Some," Reed said, nodding again.

"And now," Sue said softly, "if we can't make things work on our own, we have only ourselves to blame."

"Amen to that," Ben responded. After a moment, both of the other men repeated his words.

The Vault, Colorado:

Seated on the edge of his bunk, the Thinker made a sound of disgust, but he was careful to make it softly enough that none of the prison surveillance microphones could detect it. He folded the newspaper that he had been reading and added it to the eleven-inch stack that rested by his right foot. He folded it with some precision and stacked it with care; the Thinker did not care for untidiness. The other pile of newspapers, the one by his left foot, had dwindled by more than half since a Guardsman had delivered it an hour ago, and he knew that it would not last much longer at the rate he was reading. That annoyed him. Since Richards had installed his blocking device, the Thinker could no longer leave his body, and had reverted to his normal sleeping patterns. That left him some twenty-two hours a day to fill, a task that was becoming steadily more difficult as he used up the limited reading material resources of the Vault's library.

This paper was a New York tabloid, the *Daily Bugle*. An attractive woman with good teeth smiled out at him from under a headline that announced, APES HELD ME PRISONER IN NEW JERSEY! The face belonged to Jenna Villanueva, the WNN reporter who had recently enjoyed his hospitality, but the words apparently belonged to some anonymous *Bugle* staff editor. Below the photograph, another, smaller headline read, KILLER APES: WHAT'S SPIDER-MAN UP TO NOW? announcing a front-page editorial by J. Jonah Jameson, noted arachnophobe. The Thinker did not anticipate taking long to wring this publication dry of useful facts. More to the point, he expected to learn nothing that he did not already know.

To the Thinker's practiced eye, a dozen apparently unrelated news items told one story, confirming what he already knew. Economic indicators were on the upswing in most of the industrialized world. Three of the five largest Internet service providers were increasing service, not reducing it. Key leaders in America and abroad had spoken out against hate crimes, and, incredibly, polls indicated that their audiences had listened. More and more, the data pointed to a specific conclusion, one that the Thinker hated, but could not deny.

The crisis point had passed.

Richards had won. Somehow, impossibly, the world had staved off the collapse that he had so painstakingly engineered. Too many unforseen facts—Grimm's need for a new coat, the arrival of the Inhumans, Richards's escape—had intervened. The fact that those developments were not only unforeseen but unforeseeable was small consolation.

Only two more papers remained now. He scanned them hastily, still finding nothing that he did not already know, then set them aside. He lay back on his bunk and did what he did best.

He thought.

More years and effort than he cared to quantify had gone into this campaign, and they had all gone for naught. Too many of his resources had been forfeit to failure, and only a few of his most treasured secrets remained—key among them, the secret of his multiple bodies. None of his adversaries had yet ferreted out the solution to that puzzle, and it seemed unlikely that any would. Richards had detected the carrier wave and found a way to block it, but, predictably, the man's lesser intellect had not divined the true secrets of what he had found.

That left Kragoff, still at large, still hungry for his own measure of power.

The Russian was a simple creature, scarcely more complex than his apes, but possessing useful skills. The Thinker had spent many hours cultivating the Red Ghost's trust, encouraging his loyalty. He knew that the Thinker was his best, most likely partner in future campaigns. That knowledge, coupled with the Russian's own ambitious nature, held the key to the Thinker's freedom.

In yet another hidden location, in a room without windows and doors, a button waited. A single push of that button would shift the psionic carrier wave that Richards had detected a full eight cycles out of phase with its present frequency, and well beyond the limited spectra that Richards's toy blocked.

Kragoff knew of that button, even if he did not know precisely what it did.

A single press of the Red Ghost's finger, and the Thinker would be free again.

And if Kragoff should fail him? The Thinker smiled.

There were other ways.

Elsewhere, around the world:

In Sylvania, a new round of talks opened between the German and Gypsy factions, hosted this time under the watchful eye of a representative from neighboring Latveria. At the opening session, the Latverian emissary read a message from his own ruler, Victor Von Doom: "This nonsense must cease." It did.

In California, Morrie Kalman typed a dozen letters and numbers into his computer's keyboard. An instant later, BizNet's log-on screen faded into nothingness, to be replaced by a directory of services. A flat, neutral voice welcomed him and told him that he had mail waiting. Morrie responded with a muttered, "It's about time!" and then set about the vital business of meeting the world's supersonic emulsification needs.

In New York City, Jenna Villanueva went from covering news to being news, and then back again. She was interviewed a dozen times in as many days about her involvement in the mysterious wave of abductions that had swept the world. For three months, she was famous, and she used her fame to leverage a new contract from WNN's notoriously stingy management. By the time the surge of interest ebbed, she had established her own journalistic credentials and was, if not a power in the local broadcast media, at least a definite presence. A month after that, the first of the unauthorized fan clubs had formed, and network representatives were calling periodically, "Just to stay in touch."

In Rhode Island, newly divorced and newly lonesome Aspidistra Paltrow, née Smith, answered a phone and blinked in astonishment as a voice she had not heard in eight years sounded in her ear. An hour later, she had made a lunch date with a man from her past, a man whose increasingly heartless business practices had prompted her to drive him from her life. Now, however, he claimed to have changed, and seemed sincere. When she returned the receiver to its cradle, Aspidistra realized with some surprise that she was eager to see Michael Brady again.

In Washington, D.C., Omegatron Productions, producers and syndicators of the popular *Fred Raven's America* radio program, announced an end to the long-running drive time talk show, citing poor ratings. Industry insiders blamed the cancellation on the "kinder, gentler" approach Raven had taken in recent months, but he proved them wrong by taking the show to another network and making it a success again.

In Baktakek, Hungary, an elderly American felt his blood grow cold as he saw with his own eyes what horrors had been wrought in his name. The past years had been hard ones, spent behind prison bars and cut off completely from civilization. The past months had been difficult, too, as he took up once more a life that the world had thought ended some five years before. Now, however, he knew that the real challenge still lay ahead of him, the challenge to make whatever amends he could for the terrible wrongs that had been done by someone wearing his face. There was much that could never be corrected, of course—but Montgomery Burns promised himself that what could be fixed, would be fixed.

In Moscow, Russia, a wary woman named Dina Rosengaus met with the other directors of URSA and attempted to explain, without much success, why the organization's plans had come to naught yet again. Kragoff had failed her, she explained, and disappeared, and the elaborate scheme he had outlined had never been fully implemented. It wasn't her fault, she argued. She was still arguing when she felt the telltale sting of a hypodermic needle, and she was still trying to argue when her last breath left her lungs.

In Madripoor, in Italy, in Costa Verde, and in France, on all the world's continents and in most of the world's nations, a thousand men and women took up once more the lives that had been denied them. Some were famous, but most were not. Some had emerged from their harrowing experiences bettered by them; some had not. Now, upon their return to reality, all lived their day-to-day lives as best they could, guided by their own wits and desires and needs, rather than by a mastermind's schemes. Countless other members of the world's populace did the same, no longer the unwitting subjects of a madman's experiments, no longer at the mercy of a thousand carefully placed agents of chaos.

Life went on, much as it always had.

A shining beacon of hope to his friends, a shadowy figure of terror to his foes, **Pierce Askegren** has drunk deep of life's rich cup, and spat its dregs in destiny's dark eyes! Esthete, scholar, philosopher, jerk—others have called Pierce all these things and more, yet no single word can come close to encompassing his complex majesty. Some three other writers are blessed enough to call him "collaborator"—Danny Fingeroth and Eric Fein on the epic "Doom's Day" trilogy of Spider-Man team-up novels, and John Garcia, on the story "Better Looting Through Modern Chemistry" in *Untold Tales of Spider-Man*. Loyal readers know him as the guy who brought back the Painter of a Thousand Perils (in *The Ultimate Super-Villains*) and contributed to *The Ultimate Silver Surfer* and the forthcoming *The Ultimate Hulk*. Comics fans with extremely long memories for obscure anthology stories know that he wrote for Warren Publishing's *Creepy* and *Vampirella*. And fans of novels based on role-playing games will be familiar with his novel *Gateway to the Stars*, based on the *Marc Miller's Traveller* RPG. These days, the laughing daredevil of literature dwells in a bucolic land named Virginia, works as a technical writer, and continues to create stories featuring other people's characters. What's next on the big man's plate? Well, even as this is written, he's busily developing an Avengers/Thunderbolts team-up novel, and there are plans afoot for him to take his derivative genius into new venues, which may or may not include the word *Ultimate* in their titles.

Paul Ryan is a New England-based cartoonist and a graduate of the Massachusetts College of Art. He worked as a graphic designer for eleven years, then as an assistant to artist Bob Layton. In 1985 he struck out on his own, and his artwork has graced the pages of *Squadron Supreme*, *DP7* (which he co-created with Mark Gruenwald), *Quasar*, *The Avengers*, *Aveng-*

ers West Coast, Iron Man, Ravage 2099 (which he co-created with Stan Lee), *The Flash*, *Superman*, and, naturally, the monthly *Fantastic Four* comic.

Jeff Albrecht has worked as a commercial illustrator inside and outside the comic book field for over ten years. He has extensive credits as an inker for the major comic book publishers, and occasionally serves as penciller. In addition to comic book art, he spends a large part of his time creating licensing artwork for Warner Brothers, the Walt Disney Company, DC Comics, and others. His other book illustration work can be seen in *Spider-Man: The Octopus Agenda* and the *Untold Tales of Spider-Man* anthology. He lives with his wife, Dorothy, and son, Lucas, in Missouri.

CHRONOLOGY TO THE MARVEL NOVELS AND ANTHOLOGIES

What follows is a guide to the order in which the Marvel novels and short stories published by Byron Preiss Multimedia Company and Boulevard Books take place in relation to each other. Please note that this is not a hard and fast chronology, but a guideline that is subject to change at authorial or editorial whim. This list covers all the novels and anthologies published from October 1994–September 1998.

The short stories are each given an abbreviation to indicate which anthology the story appeared in. USM=*The Ultimate Spider-Man*, USS=*The Ultimate Silver Surfer*, USV=*The Ultimate Super-Villains*, UXM=*The Ultimate X-Men*, and UTS=*Untold Tales of Spider-Man*.

If you have any questions or comments regarding this chronology, please write us.

Snail mail: Keith R.A. DeCandido, Marvel Novels Editor
               Byron Preiss Multimedia Company, Inc.
               24 West 25th Street
               New York, New York, 10010-2710.
E-mail: KRAD@IX.NETCOM.COM.

                      —Keith R.A. DeCandido, Editor

"The Silver Surfer" [flashback] [USS]
by Tom DeFalco & Stan Lee
  The Silver Surfer's origin. The early parts of this flashback start several decades, possibly several centuries, ago, and continue to a point just prior to "To See Heaven in a Wild Flower."

"Spider-Man" [USM]
by Stan Lee & Peter David
  A retelling of Spider-Man's origin.

"Side by Side with the Astonishing Ant-Man!" [UTS]
by Will Murray
"Suits" [USM]
by Tom De Haven & Dean Wesley Smith

FANTASTIC FOUR

"After the First Death . . ." [UTS]
by Tom DeFalco
"Celebrity" [UTS]
by Christopher Golden & José R. Nieto
"Better Looting Through Modern Chemistry" [UTS]
by John Garcia & Pierce Askegren
These stories take place very early in Spider-Man's career.

"To the Victor" [USV]
by Richard Lee Byers
Most of this story takes place in an alternate timeline, but the jumping-off point is here.

"To See Heaven in a Wild Flower" [USS]
by Ann Tonsor Zeddies
"Point of View" [USS]
by Len Wein
These stories take place shortly after the end of the flashback portion of "The Silver Surfer."

"Identity Crisis" [UTS]
by Michael Jan Friedman
"The Liar" [UTS]
by Ann Nocenti
"The Doctor's Dilemma" [UTS]
by Danny Fingeroth
"Moving Day" [UTS]
by John S. Drew
"Twelve Tons" [UTS]
by Dennis Brabham
"Deadly Force" [UTS]
by Richard Lee Byers
"Improper Procedure" [USS]
by Keith R.A. DeCandido
"Poison in the Soul" [UTS]
by Glenn Greenberg
"The Ballad of Fancy Dan" [UTS]
by Ken Grobe & Steven A. Roman
"Do You Dream in Silver?" [USS]
by James Dawson
"Livewires" [UTS]
by Steve Lyons

"Arms and the Man" [UTS]
by Keith R.A. DeCandido
"Incident on a Skyscraper" [USS]
by Dave Smeds
These all take place at various and sundry points in the careers of Spider-Man and the Silver Surfer, after their origins, but before Spider-Man married and the Silver Surfer ended his exile on Earth.

"Cool" [USM]
by Lawrence Watt-Evans
"Blindspot" [USM]
by Ann Nocenti
"Tinker, Tailor, Soldier, Courier" [USM]
by Robert L. Washington III
"Thunder on the Mountain" [USM]
by Richard Lee Byers
"The Stalking of John Doe" [UTS]
by Adam-Troy Castro
These all take place just prior to Peter Parker's marriage to Mary Jane Watson.

"On the Beach" [USS]
by John J. Ordover
This story takes place just prior to the Silver Surfer's release from imprisonment on Earth.

Daredevil: Predator's Smile
by Christopher Golden

"Disturb Not Her Dream" [USS]
by Steve Rasnic Tem
"My Enemy, My Savior" [UTS]
by Eric Fein
"Kraven the Hunter is Dead, Alas" [USM]
by Craig Shaw Gardner
"The Broken Land" [USS]
by Pierce Askegren
"Radically Both" [USM]
by Christopher Golden
"Godhood's End" [USS]
by Sharman DiVono

"Scoop!" [USM]
by David Michelinie
"Sambatyon" [USS]
by David M. Honigsberg
"Cold Blood" [USM]
by Greg Cox
"The Tarnished Soul" [USS]
by Katherine Lawrence
"The Silver Surfer" [framing sequence] [USS]
by Tom DeFalco & Stan Lee
   These all take place shortly after Peter Parker's marriage to Mary Jane Watson and shortly after the Silver Surfer attained his freedom from imprisonment on Earth.

Fantastic Four: To Free Atlantis
by Nancy A. Collins
"If Wishes Were Horses" [USV]
by Tony Isabella & Bob Ingersoll

"The Deviant Ones" [USV]
by Glenn Greenberg
"An Evening in the Bronx with Venom" [USM]
by John Gregory Betancourt & Keith R.A. DeCandido
   These two stories take place one after the other, and a few months prior to The Venom Factor.

The Incredible Hulk: What Savage Beast
by Peter David
   This novel takes place over a one-year period, starting here and ending just prior to Rampage.

"On the Air" [UXM]
by Glenn Hauman
"Connect the Dots" [USV]
by Adam-Troy Castro
"Summer Breeze" [UXM]
by Jenn Saint-John & Tammy Lynne Dunn
"Out of Place" [UXM]
by Dave Smeds
   These stories all take place prior to the Mutant Empire *trilogy.*

COUNTDOWN TO CHAOS

X-Men: Mutant Empire Book 1: **Siege**
by Christopher Golden
X-Men: Mutant Empire Book 2: **Sanctuary**
by Christopher Golden
X-Men: Mutant Empire Book 3: **Salvation**
by Christopher Golden
　　　These three novels take place within a three-day period.

"The Love of Death or the Death of Love" [USS]
by Craig Shaw Gardner
"Firetrap" [USV]
by Michael Jan Friedman
"What's Yer Poison?" [USS]
by Christopher Golden & José R. Nieto
"Sins of the Flesh" [USV]
by Steve Lyons
"Doom²" [USV]
by Joey Cavalieri
"Child's Play" [USV]
by Robert L. Washington III
"A Game of the Apocalypse" [USS]
by Dan Persons
"All Creatures Great and Skrull" [USV]
by Greg Cox
"Ripples" [USV]
by José R. Nieto
"Who Do You Want Me to Be?" [USV]
by Ann Nocenti
"One for the Road" [USV]
by James Dawson
　　　These stories are more or less simultaneous, with "Child's Play" taking place shortly after "What's Yer Poison?" and "A Game of the Apocalypse" taking place shortly after "The Love of Death or the Death of Love."

FANTASTIC FOUR

"Five Minutes" [USM]
by Peter David
> *This takes place on Peter Parker and Mary Jane Watson-Parker's first anniversary.*

Spider-Man: The Venom Factor
by Diane Duane
Spider-Man: The Lizard Sanction
by Diane Duane
Spider-Man: The Octopus Agenda
by Diane Duane
> *These three novels take place within a six-week period.*

"The Night I Almost Saved Silver Sable" [USV]
by Tom DeFalco
"Traps" [USV]
by Ken Grobe
> *These stories take place one right after the other.*

Iron Man: The Armor Trap
by Greg Cox
Iron Man: Operation A.I.M.
by Greg Cox
"Private Exhibition" [USV]
by Pierce Askegren
Fantastic Four: Redemption of the Silver Surfer
by Michael Jan Friedman
Spider-Man & The Incredible Hulk: Rampage (Doom's Day Book 1)
by Danny Fingeroth & Eric Fein
Spider-Man & Iron Man: Sabotage (Doom's Day Book 2)
by Pierce Askegren & Danny Fingeroth
Spider-Man & Fantastic Four: Wreckage (Doom's Day Book 3)
by Eric Fein & Pierce Askegren
The Incredible Hulk: Abominations
by Jason Henderson
> Operation A.I.M. *takes place about two weeks after* The Armor Trap. *The "Doom's Day" trilogy takes place within a three-month period. The events of* Operation A.I.M., *"Private Exhibition,"* Redemption of the Silver Surfer, *and* Rampage *happen more or less*

simultaneously. Wreckage *is only a few months after* The Octopus Agenda. Abominations *takes place shortly after the end of* Wreckage.

"It's a Wonderful Life" [UXM]
by eluki bes shahar
"Gift of the Silver Fox" [UXM]
by Ashley McConnell
"Stillborn in the Mist" [UXM]
by Dean Wesley Smith
"Order from Chaos" [UXM]
by Evan Skolnick
   These stories take place simultaneously.

"X-Presso" [UXM]
by Ken Grobe
"Life is But a Dream" [UXM]
by Stan Timmons
"Four Angry Mutants" [UXM]
by Andy Lane & Rebecca Levene
"Hostages" [UXM]
by J. Steven York
   These stories take place one right after the other.

Spider-Man: Carnage in New York
by David Michelinie & Dean Wesley Smith
Spider-Man: Goblin's Revenge
by Dean Wesley Smith
   These novels take place one right after the other.

X-Men: Smoke and Mirrors
by eluki bes shahar
   This novel takes place three-and-a-half months after "It's a Wonderful Life."

Generation X
by Scott Lobdell & Elliot S! Maggin
X-Men: The Jewels of Cyttorak
by Dean Wesley Smith
X-Men: Empire's End
by Diane Duane
X-Men: Law of the Jungle
by Dave Smeds

X-Men: Prisoner X
by Ann Nocenti
> *These novels take place one right after the other.*

Spider-Man: Valley of the Lizard
by John Vornholt
Fantastic Four: Countdown to Chaos
by Pierce Askegren
> *These novels are more or less simultaneous.*

"Mayhem Party" [USV]
by Robert Sheckley
> *This story takes place after* Goblin's Revenge.

Spider-Man: Wanted Dead or Alive
by Craig Shaw Gardner

X-Men & Spider-Man: Time's Arrow Book 1: The Past
by Tom DeFalco & Jason Henderson
X-Men & Spider-Man: Time's Arrow Book 2: The Present
by Tom DeFalco & Adam-Troy Castro
X-Men & Spider-Man: Time's Arrow Book 3: The Future
by Tom DeFalco & eluki bes shahar
> *These novels take place within a twenty-four-hour period in the present, though it also involves travelling to various points in the past, to an alternate present, and to five different alternate futures.*

SPIDER-MAN ®

__SPIDER-MAN: CARNAGE IN NEW YORK by David
Michelinie & Dean Wesley Smith   1-57297-019-7/$5.99
Spider-Man must go head-to-head with his most dangerous enemy, Carnage, a
homicidal lunatic who revels in chaos. Carnage has been returned to New
York in chains. But a bizarre accident sets Carnage loose upon the city once
again! Now it's up to Spider-Man to stop his deadliest foe.

__THE ULTIMATE SPIDER-MAN   0-425-14610-3/$12.00
Beginning with a novella by Spider-Man cocreator Stan Lee and Peter David,
this anthology includes all-new tales from established comics writers and
popular authors of the fantastic, such as: Lawrence Watt-Evans, David
Michelinie, Tom DeHaven, and Craig Shaw Gardner. An illustration by a well-
known Marvel artist accompanies each story. *Trade*

__SPIDER-MAN: THE VENOM FACTOR by Diane Duane
1-57297-038-3/$6.50
In a Manhattan warehouse, the death of an innocent man points to the
involvement of Venom—the alien symbiote who is obsessed with Spider-Man's
destruction. Yet Venom has always safeguarded innocent lives. Either Venom
has gone completely around the bend, or there is another, even more sinister
suspect.

®,™ and © 1998 Marvel Entertainment Group, Inc. All rights reserved.

IRON MAN ®

___ THE ARMOR TRAP   1-57297-008-1/$6.50

By Greg Cox

When millionaire industrialist and scientist Tony Stark puts on his gleaming, high-tech armor, he becomes Iron Man! When Stark is kidnapped, his corporation must turn to another armored hero, and Stark's best friend, War Machine, to fulfill the ransom. And War Machine won't just take orders from kidnappers...

___ OPERATION A.I.M.   1-57297-195-9/$5.99

By Greg Cox

The product of Advanced Idea Mechanics (A.I.M.), MODOK: the Mental Organism Designed Only for Killing is out to duplicate the incredibly powerful energy chip Iron Man used in *The Armor Trap*. But the chip is only the first tool needed to create the ultimate weapon...

Now Iron Man must recruit fellow heroes Captain America, War Machine, and the Black Panther to help stop MODOK before it's too late...

VISIT PENGUIN PUTNAM ONLINE ON THE INTERNET:
http://www.penguinputnam.com

®, ™ and © 1998 Marvel Entertainment Group, Inc. All Rights Reserved.